DESTRUCTIVELY
MINE

KRISTA RITCHIE AND
BECCA RITCHIE

BERKLEY ROMANCE
NEW YORK

BERKLEY ROMANCE
Published by Berkley
An imprint of Penguin Random House LLC
1745 Penguin Random House LLC
penguinrandomhouse.com

Book design by George Towne
Interior Art: Spider Web © Sveta Aho/Shutterstock

Library of Congress Cataloging-in-Publication Data

Names: Ritchie, Krista, author. | Ritchie, Becca, author.
Title: Destructively mine / Krista and Becca Ritchie.
Description: First edition. | New York : Berkley Romance, 2025.
Identifiers: LCCN 2024042049 (print) | LCCN 2024042050 (ebook) |
ISBN 9780593549575 (trade paperback) | ISBN 9780593549582 (ebook)
Subjects: LCGFT: Romance fiction. | Novels.
Classification: LCC PS3618.I7675 D47 2025 (print) |
LCC PS3618.I7675 (ebook) | DDC 813/.6--dc23/eng/20240906
LC record available at https://lccn.loc.gov/2024042049
LC ebook record available at https://lccn.loc.gov/2024042050

First Edition: April 2025

Printed in the United States of America
1st Printing

The authorized representative in the EU for product safety and compliance
is Penguin Random House Ireland, Morrison Chambers, 32 Nassau Street,
Dublin D02 YH68, Ireland, https://eu-contact.penguin.ie.

Believe nothing you hear,
and only half of what you see.

—EDGAR ALLAN POE

PROLOGUE

Phoebe

EIGHT YEARS AGO
THE RIP DEAL
Malibu, California

I stare wide-eyed at a pink, a black, and a bright neon-green bikini splayed on the king-sized bed—a bed that I've called mine for four whopping whole days. "Why is this so hard for you?" I mutter to myself. "It's an outfit, not a math problem. Get your shit together."

Don't talk to yourself out loud, bug. It's a bad tell. Keep that up here. I hear my mom's tip and imagine her tapping her temple with a wink. These four walls don't need to know I'm an anxious, nervous mess. Lest I slip up in front of the things that *do* matter.

The four-poster bed!

The joke falls flat in my head, and I let out an audible wheezy laugh. Am I really this pathetic?

No.

I'm adept. Savvy. *Confident.*

I won't slip up in front of any mark. Not for this job.

Seduce a self-absorbed, self-proclaimed "rich kid" from Malibu. In the ever-moving career of swindling the rich and handsy assholes of the world, I've been granted a new project. Hailey's mom and my mom are trusting I can knock the pants off Kellan Fields while they handle more complicated threads to the larger Rip Deal, which involves screwing his father out of half a million via an under-the-table cash deal and sleight of hand. I know I have one of the easier roles.

It shouldn't be that hard.

I'm sixteen.

This really isn't my first rodeo. I've batted my lashes at boarding-school boys, and they've fallen for every trick in the temptress handbook. I've made out with an older guy in his Lambo, too, even if the actual act of being lip-locked with him is hazy in my head. I can't remember what I did.

My short time here in Malibu has been going . . . okay. Day one, I "accidentally" bumped into Kellan on the pier. Day two, I went on the most boring coffee date where he name-dropped A-listers and spent a solid hour listing off the specs of his Ferrari and yammering on about his father's yacht.

It'd been fine.

Until the end of the date when we kissed, and he reacted . . . *strange.* It caught me off guard. He thinks I'm eighteen like him, and I'm afraid my mere persona screamed *adolescent!* at some point. This con can't unravel because of me.

Now he's invited me to a beach bonfire with his friends, and I'd like to open the sliding glass doors to my new bedroom, step onto the porch, fling all three bikinis at the million-dollar ocean view, and hope the wind carries them into the Pacific.

Then my decision would be made for me.

I could just go *naked.*

Problem solved. The fact that I'm a second from Googling whether this is a nude beach means I've really lost it.

A knock sounds before my door creaks open. A second opinion. Thank God. I exhale. "Hailey," I say without turning. "I need your help. Please, *please* rank these from classy slut to trashy slut. I can't figure out what I should be wearing tonight." I pick up the black bikini with the low-cut top and G-string bottoms and whirl around to . . .

My face flames. "Not Hailey." So much for keeping my inner thoughts to myself.

Rocky raises his brows. "Not Hailey."

My entire body roasts on a spit at being caught in a distraught state about an absurdly dumb thing like clothes in front of my best friend's *older brother.*

After shutting the door, he strides farther into my room. My heart flip-flops as the space between us depletes.

His gaze falls to the bikini I'm holding. "That one is fucking trashy."

"You haven't even seen it," I combat. It's balled in my fist.

He extends a hand. "Pass it then."

Heat bathes my face ten times more, and it's not like I haven't worked a con with Rocky. I've worked *most* cons right alongside him, but I would greatly like to default to his sister's advice right now because A) Hailey is a beautiful genius and B) she's not the one I have a crush on!

Except, the idea of *not* giving him the bikini, of *not* reeling him closer and finding out what happens next—that sounds boring. My pulse speeds as I place the bikini in Rocky's hand, and I bask in the adrenaline rush.

It's me, deciding my fate, my next move.

It's him, his eyes on mine for an extended beat. Like he sees who I am before he sees the shape of my body.

Our fingers brush as I retract, and a weird sensation pulsates inside me and tickles my skin. I try not to wobble at his closeness or how he's touching the string that might go between my legs tonight. *You don't like him. He's annoying. He's ugly.*

Yeah. Right.

He needs to do something supremely aggravating right fucking now, so I can ignore the Jupiter-sized crush I have on him.

He lifts the skimpy bottoms with one finger, almost suggestively. *That's my job*, I want to say. I'm the one who's supposed to be alluring and sexy, but the role reversal piques my interest enough that I stay quiet.

He glances at the bikinis on the bed, then back to me. "Yeah, I stand uncorrected. This is the trashiest." His voice is coarse.

"Thanks for the assessment." I plop down on the bed beside the pink and neon-green bikinis. "You know, some guys like it." I'm trying to mask how attracted I am, but he's so good at reading people, the best I can do is fuss over the clasp on the pink halter top. "Kellan might."

Rocky tosses the black G-string to me. "He might be the kind of guy who'd be angry or mortified if his girl went half-naked to a party among his peers."

"I'm not really *his* girl," I shoot back.

"No shit." The words are biting, but not at me. His jaw muscle tics. He cuts his gunmetal eyes to the wall. I'd like to think the idea that I could be anyone else's girl grates on him. Disgusts him. That really, I am *his*. But this feels like the bigger make-believe.

It's my stupid fantasy.

Because when has Rocky *ever* made a real move on me?

My face burns with more frustrations, and I exhale them

out to say, "Kellan could see me like a prize. He might want to show me off."

The award for farthest eye roll distance goes to Brayden Tinrock. He lets out a low groan that sounds sensual yet animalistic. His entire being balances between *fuck* and *fight.* Like he's a second from doing both to me.

It's extremely hot, but I avoid blatantly checking him out. He knows he's attractive. He does *not* need my stamp of approval. I ball up the bikini and say, "I take it you're the angry or mortified kind of guy."

"No, I'm the kind of guy who doesn't bring the girl I like around insufferable pricks like Kellan and whoever the fuck his dumbass friend is." Rocky never forgets a name.

"Jackson."

"*Right.*"

I smile at his dry tone.

He sees, and his lips just barely twitch upward, then he peers over at the glass double doors. The sky is a stormy gray. Aggressive sounds of gathering waves fill the quiet.

While Rocky stands only a couple feet from me, I envy his demeanor. How his navy-blue suit never wears him. How his broody disposition can't cloud his real confidence. He presents himself like he's powerful enough to be elected Roman consul at seventeen. It's not manufactured. It's not fake.

It's a part of him.

He never really acts like being rich is a façade. He *is* rich, and why should I feel any different? I have the same safety net of wealth as him. I've grown up in the same affluent social circles. Fabrications of our own making, *yes.* But is it an illusion if it's our reality?

Then why do I feel like a fake rich girl? Is it because I'm in more positions that feel . . . degrading?

No, *no*.

My mom says there is power in screwing over egotistical, vain men. The ones who act like we're accessories to their expensive cars and overpriced toys. I don't feel humiliated at the end of a con. There've been several times where I've felt triumphant.

In this second, with Rocky taking a seat on my bed, I feel . . . *confused*.

"Why'd you come in here?" I ask him.

"To see if you needed help."

"Seriously?"

He gives me a hard look. "No, I wanted to take a bubble bath and braid your hair."

I scrunch my face. "Like I'd let you touch my hair."

Rocky leans his hands back on the mattress. Getting comfortable. He's zeroed in on me, but I'm not his prey. I don't care if he thinks I'm full of shit either. He can believe I have the hots for him—he wouldn't be wrong. But I'm not going to melt all over him like ice cream on a sweltering summer day.

"Where's your martini glass?" he asks. "The strawberry one?"

"Why? You plan to drink out of that while you're in my bathtub and doing a piss-poor job at braiding my hair?"

"The hair you won't let me braid," he points out.

"Exactly." I go to stand, but Rocky catches my wrist. He's sitting up now, and he keeps me seated next to him on the bed.

My heart rate pitches up at the warmth of his palm on me. He lets go, and my skin goes cold. I don't let him speak. Instead, I say fast, "You're not allowed to touch my martini glass. I went to *great* lengths to secure that one."

"You steal it from a little old 'quirky' lady in her brownstone?"

"I didn't *steal* it."

"I don't really care if you did."

I feel another smile pull at my lips. "You wouldn't," I mutter.

We are lawless, caustic things. Our ethics are twisted, and I like Rocky because he's someone who will choose immoral paths when needed. Dark shadows aren't something to avoid but something he'll walk into.

Tension thickens in the silent beat—it's not awkward. There is a pulsing heat that burns me alive. That tempts me to move closer to the scorch. To him.

Ignoring it, I end up explaining, "The martini glass was an online purchase. And we were on the *road*. It was complicated. I had to get it shipped to the front desk of the Motel 6 and it almost didn't arrive before we left."

"You never even drink out of it." He combs a hand through his hair while maintaining supreme eye contact. It's intense. Intrusive. The way he stares so deeply into me, as if he's carving out chunks of my soul and inscribing himself there. If I weren't stubborn, maybe I'd be shy. Maybe I'd blush.

But I want to intrude on his soul, too.

I stare him down. "It's decoration, and martinis are gross. I hate when guys order them for me."

"Yeah, well, maybe they should fucking *ask* first."

"Ask what I like to drink?" I raise my brows.

"It's not a novel concept, Phoebe."

I shrug. "It is when they really don't care about who I am. They just want to sleep with me, Rocky."

He's radiating with hotter heat. "Are we talking about marks or about guys you're actually dating?"

I'm not dating anyone. Not for real. None of us have the luxury of keeping a relationship with *anyone* when we pack up and go so frequently. We're basically nomads.

"Marks, I guess," I answer.

He smears a hand down his mouth. It doesn't wipe his anger away. He hates all marks. The people we deceive and scam. They're not *good* people. Most of them would never receive one-way tickets to the pearly gates.

I hate them, too, but my anger isn't a constant dark passenger like Rocky's. My rage appears, then dies. In a vicious cycle of rebirth.

Rocky won't mention my age. He won't say how I'm only sixteen. How guys shouldn't be ordering me alcohol. He's been in similar situations even younger. At gentleman's clubs with sons and fathers, he's had to smoke cigars and sip whiskey to assimilate to wealthy elite culture.

Drink young. Ages aren't restrictions when you're rich. They're just yellow caution tape, and you better have the expensive scissors that can cut it. Or else, maybe you don't really belong.

Belonging is what we're taught to do.

I check the tag on my pink bikini. He's so close, hairs rise on my arms. Will he inch nearer?

He's studying me, his eyes dipping up and down me. "Phoebe—"

"You want to help?" I ask fast.

"Yeah. That's why I'm here." He rakes a hand through his hair. "Hailey had to leave with the godmothers." *Our moms*, he means.

I can't even remember when we started calling them the godmothers. Was it before or after we nicknamed his dad the godfather?

"Right." I nod.

Oxygen seems thinner in Rocky's presence, but I must like

the feeling of being asphyxiated. *That's mildly disturbing, Phoebe.*

"I can help you pick out a bathing suit, but I need to know more about this guy," Rocky says. "The insufferable prick."

"Kellan."

"Whatever the fuck."

I want to smile, but Kellan's face flashes into focus, and I cringe. "He's a show-off. He likes flaunting his family's money, and he's not discreet about it. It's tacky. I think he's overcompensating because his two friends come from inherited wealth, and his dad is just a hedge fund manager."

"He sounds riveting."

I reexamine the neon-green bikini. "Glad you think so, maybe you can kiss him for me." I'm not looking forward to this cozy beach bonfire. At all.

"Is he into guys?" Rocky says casually, like he'd consider taking him off my hands.

"Straight." I wince at myself as I reimagine my first and only kiss with Kellan.

"Phebs?"

I bury my hot face in my hand. "Ugh, the kiss. It was so bad, Rocky." I'd rather be admitting this to Hailey and not her brother, but it looks like I'm getting this off my chest with him. So far, I don't hate it.

"Bad how?" He clasps my wrist and lowers my arm.

My palm slips off my burning cheeks. Dark concern shadows his gaze, and I wonder if he thinks there was full-face grabbing and ass groping.

It wasn't like that. "After the coffee date, we got up to say goodbye and we kissed. Then Kellan looked at me like I gave him a juvenile noogie to the head."

He's confused. "That doesn't explain the actual kiss." He rotates more to me, his thigh and knee on the bed now.

"Well that's because it's . . . hard to explain," I say pointedly. I'm partially distracted by him caring about me enough to be here right now. He's trying to understand me and this strange situation.

"So you got up to say goodbye, and in that moment, who kissed who?"

"I came in for the kiss. He looked at my lips. His hand was in mine." I recite this with little to no emotion. The event was as mundane as toasting bread. In fact, watching Starbucks baristas pop a bacon-and-gouda in the toaster would elicit more excitement *within me* than kissing Kellan.

"And?" Rocky asks.

"And then I did this . . ." Without thinking, I lean into him, and I kiss Rocky. My lips are on his lips, and my pulse explodes.

I can't gather enough breath in my lungs. I pull back fast— to where it lasts two seconds. Tops.

His brows arch.

Oh my God. "I'm *so* sorry, that was . . ." Unconsented? Abrupt?

"A peck," he states.

"What?" I'm whiplashed, out of breath.

"You pecked him on the lips," Rocky says, but that's not what has me so flustered.

"I just kissed you," I say, needing him to acknowledge this like right fucking now.

He gives me a narrowed look. "We've kissed a thousand times, Phebs."

Am I making this weird? "On jobs, *Rocky*." I force myself not to grab a bed pillow and hide—or throw it at him.

"This is about a job." His chest rises and falls a little heavier, and he avoids my gaze for a tenser second. I'm just his partner in crime. He's not going to pursue anything real with me. Clearly.

Stop getting your hopes up, Phoebe.

"Yeah, you're right," I say, and tuck a piece of my hair behind my ear. "This is basically con adjacent." Disappointment sinks my stomach, but I try to push the awful feeling away. Especially as our eyes latch.

As a slight acknowledgment passes from him to me and from me to him. As our gazes flit a little more carelessly over each other.

There is attraction.

That is real.

But like hell am *I* acting on it *for real*. Being rejected by Rocky sounds like utter hell, and if he wants me, then maybe I want to be chased. Maybe I'd rather reject him. How about that?

I cross my arms hotly. "How should I have kissed him, anyway? It was a *goodbye* kiss in the middle of the afternoon in public, you realize that? I couldn't go for tongue."

His gray eyes lift back to mine. "I'm you," he says, and my heart rate goes from sixty to two hundred realizing he's going to show me.

He cups my cheek, as lightly and softly as I would another guy, and with his gaze fastened on mine, he bridges the distance slowly, gradually, and the unbearable, inescapable tension winds inside of me. His lips close against mine as he kisses me, making it feel deeper, then he nudges into a more forceful, sensual kiss. With his hand against my jaw—he draws me closer.

Holy shit. His touch sends a shock wave down my neck and arms and legs, thrumming my pussy. Lighting my core.

He pulls back, both of us searching for breath. "Like that."

I don't want to catch my breath—I don't want this to end. "Like this?" I clasp his face with the same softness, and our gazes dive into one another as I drag myself closer. My lips ghost over his, and I sense his muscles contracting, his body shifting nearer. Then I kiss him with the same sensual undertones, and my heartbeat skyrockets.

I nudge into a deeper kiss without tongue, like he did.

His hand claws at the side of my face, and I feel his fingers sliding to the back of my head. *Yes.* I think he's going to grip my hair. I think he's going to plunge his tongue into my mouth. I think he's going to push me to the bed and do dirty things to me. *Please.*

He cuts the kiss short.

I internally groan. *Why, why, why?* No, no, *this is good.* We shouldn't be together. My mom will be intolerable about it. She's *obsessed* with the idea of us—more than even I am.

This is just for a con. It's exactly what it should be.

Rocky exhales hard and looks me over. "You okay?"

"Just waiting for my review." I lean farther back and brush hair off my tight shoulder.

He forces a smile. "Adequate."

"My kiss was better than yours."

"True."

The sudden compliment eases me, and maybe he knew it would. My joints loosen and shoulders slacken.

He checks the door. "We could keep practicing."

Who would turn down a make-out session with their biggest crush? *Not me.* So that's how I spend fifteen minutes in heaven with Rocky. I taste him on my lips. His chest melds against my breasts, but we sit upright. Never lying down.

We teeter on the edge of self-destruction, toying with the

idea of French kisses and hair pulls, but we crumble under the parameters we've set.

Practice a public goodbye kiss.

Somehow, the tension amasses to new heights from our self-control, and these become the hottest goodbye kisses of my entire life. My lips sting against his, and my skin hums, like with one simple brush against my elbow, I might release a sudden moan.

"Brayden!" his dad calls from outside my room, and we break apart. Rocky shoots to his feet, his lips reddened, and he combs two hands through his hair. We hear his dad again. "Brayden!!"

"I'll be there in a sec!" He's about to glance over at me when the door just *whooshes* open. No knock. No true warning.

Everett Tinrock graces my bedroom like the jute rug and modern bed and beechwood dresser belong to him. I mean, they're only *temporarily* mine. This place in Malibu came fully furnished, and he did help find it. So maybe they are partially his, too?

Rocky is pissed. "Whatever you want, we can do it outside her room."

"No. Stay." He holds up a stern hand.

"I'm not a fucking dog."

"Then maybe you shouldn't respond to *Rocky*."

I glare.

Everett dislikes the nickname and has tried to dissuade his son from choosing it more than once. The number of times he's brought up Rocky Balboa—and not lovingly—has made me never want to watch another *Rocky* film again.

Still, Rocky . . . my Rocky . . . hasn't discarded the name. Sometimes I wonder if he loves it more because his dad hates it.

Everett and Addison prefer to call him Brayden. It's what they called him as a baby, and Rocky has let them continue to use it.

Rocky forces an acidic smile. "And maybe you shouldn't barge into Phoebe's room without knocking first."

"*You* were in here. Don't act like I'm invading her privacy when you two were doing . . . what exactly?" He focuses on me now like he's a strict senior detective with polished loafers and the rich stench of eight-grand cologne.

Which I actually smell on him from five feet away.

I'm pretending like Rocky and I didn't just make out. Thanks to my above-average acting skills and my interest in these bikinis, I'd say I'm doing a damn good job, but conning a con artist takes advanced skill that I might not have yet.

"I was helping her for the job," Rocky bites back. "That's *it*."

Everett is staring at my mouth. God, I hope my lips don't look just kissed. I make a great effort not to lick them or chew them or draw any more unwanted attention to them.

I lift the neon-green bikini. "I was just having trouble with my outfit for the bonfire tonight," I tell him.

He slowly nods. "You shouldn't scowl like that when you're with Kellan. You're a beautiful girl, but that's unattractive."

I try to take the pro-tip with grace. He's just ensuring I don't screw up, but Everett isn't exactly my favorite person. "I won't scowl on a job."

Rocky is grinding his jaw. He moves to the door. "I'm leaving, Dad, so whatever you want to tell me, you can do it in the hall—"

Everett grips his elbow, stopping him, and Rocky slides easily out of the hold. His father says, "It's not important. You can stay here."

"It's not important?" He's skeptical. "You called my name like the fucking house was on fire."

"Later," Everett says. "You should help Phoebe. That matters more." So Rocky helping me is most important to him. If his dad believes we *were* hooking up, is he suggesting we should continue? My head pounds, and I try not to think too intensely about it.

Especially when my mom calls him and he puts her on speaker. They're discussing logistics for tonight, and it's all pretty routine. Things we've been through. I'm not shocked that Everett isn't advertising how he caught Rocky in my room. For one, it's not that unusual for us to be alone together when our roles are often intertwined.

For another, Everett is all business, and that reeks of soap-opera-level drama.

Mom sighs. ". . . this would be easier if one of them were a little younger. I miss the days when you were a baby, bug." She's speaking to me.

"I don't," I say with a rising smile. "I like being older." When we were kids, they gave us so little responsibility, and I like being valued enough to hold the rope and be the one to pull.

"You were so cute, though." I hear the smile inside her words, and it makes mine grow. "And babies are the *best* social proof. No one doubts a single lie with a cute little squishy baby on your hip."

She's not wrong, and hearing her voice makes me wish she were physically here and not Everett. When I see Rocky's intense glare at the phone, I wonder if he's thinking about his little brother.

Poor Trevor. He's aged up out of the adorable, innocent, doe-eyed phase, but he hasn't really locked down a specific role outside of sleight of hand—which we all can do. Every time he wants to be paired with Rocky on a job, they say *no* and just put Rocky with me.

I'm pretty sure Trevor hates me for it, and I can't really blame him. But it's not like I'm calling those shots.

Once my mom hangs up and Everett is gone shortly thereafter, Rocky stares at the shut door like he's throwing daggers with his eyes.

"Thanks for the assist. Earlier, I mean. Us practicing," I tell him, and I mean it. When I kiss Kellan, maybe I can imagine I'm kissing Rocky. Would that be a bad thing? Who cares, as long as I succeed tonight. That's all that really matters.

I won't fail the team.

He nods but says, "I can't stay."

"I didn't ask you to," I remind him. "Your dad did."

Rocky eases a fraction. With a hand on the doorknob, he glances back at the bikinis on the bed. "The pink one."

"What?"

"It's my vote."

I eye the halter top and high-rise bottoms. It's probably the best route. "It's the safe choice," I say out loud.

"It's pink." He's out of my room too quickly for me to ask what he means.

Then it dawns on me.

He knows my favorite color is pink. In a world of deception and aliases, Rocky is one of the few people who truly knows the real me.

ONE

Phoebe

I'm so far from normal, I should probably give up on figuring out the true meaning of the word. But what's happening right now in the dining room of a snobby country club with hundred-grand membership dues—it's not even *my* normal. The normal of a so-called "daughter" of a con artist—raised to rip off egocentric assholes and board fancy yachts and live lavishly until the money runs dry. Then do it all over again.

No, this right here is not my normal at all.

It's bizarre.

Terrifying, even.

My mom is in Victoria, Connecticut, with her best friend, Addison. And they're pretending to be fucking *matchmakers*. Probably to matchmake me and Rocky for a payout. They're here without warning. Without a text or a smoke signal.

And to pile it on, my mom might not be my mom.

It's been a literal *day* since I learned that we might not be related. She might've kidnapped me and my brothers.

Addison most definitely isn't biologically Trevor's mother. So where the hell did he come from?

There is a foundational rule to what we do. We deceive other people. We *never* deceive each other. Yet, our parents lied to all six of us.

They conned us.

I didn't realize how mad I was, not until this moment. Seeing them here. Facing them. An inferno builds in my lungs and combines with extreme levels of unease. I'm crawling out of my skin, but no one can see the alarms going off in my entire body, telling me to evacuate from this fucked-up situation. To find Rocky. Find Hailey. Find my brothers.

While I stare right at Elizabeth Graves and Addison Tinrock, the country club doesn't fall hushed. No spotlight is shining down on little ole me—the blue-haired, drama-filled server at Victoria Country Club.

The midafternoon lunch crowd has packed the dining room, and everyone is absorbed in their own social sphere. Pickleball-clad ladies chitter-chatter as they stab forks into shrimp Louie salads. Full-bellied laughter bellows from rich men over their tuna tartare. Clinks of silverware on plates sound obnoxiously loud, and flames roar in a fireplace behind my mom.

I'm the only one who knows two con artists have just slithered their way into this town's cracked foundation, and they're going to sink their poisonous fangs into someone.

Not me.

They won't trick me?

My pulse won't slow. Because that's never been a question before. Now all I have are furious questions for them. The most pressing one: *Why the hell are you here?*

"It's so nice to meet you, Phoebe," my mom says with a

charismatic smile. She brushes her blonde hair off her shoulder and extends a hand to me. "I'm Isla Rivers." Aka Elizabeth Graves. Do I even call her Mom?

Do I want to?

Not really. She doesn't deserve that, does she? Even if I'm biologically *her* daughter. Even if I am a triplet with Nova and Oliver. Even if this is all true—she's an accomplice to something nefarious with Trevor. That makes her just as guilty for duping us.

What else could she be hiding? Would she ever admit to the truth? Can I trust *anything* she ever says?

My head spins, and I wish I were holding a serving tray right now—something that'd give me an out from shaking hands with a . . . devil? *I don't know what she is.*

I always figured if my mom were a devil, then so was I. The Graves and Tinrocks—we were all just a merry little gang of heathens in hell together.

I loved it that way.

Everything is off-kilter now. My world is tipping at the axis.

I shake her hand and try to throttle myself out of this hot stupor. "Sorry, I missed what Stella said about you being . . . professionals?"

In my peripheral, I catch Stella bristling in her Chanel getup. "It's Mrs. Fitzpatrick, sweets." Her tight, acidic smile deserves one in return, and I could force one back—but I like this job.

I want to keep this job. And I'm clearly not on a first-name basis with Mrs. My Shit Doesn't Stink. I am still just the lowly server who happens to be "dating" town aristocracy, and Stella is the rich best friend of Claudia Waterford.

And Claudia—she's the mother of my fake boyfriend, Jake

Waterford. Oh, and they all despise the idea of a Phoebe and Jake union. Which should be fine. *Just fine.* Because today, I was supposed to be ending this fake dating scheme so I can truthfully (and finally) date the guy I actually love.

Rocky.

Now, whatever boat I've boarded is being capsized, and I'm used to it. I'm also used to having backup—where people wait in a life raft and pull me from the rough ocean. Then we flee unseen together.

None of them are here. I am alone.

Drowning.

Leave, Phoebe.

"She can be a little slow," Stella tells Elizabeth into a sip of mimosa. They're all appraising me like I'm a pet project. Great, I've become the fascination of the bored elite.

"This is Wendy St. James." Elizabeth motions to Addison at her side. "We own the northeast's most prominent and exclusive matchmaking service. *Eros.* It's designed for individuals who require a similar lifestyle to their own."

Similar lifestyle is code for the rich just wanting to date rich. Tempering my feelings, I plaster on the world's fakest smile and ask, "And you think I fall into that category?"

"Absolutely not," Stella answers first. "You could never afford them or even qualify, but these lovely women have so *graciously* agreed to extend their services to you at the request of Claudia."

Correction: Claudia is *paying* these women because she hates that I'm dating her son. Eros isn't real, and Elizabeth and Addison are already profiting from this scam. How long have they even been setting this up?

Elizabeth smooths out one of her blonde curls and looks me over with a slow, excavating gaze like she's hollowing out bones from beneath the earth. "Hmmm," she muses. "We might need to work on some things to make you more . . ." Her eyes hit mine. "Just *more*."

Heat bathes my cheeks, and a memory floods me.

I was thirteen.

My mom had slipped into high social circles in Charleston and landed on the cotillion's board of directors. She'd pretended to be my wealthy aunt who was presenting me to society at the upcoming debutante ball. She examined the length of my thirteen-year-old body with the same intrusive gaze, and she said, "We might need to work on some things to make you more . . . just *more*."

This is a way for her to tip me off. To let me understand this is a ploy like in Charleston. An act. She might as well be winking at me.

It just makes a wave of sudden grief roll over me, and my eyes burn. I'm trying not to glare like I have gnarled, rooted history with her.

Stella fingers her teardrop diamond earring. "Like I was telling you"—she speaks to Elizabeth and Addison—"Phoebe is a work in progress, but if you'd seen how rough around the edges her ex-husband is, you'd understand how perfect they are for each other."

Little does Stella know, my mom has always drawn hearts around me and Rocky and tried to smush us together like two slices of PB&J.

Nausea flips my stomach. *Rocky.* I need to find Rocky.

The urge grows tenfold. At least Hailey is safe from our moms. If she was at work serving with me today, she'd go sheet white seeing Addison. I rest easy remembering she's at the loft and taking care of Trevor after the Halloween horror story from last night.

He was stabbed.

I feel like I'm being metaphorically stabbed, so there's *that*.

Stella adds, "Grey makes much more sense than pairing her with Jake Waterford."

"She has good bones," Addison announces, pushing her tortoiseshell glasses higher on the bridge of her nose. "We can work with it."

I don't want them to work with *anything* that belongs to me. Not my body, not my mind, and stay the hell away from my heart. It already feels pulverized from one betrayal. Before anyone can stop me, I say a quick "I'm not interested" and beeline for the exit.

Katherine Rhodes, the manager of guest relations and *my boss*, intercepts me. "Where are you going?" Her red eyebrows arch in both panic and disapproval. "We're swamped, and ladies are waiting at the bar."

"I don't feel goo—"

"No, *no*. You leave now, I'll have no choice but to terminate you."

I use the only card I have. "Jake won't be happy about that." It comes out sharper and more threatening than I intend.

She bristles.

Jake Koning Waterford is a Koning boy. It's Claudia's maiden name and often touted over *Waterford* since *Koning* is the true source of their wealth. Jake is an heir to one of the oldest beer companies in America, and his family owns this country club.

I might be two seconds from breaking up with him, but Katherine doesn't know that.

Surprisingly, she waffles. I thought it'd be a knockout punch. An ace in the hole. What the fuck? "You'll be suspended then," she snaps. "He'll compromise with me on this."

"Will he? I'm his *girlfriend*."

"I'm his godmother."

I blow back a little. I did not think they were that close. "Jake never said . . ."

"Well, I'm not shocked. You've barely been dating." *Not wholly untrue.* She's eagle-eyeing the restless ladies at the bar. "You leave, you're suspended for two weeks. No pay."

I need the money.

I've been trying to make an honest living in Connecticut with Hailey, and that also means relying on my paycheck to cover rent. She took off today, and I don't think we can both afford to skip.

Money wins over my emotional state, and I hightail it to the bar. Thankfully I'm not being approached by Stella and her new matchmaker—sorry, I mean, *con-artist* friends.

While assisting the four women in pickleball skirts, I practice *patience* as they ask for mimosas. Being short-staffed really sucks. There is no bartender I can tag in, and so I quickly pour champagne into the polished flutes.

"I'm telling you, Jem, he made an appearance this morning. *Early.* We were the only ones here."

"She's right," a freckle-cheeked early riser named Laura vouches. "You can't blame him for not wanting to be a part of the afternoon rush. He's so sweet and tenderhearted, and after what happened . . ." They let out a collective pity sigh.

I'm . . . so lost.

I'd love to soak in the juicy gossip, but my head is already crammed full.

"Did you see him, Phoebe?" Jem asks. So much for staying out of this.

"Who?" I splash orange juice in the glasses.

"Trent Koning Waterford," Laura tells me like she's introducing Angelina Jolie. Full name status.

Trent is Jake's oldest brother. A brother that I've *never* met.

"Huh," I say, my interest piquing. "I did not happen to see this specter of a man." Hailey thinks Trent doesn't exist. He's been the Bigfoot of Koning brothers, rarely appearing at town gatherings. Always spoken of in hushed settings.

Case in point.

"Well, he *was* here," Laura defends. "He even said hello to Anika."

"He did." Anika smiles proudly while I hand her a mimosa. "I just wish he felt like he could be a part of the community. We're all here for him after . . ." She leaves the sentence hanging.

They're waiting for me to ask. They're not going to leave until I do.

Fine.

Admittedly, I kind of want to know. "After what?"

"His wife's passing," Laura says solemnly.

My brows jump. "He was married?"

"He's thirty-two, dear," Jem tells me, sipping her mimosa. They all now have their drinks.

Laura bows closer to ask me, "Doesn't the staff here call him the 'unofficial fourth widower'?"

"Um, I haven't heard it if they do, but I'm sort of still new." And maybe the other servers wouldn't want to talk about Jake's brother in front of his "girlfriend"—so I've been left out of the staff gossip, too. Maybe Hailey has as well, just by association with me.

Being ostracized by both the elite and the service is not a great feeling. I wipe down the counter. "Why is he an unofficial widower and not just official?"

Jem says, "I suppose it'd be more official if Trent stopped by the club more than once in a blue moon."

"Right." I toss a towel under the cabinet.

"He married his prep-school sweetheart right after graduation," Anika fills me in. "She passed away suddenly."

"Aggressive stage-four melanoma. It was four years ago," Laura chimes in. "He's sworn off dating ever since. He'd be the most eligible bachelor in town, but Scarlett was his truest love."

They all admire his devotion to his late wife, and I'd be more touched by the story if I weren't so confused.

I've gotten the strong impression that Jake *hates* Trent. He not-so-lovingly has Trent's ringtone set as "Highway to Hell" by AC/DC. He grumbles Trent's name under his breath. Groans whenever he has to answer his calls.

Surely Jake, who's empathetic toward his little sister's plights, would have a soft spot for his grieving brother?

It's starting to feel like Jake is the actual asshole. But I can't worry about the Koning boys. I have a bigger mess to trek through.

After I entertain the ladies for another few minutes, they take their mimosas to the sunroom, and I check on the status of my boss. She's on the phone at the hostess podium and jotting on a notepad.

All clear.

I hustle out of the dining room, and my soles squeak on the marble floor in the rotunda. I spy the cucumber water. *For guests only.* Fuck it, if I'm suspended, then I'm going to be a hydrated suspended bitch. I pour a glass and chug the water on my route to where I believe Jake probably went.

I can't believe I'm hunting for my fake boyfriend before even contacting Hailey and Rocky. This feels so wrong.

But finding Jake seems imperative. And not just so he can reason with Katherine and help me take the day off *with* pay.

He said he'd call Rocky, and he's likely *pitching* the extension of this fake dating scheme to him—and things have just drastically changed.

TWO

Rocky

Sixty miles out of Victoria, I'm in a drugstore stocking up on bandages and other shit my teenage brother might need to recover from a stab wound. Just a regular Friday afternoon for a Tinrock.

I'm tossing antiseptic cream into a basket at my feet when Jake calls me.

Phoebe. She's the first person I think about.

Phoebe is at the country club today.

Phoebe is with Jake.

Phoebe is supposed to break up with Jake.

Raw concern for her is a shot of adrenaline, and I answer on the first ring. "Hi, Jake." I narrow a glare at bottles of supplements. *Magnesium. 250 mg. Melatonin.* I calm down so my voice isn't caustic. "This better be about my new equestrian purchase."

I hope this has absolutely nothing to do with Phoebe. But it doesn't hurt to remind Jake of two things. One, that I've recently done him a solid by buying his dead sister's horse. And two, that I know he helped fake her death.

So if he fucks with Phoebe, I will *bury* him.

"It's not about that." Jake sighs like talking to me isn't on his top-ten list of daily desires. He wouldn't even make my top one hundred, so why *the fuck* is he calling me? "Listen, Grey . . ." He lets his voice taper off.

I wait and wait for more. There's nothing.

"You afraid to talk to me, Jake?"

"I just want you to think about what I'm going to say rather than react," Jake explains. "Please." His voice has lowered to a whisper.

I scan the wellness aisle and smile kindly at an older woman who passes by. She beams back, and I tell her, "Have a good day" before she leaves for a beauty supply section.

"Where are you?" I ask into the phone.

"The country club."

"But where?"

"The hall . . . outside guest locker rooms."

Interesting. He wants something from me, but if he didn't want anyone to overhear, he should've gone to the bathroom or slipped into a closet. While I read the label on the melatonin, I say, "I'm listening."

"I know you want Phoebe to break up with me."

"*She* wants to break up with you, too."

"She also expressed that," he says. "But I really need this to continue, at least until my family dinner."

Hell no. "We're *together*," I force out. "Me. Phoebe. We got back together." *So fuck off.*

I couldn't care less that he's the first to know. I want it to be *vitally* clear that she's mine and she'll never belong to him.

"Yeah, Phoebe told me," Jake whispers.

A smile tries to pull at my lips. *She already told him we're together.*

Then I realize Jake likely couldn't accept Phoebe saying "We're breaking up right now," and so she had to throw out the truth to get him off her back. Or half-truth—considering this isn't two divorcés mending a relationship.

The entire town and Jake believe Phoebe is my ex-wife. When in reality, we've never actually been together outside of a con. Not until now.

I just hate that he's pressuring her to keep this shit going.

Jake adds, "She even warmed up to the idea of staying with me—which is why I'm calling you. She told me I needed you to say *yes*, basically."

Why would Phoebe want this to continue? What'd he pitch to her?

I return the melatonin bottle to the shelf. "I'm saying *no*."

"Hear me out, please." He's desperate. Then I hear the pitch that Phoebe likely got. He goes into this whole spiel about his overbearing mother pairing him off with Julia Kelsey, a shy twenty-two-year-old who's susceptible to manipulation and won't survive the cutthroat nature of the social elite. He's protecting Julia—a girl I've met briefly in town.

And yes, she's quiet. Yes, she will be chewed up and spit out.

"But what about Phoebe?" I ask him.

"Phoebe's different. She can handle this family dinner."

Fire brews in my chest, burning my lungs. "Your mother hates her."

"Phoebe can hold her own. She's capable and something of a spitfire."

Hearing him describe Phoebe to me like I don't really know her is aggravating on several accounts. "She's capable," I repeat. "You want her to take *shit* from your mom while you protect soft little Julia. Just because Phoebe can take it." Fuck him.

"Phoebe wants to help," he counters. "She cares about Julia, too."

"The answer is *no*." While he's out here protecting Julia, all I care about—all I can think about—is protecting Phoebe. She's not his tool, and it pisses me off that he's trying to use her under some moral pretense.

"Can you please think about this?" he whispers. "*Please.* Phoebe is okay with it. Why can't you be?"

"Because I don't care about little fucking Julia," I whisper coldly into the phone, then I eye a middle-aged man who enters the aisle. I exit with my basket and slip into a quiet section stocked with condoms and lube.

I don't tell Jake that I care about five people. Just five. For that list to grow, *I'd* be more susceptible to manipulation. So I have no soft spots for these "damsels" that Jake is so adamant on shoving out of his social circle. And clearly, he hopes to save them from becoming distressed.

"Julia, who by the way," I add with heat, "isn't much younger than Phoebe."

"Phoebe acts—"

"I swear to God if you say *older*, I'm hanging up on you."

"I was going to say more mature," Jake retorts. "Phoebe has clearly dealt with more in her life than most people her age."

I clench my jaw. "You mean she's had to deal with me."

"A marriage and a divorce aren't little things," Jake reasons, like it wasn't a personal slight. "And you're not the easiest person to get along with. And still, she's choosing you for whatever reason, and I'm not asking you two to split up."

"What am I supposed to do?" I hiss into the phone. "Let you fake kiss my wife? You want to fake fuck her, too?"

"I . . ." His sigh turns into a frustrated noise. "Look, we can work out those details."

I drop the basket so I can pinch my eyes. I wish he were here so I could punch him in the face. "How do I know this isn't your way of convincing Phoebe she's better off with you?"

"It's not like that, Grey. I promise, I'm not trying to be with her for real or to win her over. I just need her help."

I shake my head a few times. This isn't happening. I partially believe he doesn't really want Phoebe—only because I have enough dirt on Jake to sink him deeper than the *Titanic*. So he'd have to be head over heels, foolishly in love with her to risk lying to me right now.

And I don't think he's in love with Phoebe—or else he'd be the one trying to protect her from his family. "I heard you," I say. "I listened to you. And the answer is still *fuck no*."

The line goes quiet, and I frown at a box of Trojans. My ears catch muffled noises over the phone. *Someone is with him.*

"This conversation is over," I tell him, about to hang up.

"No, wait. I'm still here," Jake says with a heavy breath. "Your ex-wife just dragged me into a closet with her."

My muscles contract in tensed bands.

At least Phoebe understands the importance of privacy, but I remember being crammed in the country club's storage closet with her. I remember pulling her hair and the hitch of her hot breath up against my skin. I remember wanting to thrust my cock inside her so badly, I could've wished upon every star for the ability to fuck her without consequence.

I hear Phoebe in the background. "Can you put him on speakerphone, please?" And then more clearly, she says, "Rocky?"

"He's not dating you—"

"It's not about that," she cuts me off, panting.

Alarm jars me, and I immediately go to the cashier to check out. *I'm not in town*, I'd tell her if she wasn't around Jake.

"What's wrong?" Jake asks her.

"We have a major problem," Phoebe tells us. "Claudia Waterford hired two matchmakers to try to pair me with Rocky. She's dead set on getting us back together . . . and now she enlisted the help of these . . . fairy godmothers like I'm their Cinderella."

I freeze.

Godmothers is code for Elizabeth and Addison.

Our mothers are in town. We all figured they'd arrive sooner rather than later. I didn't think they'd entrench themselves this quickly into the Waterford family, but it's not shocking they chose a role that'd put me and Phoebe together for a quick payout.

I should've known our moms would insinuate themselves in the town before arriving, but I heard nothing about them. No whispers, no gossip. Which means, I'm not exactly in the inner circle in Victoria.

I haven't really tried to be. It wasn't such a necessity.

Now, though—it definitely is.

I lose track of where I am, and things come into focus when the cashier scans a box of tampons my sister requested. When I've paid, I'm out of the drugstore and slowing my heated stride. "Hold on," I tell Phoebe.

An athletic-built man in track shorts and a Nike wick-away shirt is snapping photos of my parked black McLaren. It sticks out like a shiny new toy among hand-me-downs.

He's admiring it.

I jog to the driver's side, acting in a hurry, and collide with the man.

"Sorry, sorry," I say, in a rush.

"My bad." He's flustered, and we fumble with my plastic bags.

"No worries." I detangle from him, then slip into the front seat. Door shut, I unpocket the phone I just swiped off him, and I delete every photo he snapped of the car. I check his iCloud settings and see he has it disabled.

I'm cautious. Paranoid. I'm not taking any chances, and I don't need him to post this shit on social media and for anyone to trace me to a drugstore out of town. *Shouldn't have taken the McLaren.* It seemed like a minor risk before now.

Before knowing we're several steps behind Elizabeth and Addison.

Once the man disappears inside the store, I roll down my window and toss his phone on the pavement where we made impact. He'll think he just dropped it.

I peel onto the road and use my burner phone to text my siblings, Phoebe, and her brothers.

Godmothers are in town 🕷

I have no idea where my father is, but if they're here, it's likely he's not far behind.

"I'm in the car," I tell Phoebe and Jake. *En route to Victoria.* "Who are the matchmakers?"

"Isla Rivers and Wendy St. James," Phoebe says.

So our moms are using aliases. Phoebe's voice sounds strained, and I hear a *thump* of a tennis ball or racquet.

I forgot they're sharing a closet. "Let's video chat."

"You're driving," Jake says like it's unsafe.

Jesus Christ. "I'll pull over just for you, sweetheart."

THREE

Rocky

I drive into an old historic cemetery and park in the back where fog hangs over mossy headstones. It's quiet and only filled with the dead. Then I switch to video.

Jake comes into the frame. Just his too-fluffy, light brown hair and uptight face. I think a bucket of golf balls is on a shelf beside his head.

I adjust my phone and see my scowl in the minimized frame. "Where's Phoebe?" I ask.

"We're in a closet," Jake says, like that explains why I can't see her.

I glare. "Hand her your phone."

"I'm right here. It's fine," Phoebe says, trying to problem-solve. Only, her way of problem-solving involves slipping in front of Jake's body. His long arms must wrap around her. How else would he be holding the phone and have Phoebe in the frame? Her back is flush against his chest.

What kills me is her expression. It's flat. No fire. No flame. No *anything*. She's dissociating from her body, and I crave to reach inside the phone and cup her face until her eyes wield more than an empty vacuum of nothing.

"Phebs," I say slowly.

"What?" she snaps, blinking a few times. "We're fine. We're figuring this out. Right?"

"Right." I rake a hand through my dyed-black hair and skim her again. Her dark blue hair is falling out of a pony, and pieces brush against her beautiful heart-shaped face. Her brows crinkle, and a scowl forms the longer I stare. *She's okay.*

"I didn't know about the matchmakers," Jake says with a heavy, aggravated sound. "It *is* something my mom would do. She must feel threatened by my relationship with Phoebe."

"Why?" I ask him.

"Because she can't control her. Which means, she's losing control over me."

It's a motive for Jake.

A desire. To be free from Mommy's gilded prison.

Is Phoebe really the key? It doesn't matter to me if she is. These are Jake's interests. Jake's hopes and dreams. But what about hers? What about ours? This has *nothing* to do with us.

"People in this town are too invested in our love lives," I tell her. "You sure you don't want to pack your bags, Phebs? Catch a one-way ticket to anywhere else?"

We could leave. Run. Start over again. But she's expressed multiple times that she wants to stay in Victoria. To plant roots. Whatever the fuck that means.

So I'm not surprised when she says, "I'm staying here. We just need to decide what we're doing next with the whole fake-dating thing."

Jake shifts uncomfortably behind Phoebe.

She stiffens. "I can move to the side?"

"No, you're okay," he says. "I just need to shift my arms a bit. Can I touch you?"

I glare out at the headstones and breathe out fire from my lungs.

"Yeah . . . sure."

Back to the phone, where my gaze darkens on Jake. "You touch her ass and you're dead, Koning."

"How about her collarbone?" Jake asks. "Is that off-limits, *Phoebe*?" He specifically asks her like he knows it'll piss me off, and he's probably reaffirming she's the only one who can give permission over her body. Jake Waterford has a *thick* moral bone.

I'd like him to choke on it.

And I know exactly what that says about me.

Though, there is still a part of me that wishes I could be *better*. To have somewhat of a moral compass. But times like this, where he's so goddamn infuriating, I would rather not take a single note from Jake's virtuous handbook.

"The whole savior complex is tired," I snap at him. "Get a new bit."

"It's not a *bit*. But I wouldn't expect you to understand consent."

I let out a dry laugh. This guy. He knows *nothing* about me. "You're such a little—"

"Guys," Phoebe cuts in, wide-eyed. "I thought we were friends." She's glaring at me like I have the power to play nice, and I do. I should. I need to.

Things have changed, I remind myself.

Jake cools off, and there's a brief second where I remember our conversation at the horse stables, where he broke down. Where *I* broke him down. Where I agreed to help him.

Still, I don't fully trust him. I'm too cynical. Too paranoid. I just can't.

"We're something," I mutter as Jake wraps an arm around her collarbone and leans his other elbow on the shelf. He's long limbed and cramped, and he exhales in relief at the new position.

Phoebe relaxes, but I think it's mostly because she can't see him—and her eyes are only on mine.

We watch each other while Jake talks. "Personally, I don't want my mother to get what she wants, but for you two to be together, the matchmakers will have to succeed, right?"

"They're not matchmaking us," Phoebe says before I can. "I'm not agreeing to it, so your mom can fire them."

It'd end their con, and it'll raise red flags in front of our parents. They'll wonder why Phoebe, the greatest team player of all fucking time, is sabotaging easy earnings.

Getting out from under them was always going to be a mess. I'd rather create it with her than keep living inside their lies.

Jake looks more hopeful. "Would you be willing to fake date for a couple more months then?"

She winces. "I don't think I can, Jake."

"It won't be that long."

I glare. "You're not fake dating Phoebe while I'm with her. Break up with her within the week." He's lucky I didn't say within two minutes.

I see Phoebe's lips begin to rise.

Jake doesn't notice her smile. "Phoebe?" he asks her.

She looks steadfastly at me. "I'm with Rocky. It's over, Jake. Sorry."

"I'm not sorry," I say.

Jake rubs at his eyes, which causes the camera to shake. Then I hear Phoebe's phone buzz. "It's Hailey," she says, and before long, she's out the door to take my sister's call.

I'm left with Jake.

He drops his hand off his face, and his eyes are noticeably reddened with grief. Like he's lost a lot more than a fake romance.

"She's not your meal ticket," I tell him.

"You don't understand," Jake says in a pained laugh. "You can't understand."

I frown. "Then help me to."

He considers but then slowly shakes his head.

"I don't have many friends here," I remind him. "It's not like I'll rat out your secrets to your brothers or your mother or anyone at the club."

"You might not have many friends, but you've rubbed enough elbows. And locals, they love talking about you." He sizes me up through the phone. "Grey Thornhall. The man who chased down his ex-wife in hopes of winning her back. It's romantic to some."

"Creepy to you," I add.

He doesn't deny it. I'd think he was full of shit if he did. "If you gave anyone here *anything*, they would fall all over you, Grey. They want to know you. They want to be close to you. They want to be the one you share everything with. You're a part of the social ether of Victoria. And that is . . ."

Power.

He's scared of me. Because he trusts me about as much as I trust him. Again, we're on a trust teeter-totter, and I've never dealt with a situation this fragile. He's not a part of a job. He's not someone I'm supposed to manipulate. He's just Phoebe's fake boyfriend and my sister's landlord.

"You're going to have to trust me again," I say to him.

Jake has a weighted frown. "I don't know if I should."

"I'm keeping your secret about your sister. What's bigger than that?"

His long neck strains. His squared jaw noticeably tightens. He's protective of her, and Jake on the defense is like a knight from King Arthur's round table grabbing a sword. He looks like he wants to cut my throat. "And you keep mentioning Kate."

"It's leverage. Wouldn't you bring it up if you had it on me?"

"Maybe," he admits, and cools off at my honesty. "How's your sister doing?"

I narrow my eyes. Tit for tat, huh? "Why do you care?"

"She didn't show up for work today."

"She's fine, Jake."

He nods.

I nod back.

We're not getting anywhere I want to be. "Trust me or don't. You're the one with something to lose. Not me." I give him a few seconds. His indecision is killing me, so I hang up. If he's serious, he'll call me back, but I have more important things to deal with.

The godmothers are in town.

I switch gears to the car. My life has been wrapped up in my parents' plans, their jobs, their decisions. Phoebe and I and our siblings have always said *yes*, and we're about to find out what happens when we finally try to take control.

FOUR

Phoebe

"How does it feel?" Rocky asks me late at night.

We're in the tiny kitchen of my cute and quaint loft that resides above Baubles & Bookends. Sharing a cheap bottle of Pinot Noir, which I bought last week for a girls' night with Hailey. It's probably sacrilege drinking it with her older brother while she's asleep. Especially knowing that she's clueless about me and Rocky hooking up.

She doesn't even know that I love him—let alone *like* him.

I'll be a better friend tomorrow.

Tonight is a wine night. Or a date night? I don't know what this is with Rocky—other than the aftermath of total chaos. It's one a.m. It'd be normal to be tired from the endless curveballs thrown at us in just forty-eight hours. But I'm seated on a high.

The roller coaster of our lives never stops plunging. I've never experienced a true calm, and weirdly, I don't think it's what I've been searching for in Victoria.

"How does what feel?" I ask . . . my boyfriend? Is that even what he is? I take a hearty sip from the bottle. Not tensed or uncomfortable. I'm just taking it *all* in. Me. Him. The newness of us together for real.

How I'm sitting cross-legged on the counter.

How he's standing and angling his weight against the cupboards, just to face me. Just to be inches away. Just to be near.

"Telling your mom *no* for once," he clarifies. "How does it feel?"

I texted my mom a short voice memo. I told her she's not matchmaking me and Rocky. Straight to the point. Nothing incriminating. If she wants to delete it, she can.

"It feels like she's blowing up my phone," I say as the screen lights up on the counter beside my kneecap.

My stomach plummets seeing her panic in real time.

"You care for her still?" Rocky asks.

"Not like I did," I say sourly, and pass him the Pinot. "It hurts. She *hurt* me, and I guess it feels like the woman I knew died. I don't even know who this person is anymore." It's why I'm not reaching for the phone to respond.

She can wait.

Rocky seems understanding. We're all slowly coming to terms with our parents' betrayal, and I don't expect either of my older brothers to have the same exact reaction as me. Not when we all had different relationships with our mom.

"What about you?" I ask Rocky. "How does it feel taking several hundred steps away from them?"

He lifts the bottle to his mouth. "Like we could take several hundred more." He swigs.

I wonder what will satisfy him. If anything really can. "We could be on different continents from them and I bet it wouldn't be far enough for you."

He licks wine off his lips. "Distance doesn't make my heart grow fonder."

"What does?" I ask. "Death?"

He widens his eyes. "Now there's an idea." He forces a dry smile.

"Plan to kill me, too?" I force a tight smile back.

He sets the Pinot on the counter. "My heart, or whatever's left of it, is already too fucking fond of you."

Breath sputters in my lungs, and my smile goes unsteady when his smoldering gaze traces over my features. We've only had sex once. But it was also with the pretense that we would be together for real and that the one time would turn into two times, then three, then a hundred thousand.

If this is actually a date, which I'm starting to believe *yes, it is, Phoebe,* then I imagine sex will follow . . . or start?

Honestly, I never really conceptualized what a real date with Rocky would be like. But regardless of what happens next, sharing time alone in a kitchen sounds about right.

I'm not dressed to the nines. I'm just wearing white sweatpants with an embroidered strawberry on the butt pocket. Wet strands of my hair stick against my chest and soak my cropped blue T-shirt from a recent shower.

My face is bare of makeup. My lips are only coated with Aquaphor to combat cracking.

Whereas Rocky is still in expensive navy-blue slacks and a black Calvin Klein tee. The cotton molds to his biceps, and I ache for those strong arms to wrap around me. To hold me so tightly and throttle feelings that I only ever feel with him.

Without thinking, I rest my palms flat behind me and uncross my legs. Spread my knees apart. "You want to fuck me, Ex-Husband?" I ask him quietly.

"*Fake* Ex-Husband," he corrects, his eyes glued to mine. Somehow, it's more intimate—Rocky staying fixed on my face rather than my pussy. His control heats my core.

"Fake Ex-Husband," I echo. "And Real . . . ?"

"Boyfriend," he declares. "That okay with you, Fake Ex-Wife?" *Yes, yes, yes!*

I smooth my lips together, a way too big smile trying to form. "It kind of sucks." I shrug.

"Liar," he calls me out casually, lovingly.

It softens my smile, and I peer past the cozy living room where two bookshelves flank a brick fireplace. A tiny hallway leads to two bedrooms, and right now, those doors are shut. I told Hailey to take my bed since Trevor has been crashing in hers.

The sofa has my name on it tonight.

There's such a slim chance either of them will wake up, and the risk that they might sounds oddly exhilarating.

Looks like I still love Danger with a capital D.

So I tempt Rocky a little more by lifting the hem of my shirt to my collarbone. No bra. I let him see my breasts and hardened nipples. The left one has a barbell piercing.

Again, he doesn't look.

What the hell.

My pulse suddenly races at the unknown trajectory of us, and my cheeks warm. "Afraid someone might walk in?"

"Of all the things to be afraid of?" He arches his brows. "That's not on my fucking list."

"Your fear of geese ranks higher?"

"I don't *like* geese. I'm not afraid of them."

I point a finger. "If you see *one* on a sidewalk, you will go out of your way to cross the street to avoid it. That is fear, not aversion."

He's struggling not to look at my boobs now, and a guttural, sexy noise rumbles in his throat.

I smile, more satisfied.

"Pull your shirt down."

"Take your shirt off," I counter.

Rocky grips the back collar of his tee, then pulls it over his head. Bare chested. Ridges of his abs and sculpted muscles capture my attention for a sweltering second, and the V line leading toward his cock almost seduces me forward.

Forcing my gaze to his, I remain cool, composed, not at all suffocating inside the toxins of arousal. Nope.

My lungs are on fire. "Nice abs."

"Nice tits." He's removing his belt.

My pulse pitches. *Where is this going?* The thrill is pure headiness, and I cling to the exhilaration for dear life.

Still, I bristle at the idea of being too easy. I want to be what I feel I truly am—rough around the edges, antagonistic, a sword to his sword. Fire to his fire.

Lounging back on my hands, I touch my foot to his chest. Keeping him at a distance. My heartbeat pounds so loud I'm surprised he can't hear it. "Maybe I don't want you," I say with slight rasp.

He devours me with one all-consuming look. "Maybe you know this won't stop me." He pushes my foot off like I'm putty and not steel.

As a counterstrike, I hop off the butcher-board counter. "Maybe this was all just for show." I tug my shirt down, hiding my tits.

He blocks me from passing, and the air strains when we go head-to-head. We're the apex predators, the ones in a molten standoff, the ones who clearly want to copulate.

He's fisting his belt.

I hear my shallow breath as he bows his head closer to my cheek, and in a deep, husky whisper, he says, "Maybe you're doing what you were born to do."

I stare him down. "Be a tease?"

"Lie through your fucking teeth." He stalks forward.

I step back.

Holy shit.

Our chests bump, and my knees threaten to buckle with unconscionable longings and more brutal desires. I crave for him to chase me. I crave for him to manhandle every vibrating inch of me. Until I don't know what's up or down. Until I black out.

He corners me against the cupboards. His left hand clutches my face. Possessive, forceful aggression. It's detonating. I almost slacken against his muscled build and succumb right here. I swallow a moan. "Rocky," I warn, glaring.

He eats it up. "Shall we count the fucking lies?" He threads his leg between mine, and I feel his weight against my body. Bearing on me so I can't move away. His lips touch my ear as his hot whisper ignites me. "One: you don't want me."

"Two," I say with heat. "You can't have me." I wrestle against him.

"Three." He pins me harder with his body. "You. Hate. *This*," he growls from his core, and I pulsate because I. Love. *This*. "Four: you hate how I'm never letting you go, no matter how much you protest."

My lips part to object, but an aching sound threatens to escape instead.

His fingers slide into my hair. Gripping the blue, wet strands. "Five: you hate how I'm going to destroy your little cunt tonight." Oh fuck. "Six: you hate how I won't stop. I'll never fucking stop. Railing you. In and out. Loving you. In . . . and out."

I'm trembling against him, and a noise squeaks out of me I've never heard before. I'm dizzy and miss the opportunity to shove him when he hoists me up on the counter.

"*Rocky.*" It's more wanting than combative this time. His lips graze my lips, and the almost-there glimpse of a kiss is obliterating me in . . . and out.

"Phoebe." Veins protrude in his neck as he keeps from exploding forward. He's edging us, and I have a very good feeling this is as big of a turn-on for him as it is for me.

Then suddenly, he captures my wrists.

Using the belt, he starts fastening them to the rattan handles of the seafoam-green cabinets above my head. "Safe word. Remember it?" he asks in a whisper.

I nod, trying to capture my runaway breath.

"Say it," he demands.

Then what? It's over before it starts. "You know, actually . . ." I cock my head, feigning confusion while I tug at the restraint. "It's not ringing a bell."

He narrows his eyes. "You really want me to leave you tied up all night, don't you?"

I glare. "You wouldn't."

"Safe word."

"Asshole." I scowl.

He flashes a dry smile. "Wrong one." He presses forward and grips the wooden counter beside my thighs, forcing my legs to spread open around him. He's assessing me, how I'm barely fighting against the leather belt, how I'm stalling—but not because I dislike being restrained by him. Then he asks, "You're afraid this is going to end soon? Is that it?"

Yeah. I inhale deeper.

It's attractive—how much Rocky can read into my actions like I'm an open book, when I feel like I've always lived untouched and lost on a dusty shelf. How long has he held the pages of who I am? How long has he loved each messy line?

How long have I loved the pages of who he is?

"Are *you* afraid it'll end soon?" I whisper.

He's gripping the back of my skull with an affection I could melt into. "No. Because I'm going to take my excruciating . . . long . . . hard time with you."

"Miami," I breathe out the safe word. Finally giving in to him.

There is only hunger and need in his eyes, and I return the sentiments in mine before our lips collide to a vicious beat inside me. *Holy . . . fuck.* His clawing, forceful kisses shove me harder into the cabinet. *Yes, God.* I instinctively jerk against the belt—to touch him.

I can't . . .

But his hands—they're on me. He's tearing my sweatpants to my ankles. "Be fucking quiet."

"You be fucking quiet," I hiss in a shortened, hot breath.

Sweatpants off. Pink lacy panties on. I think he's going to strip me completely naked, but Rocky fishes for the button of *his* slacks. He steps out of his navy-blue pants, then tugs off his boxer briefs with the confidence of a fucking god.

He is well endowed, extremely hard, and *very* naked in my shared kitchen. I like this—no, I'm *obsessed* with this. He's the one who's bare first, and maybe from our first time together he knew I really enjoyed seeing him strip.

He's not lifting my shirt to peer at my tits. I'm curious to see what turns him on, too. We're in an exploration phase, and sexual intimacy with Rocky is so enthrallingly new.

He slips my panties roughly off my legs, then grips my kneecaps and splits them back open. He's looking at my bare pussy with a primal expression. My heart rate accelerates at the vulnerability with him. Being naked from the waist down, I could probably do this anywhere and feel fine. If *fine* is hollow.

Now, I don't feel fine.

I feel combustible. On the verge of a volcanic eruption.

"Like what you see?" I rasp.

"Yeah," he says while staring deeply into my eyes. "I'm going to eat you alive, little nightmare." *Fuck me.* I can't even think before he has my ass in his hands. He hoists me upward while I instinctively hook my legs over his shoulders. My wrists pull at the cabinets, but Rocky keeps me steady.

He's face-to-face with my cunt, and I'm a withering, wet mess for him. All the while, his gaze is fixed on mine.

He never breaks.

Not when his mouth closes over my sensitive bud. Not when my thighs tremble against his shoulders. Not when he licks and sucks.

Ohh God . . . I imprison each moan in my throat, smothering the high-pitched, pleasured sounds. I'm breathy and losing sense of time as sweat builds, as Rocky's possessive hand rises against the curve of my hip.

His touch, his tongue, his presence electrifies every single inch of me.

But it's his eyes causing critical damage. I'm caught inside those gray swirls of tempestuous storms. It's a vortex he's dragged me into, and I'm wrenching him into mine. We're locked in, as if hurled into our twisted past—the years upon years of *longing* and grief of *needing.*

The intensity is unlike . . . anything.

I'm lost inside the transcendent moment, ripped into shreds by the way he works my arousal and emotions into a tight coil. I'm on an ascent for I don't know how long.

My breath heavies, and I'm struggling to stay silent. "Rocky." My warning turns into a quiet, *quiet* whimper. *"Please."* I need to come. I take it back—I don't want this to last forever. I'm going to be really fucking loud if he keeps stretching out this insane pleasure.

"I'm not done with you." His graveled voice sounds hoarser with need, and I try to glare, but I'm being eaten out by *Rocky*. The guy who's protected me my entire life. Who's always been there for me. Who will be there for me in new, exciting, unbelievable ways. *We're really together.*

He's all mine.

"*Please*," I whine. God, I can't believe I'm *whining* for him to make me come.

"Impatient much?" His graveled, asshole voice shouldn't be such a turn-on.

I groan, and despite my wrists being bound to the cabinet, I flip him off. He sees, and I swear he smiles before his tongue enters me.

This is torture.

The greatest kind.

The next time he sucks my clit, he drives a toe-curling orgasm out of me. My gasp turns into the start of a cry—he quickly plants a hand over my mouth and drops my legs and ass to the counter.

I'm shaking from a full-body climax. Spurred on from *oral*.

I'm a goner. Done. Deceased.

This can't be real life. My breath sputters from the aftermath of the shock waves, and Rocky is eye level with me once more. He brushes back pieces of my damp hair that have fallen in my face.

In the wake of his demolition, the softer gesture causes weird butterflies to flap inside my body.

"Can you keep going?" he asks seriously.

I intake sharp breaths. "Does it look like I can't?"

His brows spike. "You seriously want me to answer that?"

I scowl and make a point to inhale *mega* lungfuls of oxygen. "I'm not done with *you*," I retort and tug on the belt again. Frustrated that I can't put my hands on him.

He's near laughter.

I grow hotter. "It's not funny."

His smirk only widens. "It's really fucking funny, actually." He stands between my legs, and his masculine palms slide up my thighs to my hips. Oh, wow. My pulse skids, and I'm fastened to his assured movements and how he's drinking me in. "You don't want to fuck me, Phebs. You want me to fuck you."

"You can't know that," I whisper, cheeks heating. I'm both loving that he sees me so well and also hating how unraveling it feels. "We've only been together for a week, Rocky."

"Then let's go to the couch. You can fuck me while I just lie there with my hands behind my head."

I stubbornly ignore the roil of my stomach. "Fine. Let's go." I wait for him to untie me.

FIVE

Phoebe

Rocky moves *zero* muscles. He's staring through me. I wonder if he's crawled deep enough to smell the truth like a bloodhound. "Yeah? You want to rock my fucking world, Phoebe Graves? You want to ride me all night while I just come over the mere sight of you?" He pauses. "You're cringing."

I am. "I've done that before and liked it fine. I'm not selfish in bed." And I hate that I'm surfacing past hookups while *we're* in the midst of hooking up. This feels like a huge relationship faux pas. I did not want *failure at first real relationship* to be attached to my good name.

His brows furrow. "What makes you think what we're doing right now is you being selfish?"

"I'm not even touching you," I whisper hotly. I kind of want my wrists back, but then I don't. Am I a needy bitch with Rocky? Do I want to be *that* girl?

Yes.

And no.

Yes-no?

Choices are hard, and it feels like ever since I arrived in Victoria, I've had to make bigger ones. Which I should know how to do. I'm twenty-fucking-four, but since I've been raised as a follower—rarely the leader, rarely the dictator of where I live or what I'm doing in a job—making my own decisions hasn't been innate.

I'm used to conferring with the team. Taking a vote. Reasoning with others—like with my best friend. But I can't think of anything more awkward than asking Hailey to help me decide if I should fuck her older brother on the couch or let him fuck me against the cabinets.

No thank you.

Rocky hasn't shifted away. He's still intimately close. "I get off doing this to you. So are you really fucking selfish, Phebs? I could say the same thing about myself."

I contemplate this. "You prefer being in control?"

"All the time." His eyes skim me again. "But being this close to you makes me feel very, *very* out of control." By the depth of his expression tunneling through me, he clearly likes the unhinged feeling, too.

I breathe in. "Okay."

"Okay," he murmurs, "and so you know"—he pulls away and finds his slacks on the floor—"when I fuck you tonight, you're going to feel a lot more than just *fine*."

Arousal bathes me inch by inch. I squirm for him.

I watch Rocky fish out a condom from his slacks pocket, and I cast a quick glance to the two bedrooms.

His brother or sister could still walk in, and it's not stopping him. Not as he sheaths his erection and moves back between my legs.

I love the stakes.

The danger.

But really, I love it with Rocky. It's danger with a soft, padded cushion at the bottom of the fall. It's danger with an antidote to the poisoned draft. It's danger with the security and safety of him.

I scoot closer to the edge of the counter. He's at the perfect height, and as I wrap my legs around his waist, our pelvises are aligned.

Now he lifts my cropped tee back to my collarbones. Cold air hits my nipples, but as he kneads one tender breast and crushes agonizing kisses to my lips, all I feel is heat.

His mouth veers to my ear. "You need to know something while we're together."

"Hmm-mm, sure." I'm *so* composed and not at all an emotional fool for him.

"This." He slips his finger against my swollen clit. *Oh my God*. His whisper pricks my ear again. "*This*." He teases his finger into me. "Is mine."

I shudder and a noise catches in my throat.

Then his hand leaves the warmth between my legs. He's suddenly pushing his thick, hard cock into my heat. I try not to unravel at the fullness. Rocky whispers how deep he's inside me, how my tight, wet pussy belongs to him, how he's going to take me without pause or restraint—and every carnal word *soaks* me.

He thrusts at a rough, hypnotic tempo. Since I've already come once, the friction and sensitivity sends me so fast.

My eyes threaten to roll back.

"Look at me." He has two bunches of my hair. Holding my head, he's guiding my line of sight downward. "See what I'm doing to your cunt?"

He flexes in and out, and I watch his veined shaft disappear inside me. I'm surprised I'm not falling apart. It feels like he has all of me, to do whatever he wants with me, and I am more than happy—and trusting—to place myself in Rocky's care.

His lips press to the top of my head, and I feel him muffling a "fuck" and grunted groan into my hair. Then he kisses my temple and yanks my hair, causing my scalp to tingle. *Ah yes, yes!* I don't just love this.

I love him.

He rams deeper. "Can you keep taking my cock, Phebs? Think your little pussy can handle me? Because I'm not so fucking sure."

"Yes, and fuck you," I whisper-*moan*.

He clutches my face while pounding inside me. "No, *fuck you*." Our glares make brutal love, and he thrusts so quickly, I see stars. His hand shields my mouth while my body jostles against him, while his heavy breath is the only sound in the tensed, pleasured air.

Rapidly, he's unbuckling the belt while he's thrusting. He frees my arms in milliseconds, but I'm weak as I ascend toward another climax—only able to loosely hold his neck. He takes me off the counter. He has me in his strong arms and melds me to his muscled chest. He bounces me on his cock and then flexes up into me.

This is too much, and yet, I want more. I fear it'll all stop.

His forehead is on mine. He's chasing after the heady look in my eyes. I almost scream out his name, but somehow, it's lost in the haze as I clench around him. Coming in powerful, electric waves.

I gasp into his muscled shoulder.

I feel his cock twitch inside me, and he milks the climax by arching up into me. Once we're done, he picks me off him and carefully sets me on my feet.

I stumble back against the fridge. Holy shit. That was . . .

wow. I think I finally understand the term *fuck your brains out*, because I can hardly think straight right now.

He discards the full condom in a paper towel, then throws it in the trash bin. He washes and dries his hands in the sink. Thankfully, I'm not the only one speechless. He's catching his breath, and when our eyes meet across the kitchen, we both start to smile.

I haven't had much time to think about what our relationship or sex life would look like together. I probably hoped it'd be this fulfilling, but never, in my wildest dreams, did I think it'd be this fun.

I manage to whisper, "I honestly wasn't sure if anything could top our first time together." *Where I came four times.*

"This beat it?"

I shrug. "Came close." I pull down my tee. "You'll have to try harder next time."

"I'd believe you were flirting with me if you didn't sound so snide." He wears a sexy smile, and he runs his fingers through his sweaty hair.

I don't know why I'm blushing.

What's happening to me?

Rocky squats at my feet and picks up my panties. He's about to put them on for me, and my pulse races.

I start to say, "I can . . ." *do it myself.*

Yes, I am fully capable of putting on my own panties, but I falter. Because maybe I don't hate the idea of Rocky being sweet after a rough fuck.

He's waiting for my response. What I choose might set the standard for our relationship going forward. What if I pick wrong? What if seven years from now, I regret shutting him down, and I'm going to wish Rocky dressed me after he undressed me because he'll never try again?

He's about to stand up.

"Wait." I stop him.

He's assessing. "You want me to or not?"

"Well, when you say it like that," I bite back.

A smile flickers across his face. "We're not solving world hunger here, Phebs. It's not that serious."

I ease back against the fridge, and I nod, seeing this isn't going to make or break the situation between us. *What do you want from him, Phoebe?* "Yeah. You can," I murmur.

He helps shimmy my panties up my legs, then my hips. Letting them ride high. He stands opposite me, his hand on my waist, and tension weaves between us, making the air thicker. It's hard to breathe.

"You're killing me," he whispers into a frustrated growl, then he breaks apart to collect his clothes. I find my sweatpants, too.

"I could spend the night at your place." I suggest the boathouse he's renting in case we want to hook up again. Less chance of anyone discovering us.

"Your brothers still live with me."

I give him a weird look. "Your sister and brother live with me." I motion toward the short hallway where the bedrooms lie. "They're right there."

He whispers back, "Neither of which will punch me in the face if they catch me hooking up with you."

"You're scared of Nova?" My oldest brother has never gelled with Rocky, but they buried a small hatchet during Halloween. They're very much on the same can't-trust-our-parents side now.

Surprisingly, we all are.

Rocky fishes his belt through the loops. "I'm not scared. I just don't want a black eye."

"Understandable."

Nova and Rocky have brawled over less.

Once we're fully dressed as if nothing indecent just occurred, he comes closer when he sees me rubbing at my sore arms. Rocky massages my biceps and forearm with careful pressure, and my heart flip-flops in new patterns.

He's been kind to me after many jobs before. He's wrapped his arms so fiercely around me, hugging me for minutes on end. I fell deeply into those death-gripping seconds with him. I believed he needed the embrace, too.

I sensed him feeling how I was in one piece. I sensed him trying to hold us together. To physically feel that we made it through that city, that moment, that con.

But tonight is different. This isn't about the end of a job.

A real relationship. Me and Rocky. Yep, it's still dawning on me that this is happening.

"Thanks," I murmur.

Quietly, he asks, "Have you eaten anything today?"

"Not that much. You?"

"I could eat."

So I whirl around to open the fridge. Behind me, Rocky weaves his arms around my frame, and on pure instinct, I lean my weight against his body, knowing he'll hold me tighter. He does. When he plants a kiss to my hair, a stupid smile spreads across my face.

"I didn't realize you and my sister are living off of . . . pickles and string cheese?" The shelves are mostly bare, except for a handful of quick snack foods.

"I take offense that you're outing my string cheese. It's nutritious and *fun*."

"For a four-year-old."

Smile *gone*. "For a *twenty*-four-year-old. And who made

you the string cheese police?" I rotate on him, almost wishing I didn't because his arms drop off me.

"You, apparently." He sweeps me with a dark yet caring look that skips my pulse, then his brows do this deep, concerned furrow at the barren state of my refrigerator.

"Groceries are expensive," I remind him.

"Still penny-pinching?" He says it like it's dumb since I have the tools to trick people into giving me money. But Rocky also isn't actively roping me into rejoining a life of deceit. Technically, I haven't really left since I've been fake dating Jake.

Deciding what I want to do with my life feels a lot less critically important than figuring out what our parents have hidden from us. Even if Hails orchestrated this move to Victoria so I'd stop grifting, I don't feel in a rush to quit cold turkey.

I'm just taking everything day by day.

"I know it makes zero sense to you, Rocky, but I haven't hated being a server."

"What do you like about it? Seeing as how you're not in it for the money."

I shrug. "I'm more myself there than I've ever been . . . *anywhere*, and when it does suck, I can commiserate with Hailey. Plus, it can be entertaining. I get to see the nucleus of the town drama."

"You're in the nucleus, Phebs." He reaches around me to open a fridge drawer. Empty. "Is this really a product of lack of money or because you can't cook?"

"I can cook."

"Microwaved mac 'n' cheese doesn't count."

"Then you can't cook either," I say, sounding hostile.

All of us were taught to order food at five-star establishments, not consult a recipe to make it ourselves. Oliver is the only one who's gone out of his way to learn how to properly sauté a scallop and make hollandaise.

And that's because he was a sous chef for three weeks.

"Yeah, I can't cook," Rocky says roughly, "but I'm the one eating rib eyes from James Beard Award–winning chefs. What are you doing?"

"Thriving."

He laughs.

I glare. "I hope you choke on those hockey pucks, by the way." Okay, yes, the award-winning chef isn't serving charred meat. I've smelled those perfectly seared steaks on scoops of garlic mashed potatoes, and my mouth has watered serving them to this old biddy named Margaret at the country club.

"Not hockey pucks. They're never overcooked. Always rare. *Bloody.*" He tips his head to the side. "Just how you like it—since you were, what? Fourteen?"

I flush. "Maybe."

"Maybe." He gives me an exposing once-over. "You copied me."

"What?" I balk.

"I ordered a prime rib so bloody at Spear & Knife in Dallas that it was practically raw, and after that, you kept ordering your steak the same way." We were teenagers. He's unearthing ancient fucking history.

I scoff. "Coincidence."

"You're beet red."

"Out of *anger.*" Truth: I'm embarrassed because I might have, maybe, learned to order my steak the same way as Rocky, and this shouldn't even be something mortifying. So what? Except, I don't want him to think I was an impressionable youth, and he made such a *big* impression on me.

He might've made a small, microscopic, *hardly there* one.

But I realize . . . "You remember that moment? From that long ago?"

"My memory isn't shit."

"No, you were paying attention to me," I reason. "You were *obsessed* with me."

He says nothing. He doesn't deny it like I imagined he would, and in the silence, my pulse has boomeranged across the kitchen and returned to me. His voice is deep, rough, low. "I've loved you since I was fifteen; of course I focused on you."

I intake a staggered breath, a heady feeling washing over me like I was just dunk-tanked in ice water.

It's strange how much he's verbalizing our love. It's not that strange how much I tailspin at hearing it. I open my mouth to find the words to say back, but he's inspecting the fridge again.

He picks up a jar with one pickle floating in murky juice. "Eating dill spears for breakfast?"

"*Spicy* dill spears, sir."

He rolls his eyes but he's starting to smile. "Whatever the fuck, *ma'am*. That's not a breakfast."

"It's a snack," I agree. "And Hailey and I mostly eat out."

"Figured that." Placing the jar back, he unpockets his phone. "Seaside Griddle is still open. I can order us takeout." The local breakfast joint is open 24/7 and a short walk down the street.

There must be something worth eating here, though. I'm not ready to give up. "We have milk." I tug out the half gallon of one percent. "And I know we have cereal in the pantry."

That's how I find myself eating bowls of Froot Loops and Fruity Pebbles past one a.m. with Rocky. Lights still on, we're settled comfortably on the sofa, where I've tucked in sheets on the cushion and brought in my bed pillow.

He's scrolling through Netflix for a movie, and he's not

even asking which genre. He's already clicked into *horror* for me.

Giddiness is an overwhelming ingredient in our relationship. The addition almost makes me feel high.

And we're not even screwing some douchebag out of millions. No one is being double-crossed by our duplicitous hands.

This is just . . . normal.

I scoop up some Froot Loops and look over at him. By his brooding face, you'd think the TV fleeced him and he's plotting murder. That's just Rocky. Sitting in cynicism and hatred, but I'd like to believe he gets enjoyment from being here with me. Or else he'd be long gone by now, and he's never really left me.

"Would you consider this a date?" I ask him.

His head jerks in slight surprise, but I *am* confident. I stand fully by this pressing question. He sees and answers honestly. "Sex, dinner, and a movie. Sounds like a date to me."

"Same."

"Glad we could agree on something."

"And look, the earth didn't rip in half," I joke.

"There's still time for that."

We share a brief, rising smile. *Brief* because the front door suddenly jostles open. I freeze.

Rocky is a shotgun. He's quick to his feet, the bowl of Fruity Pebbles in his hand like a projectile weapon, and he's standing in front of me. First thought is, *our parents*. They found my address.

They're making an unwanted visit.

Fear recedes into a mountain of concern as I see who shuffles inside.

SIX

Phoebe

I frown. "Hails?"

She should be fast asleep in my bed right now. Not only is she wide awake, but she's carrying a stack of worn leather-bound books against her small frame. I'm not sure she even heard me since she's not responding.

Struggling to hold the hardbacks, she blows a strand of platinum-blonde hair off her chapped lips and nearly loses the stack trying to shut the door.

I run over to her before Rocky can, and I gather several books in my arms.

"Thanks, Phoebe." She's on a mission, barely pausing as she plops her stack on our two-seater bistro table.

Too many alarmed questions zip through me at once, and I go with the most useless one (don't come for me). "Who do these books belong to? A crypt keeper?" I pile my stack on top of hers.

"Jake."

My eyes bug. "Excuse me? Jake, as in our landlord?" *And*

soon to be fake ex-boyfriend, but I don't want to say the words and remind everyone of my current fake relationship. Mostly for Rocky's sake.

Hailey isn't answering. She's flipping open a book.

I swing back to Rocky, and his dark concern is palpable. Jaw locking, muscles tensing, eyes narrowing—Hailey sees *none* of her brother's protective storm cloud. No, she's reading these yellowed, crusty pages at a mile a minute.

"Hailey," Rocky calls out.

"Huh?" She doesn't look up.

Okay, this is way more serious than I realized. Her plum-colored lipstick is faded in certain spots. Has she been biting her lips? Bluish tint circles her eyes and appears like makeup, but now I'm seeing it's not from an eyeshadow palette. It's from being sleep deprived.

I scoot the second chair next to hers. Sitting, I hesitate to reach out a hand and disrupt her mental focus too much. "Have you slept, Hails?"

She flips a page.

"Hailey?" I ask again.

"Yeah."

"She doesn't know what she's responding to," Rocky tells me, coming over to us. It's very clear Hailey is about one-tenth listening to me and zero-tenths listening to Rocky. She's tuning out her surroundings to concentrate on these dusty texts.

Rocky grabs a faded gray book.

"St-stop," Hailey stammers. "Put it back, Rocky. *Please*."

"Put it back," I tell him. Her distress is like a knife in my gut, and I want to yank the blade out like right now.

Rocky gives me a sharp look. "I'm not hurting it." He examines the title on the spine. "Why would Jake lend you a book on the history of Victoria's seaports?"

"I-I can't . . . Put the book back. Put it back." She's on the verge of shaking. "Phoebe."

I stand. "Rocky." I'm a second from tugging the novel out of his hands.

His gaze darkens. He passes me to set the novel on the stack. She relaxes, but he whisper-sneers against my ear, "You're not helping her."

"Neither are you," I sneer back. We're both hot blooded over how best to take care of her. There've been a few instances where I've seen Hailey spiral this way, but not enough that Rocky and I have a well-formulated mode of action to help her. And when she's pleading for me, how can I not come to her aid? How can I not do what she asks?

His hand stays on the small of my back, and we both take a few silent breaths, trying to extinguish the heat. Being pent up with aggravation isn't going to help her either.

Hailey muffles her ears with her hands. Not wanting to even hear us anymore. She's just skimming the books at rapid-fire speed.

I lower back into the seat.

"We need to take the books away," Rocky says.

"She'll freak out."

"She won't stop reading."

"You know she'll just go grab her computer and do research."

"Then we take her fucking computer."

"I'm not locking her in a padded room!" I shout, and my throat swells painfully.

Rocky rakes two hands through his dyed-black hair. He's torn up. "She's not blinking."

I know.

I know.

I manage to croak out, "We're not doctors, Rocky. We don't know what's right."

"You don't leave a drug addict with a syringe and a vial."

He's not saying she's addicted to books, but obviously she's obsessing over them right now. My face twists at the idea of removing the subject of her hyperfixation. "What if it makes things worse? What if it's not what you're supposed to do in this situation?"

"Well, it's not like she can go to a fucking psychologist and figure it out." His bitterness drips off the words. Just another product of our criminal upbringings, really. We can't unleash our history on a doctor without basically sending ourselves to jail.

It sort of feels like the six of us live in a Middle Ages fantasy world like Westeros, where physicians wouldn't have a modern diagnosis. They'd probably just think Hailey lost her mind.

"Phoebe," Rocky says, trying to sound gentle (he sucks at it). "We'll never know if it's the wrong or right thing unless we try."

"Okay, okay," I agree, but my ribs are squeezing around my lungs. Together, Rocky and I swoop in and scoop up the hardbacks.

"N-no, *no*, please. Phoebe." Her breathing pattern sounds hoarse and *awful*. Like she's sucking in a plastic bag.

"Rocky, I can't." It hurts. My entire body is being crushed, and I immediately place the books within his sister's reach. "I'm sorry." I can't even look at him. Defeated, I take a stiff seat beside Hailey and do my best not to cause her more panic.

Rocky lets out a deep sigh. When his hand suddenly warms the back of my neck, I ease at the unexpected comfort. I look up at him, but his gaze is planted on his sister.

"You might be right," he says.

I shake my head, feeling like I'm making this worse.

"Just try talking to her, Phebs."

I swallow a lump in my throat and shift closer to my friend. "Hailey? How long have you been awake?"

She mutters to herself. I think she's reading out loud.

"When did you go see Jake?" I ask.

Nothing.

Rocky is a rigid tower beside me.

She's not covering her ears again, so I take this as a sign we're making progress. Baby steps. "Hey, can you tell me what you're reading?"

"St-stuff about Connecticut. The history . . ." She scoots farther into the table, practically pressing her face into the book. The chain on her black cargo pants jingles while her leg jostles. "I'm-I'm figuring it out." She rubs at her watery eye and flips another page. "I'm going to figure it out."

"Figure what out?" I ask.

"Who we are."

The bottom of my stomach drops.

Rocky shifts his weight. "What does Connecticut have to do with that?"

"I-I don't know yet." She blinks a few times. Good. Yes! *Keep blinking, you beautiful genius.* "We can't trust . . . we can't believe anything. She-she might've even lied about her blood type, and then who knows what anymore? We know nothing. We know nothing." Her eyes are glazed, staring off into the middle of the room.

She must be her mom. Addison.

"You need sleep," I say so softly to Hailey, and somehow this draws her gray eyes to mine. "Real sleep, Hails. Can you go to bed? Please? For me?"

Her eyelashes flutter, and very zombielike, she rises and

spins three sixty. Rocky reaches out to steady her, but she's not in danger of falling. She's just lost. Like she's searching for something.

"Where's Olly?" she whispers.

"It's late. Oliver and Nova are back at the boathouse," I tell her. "Trevor is asleep in your bed. You're going to crash in mine, okay?"

Hailey nods slowly. "Yeah . . . yeah." I guide her into my bedroom, and Rocky pours his sister a water while I help her take off her Converse sneakers and climb beneath the fluffy marshmallow comforter.

Rocky places the water on the nightstand. "You need to drink something."

She takes a few sips, and when she looks up at her brother, her round eyes go glassy, like snow globes pooled with water. "We-we might not be . . ."

"You will *always* be my sister," Rocky professes. "There is nothing in my lifetime that could change that, Hailey. Not one fucking thing."

This eases her enough that she lies back.

I tuck her in. "Just shut your eyes and brain. Don't think about anything except your body sinking into the mattress."

She shuts her eyes, and I wipe the involuntary tears from the corners with my thumb. My heart is aching, especially as she croaks out, "Thanks, Phoebe."

"No *thanks*. Just sleep."

Before we leave, she mutters one thing. "He-he once told me about his family's library. I asked if I could borrow the books . . ."

Jake, she means.

"Okay," I whisper. "Sleep."

Once we switch off the lights and quietly exit, Rocky

checks on Trevor and says, "Asleep." At least his little brother didn't sneak out.

I release the tensest breath of my life, and Rocky's concern is on me. "You okay?"

I nod a lot. *Yeah.* The word sticks to the back of my throat. I just want Hailey to be okay.

Rocky threads his fingers behind his stiff neck. His glare is lethal, and he's doing everything not to place it on me.

"I'm going to kill him," he fumes. "I'm going to fucking *kill* him."

"Jake?"

"Who else?"

I make a face like he's scaling Mount Everest when we should be climbing K2. "Jake was only trying to help her. They both like books. It's been a commonality between them since we moved here, Rocky. Can't you picture a scenario where Hailey reaches out to Jake, asks for a favor, and Jake gladly abides because he's *nice*? Because I can."

"This was a face-to-face meetup. *Face-to-face.*" He manages to keep his voice down. "He physically handed her the books, and he didn't think to shoot you or me a text about it? He didn't *think* to tell us Hailey looks a little fucked up? He didn't see her and go, *Gee, maybe this girl is an insomniac?* Is he really that dense, Phoebe, or are we being played?"

I frown. "Hailey probably brushed it off or told him not to alarm us. Because I can't see a situation where Jake doesn't care about her. He cares about people he doesn't even know, and he knows Hailey. It'd be cruel, and he's so far from that."

"That we know of."

"He would be a sociopath."

Rocky outstretches his arms. "Maybe he is one."

"If you really believed that, then all of our bags would be

packed, and Victoria would be in our rearview mirror." Jake has never been a real threat to Rocky.

He smears a hand down his face, then breathes out the coarse grit in his throat. "Fine."

"Fine . . ." There's one thing about Jake that I've just learned today. That I need to share, but Rocky reclaims his seat on the sofa.

I follow and pick up my bowl of cereal. The Froot Loops are mushy, but I swallow a scoop anyway. Is Toucan Sam courage a thing? Because I could use some right now. I just don't want another reason for Rocky to doubt Jake when he's been an ally, but the seed is already planted. It's sprouted into a beanstalk, and I'm not capable of chopping it down.

He reaches over and shuts off the lamp for the movie. Light from the TV brightens the dark living room, and we decide on *The Texas Chainsaw Massacre* from 2003. I'd rather just watch the slasher flick, but he's too good at reading body language.

"We can forget about Jake. He's breaking up with you within a week, and what I feel about him doesn't matter anyway. Right?"

"Yeah." I nod tensely.

He nods back, seeing. "What's wrong?"

Rotating more to him, I lift my legs up, and before I can tuck them under my butt, he seizes them, letting me stretch out over his lap. His hand stays protectively, comfortingly, territorially over my calves.

It's such an intimate gesture. It reminds me of how we are on jobs, not in real life, and knowing this is now my every day, I almost melt into the side of the couch cushion.

Maintain composure.

I can do that. I'm a fucking professional.

"Remember how I didn't eat much today?" I start off.

"Yeah?"

"It's also why I didn't see Hailey until . . . like right now. It's because work was hectic, and by the time Jake convinced Katherine to let me go early, my shift was thirty minutes from ending."

"Jesus Christ." He rolls his eyes into a heated glare. "What does she have on him?"

"Nothing. He just respects her, I think, and apparently, she's his godmother."

His brows jump. "Come again?"

"She was first his nanny. That's what Jake told me, at least. His family loved her enough that they wanted her to stick around after their youngest was grown, so they hired her to manage the country club."

I explain further how I've noticed that Jake has mannerisms eerily similar to Katherine's. The sharp side-eyes, the disappointed parental expressions. I believe she helped raise him.

Rocky pinches his eyes, then rests his arm on the back of the sofa. "He's hiding too much."

"*We're* hiding more."

"If he's anything like us, then it really isn't safe to be here."

I watch him fixate on the paused intro of *Chainsaw Massacre*, and I tell him, "I don't see you preparing for a big move."

"That's because I'm on a date with my girlfriend."

My lips turn up. "I'd think you were flirting with me if you didn't have a sarcastic fucking smile while you said it." I use some of his words from *much* earlier in the night, and he must remember.

Because he laughs for real.

After abandoning the cereal on the coffee table, I sink

against his chest, feeling the rumble of the last bits of laughter, and with his arm around me, he presses play on the remote. Not even three minutes in and his phone rings.

"For fuck's sake," he mutters, digging it out of his pocket. There's only a handful of people who'd contact us at this hour. He flashes the random number to me. "It might be someone calling from a burner phone."

I worry about my brothers. Until Rocky answers the call on speaker and his father's stringent voice floods the room.

"Brayden? Are you alone?"

We've all been screening our parents' incessant calls and texts, but we've known we'd need to confront them soon. I just didn't think it'd be *tonight*.

He pries his bicep off my shoulder, then sits forward. "Yeah, I'm alone," he lies. "It's late, Dad."

"We need to talk about what's going on." The urgency in his tone pricks the hair on my arms.

"What's going on?" Rocky spits out. "Mom and Elizabeth show up here, *unannounced*—"

"Shit happens," Everett cuts in. "You've been taught to coast into a con, have you not?"

"We're not riding a fucking Malibu wave—"

"This isn't new," he interjects again, and Rocky's annoyance could sever the air. He swallows the feeling and listens as Everett continues. "Your mother and Elizabeth showing up out of the blue is something you *all* should be prepared for. You're not little kids anymore. You don't need your hand held."

Usually, I'd agree. Yeah, he has a point. The shock and awe shouldn't startle us, but that was before we knew they've been actively *lying* to us. Rage swarms me just hearing his condescending lecture, on top of the fact that he might not even be

Rocky's dad! He might've stolen him out of an orphanage, a bassinet—hopefully not a womb, or I will *murder* him myself.

"Thanks for the pro-tip," Rocky says coarsely. "Why'd you even call?"

"The rainmaking job." It's what the matchmaking con is technically called.

Rainmaking.

It's where we promise a mark that we'll use our influence to "make it rain" for them. In this case, our moms are likely promising Claudia Waterford they can break me and Jake apart by matchmaking me with Rocky.

"It's not happening," Rocky says. "Phoebe already told Elizabeth."

"It's a short con. It'll last a week, tops. You can convince her to do it."

My mouth drops. *What?* I mouth to Rocky.

His nose flares. "That's *not* fucking happening," he whisper-sneers into the phone. "Pocket whatever Claudia paid you and call it off."

Everett sounds exasperated. "Whatever job you've started, you need to end it."

We're not here to scam anyone.

Rocky conceals this card. "Why?" he asks.

"It's not safe for your sister or your brother or the Graveses to be there. Understand? You either need to do the short rainmaking job with your mom or finish what you're doing and get out. We don't pull jobs in Connecticut."

I blow back, and my head whirls in blistering confusion.

"Since when?" Rocky barks.

"Since *forever.*"

No, this is a rule we've never been told until now. If I forgot it, then Nova would've remembered, and my brother never said Connecticut was a danger zone.

The line is dead quiet, except for Everett's labored breaths. I'd believe he was jogging around a track if I could hear his footfalls. "You have one job, son. The most important job of your life—"

"Protect them, I know," Rocky says, glancing briefly, almost painfully, to me before dragging his harsh gaze across the coffee table and our soggy bowls of cereal. "We'll all need to get together. Safe location. The six of us will pick the place. You can pick the time. We'll talk more then."

"Okay. I'll confer with your mom and Elizabeth." At this, they hang up, and neither of us releases any breaths this time.

There is no relief. Just a tsunami of uncertainty and doubt, and the wave is cresting over our heads, threatening to envelop us whole.

He taps the phone in his palm, thinking. "When we first drove here, I thought about how unfamiliar Connecticut is to me, but I couldn't be sure. Now . . . I'm almost certain. We've never pulled a con in this state before."

"But maybe our parents have," I realize.

There are very few reasons to avoid an entire state like the plague, and one of the greatest is a con gone wrong or a job so big that you can never go back.

Only, Elizabeth and Addison showed their faces at the country club. They *appeared* there for the rainmaking job.

A short con.

In hopes of getting us to leave Connecticut faster? If they think we're pulling some lengthy, drawn-out scam here without them, then yeah, it'd be a good ploy to draw us back and get us to pack our bags.

Rocky peers over his shoulder toward my bedroom, then to the deserted hardbacks on the bistro table. "Hailey is always five steps ahead of us, Phebs. If she's digging into Connecticut, into Victoria, then she must believe it's all connected. Who we are and why we've never pulled a con here."

I scrunch my face. "Doesn't it seem too coincidental? That out of everywhere, we just so happened to stumble on the one place that could tell us about our births?"

Rocky leans back beside me. "I don't care if it is or isn't. If this state has even a single answer to what our parents are hiding about us, then I want that truth."

Clarity.

That sounds like real relief to me. I nod a few times. "Yeah, I do, too."

SEVEN

Rocky

I've hated it here, but Victoria isn't special. I've hated it everywhere I've *ever* been for the past twenty-some years. But as I wake up on a lumpy sofa with a blue-haired girl asleep on my chest, with the TV paused on Leatherface and rain beating the panes of a foggy window, there is nowhere else I'd rather be.

No one else I'd rather hold. No one else I'd rather love than my Phoebe.

My lips tic in a slight smile. I remember our childhood. Where we claimed each other like we knew we'd fall in love eventually. *My Phoebe.*

Being sentimental is for the fucking fools, and I feel myself being grossly sentimental over her. I can't stop it. I don't even really want to.

Preserving this, protecting her—it consumes my waking thoughts. It's to the point where I'd claw through stone to keep her and rip apart any fucker who tries to take her from me.

"Mmmhmm," Phoebe moans while her eyes fight the morning light.

Not wanting her to shift off my body, I skate my fingers through her hair. Over and over. As I continue the melodic movement against her scalp, her limbs slacken, and she falls back to sleep.

Dipping toward her, I press a kiss to her head. *I have her.* In my arms. Amid a lot of bullshit and torment in our lives, this is the *one* reassuring feeling.

I have Phoebe.

For now.

It's fear. That with any wrong turn, I could lose her. At any moment.

Fear is just a monster created by another monster. My father. So how much of it is real and how much of it is just him *manipulating* me?

Before I let him ruin this quiet, warm moment in my brain—someone else does. A knock raps against the door, and Phoebe jolts at the same time I sit up.

Our foreheads bang.

"Shit," I curse, while she says, "Ow, fuck."

I clutch her head protectively, kiss the reddened spot, and stand fast to answer whoever the hell is on the other side of the fucking door. It's not even eight a.m.

"Don't your brothers have keys?" I ask her.

She's on my heels, following. "Yeah, they do. Nova made copies."

"Breaking one of your landlord's pointless rules," I mention.

"Don't tell Jake that," Phoebe warns. "He's already upset about calling off my fake relationship with him—"

"Which he hasn't done yet," I cut in, just as we hear another three knocks. They sound less aggressive. More polite.

I sincerely hope it's only Oliver and he's lost his key.

"We gave him a week to break up with me," Phoebe says.

"He'll do it, or we will. And I don't want Jake to have any reason to end our lease."

Irritation mounted on burning anger—that's what's eating through me. "If he ends your lease over you making copies of your keys or because he's not getting his fake girlfriend for another two months, I will leave him broken on the floor."

She's trying not to smile. "Don't."

"Be a little more convincing next time and maybe I'll consider it."

She groans out like I'm horrible, but she's also fighting a grin.

Then I swing the door open. All dark banter vacates the loft. Because I face the ever so fucking tall Jake *Koning* Waterford.

"Hey, sorry." He's out of breath, and he looks like a sopping-wet golden retriever.

Water drips off his light brown hair, and a soaked blue button-down suctions to his six-pack and chest. Look who forgot an umbrella and probably sprinted through the rain.

I hope he drowns in the thunderstorm and slips into a sewer and eats shit.

"Are you all right?" Phoebe asks.

Is *he* all right? "He's fine, Phebs."

"I am fine," Jake interjects, finally filling his lungs with oxygen. He wipes the wet rain trails off his face with one hand. "I just got caught in the rain, and I wanted to check on Hailey. She asked me for some books from my family's library, and I met her last night at Seaside Griddle to give them to her . . . but she seemed off. She wouldn't let me walk her home, and it's kept me up all night. She is here, right?"

Phoebe sends me an *I told you so* smug expression. She's just short of saying, *See, Jake cares.*

I grip either side of the doorframe so Phoebe doesn't butt in and soften this exchange. "Ever hear of this modern device used to call people?" I mime a phone with my hand. *"Hey, Grey, how's your sister doing? Good? Great. Bye."* I hang up and force an acidic smile. "Is it that hard?"

"With you, yeah." He nods strongly. "Yeah, it can be, Grey. You're a real fucking piece of work, and it boggles my *mind* how you could even have a sister as nice as Hailey and a wife like Phoebe—though, the *ex* part of *wife*, I definitely get."

I boil. "Your presence is unwelcome."

Jake has a hardened scowl.

"It irks you," I say. "Mr. I Own This Town being told he doesn't belong somewhere."

"You're in my loft."

"Yeah." I look at him head-on. "I fucked your fake girl-friend in it."

Jake is borderline enraged.

"On your kitchen counter. Against your cabinets. And I'll continue fucking her. Over and *over* again."

He controls his anger enough to find Phoebe behind me. He's protective of her—that is vitally clear now.

But as soon as he catches sight of Phoebe, something switches in his face. Uncertainty?

It's this moment that I peer over at her.

Her breath is shallow. Each lungful pushes her perked nipples against her cropped blue T-shirt. Jake sees that she's turned on by me, and I hate that he's staring at her tits.

I shove him back from the entryway and grip the door, about to slam it closed and meet him on the landing in private.

But Phoebe grabs the knob. "Rocky, seriously, *don't*."

She can keep the door open. It isn't stopping me from push-ing Jake up against the fucking wall. At the top of the stairwell, he extends his arms in a slight surrender, but I say between gritted teeth, "You're pissing on the wrong grass. Find a new plot of land that doesn't belong to her or my sister."

Jake exhales a slow, taxing breath, and his muscles loosen like he's relinquishing this fight. "Okay, *okay*." When I let him go, I expect him to say a quick goodbye to Phoebe and get the hell out of here, but he *lingers*.

I run my tongue against my molars.

He expresses deeply, "I only want to check on Hailey. Then I'll go."

Jesus, he's not giving up. I would respect it more if I liked him more.

"Rocky, it's okay," Phoebe says. "It's pouring out. Just let him inside. We can ask Hailey if she wants to see him."

"We're friends," Jake professes to me. "We go to the same book club on Tuesdays. Look, I just need to know she's all right."

"You don't believe me when I tell you she is?"

"No offense, but I'd feel better if I saw with my own two eyes."

Funny enough, I relate to that feeling. I understand needing more than words so you aren't sold a bag of lies, and it's not the first time I've found Jake relatable. I hate that it's swaying me, but here we are.

Against sound judgement, I let him through.

We're not even two steps into the kitchen, and I instantly regret it. Because my nineteen-year-old brother stumbles weakly out of Hailey's bedroom in a slim, black Brioni suit with various white gold rings on each finger like he's planning to dine at a three-Michelin-star restaurant.

"Where are you going?" I ask him, trying to ignore the confusion radiating off Jake.

"Out."

I put a hand to his chest. "Like hell." He can barely stand up straight without wincing. His arm is hovering over his abdomen. And underneath the designer suit is a bandage, stitches, and a fresh stab wound.

"Have you checked the fridge? I'm starving, Rock." Then he slings his head to the side, seeing Jake and Phoebe. "Put some clothes on, PG. No one wants to see your pierced nipple."

"Knock it off," I growl.

Phoebe slings back at him, "No one wants to see your face. Dead in the eyes."

Trevor wheezes out a dying laugh. "I might be dead eyed, but at least I'm not fake banging my landlord."

Fuck. Trevor.

Jake's jaw unhinges in shock, turning from me to Phoebe. "*He* knows we've been fake dating?" Jake isn't aware that we've told *anyone*. When, in actuality, we've shared the truth among my siblings and Phoebe's. He motions back to Trevor. "Who even is he?"

Trevor hasn't picked an alias yet, and I'm prepared to jump in and open an escape hatch so he won't have to answer.

But then he announces, "Trevor Thornhall. Younger brother to Grey and Hailey." He lifts three fingers in a stiff but casual greeting, still slumped a little in pain. I'd put an arm around him, but he'd just shove me off.

We share a small beat, our gazes meeting in a sentiment close to love. For him to choose to be my brother in this town—after knowing we don't share the same DNA—it means something to me. It's also another thread of realism sewn into our lives within Victoria.

"Hailey wants her brother to crash here," Phoebe explains fast. "I know you have a two-tenant rule, but it's temporary."

Jake pulls at his soaked button-down, his face still contorted. "Hailey never said she had another brother. You never
said anything." He's accusing me now.

I grip the butcher-block counter. "We didn't have the rosi-
est upbringing, and we're protective. So no, we weren't going
to share our family tree with you. Just like you never told me
Katherine Rhodes was your *nanny*."

He inhales a sharp breath of understanding. "Right." He
surveys the kitchen, the living room, and when his attention
flits past the sofa and coffee table, I'm glad Nova brought over
a Turkish rug. It hides the bloodstained floorboards. Where
Trevor almost bled out on Halloween.

"Let me check on Hailey first," Phoebe says. "If she's sleeping, we really shouldn't wake her."

"Agreed," I chime in, and surprisingly, Jake is nodding, too.

Phoebe slips down the short hallway.

To Trevor, I say, "I'll pick up breakfast for you. What do
you want?"

"Pancakes." He's squinting at Jake. He already revealed
something he shouldn't, and he's not well trained in the art of
face-to-face manipulation.

He's not here on a job. He's not supposed to be screwing
Jake over.

But we have enough baggage that could bury all of us. Our
parents kept him on a tight leash because they knew he's impulsive and unpredictable. Still, all he has *ever* wanted is their
approval to do more than creep in the shadows. All I have ever
wanted is for him to be less of a bitter, angry cynic like me.

"You know, if this thing with Phoebe doesn't work out"—
Trevor sifts through a basket of sunglasses—"you could always fake date me."

It'd be funnier if I weren't holding my fucking breath.

"I'll even put out," Trevor offers.

"No, he won't," I cut in.

"Yeah, I will." Trevor closes one eye in appraisal and uses a single finger to outline Jake's tall, athletically fit frame in the air. "I can work with it. He's about a nine out of ten."

Jake's brows are permanently crunched. He raises two hands to pause the show. "Thanks for the offer, I think, but my mother wouldn't really approve. She almost wrote me out of the will when I dated a guy in boarding school."

I'm genuinely shocked, but I smother that emotion so deep.

"Gay?" Trevor wonders.

"Bi. I like women, too. And you're . . . ?"

"I don't really do labels." He slips on a pair of Prada sunglasses, probably to hide the fact that he's wincing in near-severe pain. "Neither does my older brother."

"Shut the fuck up," I whisper through my teeth at him. "And sit down."

At least he lowers into a bistro chair, and I relax when he swallows like the pain is ebbing. Wanting Jake a whole football field away from my brother, I tell him, "Let's check on Hailey." Phoebe shouldn't be taking this long.

Once we make our way into the short hall, I push the cracked door farther open, and my muscles flex into burning bands seeing Hailey hunched over a laptop with her eyes wide on the lit screen. Phoebe is beside her on the bed, trying to entice my sister with a glass of water.

Our presence only captures Phoebe's attention. She gives me a slight worried shake of her head and shoos us out with her hand.

I shut the door, hoping Hailey at least slept a couple hours last night.

"She didn't look good," Jake whispers to me, skating a

hand through his damp hair. Worry pleats the space between his brows. "Did something happen . . . ?"

We learned our entire existence might be constructed on a lie, so yeah, something happened. "It's a situation from back home. Phoebe is taking care of her."

"Right," he says, more sharply this time. He can tell I'm being evasive. I'm not letting him in. It's frustrating him.

Welcome to the fucking club.

He has no idea that I could so easily spout off a wild, fabricated story. He'd buy the tall tale, and I wouldn't have this massive, brain-splitting headache. Instead, I am *actively* trying not to outright deceive him.

And unfortunately, I have to share his company for another five minutes. I escort him out of the loft, and since I need to pick up breakfast for Trevor, I'm descending steps in the echoey stairwell with Jake.

He's ahead of me.

Which is annoying because he stops midway and turns. Blocking me. "So you aren't straight?" he suddenly asks.

"You hitting on me, Jake?"

"No," he says pretty causally. "You're not my type."

"Too mean?" I mime crying fists to my cheeks.

"Too short, actually."

I almost, *almost* smile at that one—since, when we first met, I said he was too tall to be my type. "Funny."

The air unwinds. Strangely. Considering seconds ago, we both looked ready to fling each other out the window. Common ground is the best brick to build bridges, but never did I think we'd have this in common.

I don't hate it.

He has a foot above the stair, a foot below. He's practically dry by now, and I hear the rain letting up. Yet, he's not moving.

"Jake—"

"You're right," he interjects. "I do have more to lose than you. I *really* need Phoebe, and I want to tell you why. I do, and . . ." His voice tapers off as a song blares out of his pocket and echoes throughout the stairwell.

He sets ringtones for family members. "Chiquitita" for his beloved little sister, Kate. "Highway to Hell" for his oldest brother, Trent. "Bad to the Bone" for his *lovely* mother, Claudia.

But this particular song is new. "Is that 'The Boys Are Back in Town'?" I ask.

"By Thin Lizzy," he confirms, as if this entire situation isn't suspicious. He's hurriedly digging out his phone.

Who could possibly warrant this type of urgency? An uncle? None are present in Victoria that I'm aware of. A grandparent? All deceased, unless he faked those, too. *Doubtful.*

I'm scrutinizing the fuck out of him.

"Sorry," he apologizes. "I should take this. He rarely calls."

"Who?" I ask.

"My old boarding-school roommate." He *jogs* down the stairs.

"Where'd you go to boarding school?!" I call out.

He has the phone to his ear. "Faust. It's in upstate New York." Of course I recognize the name of the all-boys boarding school. Once upon a time, we all attended a coed one only an hour from Faust. It was where we'd meet at the cemetery every Thursday night.

Jake slows to a sudden, eerie stop at the exit, then he asks his friend, "Who died?"

EIGHT

Rocky

re you going to the funeral?" Oliver asks me in the bathroom of the boathouse.

Yeah, I learned who kicked the bucket. Jake offered the
information freely in the stairwell. It quickly became public
news, and it's all this town could talk about for five days
straight.

Emilia Wolfe.

She was cresting eighty-eight, and it's not that she was re-
vered or benevolent or charitable. As far as I'm aware, most
people found her to be crotchety and shrewd. It didn't take
Sherlock fucking Holmes to figure out why everyone was acting as if British nobility died.

She was a Wolfe.

The Wolfes are the first of three founding families in Victoria. The Konings being the second. The Bennets being the
third.

What I've heard about the Wolfes sounds more like urban
legend. The family are shut-ins who live in a hundred-year-old

mansion affectionately named Stonehaven. The three-story shingled dwelling is constructed on one tiny, jagged, stony island. It's like they dropped a house on a rock and called it a day.

Stonehaven. The infamous residence is mentioned on walking tours and historical brochures in the welcome center. "Skunks" (out-of-towners) will even take boat excursions to the mansion. Harbor waves ripple against the girthy stone foundation, and tourists will snap pictures of the foreboding home, hoping to catch a glimpse of Emilia. Or her recluse of a son-in-law: Varrick.

I've seen the weathered oak shingles and the shuttered windows from the dock. The house itself is only accessible in and out by boat.

It doesn't matter who you are—a college student (not calling them *caufers*), a local, or a skunk—everyone is crossing their fingers they'll spot the elusive Varrick Wolfe at the public memorial tomorrow.

"All of Victoria is attending," I tell Oliver while I stand on the top of a ladder. Still in our shared bathroom. "It'd be social suicide not to go to the funeral."

Oliver moisturizes his face at the sink. "Social suicide, a fate worse than actual death according to our mothers." He gasps at the mirror. "But *are* they our mothers? Perhaps we're just test-tube babies. Brought into this corrupt world via science." He twists toward me. "We are a *failed* science experiment. Six botched test subjects."

I give him a look. "How many dystopian melodramas have you been watching?" I bite on a screwdriver and try to pry this fucking bolt out of the air vent.

"Can you hurry up?" Nova barks up at me. He's gripping

the metal ladder, keeping it steady while I have my bare feet near the top rung. I'm attempting to unscrew the ceiling vent.

"Can you shut up?" I mumble back, mouth full of screwdriver.

Oliver slows his lengthy eight-step morning routine, eyeing his brother. Light rarely dims inside Oliver Graves, even when he's concerned about those he loves, even when he's in the center of a grotesque job neither of us really want to be in. He is a people-pleaser. Peacemaker. Pacifist.

A true middle child in the fact that he's never celebrated or patted on the back enough for all he's done.

Sometimes I envied how he could find joy in a youth that seemed joyless.

He reties a white cotton towel, wrapping it low around his sculpted waist. He just took a shower, and his wet, dyed hair looks closer to his natural dark brown shade. He has the same olive skin tone as Phoebe. Same dimpled chin. Hell, even *Nova* has a chin dimple. It'd be stranger if they weren't siblings.

Despite Oliver obsessing over his appearance, he's still partially focused on his brother. "What are you thinking, Nova?"

I realize how darkly Nova is staring off at the Italian painting on the wall. The art is insignificant to me. Just a canal in Venice. A gondola under a bridge.

He could have an aversion to Italy just as much as his mind could be five thousand miles away from the country. I'm good at reading people, but I'm not in his head.

Yet, I know him better than ninety-nine percent of the population. He attempts to walk an ethical line in this immoral lifestyle, but all ethics will be thrown out the window if it means going into battle for his siblings. Loyalty over integrity is the Nova Graves way.

Also, he currently has a fucking mustache.

I'd say he looks comical, but he was bestowed with good genes. Am I jealous he can pull off the heinous facial hair? *No.*

"I'm thinking we should leave." He clenches the ladder with two hands like he's strangling the metal. "We should all grab our shit. Get the girls on board. Get Trevor. Never say a word to the godmothers, the godfather. We escape them. This town. And we're gone. Together."

"And then what?" Oliver asks.

"Then we pull a job somewhere they can't find us."

"They'll make it their goal to find us," I chime in, screwdriver in my hand. "We're assets twenty-five years in the making. You don't throw that away this fast."

"We'll keep moving every time they track us down."

"Says *the getaway*. All you know how to do is run."

Nova jostles the ladder, and I seize the top so I don't fall off. When I'm stable, I give him a middle finger.

He glowers. "You have a better idea, asshole?"

"Yeah, fuck-face, we stay and figure out why they want us to leave Connecticut so badly."

"I'm not surprised." He runs his hand back and forth across his buzz cut, then motions to me. "You always want to do the antithesis of what they ask. They say *leave*, you say *never*."

"You want to give in to what they want, Winchester?" I use his nickname from *Supernatural*. "You want to go back to sucking the godfather's toes? We don't even know who the fuck he really is. He could've been a serial killer in the seventies and dumped bodies in the fucking Everglades."

"I know!" Nova yells. "God, I fucking *know*. I can't stand the idea of any of us around them, Rocky. And now, we're setting up a family *dinner*. To discuss what? How they fucked us all over? Are you packing or am I? Because they might kill us before dessert."

"Again, you don't get rid of assets twenty-five years in the making, and we're using the dinner as a way to get their DNA."

Oliver tips his head to Nova. "You should take the Glock."

"I am taking the Glock." He's staring up at me. "They don't want us here. It's still safer to leave."

"Your sister wants to stay, too." I remove the ceiling vent and glance over at Oliver, who's suddenly very preoccupied with tweezing an eyebrow hair. "And so does your brother."

Nova twists around to him. "Ol, it's better if we go."

"There are answers here, Nova."

He lets go of the ladder. "Those answers could come at a cost I'm not willing to pay. What matters is our *survival*."

"Not getting answers could come at a higher cost, Nov." His brows rise. "I might not need them, but Hails does." He drops his voice to a whisper, but I strain my ears to hear him. "I spent *five hours* just trying to get her to close the computer yesterday. She's blaming herself for not seeing this sooner."

"It's not her fault," Nova whispers back.

"We dubbed her the mastermind."

"We were kids."

"Her role. Her responsibility. How deep is it drilled in us, really? How deep is being the getaway in you? The seductress in Phoebe? Because I think it's at least one half of who we are."

"Ol," he whispers, sounding softer than usual. I shouldn't be eavesdropping, but I'm on autopilot now.

Oliver bows closer to him. "She thinks she failed us, and I highly doubt anything will curb her anxiety except for the truth. She needs answers, and I'm afraid of what's going to happen if she doesn't find them. So I have to stay for her." His brown eyes shift to me. Realizing I can hear him, he returns to the sink and busies himself untwisting an expensive canister of shave cream.

She called out for him. The night she entered the loft in a distraught state with a pile of old books.

He's been visiting the loft twice as much. Canceled therapy appointments with his clients. Phoebe said he was the one who got Hailey to take a bath.

I don't know how. I don't want to know why.

Sticking my head in the sand sounds *great* when it comes to the idea of Oliver with my sister in any way that's not chaste and virginal. I think I'd rather choke on the desert dunes of Namibia than picture them having sex.

I hand Nova the ceiling-vent cover. "Have you talked to your mom at all?"

"She's not my mother."

"That would be a *no*."

"We don't know with certainty that she's not our mom," Oliver reasons with him. "We could still be related to Elizabeth."

Nova unzips his cargo jacket, heating up. "I don't care if we share her DNA, or that she raised us. The more and *more* I think about what Elizabeth, Addison, and Everett could've done to take Trevor, the sicker I realize they are, Ol."

He frowns. "It could've just been Addison and Everett behind that. No offense," he adds to me, since they're my parents.

"None taken," I deadpan, having little love for any of them. It's more jarring seeing Nova join me to *this* degree.

Nova spreads out his arms. "Our mom was an accomplice to likely kidnapping a *child*. That doesn't make it any fucking better."

On the ladder, I rotate more to him. He's done a complete one-eighty on the people he worshipped. It's like he discovered the regular man behind the Wizard of Oz, and he's mad. I never thought anyone would be as anti-godmothers and anti-godfather as me. But Nova has boarded my raging ship of one. Or maybe two . . . considering Phoebe is also pissed.

I'm not sure how this much anger can sail it out to sea.

"They've never been *good*, Winchester," I say. "None of us have been. We aren't doling out Candygrams for a living. We screw people over."

"There's a line we don't cross." He threads his arms and lifts his stiff shoulders. "But *fuck me* for thinking they'd never put a pinky toe on it."

"No, fuck them," I tell him.

His nose flares. He holds my gaze for a long beat and nods a few times, his pain palpable. Oliver reaches out a hand and touches his brother's head with love. Nova pushes Oliver off with playfulness he only shows his siblings.

I feel around inside the duct. Grabbing three metal boxes, I slide them out and pass a couple to Nova. I climb down with the third in hand.

I shouldn't still be living with Phoebe's brothers. And technically, they're living with *me*. I'm the one renting the boathouse in Victoria, and they decided to crash here short-term. The longer we're in this small town, the less vague we can be about who we are and where we come from and our relations to one another.

Our backstories need to be infallible. Never contradictory.

"Why are you living with me at the boathouse?" I quiz them.

"We're new to the area," Oliver says smoothly, opening his box. "I'm Oliver Smith, a licensed marriage and family therapist. My brother is Nolan 'Nova' Smith. Art curator at the local museum. And we're still looking for suitable housing, but in the meantime, we've always been friendly with our sister's ex-husband. She's still friends with him, after all."

"And we can't stay with her. Her loft is too small," Nova concludes with a sterner tone. He's surly while flipping through IDs in his box. "But we would rather be there."

I slip him a tight smile. "Trust me, I'd rather have her as a roommate, too."

Nova glares at me like I said I wanted in her pants.

Already happened. He is not going to take me dating her well. At all. Especially considering he liked her "options" in this new town. Really, he'd like her with anyone *but* me. It's annoying as hell, but I can't say I'd feel any different if my sister were romantically involved with either of them.

Hypocrites-R-Us.

But I realize there aren't many lies in our personas in Victoria, Connecticut.

Sure, Oliver isn't really a therapist, and I'm not really an investor.

But the town knows Nova, Oliver, and Phoebe are triplets. They know Hailey is my sister and, more recently, that Trevor is my brother. They know we're all cordial and close enough to live together.

This is the only place where we've ever established who we truthfully are to one another.

Some people even know our real personalities. I came in like a jealous, territorial, cold jackass who loves his ex—which is a big part of who I am.

It's been therapeutic not giving a shit about the consequences that come with being myself, and I've understood why Phoebe wouldn't want to walk away from that either.

The desire to maintain it for her, and maybe for me—it grows stronger.

We thumb through the metal boxes. IDs. Passports. Social security cards. Hell, I even have memberships to Costco and Sam's Club under random names. *Bernard Higgins. Ansel Odell.* I take a new ID for the short time we'll be out of town this week.

To meet our parents for dinner.

Oliver chooses one and latches his metal box closed. He's picking up a razor when my phone buzzes.

I click into a text from Jake.

Strange.

Jake: Can you meet me tomorrow before Emilia's funeral? I want to tell you the truth.

I read the text to Phoebe's brothers. Oliver says, "Ask him if you can bring someone." I do, and Jake is fast to respond.

"He said to come alone." I reread the text. *Great.* "So I might die tomorrow," I joke with the raising and lowering of my brows. Not enthused by this meetup, but I'm interested to hear what this so-called truth entails.

"I'll wait outside the location," Nova says, already planning my escape.

"You could wear a mic," Oliver suggests. "The rest of us can listen in in case it gets dicey. Jake doesn't strike me as the type to pat you down. Or would he?"

"He wouldn't think I'd come in with a wire."

He flips his razor between his fingers. "Perfect."

I like the plan, so I ask Jake where we're meeting.

Jake: My catamaran.

NINE

Rocky

Thank God Jake and I aren't in a boat-measuring contest and we're not comparing the size of our masts or length of our bows. Because I would fucking lose.

I have a perpetual scowl the moment I board the glittering sixty-five-foot *Ananke*.

"Don't love the name," I tell Jake as we go down into the hull.

He's ahead of me and peers back with slight surprise. "You know your Greek gods?"

"Technically, she's a primordial deity." I duck as I descend the stairs. "You named your boat after the personification of compulsion, necessity, and *inevitability*."

He lands in the living area first. Spacious, clean, hardly touched. Exactly what I'd expect from a billionaire. "Ananke is also the only one who has any influence over her daughters," he tells me. "The three fates."

Influence over fate. The ability to change destiny.

Does that appeal to him?

I don't ask. I don't share my theories of what I think about him and Ananke. It's so easy for someone to construct a narrative around a morsel of belief. I show him a piece of the picture in my head, and he finishes it for me. That's not the truth.

That's just simple manipulation.

And whatever happens today, I won't be manipulated by him.

I'm feeling hostile (being honest here). Like I could stick his head in a toilet and flush.

Jake can tell.

Because I'm not hiding the slow-burning irritation. It's six a.m. We're in funeral blacks. While he sports a designer peacoat, my hands are stuffed in my two-grand leather jacket. What he can't see: I have a pistol holstered against my rib cage and a wire is taped to my bare chest beneath my black button-down.

There isn't a mic in my ear. So I can't hear Phoebe, but I know she's listening in with Hailey, Trevor, and Oliver at the loft. Nova is parked at the marina and also tuning in to today's show, called *Jake Tells the Motherfucking Truth* . . . Hopefully.

I carry empty suitcases of hope, so I'm expecting him to bullshit me and for this to go absolutely nowhere.

Jake motions to two curved, white leather couches facing one another and the Lysol-scented coffee table between them. "This is the *Ananke*. A portion, at least. She has six cabins, sundecks, two bars, all the usual things." It's massive. Big enough to host at least seventy people.

"Cute. I didn't come here to play with your toys." I hear my coarse voice. "I have better things to do. Like break up your fake relationship with my wife. Seeing as how you still haven't done it yet." We gave him an extra week, and he's dragged his big feet every single day since.

He took my brief act of kindness and stepped on it. It's why I can't stop picturing him choking on toilet water.

"Your *ex*-wife," Jake corrects with a soft tone like he's padding the insult.

I arch my brows. "I married her. We divorced—"

"She divorced you," he cuts in to clarify. Annoyingly.

I glare. "And we're back together. You want a detailed report of what I did to her in bed this morning, too?"

Phoebe's brothers are overhearing this. My sister is listening in, too. None of them know I'm *truly* with Phoebe yet, and there is a ninety-nine percent chance they believe I'm just spouting bullshit to Jake.

It's what we do.

Tell lies to get the mark where we want them.

Just another day at the office.

He works his jaw, and I can't read him very well for a moment. Not until he says, "Don't hurt her."

Don't hurt her?

Don't hurt the one girl I've only ever loved. Don't hurt the one girl I would give my life for on repeat. Don't hurt the one girl who has burrowed so deep in me, I can't cut her out without *bleeding* out.

Don't hurt Phoebe.

My eyes burn. We've hurt each other through the years, by pulling away and pushing closer in a tortured, loving cycle. It's been devotion and resistance. But that type of hurt isn't what he's referring to.

"I'd never harm Phoebe," I say deeply, truthfully.

Jake must accept this honesty. He untenses. "About her," he says, then checks his watch.

My pulse tries to spike.

He glances at the hatch we just climbed down.

I'm laser focused on him. "Expecting someone?"

He avoids my gaze. "We should go to the galley." He's already leading the way.

Fuck.

I have no choice but to follow.

Leveling my heartbeat, I concentrate on the weight of my jacket on my biceps. The tag skimming the back of my neck. It starts itching. So does the thin wire brushing against my chest. I force myself not to yank at it and throw it in the trash can.

We're in the galley. It's less sterile and industrial than I imagined. The floors are scuffed and worn, and ass indents concave the blue corduroy cushions of a U-shaped couch. Nautical magnets decorate the white fridge, holding up at least a dozen photos.

He must spend most of his time here.

I scan the pictures, only seeing one family member. I recognize her from news reports online.

Jake follows my gaze. "That's Kate." Grief clouds his eyes for a second. He's lost in the memory of his little sister.

In the picture, her hair is the same light shade of brown as Jake's, and they have the same ocean-blue eyes. She's mid-laugh and trying to stand on her tiptoes to reach his height in the photo.

She looks no older than fifteen.

"You miss her." I don't ask. I can tell. Very few people would be able to fake this kind of raw emotion that throws you into the past. It's genuine, his love for her.

"Every day. The *only* solace I have is knowing she's safe and happy."

I wonder where she is. Another state? Another country? "She can't be walking around Texas or Montana as Kate Koning Waterford—a dead girl," I tell him. "So what'd you do? Make her a new identity?"

Jake stiffens, clutching the handle to the fridge. "I did what I had to do." He stares back at me. "Wouldn't you for Hailey?"

Yes. But I was born into crime. The decision would've been easy for me. "You don't want to know what I'd do for Hailey," I mutter, taking a seat on the lumpy corduroy cushion. I lean back, getting comfortable enough, and I watch him tug open the fridge.

He plucks out two bottles of Koning Lite. "Are you all right with beer?"

At six in the morning? Not really, but I like the idea of having a glass bottle I can crack over his head if this really takes a turn.

"It's five p.m. somewhere," I say dryly, taking one from him.

With the other in hand, Jake slides into the booth, sitting across from me. After he pops off the cap with a gold bottle opener, he tosses it to me. I do the same, and the growing tension between us is splitting the air into a thousand fatal shards.

"About her," I say, surfacing his statement, the one left *unfinished* from earlier.

"About her," Jake parrots. He's not blinking. He's just as laser focused on me. Neither of us have taken off our jackets. He swigs his beer. I swig mine.

Jake isn't that afraid of me in this moment. He has the confidence of someone who has the local sheriff in his pocket, but I also have dirt on him, so I'm not quaking in my boots.

"Why am I here, Jake?" I ask him.

"I need Phoebe, and you're in the way."

I'm barely breathing. I conceal it. "Yeah? What are you

going to do? Tape my picture in your diary and scratch out my eyes? Complain to Mommy and Daddy that you didn't get what you wanted? Cry in your million-dollar sandbox?"

Jake expels an annoyed breath. His smile is a grimace. "Actually, I was going to ask for your help, even though you're probably the most grating bastard I've met all year."

"Just all year?"

"You haven't met my brother."

"Jordan?"

"Trent," he clarifies. "I can't get rid of you because for some reason Phoebe likes you, and I respect her. So I need you to understand what's really going on here."

He wants me to be less of a wedge. Because I'm preventing Phoebe from saying *yes* to extending the fake-dating scheme. If I approved it, then there's a chance she would, too. He recognizes this.

Jake bows forward, elbows on the table. "I'm choosing to trust you, Grey. So if you screw her over, I'll find creative and painful ways to *ruin* you." The depth of the threat in his eyes is like looking in the mirror.

My temple pounds in confusion. "How could I screw her over, exactly?"

"She's not a normal girl. Her name isn't even Phoebe Smith."

And then he says words I never thought I'd hear from him—not in my lifetime.

"She's a con artist."

TEN

Rocky

While most parents trained their children to "never take candy from strangers" and "always wear your seatbelt"—my parents would run drills where they'd accuse us of grifting.

I've practiced this scenario *hundreds* of times. But there's a distinction here that I weigh carefully—Jake never called me a con artist.

I raise my brows. "A con artist? Phoebe?"

"I don't know her real first name, but she goes by Graves."

How *the fuck* does he know her last name? The wire is hot on my chest, and I wish I were back at the loft. She's likely freaking out hearing that she got exposed, and I'm doing all I can not to burst a blood vessel in my neck.

This has never happened before to Phoebe.

Not once.

In the short pause, my phone vibrates in my leather jacket pocket. I dig it out and peek briefly at the message beneath the table.

Phoebe: WTF

Eyes on Jake, I text back without staring at the keys. **Fuck him.**

"Graves?" I act like he's feeding me a bullshit story.

"I'm serious." His expression is grim with the gravity of what he's sharing. "She's not who you think."

I could laugh—because, really, who the hell does he think I am? But my face pulls in a painfully contorted frown. I'm going to have to borrow Oliver's retinol cream after this. "I'd know if she were playing me."

"You wouldn't. She's that good."

Well, I hope Phoebe relaxes with that small kudos.

I have so many questions. How long has he known? *How* does he know?

Jake rests back and fists his beer. "She doesn't go after regular people. She fleeces wealthy dirtbags who deserve it."

And who exactly told him this? "Yeah?" I sound skeptical.

"I figured she got cold feet with you."

I brush a hand through my hair. "With me?" I wrap my head around this. "She tried to fleece me?"

He skims my features, but my face isn't conveying a semblance of truth. "I think she abandoned her plan." *He thinks.* "Then she divorced you and tried to get away from you with Hailey. A friend she'd made when she was with you."

"Oh, is my sister a con artist, too?"

He sighs at my mocking tone. "*No.* Hailey knows nothing about what Phoebe does. She's just as in the dark as you are."

Don't laugh.

Do not fucking laugh.

I force a brittle smile before taking a hearty swig of beer.

Jake explains, "Phoebe moved to Victoria for a fresh start with Hailey. And you followed her here."

I swallow the pissy taste of Koning Lite.

He thinks I was Phoebe's mark.

A scumbag.

An *abusive* scumbag. Hence, the instant lack of trust he's had in me from day one. It wasn't just my "grating" personality then, but I'm sure that only validated his suspicions about me.

My mind rapidly backtracks to our first meeting. Hailey, Phoebe, and I were waiting on the main street for Jake to unlock the door to the stairwell. So he could give the grand tour of the loft. Once he emerged, I tried to read him, but I couldn't get a good grasp of his intentions at all.

I didn't understand the intensity with which he checked out Hailey from head to toe. Or how he did the same to Phoebe, too. I concluded that he was an uptight, snobby prick who was judging his tenants based on their appearance. That's why he was trying to get a good look at them.

I was wrong.

He was casing them.

He must've known before they even arrived that one was a con artist.

"You don't think I just followed her," I correct him. "You think I *stalked* her here."

Jake expels a resigned breath. "I don't know what the truth is there."

He is throwing darts in a pitch-black closet, and he doesn't even realize the lights are off. Being kept this far in the dark—where you can't crawl your way to the truth—it's not a pleasant spot to be in. It's where I've *never* wanted to be, but it's where I currently am when it comes to a huge portion of my life, my childhood.

Jake is giving me the type of honesty I wish my parents would. He really has more to lose by showing me his cards, but he's taking the risk anyway.

Blind faith in someone you barely trust.

It's dumb as fuck, and yet, I admire his ability to try.

Because if I don't extend the same honesty to him, am I any better than the people who raised me? I could open the door and let him see the light. Or I could keep him in the dark.

And protect the people I love.

Yeah.

I'm not spilling shit. "Phoebe told you all of this?" I ask a question I already know the answer to.

"No." Guilt pinches his Abercrombie-model face. I sincerely wish it made him look ugly. He twists the beer bottle in his hand. "She . . . she doesn't know I'm aware of what she really does for a living. I'm a little terrified of telling her because she's been helping me and I've been lying."

Oh, she knows now, sweetheart.

She's also been lying to him.

We both have been. So weighing the scales of morality when they're heavy with lies? Not our thing. No one is the better person here.

"The plan was to come clean soon," Jake professes, "but you're trying to cut the con short, so I need you to get on board first. I think there's a way we can all work together that'll benefit each of us in the end."

My head pounds. "Who told you about Phoebe? How do you even know they're a credible source?"

"I just know."

"That's too vague, Jake."

"Yeah, I thought you'd say that."

"Because you know me so well," I quip, stuffing a hand back in my jacket.

His attention veers to his Rolex again. "He's actually on his way."

My father. Did he expose Phoebe? Makes no sense. It wouldn't benefit him. And he wants us to leave Connecticut.

Jake clearly wants Phoebe to stay.

I down another gulp of piss beer.

"I know, it's a lot," Jake says, consoling me like he's petting a kitten and not a brown recluse. It's a little insulting he thinks I'm naïve enough to be played by my ex-wife.

And then I hear an old song. It's muffled in Jake's peacoat, but once he retrieves his phone, it blares more distinctly throughout the galley.

"The Boys Are Back in Town."

Before he answers the call, the sound of footsteps swerves our attention to the entryway. Blood pulses in my ears, and my muscles flex. I force myself not to reach for my gun yet.

"Knock knock!" a male voice echoes toward us. "Anyone home? Ah, I *love* this song!" His accent sounds English. East London, maybe. The familiarity explodes an ember of anger inside my chest. I grind down on my emotions until they're dust.

First thought: *I'm going to kill him.*

"In the galley!" Jake calls out.

My fingers twitch on instinct, even as my pulse slows into a calm, alert rhythm. I take off my Rolex, which feels like a thousand fucking pounds on my wrist.

The *thump thump thump* of feet headed our way dials up my vigilance.

Jake stands to greet his source, and as soon as a guy in his late twenties saunters into the galley, I try to pretend he's no one I've seen before.

He's very tall—well over six-three, Black, built like a pole vaulter, and dressed sharp in a black houndstooth twill suit like he might attend the funeral, too. He has dark brown eyes the same color as his skin, short-buzzed hair, a squared jaw, and a charming smile that I've been the recipient of once or twice.

"Carter," Jake says with a smile and hugs his old boarding-school buddy.

Fucking *Carter*. Our forger. We rely on others to keep their mouths shut, and they rely on us to do the same. It's a very, very small network of like-minded criminals, and he entered the fold when I was eighteen.

Seven years later, and he sold out Phoebe.

Fury flares inside me, but I'm burying it so far down.

"Jakey," Carter says warmly, slapping Jake's arm with lighthearted mirth as they retract from a friendly hug.

Jake smiles brighter. "It's good to see you. It's been too long."

"We won't make a habit of it now, will we?" He grins. Jake grins back, as if there's an inside joke there. The song cuts off when Jake ends Carter's phone call, and that's when they both rotate toward me.

I raise my beer to Carter in greeting. "Grey Thornhall," I introduce myself.

His face fractures in a flash of confusion. "Mate, you can't be serious. He wants to work with you, and trust, you'll want to work with him, too. And this'll be a hell of a lot harder if I got to go about lying to my oldest friend."

Jake frowns at him. "Lie about what?"

"*Oldest* friend?" I ask.

Carter swings an arm over Jake's shoulder. "Roommates grades seven through twelve. We survived Faust Boarding School together. We're bonded for life."

Jake smacks a hand to his chest. "We'd be more bonded if you stopped by more often."

"Places to be. People to see." Carter plops down on the cushioned seat beside me. I wish he'd sit five fucking *hundred* feet away. The urge to punch him is a desire I'm wrestling with. He reaches for my beer like we're besties, but I pull away.

"You mean passports to forge," I add bitterly. "Papers to counterfeit."

Jake freezes midway into taking off his own peacoat. "You two know each other?"

"You know about his extracurricular activities?" I question with furrowed brows. What the fuck?!

"Yeah, of course," Jake says. "He was counterfeiting money in school." He pauses, then decides to share, "And he helped get Kate a new name, a new passport. She lives in the countryside in France. Once I pay you back for her horse, I'm hoping to send her Bowie."

I want to inwardly groan, but I'm thrown at how much Jake is sharing. He's hoping I'll do the same, but the truth is glued to the roof of my mouth.

Carter claps his hands. "Koning, grab me a Koning, would ya?" He nudges my shoulder. "I love being able to say that."

"You're in a good mood for someone who just signed their death warrant," I tell him coldly.

He gives me a look. "Who's going to kill me? You?" He blows a raspberry. "Bruh, try to find someone who can make a better fake. I'll wait."

Jake doesn't move toward the fridge. He folds his peacoat

over the granite counter. "Is no one going to explain this?" He waves a hand from Carter to me like it doesn't compute.

I take a bigger swig of beer. I'm on the bow of the *Titanic* and I see the black depths of the water ready to pull me under.

All because I trusted Carter.

I've never blown my own cover to anyone. I can't even will the words to do it now.

"You think he needs to know," I say to Carter, "then you tell him."

Carter gives me an annoyed look like *I'm* the asshole. "You can trust Jake."

"I don't even think I can trust you anymore," I snap at him.

Carter shakes his head, a flash of genuine hurt crossing his face. "You think it'd be better if I gave your sister a brochure to Antarctica?" he questions. "I know Victoria. I know the people here. I know Jake. Here I was, thinking if she wanted to risk pulling away from your parents, it'd be better to do it in a place with allies."

He had a hand in this? He *purposefully* sent Hailey to Victoria? "Did you also give her a link to Jake's loft?"

"I said it was a good place to rent. I knew the landlord."

So it wasn't random. This place. He led her here, *knowing* Jake would be here.

Does he also know why our parents wouldn't want us in Connecticut?

I shake my head repeatedly. "Why not be up-front about it? What's with this layer of deceit?"

"I was honest with Ailey." His accent drops the *H* of my sister's name and pretty much every other word with the letter. "Just didn't tell her everything about Jake. Just like she never tells me everything about anything. We've got a system. It works. I knew she wanted a fresh break. She knew I had ties to Victoria." He nudges my arm. "I even tipped you off that she'd be coming here so you could join her, too. Though, I think she knew I'd do that." He grins. "Ailey's too smart for the likes of us, really."

I can't picture their reactions at the loft. Nova is probably cursing at his steering wheel, though.

I knew my sister reached out to Carter to get new licenses for their new start. I didn't know he was the one to suggest Victoria.

When my phone buzzes again, I'm more careful to check the text with Carter beside me.

Phoebe: Hailey is confirming his story. It's all true.

She's fast with another message.

Phoebe: Don't be upset at her. She didn't think it was something we needed to know.

Hailey withholding more than I assumed—it's not an earth-shattering revelation. It's not the first time she's thrown us crumbs when she has the whole loaf of rotten bread. I can't even be angry. Not when it's what she was taught to do.

Give selective information to us.

She was our mom's little protégée in planning and logistics, and she worked closer with the godmothers than she did with me and Phoebe. Now I wonder if they kept her close because they were afraid she'd figure out what they've done.

Unable to type out a lengthy response, I send a thumbs-up emoji.

Then I run a hand through my hair while Jake passes his friend a beer. He's waiting patiently for his turn for answers.

It's almost annoying how, even under this amount of mind-fuckery, he's not bum-rushing to cut the line for an explanation.

I look from Jake, then back to Carter. "You didn't send Hailey here to help her and Phoebe. You sent her here to help your *oldest* fucking friend."

"Not true," he defends. "Ailey reached out to *me* first. Then I called Jake and let him know who he's renting to."

Jake takes a seat across from me. "Carter explained that two girls were coming to town, and they were looking to rent the loft above the bookstore. He said their names were Hailey and Phoebe. He said one, or maybe two, but possibly just one was a con artist who screws over dirtbags."

I make a face at Carter. "One or maybe two or possibly just one?" I repeat.

Jake answers, "Carter can be elusive about the truth, and I've always understood that he can't tell me things outright. That I need to find the answers myself."

Carter slides me a smile. "And you said I wasn't trustworthy."

"Just because you failed to give him *all* the information doesn't mean you didn't leak like a sieve," I retort.

Jake frowns, his interest shifting between me and his friend like he's trying to discover a new answer in a hidden temple. He rolls up the sleeves of his black button-down. "At first I thought the grifter was Hailey," he admits, "but then getting to know them more, I was sure it was Phoebe."

"And then what?" I snap back. "You saw her as someone to use?"

"I honestly didn't even think about faking a relationship with her. Not until *she* mentioned it. Then at the clambake, the opportunity came to tell my mother we're dating, and yeah, I took it. Carter didn't bring Hailey and Phoebe here for my gain. It was *genuinely* for theirs, because he knew I'd take care of them in this town. I have influence and money and authority. But I did see a way Phoebe could help me, and I can't let go of that."

He can't let go of her.

I clench my jaw.

Jake studies the surface of me. Uncertainty in his eyes. "Carter never told me you were coming. You were rich, confrontational, an asshole. So when Phoebe said you were divorced, I assumed you must be her dirtbag mark, so obsessed with her that you stalked her to Victoria." He scans me again. "Up until five minutes ago, I still believed that."

I smile dryly. "Belief is funny like that. Whoever wields it has the most power."

He looks right at me. "So who are you?"

I tip my head to Carter and raise my brows. I won't say it.

Carter finally relents and says, "He's the guy pretending to be the dirtbag to fleece other dirtbags."

Jake's face steels itself. "You're a con artist, too?"

I force a smile in confirmation. Then I lean forward, my lips slowly turning down with my emerging glare. "I'm not her mark. I've known Phoebe since I was a child. I've known her my entire fucking *life*."

He careens back like I shoved him. "That's why . . ." He closes his mouth, realization washing over him like he's seeing the leaves on the tree for the first time. "You came here to look out for them."

"Accurate. For once."

Jake laughs, looking stunned. "It's almost unbelievable." He's staring at me like I've changed shapes. Square to octagon.

"Don't get excited. I'm still an asshole."

He's still smiling. Though, it softens.

"You never saw it?" I ask him. "Even knowing Phoebe is a con artist, you didn't think I could be one, too?"

"Honestly, no," he says. "I thought you were too unfiltered and unhinged to be one."

A laugh rumbles out of me. With Jake, *yeah*, maybe I have been those things. I never would've thought it'd help protect my identity.

Jake sizes me up. "I would think you'd be a little more . . . stoic, I guess."

"Con men aren't going to look like ice-cold killers. We're going to look like the people you surround yourself with every single day. So when we appear, you won't realize that we've crawled into your foundation. Just to tear it all apart."

He's processing with a slow nod. "So you're not rich?"

"I'm rich."

"He's rich," Carter asserts. "Self-made millionaire, this one." He shakes my shoulder.

I jerk so his arm falls off me, and I scoot farther away.

Carter tsks. "Sensitive, are you, now? I won't touch." He tells Jake, "He has a skin thing."

"It's not a skin thing." I internally groan.

"Sensitivity issues. Gets a little—" Carter makes a *brrr* motion.

"Would you shut up?"

Carter grins. "You love me, come on."

I pinch my eyes.

"You're rich by stealing," Jake concludes.

I drop my hand to the table. "Is it really stealing if they willingly give it to me?" I toss my head side to side. "But . . ." *Yeah*. I don't exactly confirm out loud.

Jake stares off for a long beat. "And Hailey?"

"Also a grifter," Carter says so casually that I slide him a deeper glare. He ignores it.

Jake dazedly rubs his mouth. "What about the triplets? And your brother?"

"Nova, Oliver, Trevor," Carter says, "are the names you currently know them by. All grifters."

"Damn." He rocks back again. "I would've never known."

"Okay, Stuart," I snap at the guy beside me.

"It's Carter," he reminds me with a flash of a smile.

"Stuart Cartwright." I say his full name now. "What is this? Your version of recruitment? Bring Jake Waterford into the family business? He has *morals*. He's not cut out for this. Leave him alone."

"See, mate, that's how I know he's perfect for this," Carter tells me. "When have you ever tried to protect someone who didn't belong to one of two families?"

I don't feel great that Carter knows this about me. We've had phone calls that've lasted five seconds to two hours. He ribbed me about why I needed a new marriage certificate and divorce papers with Phoebe, but he wouldn't pry, knowing I couldn't involve him. We always talk less about the details of a job and more about our personal affairs.

How are your parents doing, Carter? Still living the single bachelor life? Are you liking Manchester?

Over the years, he's understood that I hate everyone I'm around. Except my family and Phoebe's. That's it for me.

That's why I'm here.

I've known Jake for *three* months. I could ditch him in an instant. That's not love.

My teeth ache from grinding down on them. "Or maybe I don't want a liability."

"Is he one?" Carter asks. "His family owns half the town

you're in, and your sister wants to make a permanent residence here."

We could go anywhere. That's not true anymore. Most of us want to stay in Victoria. I physically twist more toward Carter. "Why do my parents want us out of Connecticut?"

For the first time, Carter is puzzled. "Didn't realize your parents had an issue with this state."

"Who are his parents?" Jake asks him.

"Tinrocks. Addison and Everett."

I tip my beer at him. "When did you become a name-dropping whore?"

"Only for my oldest friend," Carter says, but his grin has vanished. He's thinking.

"Tin*rock*?" Jake is staring at me. "That's where your nickname comes from?"

"No." I turn back to Jake. "My father hated my name, but Phoebe kept using it, which made Hailey and the others use it. So my parents decided that our last name would incorporate *rock* in the event that people overhear them calling me Rocky. They wanted it to make fucking sense, and I can't believe I'm telling you this."

Jake's frown deepens. "Rocky," he contemplates. "But what's your real name?"

"That is my real name."

"Your birth name," he clarifies.

"I don't know," I say, almost under my breath. Why am I sharing this?

Jake seems caught off guard. "You don't know the name you were given at birth?" His voice is nearly a whisper, as if he, too, understands the damage.

"Connecticut." Carter draws our attention away from each other and onto him. He's waking from his deeper thoughts.

"I've never made a fake for them from this state. But I know they've been here before."

"How?" I ask.

"They got my contact through my mum and dad. Both my parents are bit of sharks, ya know. Best of the best in Fortune 500s, wheeling and dealing, and they've known I am good at making fakes. Said it's a God-given *talent*. I love 'em for that, so they've always passed my name along to their friends." He takes a tense beat. "Which is how I got to know Addison and Elizabeth."

"Elizabeth?" Jake asks.

"Graves," Carter explains. "Mum to the triplets. Their dad got locked up years back for fraud."

I blink hard. This is really fucking happening. I'm on edge because Jake hasn't given enough in return. But he could give me his firstborn, a kidney, and a kneecap, and it still wouldn't feel like enough.

"Thing is," Carter continues, "my dad grew up here. We all lived in Victoria before they moved us to Stratford. I don't remember much. I was just a toddler at the time, but it's why Jake and I got on so well when we first met at Faust and part of why I came back for the Wolfe funeral. My parents wanted me to pay our respects as a family. They couldn't cancel their business meetings to make the flight."

So Carter *is* in town for the funeral, too.

With his arms crossed, he holds his chin in thought. "I'm almost positive Mum told me she met Elizabeth and Addison in Connecticut." He points. "Yeah, that's how she knew 'em. I don't know how long they were here or what they were doing. It was before me, mate, but they've been here. At least once."

They don't want us in Victoria, but we only came here

because of Carter. We only know him because of a connection they made from years past in a place that's suddenly off limits.

They're getting caught in their own web.

"Where are they now?" Carter wonders. "The godmothers and godfather?" He angles his head to Jake. "That's their code for their parents."

I have a splitting migraine. "I don't know," I lie. Evading on instinct. It's ingrained down to the bone. Do not blow their covers. Do not incriminate yourself or others. Do not tell anyone what we really do. And even now, when I wish the plague and eternal hell upon my mother and father, I'm still protecting who they are and what they've done.

My phone buzzes.

This text isn't from Phoebe. It's from a burner phone.

Tell them everything. ♥

The black heart emoji is Hailey's signifier. We each picked one out when we were teenagers.

Even knowing my sister withholds information from us, I trust her with my life, but she hasn't slept in fuck-knows how long. So, yeah, I'm hesitating to take direction from Miss Sleep Deprivation.

"Your parents are con artists," Jake realizes. "And they raised you doing . . . *this*?"

Before I can respond, another quick text vibrates my palm.

They can help us. ♥

I don't disagree. But Carter is also *their* forger, *their* contact. In my head, he is no more loyal to us than he is to them.

Carter's phone pings. His brows do a weird crinkle. "Huh."

He looks up from the message. "Your little brother just sent me a middle finger." He laughs, his charismatic grin filling the whole galley. "Is he listening in? Are you wearing a wire?"

I pull down the neck of my shirt to show it taped to my sternum. "Say hi."

Jake bows to me with eagerness. "This is great—we can bring them in." He's a puppy that just saw a bone, and I want to take it away. I can't tell if I'm being protective or petty.

"Hi, Ailey!" Carter calls out. "Miss you, hugs and kisses. Let's grab a bite while I'm in town, yeah?"

"Bring them into what?" I ask Jake.

"You all go after bad people, right?"

"A 'bad person' is subjective. To many out there, we are the bad people."

He isn't tearing away from my gaze. "You're the insidious ones who take from those who abuse their power."

"Not always. We're not fucking Batman. *Sometimes* we just take because there are easy marks."

"Am I an easy mark?"

"Yes."

"You're not actively conning me, though. Why?"

Maybe I am, I could lie.

I grind my jaw, struggling to be anything but honest with Jake Waterford. Ever since I first met him, it's been unnatural deceiving this upstanding, morally driven, do-the-right-thing Abercrombie model.

He is right in one sense.

The six of us try not to fuck over people like him, and as much as his hero antics annoy the shit out of me, he is *that*. Good. Protective. Caring.

"They genuinely like you," I tell him. "Phoebe. Hailey. Even Nova. But what we think about a person's character means less to our parents. They wouldn't care about you. You'd either be the main mark or a poor bystander getting fucked by association."

"They call the shots? Your parents?" Jake wonders.

"They're pulling away from them," Carter answers first after a sip of beer. "Ailey didn't say why. Just that she and Phoebe needed distance after a bad job. Hence, the fresh start. 'Bout time, if you ask me. Their parents sank their claws in deep. I've wondered when they'd tear them out."

Could he be on our side then?

Hope.

It's so foreign, it feels like a tumor in my chest.

Jake focuses back on me. "Your parents don't want you in Victoria, but you want to make a new life here," he says, seeing our goals in bright Technicolor now. "A *safe* life after all the crimes you've committed, everything you've done and maybe still plan to do. What if we can achieve that together?"

I'm suspicious.

Doubtful.

Cautious.

"How?" I ask. "With your so-called influence?" I sit forward, closing in on him. "You don't own this town. Your mother does, and even then, you're not the firstborn or even the second born. You are the *third-born* errand boy to your mother and brothers. You take care of the leftovers. The real estate. The rentals. The country club. You are nothing more than a gopher to them."

"You think I don't know that?" he retorts. "How they treat me—it's not even why I hate them."

I nod. "You already told me they were controlling toward Kate. That they suffocated her to the point where your sister tried to take her own life."

"It's even more than that," Jake professes. "You don't know my family. You can't even imagine what they're capable of."

"I've been around hundreds of people just like them my entire life. I think I can crack a fucking guess."

"Then you know they shouldn't have this much control over an entire town. There are *good* people here who get bulldozed and abused all the time by them."

"That's life."

"It doesn't have to be." Jake is grasping for an ideal world. "I've watched girls be torn down by my mother for too many years. Most especially the ones she sets me up with. And the greatest effect I've ever had stopping it was Phoebe."

My jaw aches from gritting on my molars. I shake my head profusely. "Your mother hates Phoebe for accidentally dumping a glass of champagne on her dress and being whiplashed at your sudden 'relationship' with her." I use air quotes. "What do you think happens to Phoebe at the end of this? Because you can't protect her from a woman who overrides you in every way, Jake."

"Help me then."

"Help you what?"

"Take control." He rests his forearms on the table, closing in on me now. "Trent stands to inherit *everything*. The land, the brewing company, the money, all assets. It *sickens* me. Knowing he's what my family's centuries-long legacy is going to boil down to. It can't end up with someone like him. It shouldn't even be with someone like my mother."

"You want to be sole heir," I realize.

"I want it all," he confirms. "If there's a way to push my mother off the board of directors for Koning, and push Trent off, it'd leave me as the most prominent voice. And then I slowly take everything else from them. The cars. The estate. The inheritance. Until there is nothing left."

He's not looking to backstab them. He wants to slit their throats. I arch my brows, almost impressed. "You want to leave them destitute?"

"I'd rather have them behind bars, but I'll take what I can get."

Yeah.

I feel that. Deeper in my soul than he knows. Because if I could put my parents in the slammer without also joining them, I'd do it.

"What you're hoping for," I tell him, "is a miracle. You're not even close to being first in line. You have *two* older brothers." I've never met the oldest, but I listen around town. "The way women talk about Trent—they act like he's Koning *Jesus*."

"It's what he likes people to believe. In fact, I'm not entirely sure he doesn't also believe it about himself."

Easy to manipulate. Hard to be around.

I don't tell Jake that. "And your other brother? He's desperate for validation from your mother. I've seen him practically slobbering at her feet."

"Jordan is . . . inconsequential, for lack of a better word. My mother doesn't take him seriously."

I widen my eyes. "Great. Now we can just give you a pat on the back and push you ahead of the firstborn favorite *and* the woman already in power." I add more seriously, "It's not that easy."

"I didn't think it would be, but with Phoebe, there's a chance. My mother feels most in control when she can toy with women to manipulate me, but Phoebe won't bend to her wishes. It makes my mother angry, and her real nature is more likely to come out."

Her real nature? What heinous things has she even done before?

"You want to blackmail her?" I ask.

"That's exactly what I want to do. We can record her. Use the damning evidence against her. We can do the same to Trent. Maybe my father, too, if he gets in the way, but I doubt he will. He spends most of his time traveling. He's never been considered a part of the Koning inheritance. He's not even on the board. He signed a legal agreement that says he'll get a small amount upon divorce or her death, and nothing more."

In this moment, all I can think about is Phoebe. Of what this would mean for her, for us.

I rake two hot hands through my hair.

Jake must read the slight anguish cinching my face. "I know it'd extend the time I'm fake dating Phoebe, but if I end up with this kind of power, I can offer it to you, too. You can *stay* in this town. You can make a home here, and I'll protect you. Even if it's from your parents, if that's what you want or need. I can pay them off. I can *keep* paying them off indefinitely."

He's offering me freedom.

In a way, I'm also the key to his.

A life without living under the control of our manipulative mothers. A life that's mine. Not theirs.

It's what I've always wanted.

But I've also always wanted to have Phoebe—for her to be mine.

The idea that she could continue to be his (even in a *fake* capacity) isn't making me want to clink beers and sail into the fucking sunset. But it also wouldn't be the first time I hated a piece of a job.

I'm expecting Phoebe and my sister to text their opinions.

When none come, I shove my phone in my leather jacket. "This is a long con," I tell Jake. "It's massive, even for us."

Carter smiles as he says, "For a job that big, you'll need all of them, mate." And that's when I realize, they're here.

It's relief and worry, seeing each person I love enter the galley and this fucked-up mess.

ELEVEN

Phoebe

By the time Hailey, Oliver, Trevor, and I meet up with Nova at the marina and board Jake's catamaran, my emotions have traveled all over the map. I went from wanting to stab Jake and Carter in the face to deciding to chuck the knife away. Am I too understanding? Because I get it.

I get the secrecy. I get not playing all your cards outright. I get needing help.

If Jake has any chance at succeeding, he definitely needs ours. Just like we need his—because is there anything more alluring than finally being rooted somewhere?

I've craved the moment where I can unpack my bags for longer than a few months. Where the next destination isn't in our headlights, and where the place I love isn't in my rearview mirror. We're out of the car. It's in the garage.

This town can be our home.

But there is one thing that's more alluring.

Rocky.

Being with him for real. In my heart, I know I'd choose to be on the run forever if it meant I could have Rocky.

The more powerful desire is him.

I might be a true needy, greedy bitch because I want it *all*. The safety of his arms in the safety of a home.

Inside the catamaran, we're all dressed in black for Emilia Wolfe's impending funeral, but today feels more like the death of our covers.

We come into the cramped galley, and Rocky and Jake stand upon seeing us. Their attention beams down on me like I'm about to be sucked up into one of their spacecrafts.

Rocky, Rocky, *Rocky*, my heart would pick for me.

Only Jake knows I've gotten together with Rocky for real. I managed to keep that nugget of truth a secret from my best friend and my brothers, and with *everything* we just heard, my love life shouldn't be the ultimate factor in what we do.

This isn't just about me and him anymore.

Instead of confronting either guy, I catch Hailey's hand and tug her into the kitchenette area, where blue-and-white striped dish towels hang above a stainless-steel sink.

"I can't do this." That's not me whispering in panic. Hailey dips down her black ballcap with red embroidery that says SATAN'S LIL HELPER. It shadows her already sleep-stricken eyes. "He's right *there*."

"Who?" I whisper back.

Her eyes snap over to Carter, and her fair white skin goes rosy.

I instantly smile. Seeing my best friend smitten instead of distraught? I will take it a *thousand* percent. "I guess I don't have to ask if your crush is still alive."

"Shhhh, *Phoebe*."

"They can't hear." *I don't think.*

"It's just a lot. There are a lot of pieces. A lot of pieces and pieces and men." Her gray eyes dart between too many of the guys in the galley. She's been making less and less sense to me, but you know what—she's *right*. There are a lot of pieces to this puzzle and there are also a lot of men.

So she's not losing it.

I touch her shoulders comfortingly. Her knit sweaterdress is soft, but an edgy black leather harness contraption is on top and matches her combat boots. "All the guys here are on our side," I whisper. "Your brothers and my brothers. Jake and Carter, too."

She peeks from under the brim of her ballcap. "They're watching us."

Aaaaand she's right.

The air has thinned, and the concern for Hailey is choking out the galley.

Carter, who's normally chipper, has a frown and bothered eyes, and he's currently leaning forward to whisper with Jake across the table. As their gazes shift to Hailey, it's clear they're whispering about her.

They don't need to act like the ground is falling beneath her feet. I have this under control. I am enough. I will catch her.

"Stop staring," I snap at everyone. "We're *fine*." We aren't the weak links, and I'm offended they're acting like she has one foot on an explosive, one foot on land. She's been doing the most of all of us. Of course she's still tired.

Rocky squeezes out of the booth, and when our eyes meet, my heart flips and I intake a sharper breath. He seems to be caging oxygen, too, but instead of coming to us, he goes to whisper to his little brother, who's raiding the fridge.

I don't expect my oldest brother to lighten the mood. Nova

is blocking the entryway with crossed arms and a stern *you fuck with them, you fuck with me* glare.

Oliver sinks down on the vacant seat beside Carter, as if there is zero tension to shred. "All I see are plotter-schemer friends here," he says casually, drawing attention off Hailey.

Thank you, Oliver.

He has on dark Ray-Bans that cost four grand and a much pricier Tom Ford suit, and his warm, dyed-brown hair is artfully styled. He lifts the sunglasses to his head. "I don't believe we truthfully met." He's speaking to Jake.

"Not truthfully." Jake assesses him.

Oliver smirks and outstretches his hand. "Oliver Graves. The cute one."

Carter laughs, then cocks his head to Jake. "He's the dodgiest bloke." He grins back at Oliver. "Missed opportunity not to call yourself Dodger, mate."

"Call me whatever you want." He lowers his shades and kicks back. "I'm just a bigger fan of *Oliver.*" He chose the name when he was ten after he read *Oliver Twist* and saw the movie. Dodger is a thief and leader of child criminals in the Dickens novel, and it would've been too on the nose to choose it for a name. But Oliver seemed to always care for the main protagonist: a young, orphaned boy born into poverty who later discovers he's the illegitimate son of a rich man.

We hadn't seen our dad in years at the time, and I wondered if my brother connected to the character's longing for a paternal figure. He's never been close to Everett Tinrock the way Nova has been.

"What do you mean by *the dodgiest*?" Jake asks Carter.

Oliver stretches out. "It means I'm the smartest." He mimes a brain explosion, then speaks in another language.

Jake shakes his head. "I don't know Dutch."

He switches to French, which we all understand certain phrases of, but not whatever he's saying now; then Spanish (don't know), Mandarin (definitely don't know), Portuguese, Turkish, Gaelic. Jake can't keep up with my brother any more than the rest of us can.

"Show-off," Trevor mutters into a mini bottle of tequila.

Rocky tears it out of his hand before he sips it.

"They call him the chameleon," Carter outs him.

An irrepressible smile pulls at my lips.

Were we all dumb to share our monikers with Carter like we were cool-ass bandits and he was the ripper of our wanted posters? In hindsight, probably, but also, it feels strangely liberating to invite someone else into our group.

It's been decades of secrecy. Trusting another person is exhilarating.

Oliver waggles his fingers at Jake. "I'd say *at your service*, but you're going to be at mine." He winks.

"Yeah." Jake seems hopeful. "I can work with that." He surveys each of us around the galley.

"The getaway." Carter points out Nova, who hasn't budged an inch. I'm fairly certain two handguns and a knife are underneath his black bomber jacket.

"Nova Graves," he reintroduces himself. "And fuck you for lying to my sister."

Rocky is smirking near the fridge. Probably *loving* the dig at Jake.

I cut in fast, "We went over this before we got here." An awkward heat bathes me. I told Nova that Jake's deception didn't matter. We're all liars, really. But my brother feels like Jake violated my trust, which is worse because he's in a power position and I'm not. "We weren't truthful from the start either. No one has to apologize."

"I'm still sorry," Jake says. "To you both." His gaze stays intimately on Hailey.

She shies at the attention. "No sorrys. Like Phebs said. Really. It-it's okay."

I squeeze her hand. She squeezes mine back tighter.

"Fresh beginnings for everyone," Carter says lightheartedly. "Beautiful, innit?" He has a megawatt flirty smile on Hailey.

Oliver shifts out of a relaxed position.

She blushes again but crawls farther back into the kitchenette alcove. Bumping into the sink. "I can't do this," she whispers again.

I'm not used to seeing her lack of confidence with guys. She's the one who will full-on approach a man at a bar and say, "*Want to fuck?*"

Literally!

I have been envious and captivated by the blunt sexiness of my best friend. Behind her RBF, she can unknowingly smolder and make men weak at the knees. Sure, sometimes the men are experiencing *fear*. But when she asks to blow them, nine out of ten—it's *lust*.

Is she freaking out now because she has real romantic feelings for Carter?

It's not just sexual desire?

She's spellbound by his forging skills and Louvre-worthy fakes, and her long-standing crush is in the flesh while she's only clocked an hour of sleep. That'd throw anyone off their A game.

"You're doing great," I encourage. "We're breathing. We're the best of the best, and they know it." I wave my hand at them, uncaring if they see us gossiping about them. I hope they do.

"Yeah." She nods. "We're cool. We're the best."

"You're the best *best*. Can't be beat."

Her soft smile appears. "No, you are, Phebs."

I smile back, and we do our handshake: two pinky hooks and fist-bump explosion. Our smiles fade fast because Jake asks, "Do you have a problem with me?" He's talking to Nova.

"Keep your word and we won't have one. Break your word and I'll break your neck."

"After me," Rocky interjects.

"I promise to be honest from here on out," Jake assures us, then focuses back on Hailey. "What do they call you?"

"Hailey."

"The mastermind." Carter grins.

She does a small up-nod, not looking out from the brim of her hat.

"Phoebe, you're . . . ?" Jake starts.

I let Carter answer. "The seductress," he announces.

Now I'm burning up at the many eyes upon me. Even being exposed to one person feels enormous. "Phoebe Graves," I tell him, more aware of how my slim, black, silky dress molds to my hips and breasts.

"I have so many questions," Jake mutters.

"She's not a prostitute," Nova slices in protectively.

Oh my God.

"That we know of," Trevor deadpans.

Rocky smacks the back of his head.

I'm *over* Trevor.

We bickered all the way from the loft to the marina, and he's made me feel fourteen, not twenty-four. I have the urge to lower myself to his lame back-and-forth insults, and I'm taking a new, mature stand by staying *silent*.

Nova is still staring down Jake. "If this whole thing is about you getting your dick wet, you can fuck off."

"Nova," I groan, my face in my palms. I peek between my fingers and see Jake glancing back at Rocky, like he'll shovel him out of the ditch he's dug with my brother.

Rocky holds up his hands. "You piss off Nova, that's your bed to lie in."

"Rocky's been sleeping in it for the past decade," Oliver pipes in with a smile.

"And you're what?" Jake asks Rocky. "The manipulator?"

"He's the silver tongue," Carter reveals.

Rocky raises and lowers his brows.

Jake nods back, and do I sense . . . a shared respect? Are they getting along? My lungs inflate, and I wonder if a team-up could really work between us.

Trevor rests a forearm on Rocky's shoulder. "You want to know what they call me?"

"A little turd," I mention. My silence lasted like two seconds. I'm only somewhat ashamed.

"Wannabe stripper," he slings back.

"*Trevor*," Rocky grits out.

"You've said worse to her, come on."

He swipes a hand across his eyes.

It admittedly turns me on when Rocky is mean. It does not turn me on hearing a stupid insult from his nineteen-year-old brother. And I am *not* about to explain that out loud.

Neither is Rocky.

"This shifty bloke here is the youngest of them." Carter motions to the lankiest in the room. "The psychopath."

"Trevor Tinrock," he says flatly.

"The psychopath?" Jake repeats with hesitance.

"It's a joke," Rocky interjects.

"That's news to me," Oliver adds.

"And me," Nova says.

"Self-diagnosed," Hailey chimes in, staring faraway.

I weave my arms. "He wishes he were one. Because it's so *cool*."

"You don't know what I've done, PG—"

"Enough," Rocky snaps.

Jake checks the time on his watch. We should leave for the cemetery, but no one makes a move toward the exit.

"So you all have different specialties?" Jake asks us.

"Sort of," I say.

"It's what we were taught," Hailey clarifies. "They separated some of us. Paired some together. We each have . . . *had* a purpose." She's unblinking and staring at everything but really at nothing.

It scares me. "Hails." I squeeze her hand.

She doesn't squeeze back.

"I think we should go," I say.

"No," Hailey breathes. "They need to know about them."

"About who?" Jake asks.

She lifts her head up, and Jake meets her haunted gaze as she says, "The people who made us what we are."

"Your parents?"

"Our parents," Hailey repeats, sounding heartbroken. She pushes down the brim of her hat, and then she shakes her head slowly.

"Hails?" I whisper.

"No," she croaks out. "They're not . . ." Her headshakes become fiercer. "We don't know . . ." She's more distraught and tugs away from me, spinning rapidly in a circle like she's searching for an exit.

I reach out for her, but she's a bullet in the other direction.

Carter, Jake, and Oliver shoot to their feet—everyone is now standing as Hailey flees toward the doorway that Nova blocks.

He lets her easily through. I think because Oliver is on her heels.

She just needs air. She'll be okay. My pulse pounds in my neck, and I chase after my best friend and come crashing into Nova's firm chest.

He fills the exit again.

"*Nova*," I say, hurt. "Let me through."

He dips his head to whisper, "Oliver is with her."

"I can be with her, too. She needs me." Why is he looking at me like that? Hot tears burn my eyes. This is cruel and unusual from my brother. "*Nova*."

His face fractures with shards of pain, too. "I love you, all right. I'm not doing this to hurt you."

"Then let me *through*."

"*I can't*," he forces out with reddened eyes. He checks on our audience behind me, then lowers his voice again. "He's the only one who's gotten her to sleep. Let him try to reach her right now without you."

Pain wells up, but it's not about me. This is about Hailey, and if she needs my brother and not me . . . I wince at myself. It's just so *strange*. Why would she need him *over* me?

Bruised ego, check.

Let it go, Phoebe.

"Yeah . . . okay." I back away from Nova like a wounded animal, and all I want to do is walk into the comfort of Rocky's arms.

He's right there. At the fridge. With a menacing, brooding look that feels naturally welcoming to me. His attention is mine—his gaze sweeping down me in a hard, caring stroke.

I stop short when Trevor whispers to his brother and steals half his focus.

Right.

No one knows we're together. I really want to change that, but not now. Not after all *this*.

Carter and Jake are still standing. Still concerned. I doubt it could evaporate at this point. It's a permanent weather condition. "What's got Ailey so knackered?" Carter asks us.

We're all quiet, casting furtive glances, wondering which one of us will spill the beans. We all end up staring at Rocky.

He rolls his eyes, then says, "Even if we tell you this, even if we agree to work together on a job, you could turn on us at the end."

"I'll give you my sister's address," Jake promises. "I love her. It's the biggest collateral I have."

"It could be easily faked, or she could move."

Jake intakes the deepest breath. "Then you're just going to have to trust me." They hold each other's gaze for what feels like a millennium.

I trust Jake, and I'm more afraid to lose him as a potential ally against our parents. Rocky is so mistrusting—he can't believe in the weapon in front of him. He'd always think it was a trick. That the weapon was filled with blanks.

This gun feels lethal.

We need him.

He needs us.

I'm surprised when Rocky relents. "All right." And he begins to tell them *everything*. "Our parents might not be our real parents. They've lied to us. That's why my sister is so distressed. She's been trying to figure out who the hell we really are."

As he continues down the rabbit hole of our fucked-up lives

and all we've learned since Halloween, Jake has a hand planted over his mouth. His brows are furrowed caterpillars of absolute shock and disturbance and . . . empathy.

Carter keeps rubbing his chin and jaw like they're aching. He's the one muttering "Bloody fucking hell" and "No way" and shaking his head like Rocky is describing the horror plot to *The Hills Have Eyes* and not, you know, our actual lives. He, too, empathizes, and I thought it'd be uncomfortable.

I thought I'd crawl into myself and want to hide behind aliases and deceit. I didn't think telling the truth would feel like purging twenty-four years of cumbersome weight.

For other people to care about us, the genuine and real *us* . . . it's overwhelming.

I breathe in helium. Dizzy and high with a newfound feeling.

When Rocky is finished, the first thing Jake says is, "I'm going to help you. All of you." It's a resolute, unwavering promise.

"You can try to King Arthur this," Rocky tells him, "but you're not wearing the crown yet, Koning boy."

"He's still an heir," Carter reminds him. "He might not be able to dupe your parents, but he can protect you while you're in town. I think I'll stick around, too."

Hailey's crush is *staying.* I smooth my lips over a burgeoning smile. Maybe her *Mystic Pizza* romance will seriously come to fruition here. My smile slowly fades as I remember how she fled the catamaran. Maybe a happy distraction will help her mind rest.

Carter moves out of the booth and tosses Jake his peacoat. Jake catches it. "You don't have to go back to York?"

"I thought you were in Manchester now?" Rocky questions.

"I'm here, I'm there." Carter smiles. "And I've got time to spare, and my grannie still lives on the harbor. Might as well pay a long-extended visit and see if she knows anything about Addison and Elizabeth." His lips drag into a frown. "I am sorry . . . about what they might've done. If I had known you weren't really theirs . . . I would've told one of you."

"Thanks, Carter," I say from the sincerest place I can.

He nods to me. "Tell Ailey we'll catch up when she's hit the hay, yeah? That Ocean Pearl needs an Uncle Ned about yesterday." He laughs to himself at my quizzical expression. I wish Oliver were still here to translate that Cockney slang for me. Then Carter's light on his feet and en route to leave the catamaran.

"Wait," Rocky calls out, stopping Carter at the exit beside my oldest brother. "They're here. In Victoria."

"Who?"

"Addison and Elizabeth," Rocky says. "They just arrived about a week ago."

Nova warns him, "We don't know if they'll be at the funeral."

I offer this fun-sized piece of info. "They're posing as matchmakers."

Jake freezes midway into slipping his arms into the peacoat. "Isla and Wendy are the women who raised you?" He glances between all of us.

"In the flesh," Rocky says dryly.

I explain, "They're hoping this matchmaking thing will be a short con and we'll leave town with them."

"I'll keep an eye out," Carter says, lost a little in thought before he disappears.

The rest of us aren't far behind.

It's pouring when we reach the cemetery. Rain slips off hundreds of black umbrellas as people surround the freshly dug grave for Emilia Wolfe. Several socialites offer parting words, including Jake's mom, but they lament more about the town than about the woman who left it.

"She lived a wonderful life in Victoria, as we all do."

"The Wolfes will *always* be a hallmark here."

"Their names are etched in the very foundation of town hall."

I see necks craning and eyes shifting. The wealthy elite are taking stock of who's in attendance, and I wonder if they're noting Hailey's and Oliver's absence, or if they're not influential enough to matter.

They matter to me.

I shoot both a text, hoping all is okay, and I ignore the knotting in my stomach.

It becomes painfully obvious I am a person of interest. Probably because I'm standing between my situationship—Jake and Rocky.

Neither one touches me. There are undefined parameters regarding *us*. But I'm sharing an umbrella with my fake boyfriend. Jake hoists it above the two of us, and rain pings against the black, tented fabric.

As the funeral winds down, whispers and disappointed frowns take flight. Most suffered through the storm and service to catch a glimpse of the elusive Varrick Wolfe, the son-in-law to Emilia, but he's a no-show.

I care less about that chupacabra and more about the ones who raised me. Luckily, they don't seem to be making an appearance today either.

The coffin is lowered into the ditch. While people begin to disperse, sloshing in the muddy terrain, Jake leads me away from the crowds and to his grandfather's grave.

It's private.

Canopies of old oak trees catch the rainfall, and fog hangs low across the historic headstones.

"Addison hates being dirty, so maybe they were avoiding mucking up their Louboutins," I theorize to Jake, of all people, but Rocky is hanging back at Emilia's grave and socializing with several contacts he's made while being Grey Thornhall.

Valentina de la Vega. (Caufield MBA student and stunningly beautiful. I have eyes.)

Damian Bennet. (Son of the third founding family.)

Collin Falcone. (Supposed loyal best friend to Trent Koning Waterford and a notorious partier.)

"I'm glad she didn't make it," Jake says, and I agree, letting the convo about Addison end there. I'm not looking to dig deep into the pain of what has happened. I'd rather move forward, and I think Jake senses that, too. He keeps the umbrella steady over us as we walk between the many grave markers. "I hate cemeteries," he breathes.

"I love them."

His laugh turns into a smile. "The horror-movie lover in you?"

"That and . . ." I look around at the names scrawled across dozens of weatherworn stones, some graves nestled only inches apart. "It's lineages of people buried together. Families. A visual representation of close bonds between those who mattered to each other." I smile back at him. "It's love in death. So in that sense, cemeteries are *romantic*."

"Okay, yeah. When you put it like that." His lips rise higher. "Does your ex-husband have the same feelings?"

Ex-husband. *Shit.*

We forgot to clear up this last lie, and is it bad if I don't want to? I love pretending to be Rocky's ex-wife. There is no better term that encompasses the messy depth of our history.

"Uh." I blink past that speed bump. "No, he hates cemeteries, like you. He's ridiculously superstitious."

"Really?"

"Oh, *to the max*." My cheeks hurt in a smile. "He would probably never step foot on cemetery grass if he could help it, but he'll do it for . . ." I flush.

"For you," Jake guesses, sweeping his eyes over my features.

"Yeah, but also for Hailey. Trevor. All of us. When I told you he'd do anything for his friends, what I meant is he'd do anything for the five of us. He has done more than you can ever know."

"I'm sure," he says, still in the slight haze of realizations.

As we draw farther and farther from the freshly dug grave, I'm afraid to lose sight of Rocky in the distance. I love casting sly glances back.

I love locking eyes in secret, pulse-pounding seconds. I love the iron-strong tether between me and him, and anyone who tries to break it will trip and fall. Maybe it's why I'm not overly concerned for our real relationship amid a potential job.

If we were going to get together, it'd always have to work inside what we do.

Unless, of course, I quit this lifestyle, but that's not even an option I want to mull over right now.

I risk a glance back at Rocky.

His dark gaze fastens to mine, and my heart double beats when he shakes Damian's hand in goodbye, then aims for us with an unyielding, confident stride.

Jake sees and slows down so Rocky can catch up. We don't

have much of an audience over here, and Rocky interrupting me and Jake would just stoke the narrative that my ex-husband is still pining after me and can't leave me alone.

"Phoebe was just telling me you hate cemeteries," Jake says.

Rocky grips an umbrella with one hand and brushes his hair with the other, all while staring intensely down at me. "Can't stop talking about me?" Okay . . . that was extremely hot.

But I'm not falling all over him. "I could go on about all the things you hate, but it'd shave ten years off my life, so you're lucky I even shared *one* thing."

His lips nearly twist in a smile. He angles his umbrella, shielding us from view of the gravesite we deserted, and using the discreet moment, he whispers against my ear, "I'd say you love me in your mouth, but I haven't been there yet."

The image of his cock between my lips causes me to throb, and I'm not even a fan of blow jobs, so what is happening?

Jake is watching my breath hitch. I'm more aware of him here, and it's a little obvious Rocky just aroused me. Minorly. *Minorly aroused.*

Rocky seems satisfied.

I might like how he came on to me in front of Jake. Is that weird? It's not a sudden revelation that I enjoy being possessed by him, and if we're extending this fake-dating thing, I hope he never stops.

"How long have you two really been together?" Jake wonders. "Were you ever actually divorced?"

I think he believes we've always been married—that there was no breakup.

I tense. "It's complicated."

"It's not that complicated," Rocky says curtly.

I glare. "But *it is*."

"Watch me explain it then." He sets his gunmetal gaze on Jake. "She's been everything to me for too many years. It's been a marriage of both convenience and inconvenience. Of pure love and pure hell, and I wouldn't give up one to have the other. They coexist *unnaturally*, but nothing about us has ever been normal. So you don't need to scrounge around for a fucking term for what we are together because there isn't going to be one bone-deep enough that fits."

My eyes burn with emotion. My lungs swell. I bite the corner of my lip to keep a smile at bay, especially while Rocky has a dark threat in his eye toward Jake.

"Is that good enough for you, sweetheart?" Rocky asks him. "Or do you want me to throw her diary at you, too?"

"Like you would let me read it," Jake quips back.

"I don't have a diary," I cut in. "That'd be careless in our line of work, and we have to be careful. Even now."

"We'll be careful," Jake assures me. "You two have history, and I know I'm in the middle of it. So you give me the boundaries. I won't cross them."

Rocky and I share an intense look, and my pulse will not slow.

We're really doing this.

"We're not even sure how long this job will take," I tell Rocky.

He adjusts his tight grip on his umbrella, staring deeper into me. "It could take a really long fucking time."

"And you still want to do this?" If it's torture for him, I'll say *no* to Jake. We can find another way. I'd drive myself over the edge watching Rocky be physically close to another person that's not me. Hell, that's all we've *done* in the past. Torment each other to no end.

So I'm not surprised when he says, "Yeah, it's what I'm used to." After a crack of lightning, he tells me, "Some things are bigger than us, Phebs. But I am always, *always* with you. There's never been a moment where I haven't been."

I breathe in the sentiments. "I know." It's why I'm also very willing to agree. This is about my best friend, his brother, and my brothers. And who am I if I'm not a team player? Who am I if I'm not even part of the team?

It's been clear all six of us want what Jake is offering when we complete this job. And the idea of turning Victoria into a "fun zone" where we can pull a con had Trevor foaming at the mouth on the car ride here.

I don't love being in the same camp as Rocky's brother, especially when I've been toying with quitting a life of deception—but diving into a job and screwing someone over, it stokes a giddy anticipation, like I'm tiptoeing to the edge of a cliff.

"I might be an adrenaline junkie," I tell Rocky.

His smile inches up. "You think?"

I smile back. "You aren't going to say we're one and the same?"

"Some things between us have never needed to be said." That's more than true, and even though we can't touch in this cemetery, in this second, I feel Rocky all over my body in ways only he can be.

There is an electric feeling that *yes, this will work between us.* If not, we'll beat against the obstacle until it does work. Come hell or high water.

We like living in that, too.

TWELVE

Rocky

The Berkshires.

It's where our parents agree to meet us. We stagger our arrivals out of paranoia. Phoebe will be there first.

Then me.

Ditching the McLaren for this getaway, I ride a motorcycle I purchased not long ago, and I come upon a modest-sized mansion with white siding and black shutters. It's situated in a thicket of orange trees. Farmland and rolling hills landscape the overgrown, weed-ridden grounds. No other house in sight.

A month ago, Nova Graves bought this seven-bedroom estate on five acres of land under an LLC he created from scratch. It'd been designated as a home base for him, Oliver, and me since we never agreed to Phoebe and Hailey's path of virtue.

It's an easy place to gather and plan a short con, so we agreed it's a perfect location to meet the godfather and godmothers for dinner. All without the entire town getting a whiff of it.

Inside, I'm caught at something in the foyer.

"Jesus Christ, Nova," I mutter under my breath.

It's not stained or peeling wallpaper. The early 1900s mansion is in decent condition with scuffed floorboards and a musty old-house smell. It's a fixer-upper, and maybe if it was used as more than a safe house, we'd collectively spend money to polish the brass.

This, however, is a bad omen.

An enormous oil painting by William-Adolphe Bouguereau hangs on the wall. Dark oranges bleed into darker grays, a winged demon flying in the hellish background on the canvas. In the foreground, two naked men are in a gruesome, endless fight in the eighth circle of hell.

The one designated for fraudsters, imposters, counterfeiters, *liars*.

The redhead pins his knee into the other man's back while taking a bite out of his throat.

It's called *Dante et Virgile*.

Dante and Virgil in hell. Nova sold a forgery to the Musée d'Orsay a couple years ago and kept the original.

Now the original is hanging in a fucking *safe house*. Because there is so much about this that screams *security*.

The painting was inspired by Dante's *Divine Comedy*. The redhead was Gianni Schicchi, a thirteenth-century Italian who impersonated a dead man so he could inherit his wealth for himself. Nova loves art, and it's his ironic love of this painting that makes me think he needs a therapist that's not his brother.

I hate housing stolen artifacts and possessions. It feels like collecting ticking bombs. He needs to put the painting in a fucking storage unit. Like tomorrow.

I'll argue about it with him later.

I'd much rather be in the company of his sister.

I enter the living room and see Phoebe on her hands and

knees in a simple but *beyond sexy* pink cotton dress. She's laboring over an old cast-iron wood-burning stove, shoving firewood in the hatch.

My cock instantly stirs. A primal instinct tries to tear through me.

The floorboards creak as I near her.

She glances over her shoulder at me, dark blue hair falling into her heart-shaped face. She brushes the strands back, and as we lock eyes, a thousand different feelings barrel through me at vicious speed, a million different memories and lives we've lived all colliding at once. And this one—*this life* is carved out as the most fragile. Most vital. The one I want to exist inside.

Because I can do this.

I drop my motorcycle helmet and cut the distance so fast, she has no time to stand.

I'm on my knees in front of Phoebe. I clutch her soft cheeks with two unforgiving hands, and she hangs on to my neck as I crash my lips against hers. Her teeny-tiny moan builds an inferno in my bloodstream.

Her body responds by bowing toward me.

I kiss her with truths. Of how we won't be alone for long. There isn't sweet, little urgency in me. It's violence against seconds, against time. I ravage the fuck out of her with my tongue, my hands, with the emotion coiling around my searing lungs.

Phoebe's fingers cling tighter as though to command, *Don't stop.*

I breathe in her intoxicating, sugary floral scent and cup the back of her head, deepening the kisses in feral, hungry waves.

More.

I need more of her.

I tear my lips off hers.

She pants out, "No *Hi, Phoebe*?" She grips my leather bike jacket with two strong fists. "No *How's it going, Phoebe*?"

"Hi, Phoebe." I slide my hand farther into her blue hair. "You want me to come inside you, Phoebe?" An aching, whimpering noise escapes her throat. *Fuck her, fuck her, fuck her now.* I want to burn her sounds in my brain.

"*So badly*," she teases, her glare ratcheting up the heat between us. "You want to ram your dick inside me?"

"Repeatedly."

Her lips part with another breathy noise. "Not now . . . ? My brothers should be here soon— Rocky!"

I lift her by the backs of her thighs. The fire in her eyes hasn't extinguished, and I tell her lowly, darkly, "You think I care if they see me fucking their sister?"

She shoves my arm. "You *should* care."

"I care about railing you so deep, you're unsure whether to cry or scream." I watch her breath shorten. "I care about making you come until your eyes roll into the back of your head and you beg me to do it all over again and again and *again*."

A flush stains her cheeks, but while I hold her, she leans close to snap back, "I'm not begging you for *anything*."

I throw her on the couch. It's covered with a white sheet, and she falls into the fabric and bounces a little on the cushion. Before I can pin her down, Phoebe pops up on her feet and backs away with a stubborn blaze in her eyes.

She's so much like me, it's almost terrifying.

I track her, but she circles me—which causes me to circle Phoebe with an unmanageable tension. Like we're assassins come to kill each other.

"I'm not wasting any moment I have with you," I warn her.

"Even if it's locked between two risks and six thousand dangers."

"Good," she snaps back.

"Great." I take off my jacket, then yank my shirt off my head while I continue tracking her. She zeroes in on my hands as I unbuckle my belt. I toss it aside, then unzip my pants. I'm shedding my clothes rapidly. To where I'm buck-ass naked. My hard cock primed for entry into her pussy.

She gathers her hair in a pony, and blood pumps hotter through my veins. It's not a cat-and-mouse game with Phoebe. We're the same wrecked, venomous breed.

"You want me?" she taunts. "Come and get me."

I stalk forward, and she steps back—but not fast enough. I catch her hips, and the inferno explodes in us—we crash together with hungry kisses. Her fingers dig into my biceps, and just as I pull Phoebe firmer against my muscles, she wrenches away and shuffles backward.

My pulse is in my ears, until I see her arousal and a daring, seductive look in her narrowed eyes. She's roping me in, winding me around her, and I won't lie—it's driving me fucking mad.

I pursue her, crawling toward the unbalanced feeling that makes me feel alive.

"You won't make it past the door," I threaten, my glare matching hers.

"Watch me." She whirls around to run, but she can't even grab hold of the doorframe before I seize her around the waist, hauling her against me.

She's a head shorter than me barefoot. I have a flexed arm around her breasts and another around her abdomen. Her back to my chest. My grip is so tight, she can't wiggle out, even though she barely tries.

I whisper against her ear, "I'll always find you. Wherever

you go, I will hunt you down with my last fucking breath." My love is as unrelenting as it is vicious. Phoebe can't contain a whimpering moan.

I need inside her. I'm feeling more feral, as if I need to mark my territory so predators smell me on her and know I'll maim and kill if they attempt to rip her from me. I practically carry her over to the wood-burning stove.

"You're going to the floor," I tell her as I bring her down with me.

"No, I'm not." She hardly puts up a fight, wanting me. Wanting this. I've become rapidly aware that Phoebe is attracted to the fact that I will do *anything* to have her. That nothing will stop me, not even her verbal protests.

I *crave* seeing her succumb to her own overwhelming arousal. I crave being in total control of her body, her heart, her soul. Mine to protect. Mine to love.

Mine to fuck.

I'm knelt behind her, and I push her flat against the floor-boards. My slacks are in a heap beside me, and while I dig a condom out, she tries to army crawl away.

I capture her ankle and slide her back.

"Rocky." She tries to turn to face me, but I bend forward and use my weight and strength to easily force her chest onto the ground.

"*Phoebe*," I growl in her ear as I tear her dress down her full breasts and to the curve of her hips. I snap off her lacy white bra. She is undeniably *gorgeous*. But I love so much more about Phoebe than her body. It's just a vessel for what I really want to touch.

"You better hurry," she snaps, her head raising toward the door like her brothers could walk in.

"You better not fucking rush me," I retort, lifting her pink dress off her ass and slipping her mesh thong off her legs. With her dress still pooled at her hips and her round, perky ass in view, all I can think about is her pussy.

I slide two fingers inside Phoebe's swollen, wet heat, and her high-pitched cry is a symphony in my ears. She's beyond ready. I brush her clit, and her whole body vibrates against the floor. *Christ.*

I quickly sheathe my erection, and again, she attempts (poorly) to wiggle out from under me. I capture both her hands in mine and stretch her arms upward. Planting her palms on the floorboard, I hold them there. My muscled body envelops her soft frame, and I use my knees to spread her thighs open.

Her breath comes more ragged, faster, in anticipation, and I grind into Phoebe, penetrating her with my hard length. She chokes on a pleasured cry, and I grit my molars as she clenches around my cock. She is *so tight.* I flex my abs to keep myself on an edge. Melded with her, I thrust deeper, harder, in a systematic, mind-numbing pace that stokes friction and heat.

"You feel my cock burrowed in your cunt?" I hold her tighter as she shudders. "You're not going anywhere," I say roughly, thick arousal raking against my throat.

I have her. I rock deeper.

I fucking have her. Harder.

No one is taking her from me.

"Oh fuck," she cries into the wood. Her body jerks forward with my thrusts, and then she tries to twist her head to see me. When she can't get a good look, she tenses a little.

I slow, watching her carefully. Then I lower my mouth to her ear. "Let go. I'm not going to hurt you."

She releases a breath, and her limbs slacken under me.

I clutch the back of her neck more protectively, my fingers rising up into her hair. I've stopped moving inside her.

"*Rocky*," she cries, a needy little fucking cry.

With a fistful of hair, I pull her head back, and her glare hits me from upside down, especially as I say, "What were you saying about not begging me?"

"Shut up," she growls.

I ram into her pussy, and her lips part while her glare remains. She likes this, though—our eyes drilling into each other while I fuck her deep.

"You need to hurry," she moans out.

"I hope they walk in," I grit back, our bodies slick with sweat. "I hope they see me destroying their sister's tight little pussy."

"Liar," she cries, giving me a hotter glare.

I'd grin if I weren't so fucking pent-up.

And then my phone rings.

"Rocky, don't—"

I'm already grabbing the cellphone. "Be quiet."

"You wouldn't," she rasps, sounding half challenging, half uncertain.

I let go of her hair and push her fully down again. Caging Phoebe with my weight, I stay inside of her. "Your fake boyfriend is calling me." I place the phone near her mouth. "Want to say hi?"

"*No.*"

"I will."

"Rock—" She cuts herself off as I hit the green accept call button, along with speakerphone.

"Jake," I answer and force all arousal out of my voice.

Phoebe stays deathly quiet. Especially as I make slow-burning, languid movements inside her.

"Are you busy?" he asks.

"No, I'm just twiddling my thumbs and waiting around for your fucking phone call." I drive deeper, flexing forward in pumps that *dig*. Phoebe presses her forehead to the floor, trembling beneath me.

"Nice to talk to you, too," Jake replies, sounding like he's in a hurry.

I fuck Phoebe without stopping. She is a swollen vise around my cock, and it's all I can do to control my breathing.

"I'm on my way to a lunch with my father," Jake tells me. "But I need to know if you play tennis."

I sit up on my knees. "Yeah, I play tennis." I clutch the crook of her hips and pound her quietly, seeing my cock slide inside her pussy. It's an image I could watch on repeat, one that likely won't leave me.

She's clawing at the floorboards, struggling not to make a noise. I suck in a breath through my nose. My muscles are on fucking fire. I want to unload in her.

"Trent needs a doubles partner on Saturday," Jake says.

"Yeah?" I hover back over Phoebe, and I pinch her cheeks and turn her head, so she sees me.

Her glare is murderous. Her lips pressed tightly shut.

I glare back and mouth, *Come.*

She shakes her head, and I grind deeper.

Her lips break apart into a breathy sound, but Jake doesn't hear. He's telling me, "Collin broke his wrist doing a backflip at the golf course, so he can't play with him. If you're serious about befriending my brother, that's your best way in. *If* you're good at tennis."

A rough, pleasured sound scorches my lungs. Not letting it out, I level my voice. "I'm good enough." The next push inside Phoebe has her pulsing around my cock, and I know she's coming. Quickly, I cover her mouth with my hand, and she releases a strangled noise. I muffle it, and I take Jake off speaker.

"I don't like this plan, just to make that clear," he says, sounding more distant.

My neck strains as I control my shortened breath, forcing myself not to hit a peak with her. "Why not?" I ask as I put the phone to my ear.

"Trent isn't an easy person to be around, and I'm . . ."

My brows arch. *He's what?* "Are you worried about me?"

"I don't like him around any of my friends."

"We're friends? That's news to me."

"What would you call us then?"

"Colleagues. Coworkers. Two guys who can't fucking stand each other but have to work together." I don't pull out of Phoebe, and I observe her catching her breath.

"Then let's put it this way, Grey. I can stand being around you more than I can stand being around Trent."

"Save the concern for someone who needs it. I can handle your brother." With a quick "Gotta go," we both hang up.

Quickly, I change positions with Phoebe. Putting her on my lap, I sink her down on my cock, and she's in a weak sex haze as I fuck her fast and hard.

"Rocky." She's gripping my shoulders, and I come when she orgasms again and cries into the crook of my neck. "*Fuck you*," she moans, her voice hoarse and raspy.

I grunt out "Fuck" as I milk my climax, pumping into her. Slow strokes. *God, that feels fucking . . .* I hold the back of her head and lick my lips before I kiss her.

She melts a little.

We're both breathing hard.

When she climbs off, she's quick to lift her dress and find

her bra and panties. I put on my clothes unhurriedly. Her eyes dart to the entryway more than once.

I buckle my belt. "Just sit with me for a second." Having sex next to the fire has left both of us sweaty, but I sink back to the floor.

Sitting, Phoebe weaves her arms over her tits and faces me, about to cross her legs until I drag her closer. Her smile fights through, especially as I rub the length of her leg, and she holds on to my knee like it's a teddy bear.

It's cute. "You liked that?" I ask her. "What we just did?"

Phoebe tucks a hair behind her ear. "You couldn't tell?"

"I just want verbal confirmation."

"Yeah, I liked it. Did you?"

"Loved it, actually."

"That's good since . . ." Her eyes flit up to mine. "I love you."

I've never heard her say that, and my lungs inflate with a power I could live and die inside. "Say it again."

"I really love you, Rocky." Her overwhelmed gaze softens on me. "Like probably way too much at this point."

"Same." I clasp her warm cheek. We kiss more tenderly, and when we retract, I think back to the sex we just had and say, "Don't get mad when I ask you this."

Her brows bunch. "That's not ominous at all."

I reword it. "Preface: I'm not trying to be a dick when I say this."

"Say what?"

"You do know what a safe word is for?"

She flinches in surprise. "What? Why would you even *ask* that?"

I pull her even closer. She's now sitting between my spread legs, and hers open around me, too. I keep a hand on her lower back. Her defenses drop while she's more up against my chest. She holds my waist in a loose hug.

Quietly, I say, "There was one moment where I thought you might've gotten in your head about something, but I couldn't see your face."

"I was fine," she murmurs.

"Yeah?" I chase after her gaze. "I'd believe you more if you looked me in the eyes while you said it."

Her narrowed eyes find mine. "*I was fine*. You don't need to worry about me when we're sleeping together."

"I do if you're too stubborn to use a safe word when you need it."

"I didn't need it."

I study her. "All right. Okay . . . but I'm telling you now, I can only read your body so much, Phebs. I can't read your mind, too."

"I know."

I kiss her again, and she kisses back in an intimate, softer moment between us. Then she rises and walks over to the bookcase. I pick myself off the floor and follow. I'm at her side as she takes a picture frame off the shelf.

Photos of two little toddlers playing in tall grass.

She flashes it to me. "This could be us."

"I doubt you were blonde as a baby." She has olive skin, likely Mediterranean ancestry, and her natural hair is darker than mine, even if my hair is dyed black right now. I'm probably of British Isles descent, if I had to guess.

She examines another frame.

"They're all stock photos, Phoebe."

"I'm seeing if the cameras are turned on." She's checking the devices embedded in the frames.

"I told Nova to turn them off." I double-check a couple

frames on a higher shelf to be sure. More mics and hidden cameras are set around the house, and a surveillance room is on the second floor. Once we ensure nothing is recording from the bookcase, we go to the dining room and set the table using white gloves.

Tonight is also about collecting our parents' DNA. One step closer to figuring out who's biologically related.

I'm meticulous about the place settings. No fingerprints. No water splotches. I repolish a gold knife for longer than Phoebe would, which is why she says, "What are you doing?"

"Watching cartoons," I say dryly, lifting my eyes to hers. "What does it look like I'm doing?"

"Jerking off a knife."

"Funny." I swipe it one more time, gaze latched to hers, and she swallows. I zero in on her throat, and as I place the knife down, I contemplate if there's enough time to take her again.

"We're still telling them, right?" Phoebe asks. "Your siblings, my siblings. We're telling them that we're really together?"

"Yeah, when they get here." I didn't seriously want her brothers to catch me in the act with her, but that would've solved the fucking orchestration of having to drop this news on them.

As the front door creaks open, I realize that time is now.

THIRTEEN

Phoebe

W e have something to tell you. Sit down, please," Hailey tells me and her older brother—taking the words right out of *my* mouth.

We have something to tell you, too. Admittedly, I did not plan to say *please*, so my best friend is more polite than I am.

Rocky and I share a confused look before we plop down on the squeaky edge of a twin bed together. The rouge comforter is a baroque, Gothic pattern. Identical thick drapes frame the ornate mahogany headboard.

We only chose to gather in one of the mansion's bedrooms since it's doubling as the surveillance area. Monitors, keyboards, and audio equipment are spread over a wooden desk and pushed against forest-green wallpaper.

Oliver spins on the office chair in slow, relaxed circles and slides a ballpoint pen behind his ear.

When I catch his gaze, I slip him a look like *what is this?*

He raises his hands, telling me, *No need to panic.*

Am I panicking? I'm staring at my best friend, who is

death-clutching an old, musty hardback to her chest like she's Gollum hoarding the One Ring to rule them all.

Thinking about *The Lord of the Rings* washes me with a wave of sad nostalgia, because we all binged the trilogy together at a Four Seasons, and Hailey and I agreed that Legolas isn't nearly as panty-droppingly hot as Aragorn.

Simpler times.

Yet, still chaotic, considering we were in Chicago to dupe a trust-fund baby and his misogynistic friends.

Now, I'm here. Sitting beside Rocky after the hottest *hello* of my life. It feels like he's still inside me, the ache and tenderness a weird comfort, and I'm simultaneously ready for everyone to find out we're together and also terrified it'll cause serious friction.

"Who's *we*?" Rocky asks his sister.

Hailey draws a circle in the air from her to Oliver. Then to Nova, who's bent over the desk, clicking a mouse, and checking the status of the camera footage. I'm shocked when her finger veers to Trevor. He's practically hugging an antique dresser while wearing black Bvlgari sunglasses and a slim black suit. I watch him wobble.

What the hell? "Is he drunk?" I ask everyone.

"Are *you* drunk, PG?" Trevor retorts lamely.

"Uh, no. I'm sober."

"Could've fooled no one." He sways, about to fall over, but he catches a drawer and straightens himself up. Rocky is about to rise off the bed, but Trevor extends an arm to halt his older brother. "Stop. I'm perfectly proficient at standing."

"Could've fooled no one," I mutter under my breath.

He hears, somehow. "Go flash a crusty old man—"

"Knock it off," Rocky growls.

Nova could've broken his neck with how fast he whipped

his head back at Trevor. I'm not bristling at that stupid dig, but Nova narrows his gaze on him for an extra beat. With Trevor's dark shades, it's impossible to tell what he's staring at.

Really, I'd bet his eyes are shut.

"And, ladies and gentlemen," Oliver says, "that is what consuming half a handle of vodka in an hour looks like."

Rocky lances a glare at him now. "And how did he come by a handle of vodka?"

"I had to stop at the liquor store." Oliver opens his hands like there was no choice. "Trev was in pain and refused to take a pill."

Trevor rests his face on his arm. "Do you know how much a Percocet sells for? I'm not swallowing money."

"You shouldn't be selling any drugs," Nova says sternly, returning his attention to the computers.

"I'm not selling in Victoria."

"I meant *anywhere*." Nova clicks through the cameras again, checking for motion near the portico outside. "You don't know who you're getting hooked on that shit."

"So?"

"I think we should focus," Hailey interjects while squeezing the book. Her black nail polish is chipped. "We don't have much time left before the godmothers and godfather get here." Her cargo pants hang loose on her bony waist, and her cheeks seem more sunken since yesterday.

"Nova, do you have a protein bar?" I ask him.

He crouches down to a duffel bag.

"We-we need to *focus*, Phebs," Hailey says, sounding frantic. "This is more important."

Rocky is biting his tongue, because the last time he chimed in after me, Hailey acted like we were ganging up on her, and he has an easier time pretending not to care. I can't hide my worry. Not for her.

"It takes two seconds to eat something," I say gently.

"Please, *just listen to me*," Hailey pleads, distraught and blinking rapidly like she's struggling to see what's up and down.

"I am, I am," I say fast.

Oliver rises casually from the chair and rolls it over to Hailey. Her wide eyes land on him, and as he holds the seat out for her, she mechanically sits down.

"Leave her alone, Phoebe," Trevor warns with no inflection in his voice. I get he's protective of his sister, but I'm not actively trying to cause her more distress.

Rocky shoots him a hard look. "Stay out of it, Trev."

He backs off.

I retreat, too. I nod her on and clutch my kneecaps, prepared for whatever bomb she needs to drop. "Let's hear it, Hails."

From behind her, I see Nova handing Oliver the protein bar.

"I've done a lot of digging about our births." She pulls at her fishnet sleeves, a cropped black Metallica shirt over them. "And there is so much that doesn't make sense." She speaks to me and Rocky. "Like how our parents said the triplets were born in Dallas. I checked the birth records of *every* hospital in the city on the day Phoebe was born. No triplets," Hailey concludes. "Then I expanded my search to the month. There were multiple full sets of girl and boy triplets born in May around Dallas, but none with two boys and one girl. Which means they're lying, possibly about more than we can imagine."

"Okay . . ." I draw out the word. "We might . . . we might not be triplets." My insides twist, and I share a pained look with both of my brothers.

Standing behind Hailey, Oliver holds the back of her chair. "We might also still be triplets. It's not a guaranteed lie."

Hugging the book, Hailey continues, "It's also totally possible Phoebe and Oliver are twins and Nova is older, but more likely, they lied about our places of birth and birth dates."

Rocky stares gravely ahead. "They didn't want us to figure out who we really are."

"I think so," Hailey whispers. "We need to start looking at the real possibility that our ages are incorrect."

My brows jump. "Like how incorrect?"

"Hailey thinks we might be off by a year or more," Nova says from the computer. "Rocky hit puberty way before me and Ol did."

"But Nova and Oliver could've been late bloomers," Hailey reasons, her voice pitching weirdly. "What else does everyone remember seeing? With your own eyes?"

We all try to recall the past.

I've been padlocking fond memories of me and my mom. Where she combed my hair late at night and called me *sweet spider*. It's all been grief upon rage, and as the tidal wave rises, I instinctively swim away.

Nova runs a hand against the back of his neck. "They hired tutors for Oliver everywhere we went. Paid for them," Nova says. "When he was little. Maybe four, five, six. They'd pull him out of pre-prep, or maybe it was pre-K, where I'd be with Phoebe."

"I was always jealous," I say. "I wanted to be in those sessions. I thought they were cool . . . but really . . . I just wanted to be with him."

"Me, too." Nova meets my eyes, then shifts to Oliver. "You remember being tutored?"

"Eight hours of eight different languages a day. It's in there somewhere." His smile is light and effervescent, like those aren't traumatizing memories. I want to believe my brother that they weren't, for his sake. "Isn't that right, Hailstorm?"

"Hmm?" Hailey lifts her chin to look at Oliver above her. "I was there."

"You were there?" Rocky's gaze darkens.

I frown, not aware of this either. "I thought Addison home-schooled you when we were that little."

I hated that Hailey couldn't go to the preppy pre-K with me, Rocky, and Nova, too. Later, around middle school, she would join us, but that was on the occasion that our parents decided to enroll us in a private school rather than teach us at home.

"She did, but sometimes she'd leave me with Oliver and his tutors." Hailey watches Oliver unwrap the salty caramel protein bar and break it.

He hands her half. "To our sequestered childhoods. May they forever be remembered." He taps his piece with hers, and my sunken heart only elevates when I see Hailey nibble on her chunk.

"I remember holding Trevor," Rocky says, looking over at his little brother. "You were a newborn. I know you were."

"I don't care if they're my parents or not, Rock," Trevor admits. "They've never cared for me—"

"That's not—"

"It is true." He wobbles, then catches his balance. "They've always acted like I'm a mistake, and maybe now we know why."

"None of us saw her in the hospital," Hailey says, faraway, "after she gave birth to Trevor. She just appeared three weeks later with the baby and no longer pregnant."

Rocky glares. "So the pregnancy could've been a scam. And for the rest of us, we have no memories of each other being that young because we're all too close in age."

"I-I just think we can't believe anything they've ever told us," Hailey says.

I hold out my hands. "What if, *what if*, Trevor is adopted, and we're just blowing this all out of proportion?"

"You would like that," Trevor deadpans.

I grimace. "No, I *wouldn't*." He might annoy me, but Rocky's love for Trevor makes me care for him, too. "It'd still mean you and the rest of us were lied to. But it also beats the alternative. *Being kidnapped*. I don't want that for you, Trevor, or for any of us."

"It's not that simple," Hailey mutters to herself, staring off at the uneven floorboards. "It can't be that simple."

Oliver lifts her wrist toward her mouth. Hailey takes a dazed bite from the protein bar in her hand. "I have a better question," he says to me and Rocky. "How exactly are we supposed to pull a job on the Konings without the help of the people who raised us?"

Rocky's face twists. "We can do it without them."

Hesitation spreads from the rest of us. Even as my stomach overturns at the idea of working with our parents, this isn't a two-man job. Plus, we're coming in at such a disadvantage.

In our mountain of silence, Rocky assures us, "*We can.*"

"Hailey and I are servers at a country club," I remind him. "Oliver set himself up as a *therapist*. What is he going to do?"

"He can pivot."

"I can pivot," Oliver agrees into a bite of his protein chunk.

I let go of my knees. "I'm just saying that outside of me dating Jake, our roles aren't that great when it comes to the setup of a billion-dollar family takedown."

"Phoebe is right," Nova says. "As much as *none of us* want to pull this with them—the godmothers are already in

Claudia's ear. We won't be getting that kind of access with our personas as they are, and we can't change them."

Rocky lets out a long, angered groan. "*Fuck,*" he nearly shouts, then scrapes his hands through his hair. "What's to say they'll even want to do this with us? They want us out of Victoria."

"We tell them the truth," Hailey says, "about everything except the end. The end. We say we'll leave with them with the payout from Jake. But we won't. We'll stay. They'll go."

Once we all agree (Rocky more reluctantly), I ask, "What's with the book, Hails?"

"It's the history of Victoria."

"Anything good inside?" I smile a little.

She shakes her head once, and her anguished eyes beg me, *Don't ask, Phoebe, please.*

So I don't pry. None of us do. "Who's attending this dinner?" I ask. "Trevor is drunk—"

"Speak for yourself."

"Again, I'm *sober,*" I point out, "and Addison is going to panic and wonder what's wrong with Hailey."

"I-I can't go down there," Hailey stammers.

"I'll stay back with Hails and Trevor," Oliver offers.

Nova hunches back toward the computers. "Count me out of dinner." He switches camera angles on the screen. "If I go down there, I won't be able to control what comes out of my fucking mouth." He's furious in his quiet, simmering Nova way.

"That leaves me and you," I tell Rocky. "Let's go." I stand.

He catches my wrist and tugs me back to the bed. "We have something to tell them."

Yeah.

I know.

But this is a *really* bad time to give Hailey more anxiety. Unloading the heavy fact that *oh, by the way, I'm with your older brother for real* sounds like a trigger for a multitude of terrible emotions. Unease. Fear. Anger.

Please don't hate me, Hailey.

Now I'm scared.

Under my breath, I whisper to Rocky, "Let's not do the thing." I try to stand again.

He pulls me down. "We're doing it," he whisper-growls back.

"*Rocky.*"

"There'll never be a good time."

"A good time for what?" Nova asks him.

"To tell you Phoebe and I are together." Rocky flashes a tight smile. "Surprise."

FOURTEEN

Phoebe

My eyes pop out. There was no lead-in. No gentle segue. No pillow placed for our siblings to land on in case they freak out like I'm freaking out.

Trevor nearly trips over his own feet.

Awkward silence follows, and my face roasts in the unbearable uncertainty of what they might feel.

"What'd you just say?" Nova glowers at him, then looks to me in confusion.

Oliver is smiling at me, like he's happy my teenage crush has been fulfilled. It makes me almost smile back.

But Hailey has her hands to her mouth, not blinking.

She's in shock. That's better than anger, right?

I shift nervously on the bed, and the springs squeak in the second wave of uncomfortable silence.

"*I'm with your sister,*" Rocky enunciates like an asshole. "It's real and recent. Jake already knows."

"Jake knows before us?" Nova spreads his arms. "What the fuck?"

"It just happened," Rocky states.

"Yeah. I don't believe that 'it just happened' with someone like you." He flings an angered hand at him like he wants to deck him, but he's too far away.

I'm on the edge of the bed. "Nova," I say softly, hurt. He intakes a pained breath but doesn't look at me.

"Someone like me?" Rocky glares.

"*Calculated.* You are a *trained* manipulator—"

"I've *never*, in my fucking life, manipulated your sister," Rocky sneers, leaning forward with his elbows on his legs. "You're mad because you think my history with Phoebe is dark, and you got it in your head that she would escape that life with a *normal* guy with no baggage. That she wouldn't be Elizabeth, that you could do for your sister what you could *never* do for your mom. Save her from being tossed around—"

Nova lunges.

I spring forward and place my hands on his chest. "Nova, *stop.* We need to stick together, not fracture apart. Okay, please?" My brothers and I have shared the same pain of witnessing our mom with horrific, abusive men. The same men she'd ultimately screw over. "Rocky isn't a mark. You know Rocky. You *trust* Rocky," I emphasize, "and I *love* Rocky." It tunnels out of me, and I hope it slams into him.

Nova isn't out for blood anymore. But he releases his bottled anger by picking up the keyboard mouse and chucking it at the wall like a Frisbee.

The plastic casing cracks.

Only Hailey flinches, and from behind the chair, Oliver covers her ears with his palms. She relaxes and focuses on her book.

Nova exhales long breaths. "And what about you, Rocky?"

His gaze jackhammers into him. "You'd really rather deny her the chance at something uncorrupted?"

"None of us are normal, man," Rocky says darkly. "*She's* not normal. *She* is just as corrupted as I am and comes with just as much fucking baggage as I do, and you can't take that away without changing her, too. And unlike you, I'm not asking for Phoebe to pretend to be someone she's not. I love her as she is. I always have."

I soften at these sentiments.

Rocky sits straighter to add, "You've really lost sense of reality if you think I'd stand leisurely by and let a man do to her what they do to Elizabeth. You're not the only one who's tried to protect Phoebe from that."

In more ways, Rocky has intervened the most. He was almost always there, one step away from cutting into the danger and saving me from a bad outcome. Only, he wasn't beside me in Carlsbad.

When I didn't want to fail the team. I just wanted to ensure we all left with money. So I had sex with the mark . . . and his friend.

I made decisions that I can't take back. "These have been my choices, too," I tell Nova.

"You wanted to quit," Nova says quietly. "You were going to quit."

He wants me to quit a life of grifting like Hailey does, and maybe he's worried that if I'm with Rocky, I never will.

"Maybe I still will," I tell him. "But right now, we have more important things to deal with."

"See, you two keep saying that"—Nova motions back to Hailey on the chair—"but the most important thing here is all of you."

"Us," I murmur. "All of *us*, Nova."

His eyes are reddened, and he reaches out an arm to embrace me. I burrow into his stiff, rigid hug that's so unlike Oliver's warm ones. But his hug feels essential, necessary. Like the last drop of water in a march across Death Valley.

"I knew they fucked," Trevor says out of nowhere. "Phoebe and Rocky."

I jolt away from Nova. Rocky's nineteen-year-old brother is still hugging the dresser and wearing his dumb sunglasses.

"What are you talking about?" I snap and ignore my speeding pulse. I cut a sharp look to Rocky, who's seated on the twin bed.

He's zeroed in on his little brother. "You know nothing."

"I know more than enough." His shades are making it harder for me to read him, but maybe Rocky can sniff out his brother's bullshit without looking at his eyes.

"How?" he questions.

"I heard you two."

Oh my *God*. Rocky and I had sex at my loft . . . in the kitchen, and Trevor, I thought, was dead asleep.

"No, you didn't," Rocky calls his bluff.

"Yes, I did." Trevor sways against the furniture—his poor balance the only sign of his drunkenness. "I watched you two fuck."

"You what?" I shoot forward with tightened, riled eyes, but Rocky bolts up and catches my waist, stopping my pursuit to strangle his brother.

"You are seriously disturbed," Oliver says nonchalantly to Trevor, as if it's not even a top-ten horrible trait.

I wrestle against Rocky's hold. "I swear to God, Rocky, if your brother stood there and got off on seeing us—"

"Sad you missed an opportunity to eat my cum?" Trevor cuts me off.

"*Fuck you*," I force out.

Rocky grits out to him, "Never. Again."

Trevor has little shame, and he's drunk.

Rocky scrutinizes him longer. "He's fucking with you, Phebs. He's lying."

"Is he?" Angry heat burns my lungs.

"Am I?" Trevor mocks.

Uggghhh!!

"Trevor, stop," Hailey says so quietly, but we all hear.

He clutches a drawer handle. "Fine. But PG wouldn't be so mad if there was nothing for me to watch, so now we all know the truth. They're boning."

I go motionless in Rocky's arms.

What.

The.

Hell.

Did I just fall for the easiest play in the manipulator handbook from *Trevor*? I'm hotter in the face and more mortified.

"My brothers are in the room," I mention like it'll change something.

"So is mine."

"*Disturbed*," Oliver says to me.

I'd like to believe I'm better at navigating these simple mind games, but I'm pretty sure Trevor just caught me in one.

"This is serious between you two?" Hailey asks me and Rocky. Her attention is off her book and now pings from me to her older brother. "Really?"

She is ten billion times more surprised than I ever thought she'd be. Did she really never catch the scent of romance between me and her brother? She saw zero breadcrumbs? Was I that good at being so anti-Rocky that it never *once* crossed her mind that I could actually be in love with him?

"*Really*," Rocky says deeply to his sister, but she's looking for that same declaration from me.

"He's who I want to be with, Hails. Long-term. For real."

"When did this happen? Where? I want *all* the details," Hailey says like she's data mining.

"You'll get them," I assure her. "*All* of them."

She relaxes even more. Maybe it eases Hailey knowing she'll have these answers, even if they aren't the ones she's actively been hunting down. It's *something*.

I feel good knowing I can give her that.

"We have company," Oliver says while facing the monitors.

Nova bends back down to the computers, and he expands the frame that shows security footage of the portico. A Bentley has just parked beneath it.

Our moms have arrived.

FIFTEEN

Phoebe

The room has not frozen over. The air has not been vacuumed out. Our moms entered the Berkshires mansion as if they belonged. As if nothing has transpired these past few months.

It's hard to pretend that we're in a normal stasis when rage and hurt have made a toxic home in my heart.

It's difficult to look at *her*. My mom—*Elizabeth*. My brain screeches like a record scratch every time my eyes meet hers, like it's trying so hard to rationalize how the mom who raised me could be the same woman who might've had a hand in kidnapping Trevor.

I'm nothing if not stupendous at putting on a façade, and I make sure to contain the swirling, pent-up anger from twisting my face. Rocky's doing less of a stellar job—but the rage in his gray eyes that screams *I hate the world and everyone in it* isn't a new feature that they're surprised by. I'm sure they think he's just in one of his many moods that could be attributed to just about anything.

Woke up on the wrong side of the bed.

Saw a black cat.

Accidentally drank expired milk.

The list is quite endless.

We've all lit cigarettes as we wait for Everett to arrive, and we've remained on our feet like he could be here any minute. The full-windowed sunroom has a view of an overgrown backyard and mossy green pond. Fallen russet leaves blow across the weeds as the evening sun descends.

Elizabeth and Addison found a crate of old records and laughed over which we should listen to. Discarding Korn and keeping the Supremes and Blondie. I dusted off a few records, and Rocky even helped fix the player.

Melodic female vocals now flood the room, and we're all casually smoking like we're catching up on lost time between jobs. The feigned normalcy draws my heartbeat to my eardrums, pounding louder.

"This place is darling," Addison compliments, her gaze roaming around the vaulted ceilings, and she tugs off her gloves. "Where'd you find it?"

"I didn't," Rocky says. "It's Nova's place."

Elizabeth seems proud. "He's always so good at finding the diamonds in the rough. Isn't he?"

"Quite," Addison says, slipping her a furtive look that I can't decipher. With her hair newly dyed a deep shade of red and without glasses, her eyes pop. She seems less mousy than when I saw her at the country club, and more like a trial lawyer who could slit my throat.

Truth be told, Elizabeth and Addison might as well be Thelma and Louise—only replace the nineties jeans with ankle-length designer dresses and trendy cat-eye sunglasses. Elizabeth perched her Dior pair atop her head, while Addison keeps her Chanels hooked in the collar of her blouse.

The music switches to a poppy tune, and Elizabeth raises her hand with the cigarette pinched between her fingers like she's trying to pause space and time. "*This* song," she says excitedly. "You remember, bug?" She whirls toward me in a sea of honey-blonde hair. Her eyes carry a vivacious energy that hasn't dulled in all the years I've known her.

But it's Debbie Harry's silky voice on "Heart of Glass" that has tossed me back into the past. I fight the urge to go there. To experience the pang and heartache of nostalgia.

"I don't remember," I lie horribly, unable to hide the bitter edge in my voice. *Be nice. Be pleasant.* But why? Why do I need to hide these feelings that torment me?

She frowns deeply, her eyes dimming. "Phoebe?"

Rocky glances to me, then to Elizabeth. "Remember what?"

She pauses briefly to slip me another confused look before she tells Rocky, "Phoebe was what—ten, eleven?" She takes another pause, waiting for me to confirm.

I don't speak. Bitterness drives into my heart. How could she dredge up this memory right now? Is it manipulation? Or is it just love?

Off my silence, she continues with a breezy smile. "Anyway, I got this call to pick her up from summer camp, and when I get to the office, she looks mad as a hornet. Ready to pluck out the eyeballs of the girl sitting next to her."

Rocky's brows rise, and he swings his head to me for an explanation.

"She called me the Scarlet Witch," I say. "I didn't know it was a comic-book reference. I thought she was just being extra cruel."

"It was still cruel," my mom confirms. "That was the day Phoebe got her period. Bled right through her jeans. On the drive home, we stopped for ice cream and *this* song came on the radio. We turned it up and sang our lungs out." Her hazel eyes meet mine, and she searches them for answers. "You do remember that?"

Of course, I remember.

I remember how she tossed my jeans in the wash and bought me my first box of tampons. I remember how she told me girls like Madeline were just unhappy with themselves, and that's why they were so mean to those around them. I remember the mint-chocolate-chip ice cream. I remember the song.

Mostly, I remember feeling like I could have lived inside that moment with my mom forever. But now . . . now it feels like swimming through tar just to reach that love.

Seeing her, I thought I could mask this hurt. But I can't. I just can't.

"I was never in Victoria for a job." I unleash that truth in one acidic second. "Hailey and I came to Connecticut to get away from everything. To quit." It feels like I'm an angsty teenager, throwing my one act of rebellion in her face.

I catch Rocky smiling before he takes a quick drag from his cigarette. He's amused by my outburst. *Lovely.* At least he's not scolding me for caving too early. We were at least supposed to wait for his dad.

Elizabeth shakes her head. "I don't understand."

"You don't have to understand," I say snidely. *God, who am I?* "I quit grifting."

They both cringe at the word. "We don't *grift*," Addison says.

"Lying, cheating, scamming, whatever you want to call it—I was out."

"*Was*." Elizabeth catches that word. Her eyes flit to Rocky, then back to me. "So this was just a break?"

Maybe. I grind down on my teeth. "I haven't decided," I say truthfully.

Elizabeth slowly sinks down onto the wicker settee and pats the floral cushion. "Here, sit, *sit*," she says to me, like we're about to have a heart-to-heart about the boy I like in school. And you know, not discuss how I was trying to leave the family business of deceit and fraud.

"I don't want to fucking sit," I tell her.

Her face pulls into confusion, hurt. I've never rebelled, not really. I've been the dutiful daughter. The team player. The one you can count on. It's what I've prided myself on, so right now, I try not to hate myself more than I hate her.

"It's not a big deal," Rocky says casually, and I love him for it. Especially since I distinctly remember he was the one who drove to a motel and told me I'd lost my fucking mind.

"So this means what?" Addison asks, putting out her cigarette on the ashtray. "You've been living in Victoria and doing what . . . ?" She gasps suddenly. "Are you and Hailey *actually* servers at the country club? You aren't shills?"

Elizabeth pales. "No." Her appalled gaze swings to mine. "You're really a *waitress*?"

"I do more than just wait tables . . ."

That explanation doesn't help much. Addison leans back like she might be sick, and she grabs my mom's hand again. "Bethy."

"I know."

"We've taught them nothing," Addison says in an anguished breath.

If Hailey were here, she'd say, *You taught us everything.*

But I just have her brother here instead, and he says, "Jesus Christ, it's not the end of the fucking world."

"Says the person she's waiting on," Elizabeth retorts, giving him a sharp glance. "Grey Thornhall."

"Phoebe didn't want to be a rich bitch like me," Rocky says, which almost makes me smile. "You two talk about *choices*. Respect hers."

They're disappointed in mine. I'm trying to get used to it, because I'm about to pile on the disappointment until it's one giant landfill.

Elizabeth taps ash to the side. "If you wanted to stay here without running a con, you could've put yourself in a position of power like Rocky did."

"Do you know how those men talk about the servers?" Addison asks me.

"Of course, I know." I hate how they believe I'm naïve in my decision to choose an honest job. Heat in my lungs, I tell them, "News flash, the world needs servers, and it's a thankless, demoralizing position at times—but I wouldn't trade it. Because I get to work with my best friend, and we're not terrible at what we do. We're actually the best ones there."

Okay, I'm not in the running for any VCC Employee of the Month awards (not that those exist), but they don't need to know that we're slowly learning.

"She's not sixteen," Rocky points out. "She's an adult. She can choose whatever bland job she wants."

"Thank you," I say.

Addison seems nauseous. "Great, she's old enough to be objectified daily by club members, and are you a part of those groups, Bray?" I didn't expect her disappointment to swing in his direction. "Have you just sat by while they dig at Phoebe? At Hailey—your sister? When there's no recourse in sight for those people? No plan to pick at their pockets? No plan to make them pay?"

Rocky grinds his molars. Before he responds, I cut in. "It is what it is," I say. "It's not something you can decide or control. So just . . . let it go."

Rocky looks at me like I just won a national spelling bee competition. He is *impressed*.

My cheeks heat, and I fixate on my mom. "I lied to you, and I thought you'd be more upset I let you believe we were pulling a job here when we weren't."

Her gaze is gentle on me. "I am hurt, but I know you must've had a good reason to lie. You didn't want to hurt me? You and Hailey thought Addison and I would disapprove?"

"Because we do," Addison says bluntly, but there's little bite to her voice. It's almost in a matter-of-fact way.

Elizabeth softens even more, like she's compensating for her best friend. "We're just trying to steer you on the right course, bug. That's all we've ever tried to do." Worry blankets her face as she looks between Rocky and me. "Which is why we're still urging you all to leave Connecticut."

Rocky mutters under his breath, "Here we go again."

Addison holds up a hand. "You don't understand, Bray."

"Help us understand then," he shoots back. "What the fuck is so big, bad, and ugly here that you want us on the train out tomorrow?"

Elizabeth and Addison share an indecipherable look, and then my mom utters three words I despise. "We can't say."

Rocky's wrath bathes him in pure ice. "You can't say?" he asks in disbelief. "I'm sorry, is the devil gripping your vocal cords? Why *in the fuck* can't you say?"

"Brayden," Addison snaps. "Don't talk to Elizabeth like that."

"He's right, though," I cut in. "If you want us out of

Connecticut, you should at least give us the decency of telling us *why*."

"It's better if you don't know," Elizabeth says and rises to her feet. She pulls the needle off the record, cutting off the music.

"I've heard that before," I say coldly. "We're not *five* anymore, Mom. You can't keep us in the dark."

"I'm sorry, spider, but this is something that's bigger than you. It's bigger than *all* of us, and it'd be worse, I promise you. It'd be *much* worse if you knew." Fear invades her eyes, but how am I supposed to trust it? Trust *her*?

My chest rises and falls heavily, the lies compounding.

Rocky is blistering beside me in his own brewing rage. "You won't tell us why?" he asks them. "Then give us something else. Because you sure as hell haven't been completely honest with us, *Mom*." The dry bitterness on that endnote causes Addison to turn a shade paler.

"What do you mean?" Addison breathes out.

"You tell me," Rocky flings back, snuffing out his cigarette on the windowsill. "It seems like you all might've kept something from us. Something else. Maybe because it's 'better if we don't know.'" He uses finger quotes.

"No," Elizabeth says quickly. "We'd let you know if there was information we were withholding."

I grimace. "I don't believe that."

Her face fractures, and I realize those words hurt her more than anything else I've said tonight.

"I don't know what you're insinuating, Bray," Addison says, putting out her own cigarette on the ashtray. "Maybe if you gave us some context."

"Context," Rocky laughs dryly. "How's this for context. Your son was fucking stabbed on Halloween by his stalker, and in order to save his life, we had to give him a blood transfusion. Except—oops—none of us even know our blood types. What an inconvenience that turned out to be."

"Is Trevor—?" Addison starts.

"He's fine," Rocky cuts her off quickly. "But six blood tests later, it looks like he can't be your biological son. So what'd you do? Steal him from a grocery store? Snatch him out of a crib?"

She shakes her head over and over and looks hurriedly to Elizabeth. My mom has a hand to her mouth, shell shocked.

"We saw you, Addison," I say. "You had a pregnant belly when we were little. Was that a lie, too?"

She touches the edges of her eyes, trying to stop the tears. "Give me a moment." She rises and flees toward the powder room.

Elizabeth shoots to her feet like she means to follow her.

"You walk out of this room, and I walk out of your life," I tell her sharply, the ultimatum spilling out of me in an uncontrolled frenzy. I'm not even sure I really mean it, and my heart thumps so loud in my ears.

She stares at me like I'm transformed. A figment of the daughter she knows. I'm glad she can understand the *feeling*. "She lost the baby, Phoebe," she tells me so softly, so painfully. "She had a miscarriage, and then she adopted Trevor. And instead of telling you all about it, Everett, Addison, and I agreed to just let you all believe he was hers. But he *is* hers. In every sense of the word."

A lump lodges in my throat.

Adoption.

I just theorized this upstairs, but aren't there holes to this story?

My stomach knots. Aching. I shake my head. "You can't adopt a kid. You can't leave paperwork."

"She had a different name. Fake identity. Fake papers." Her eyes slide between both of us, and Rocky is rigid. An ice block. "He needed a home. We gave him one."

"Where was he born? What adoption agency?" Rocky asks.

"New York. Um, I can't remember the agency Addy used. It's been so long. Like all of you, we don't like paper trails. Birth certificates get burned."

Whether Rocky believes her, I can't tell. I'm not completely sure I do, but it's not as if they can give us more proof.

"What about us?" I ask, my voice tight. *What about me?* "Are we all adopted, too?"

Her face cracks. "No, bug. I carried you three." She touches her heart. "I was pregnant with triplets. Your brothers and you. I gave birth to all three of you." She looks to Rocky. "And you and Hailey are Addison and Everett's biological children." She returns her attention to me. "Is this why you've been so . . . ?" She doesn't know the word. *Angry. Combative. Different.*

"I don't want to be lied to," I tell her. "Not by you."

"I'd like to think I raised you well enough that you could tell when I lie," she says gently, but it feels more like someone slipping a needle in my neck. Her gaze flits to where Addison left, and I think she might leave for her. But she returns her attention back on me. "Connecticut," she says. "We can't stay in the state longer than a couple hours at a time. There was a con—before your time—that we pulled."

Rocky's eyes darken. "What con is so big that you can't come back in decades?"

"And that'd make it unsafe for us to be here, too?" I add in confusion.

"One that didn't end well." She sucks in a tight breath, and I know she won't explain more. That we're going to have to be satisfied with those half answers. Now's not the time to even push. We have to get them on board with the Koning job, and it might be a little difficult considering we just made Addison cry.

I truly can't remember the last time I saw her shed a tear—and I feel a little like shit if they are telling the truth. If she did have a miscarriage. And is it my place to question that? Should I take it at face value?

I think of Hailey. The purplish crescent moons under her sleepless eyes. Her obsession with finding answers. *Proof.* We need proof.

DNA. The dinner. We have to stay the course.

SIXTEEN

Rocky

Thirteen. That's the number of side-eyes my dad has given me since we sat down for dinner. I'm waiting for one more so he doesn't leave me on that unlucky fucking number. But he's been fixated on Elizabeth for the past five minutes as she finishes explaining what he missed.

I'd have loved if we could have kept him in the dark for more than a millisecond. His green eyes darken with worry and anger, and he must be getting hot, because he starts rolling the cuffs of his heather-gray button-down. He already shed his peacoat when he walked in. His brown hair has grown out enough to touch his ears, and his five-o'clock shadow is turning into thicker stubble.

Whoever he's becoming, he appears more relaxed, carefree. Not clean-cut. Less likely to lead a Fortune 500 meeting.

Half-eaten sushi remains on my plate, and I watch my mom poke at nigiri with her chopsticks in a daze.

I *should* feel like a bastard for causing her emotional distress and flinging her into a past where she (allegedly) lost a kid. But I can't cry for her. Can't even feel a tiny particle of guilt.

In truth, I don't actually believe her.

I'm not sure I can believe anything she says. And sure, I'll be the super raging dickbag if it turns out she was honest, but I'm willing to roll those dice.

I cup my water glass and clear my throat. "He doesn't need an encyclopedia entry," I tell Elizabeth. "Just give him the CliffsNotes. We have other news to share."

My dad's brows rise. "You're not done dropping bombs tonight?"

"You're made of steel, aren't you?" I fling back. "Can't handle one more grenade?"

"Is that what this is?" he asks me. "A test of loyalty since you think your mother and I have been lying to you? Otherwise, the only thing I can think is you're being a selfish brat."

I raise my glass. "Selfish brat."

He's glaring. "We're all on the same team, Brayden."

They've reminded me of this fact over and over. Same team. Same goals. It's not entirely untrue, but somewhere along the way, I do think our desires diverged.

"It's not a bomb," Phoebe cuts in, eyeing me like *settle down*. Yeah . . . we need their help, and I'm not making this easy.

But if I had my way, we wouldn't involve them in the Koning job. We'd figure out how to do it on our own. It'd be harder, riskier, but I believe in *us*. The six of us. We don't need them. We never needed them. Yet, for how persuasive I can be, I've never been able to convince my siblings and the triplets of this.

Phoebe sips wine, then sets down the glass. "You three will probably be happy about this news."

"Good news?" My mom rouses with elation. Elizabeth reaches over and squeezes her hand.

"We're all for some good news, bug," Elizabeth says with a warm smile.

Phoebe takes a deep, readying breath. "I'm not actually dating Jake Waterford," she says. "It's all fake. I'm really, truly dating . . ." Her gaze veers to me. "Rocky." It's a head rush.

A cold shower on a hot summer day. The feeling of being so openly hers is one I'm not going to take for granted, because I know it's unlikely to happen again anytime soon.

"Phoebe," I say, like her name belongs to me just as much as mine belongs to her.

"That's it?" My dad cuts the moment with a serrated knife. "We already knew that."

I narrow my eyes. "We *just* got together. Recently."

"It hasn't been long," Phoebe confirms as Elizabeth rises from her chair and comes over to wrap her daughter in a hug.

"Everett just means we knew it would happen," Elizabeth says brightly. "You two are meant to be."

"Fated," my mom agrees into a sip of wine.

My muscles are tight, flexed bands, and I know my dad. He meant *exactly* what he said. He's always believed Phoebe and I have been fooling around with each other in secret.

Elizabeth returns to her chair. "Are you on the pill?"

"Am I on the pill?" Phoebe grimaces, and my stomach nosedives into the pits of hell. Any talk of future progeny and babies reminds me that our parents want a little shill at their disposal, and Phoebe and I are the vessels to provide that.

Elizabeth smiles like it's an innocent yet amusing question. I'm aware her prying into Phoebe's love life *is* a normal facet of their mother-daughter relationship. Hell, we'd both been given the "safe sex" talk long before we ever had sex. Pretty sure my mom and Elizabeth sat us down together in the same room.

Looking back on it—why us? Why not Phoebe and Hailey?

We all have our roles, I hear my mom say in my head, which just turns my body from glacier water to molten lava.

"What does Phoebe being on the pill matter?" I snap.

Elizabeth dips her sashimi into soy sauce. "Last time I talked with her, she didn't like the pill. I don't want you two to have an accident, unless you're thinking about having kids."

"Bullshit," I say. "You'd love a little kid." I look between her and my parents. "You all would."

"Of course, it'd make jobs easier," my mom says, "but that's not our decision, Bray." Her face fractures in hurt like I'm putting words into her mouth.

"It's not that I don't like the pill," Phoebe says gently, like she's easing back into the tension I'm spawning. "It's the process in which I have to *get* the birth control that I don't like. We've moved around too much."

It's a situation that complicates things for her and my sister. One I've tried to even help over the years. It involves pseudonyms and scamming new pharmacies, which heightens the potential risk of being caught. In the end, it's easier (and ironically safer) just to use condoms—but if either of them wanted to go a different route, I know Nova, Oliver, and I would toy with the danger to help.

"But we're not moving around right now," I add. "We're staying in Victoria, and we've heard your pleas and warnings a thousand times over. It doesn't matter. We found a job here we're going to start."

"What job?" My father is intrigued, and I begin the long process of explaining our complicated ties to Jake Koning Waterford. From the beginning. For the most part, they quietly listen with few interjections. It's only when I bring up Carter's involvement in . . . everything that their reactions turn from contemplative to annoyed.

"We're made?" Elizabeth's brows furrow in horror.

"It's just Jake," Phoebe says. "He's the only one who knows our identities."

"He's harmless," I add.

"Harmless?" My mother's eyes stake me. "Do you even know what the Waterford family is like? We were in town for less than twenty-four hours, and I can tell you that Claudia's sons are *heinous*. She's despicable in her blind love of them."

"Jake isn't like the rest of his family." I defend him so quick, it's like I'm on autopilot.

Phoebe chimes in, "He can be a little uptight and prickly about following rules, but it's endearing."

Jesus. I roll my eyes.

She shoots me a hot look. "It *is* endearing."

"As endearing as a root canal." I lean back.

"You do love pain." *Love* is a strong word for what Jake is to me, but I've surprised myself today with the swiftness with which I'd defend the guy.

"You've never even met his entire family," my mom tells me.

"And you have?" I ask, prying.

"Yes," our moms say in unison, and Elizabeth explains, "We've had a luncheon with Claudia and her oldest two sons to pick their brains about Jake and Phoebe."

"For Eros," Elizabeth adds, naming their fake matchmaking company.

"So let's get this straight, you're both in Claudia's ear," I say, "and you despise her. So she sounds like the perfect mark to me for a long con." I explain our plan to help Jake claim the Koning crown.

Elizabeth shakes her head as soon as I finish. "We can't be in Connecticut."

"It's a nonstarter," my mom says more pointedly.

No one pinches a piece of sushi, but hands are untightening on glasses. Cloth napkins are being uncrumpled in my dad's loosening fist. Tensions might be high, but they're interested. The job is tempting.

"You don't need to be in Connecticut," Phoebe says gently. "Just do your thing from afar. You already established Eros in New York. You can be a socialite without matchmaking me and Rocky."

"How much is Jake offering us?" my father wonders. "After we secure him his title and inheritance?"

"One million," I say.

"That's it?"

"*Each.*"

"For all nine of us?" Elizabeth asks.

"Yeah," Phoebe says. "Nine mil total."

My mom careens backward in the chair while cupping a wineglass. Her wide, covetous eyes shift over to Elizabeth. "Bethy?"

It's been a while since we've seen a multimillion-dollar payout.

"*No,*" Elizabeth says coldly. "No money is worth being in Connecticut. We made a promise, Addy."

"We have to, Beth," my father counters. "If Jake Waterford knows what we do and who we are, then he'll be a better asset to us when he's an heir. Right now, he's a liability."

I've called Jake a liability before, but hearing it from my father—it makes me angry. Mad that he'd think Jake wasn't on our team. Maybe it's just the pettiness in me that wants to run when my dad says walk.

Elizabeth drinks from her water goblet, and Phoebe and I are careful not to hyperfocus on her lips touching the rim.

My mother says, "It's a risk."

"Until you tell us why it's a risk," I refute, "it's one we're going to take. With or without you."

"With us," Elizabeth says quietly, placing her glass down. "If you try to pull this off, you'll need us involved."

D inner is over. After we see our parents out of the mansion, Phoebe and I return to the dining room. Wearing medical-grade gloves, Nova slips a lipstick-stained wineglass into a plastic bag, and Phoebe begins clearing the unused silverware.

She disappears into the kitchen.

I pluck two blue gloves out of the box on the table, but Nova says, "I've got it." He seals the baggie. "Let me handle this."

I glance at the staircase that leads to the second floor. The surveillance room. My family.

"Trevor passed out," Nova says, following my gaze. "Hailey has been on Ancestry.com, and Oliver has finally convinced her to lie down. He's trying to read *The Grapes of Wrath* to her so she'll fall asleep."

I could thank him for the update, but I don't. "And you're down here. A one-man cleanup crew," I say. "The fail-safe. Nova Graves."

He glares like it's an insult.

It wasn't one.

Some days, I think our worlds would all fall apart if Nova were gone. If any of us were gone . . . this wouldn't work. We need each other. I just don't want to need the godmothers and godfather, too.

TO: Helldiver101@hotmail.com
FROM: Essex Genomics
SUBJECT: Samples Successfully Submitted
DATE: 11/15

Dear Miss Hart,

Thank you for mailing DNA samples for paternity and
maternity testing. Attached is a confirmation that they
have been received. You will be notified in 3–12 weeks
about the results.

Best,
Essex Genomics

TO: Helldiver101@hotmail.com
FROM: Essex Genomics
SUBJECT: Results Ready
DATE: 2/5

Dear Miss Hart,

The paternity and maternity tests you have requested
have been completed and your results are ready. Please
follow the link and choose your preferred method of
delivery.

Best,
Essex Genomics

TO: Helldiver101@hotmail.com
FROM: Essex Genomics
SUBJECT: Confirmed Mail Delivery
DATE: 2/5

Dear Miss Hart,

Thank you for confirming mail delivery. Your results will be mailed to you in 5–7 business days.

Best,
Essex Genomics

BURNER PHONE CHAT

(HAILEY): Shiiiit. I clicked on mail delivery by accident. I meant to get the results emailed, and now they're getting sent to us via post 🖤

(PHOEBE): Where are they going? 🦴

(HAILEY): my PO Box 🖤

(ROCKY): Get some sleep. Jesus. 🕷

(OLIVER): DNA results party postponed. Slumber party instead? 🦎

(NOVA): No ⚔

(TREVOR): I'm down for a sleepover if there's vodka 🦇

(ROCKY): Sleepover canceled 🕷

TO: Helldiver101@hotmail.com
FROM: Victoria Postage
SUBJECT: Packages Incoming
DATE: 2/13

A package will be arriving at 8:00 PM EST on 2/13 and will be available for pickup.

Thank you,

Victoria Postage
Your local one-stop shop for mailboxes, shipping, and printing!

SEVENTEEN

Phoebe

I struggle to capture oxygen in my lungs. Lying sweaty, naked, but not yet exhausted under black, damp sheets, my
whole body still hums from his touch.

Sex.

It shouldn't feel this powerful, this *electrifying*. I can't ever
remember enjoying sex *this much*. Like I could keep going. I
could never stop. My nerve endings sing after hours of fooling
around in Rocky's bedroom last night and then again early
this morning.

I want to give a middle finger to his digital clock and pretend it's yesterday. It's been three months since the Berkshires,
where we collected our parents' DNA, and little things about
being with Rocky still send butterflies flapping. Simple things.
Like waking up in his bedroom.

Rocky's room.

Besides the TV, which he hung for me, his room is more
library-from-*Beauty-and-the-Beast* than actual bedroom. The
irony is that nothing in here really belongs to Rocky. Not the

Murano Glass birds or vases, the gold Venetian masks, or the dozens of 1700s encyclopedias on the many built-in shelves. The Reynoldses left their various trinkets and books when Rocky rented the boathouse, at Rocky's request and with his money.

Even if he wanted to decorate, I don't think he has enough personal belongings to do much. Unlike me, he never collected things from job to job.

Rocky walks toward the door and disposes of a condom in a trash bin. He makes a scarily attractive, naked trek back to his king-sized bed.

Scream plays at a loud decibel on a mounted TV in the background, and I try to focus more on the Ghostface killer than the murderously handsome devil that just fucked my brains out—but I am only human.

"That was . . ." I think out loud, and off Rocky's satisfied expression, I board up all compliments. "Pretty average."

His gaze sweeps my face. "Wow."

"Wow, like you're so right, Phoebe?"

"Wow, like this town is making you a *really* bad liar." He's a breath from the bed, and I throw a feather pillow at him.

He annoyingly catches it.

"I'm a *great* liar." I sit up more, the sheet dropping to my lap. His hot gaze lowers to my tits, and I ignore that to make my argument. "Case in point, this whole town believes I'm happily with Jake when I'm actually unhappily with you."

"Unhappily?"

"Uh-huh, yeah. I'm very, *very* unhappy with you."

"Yeah?" He crawls back on the bed. "You die a little inside every night?"

"More than a little." My breath snags, especially as his large palm slides up the side of my face, our exchanged desire throttling my senses. "I'm fully, completely . . . comatose."

His lips ghost over mine. "You feel pretty fucking alive to me." Just as he drags me into a body-pulling kiss and lays me against the mattress, a shrill *beeeeep beeeep beeeeeep* tears our lips apart and causes Rocky to roll his eyes into the Atlantic. "Dammit," he curses, climbing off me and the bed.

He collects his phone from a built-in bookshelf and angrily shuts off the seven a.m. alarm, then journeys around the room for his wallet, keys. Still naked. He wears rage like the warmest fur coat. His intense stride leaves flaming footprints everywhere he steps.

The fire is intrinsic to who Rocky is. But it rarely burns this many holes in the floor.

"Can't be late for your very important date?" I twist my hair into a messy high pony and ignore the clench of my stomach.

He throws dirty clothes from last night into a wicker basket. "Breakfast at Symphonies on the Pier."

"Fancy."

"Eight a.m. sharp."

"With Mr. Firstborn Fuckbag?" I ask, even if the answer is crystal clear in his hostile stance. "Your new bestie can rot in hell."

"Hell isn't painful enough," he says bitterly. "Trent would likely thrive there." The mere mention of Trent Waterford is a smoke bomb of wrath.

I inhale the fumes. "No, he wouldn't, because *I'd* be there, and I would kick his ass to some nasty flesh-eating circle."

Rocky almost, *almost* smiles. "Yeah? How exactly would you kick his ass?"

"I'm strong," I argue.

Three months into sowing seeds to gain influence over the Waterford family, and I've felt increasingly protective of

Rocky. Like I could throw steak knives and a chain saw at Trent. But I know better.

Wedging myself between Rocky and Trent isn't a good option. It'd make the situation infinitely worse, even if it's so *very* tempting.

I just wish I could do something more to help my real (but secret) boyfriend.

"I can carry a tire," I say, noting my strength.

"You can pick up a tire two inches off the ground for two seconds."

I glare. Okay, he's not wrong. I'm not out here pumping iron and working on my upper-body strength.

Still, I cross my arms. "I've thrown a punch before." At a bar many years ago. To protect Hailey after she rubbed some drunk dude wrong by merely *existing*. He said she wouldn't stop glaring at him. He was so offended that he got in her face, and so I got in his face with my fist, and then Nova intervened because Drunk Dude grabbed me by the hair.

It was a bad night.

"And how'd that go for you?" Rocky asks with more snark.

"Well, I won the fight, so it went *fantastic*."

He gives me a look. "Needing your 'older' brother to defend you isn't winning."

"Wrestling has tag-team championships, so I beg to differ." I hold on to my bent knees. "But I would kick Trent's ass solo. All on me." I flex my bicep, which produces a tiny bump of muscle. "Be fucking scared."

"I am scared," he says, "that you might pull a fucking tendon."

I flip him off with *both* hands.

Rocky abandons his wallet, keys, Rolex, and phone on the

dresser—just to get on the bed and seize my ankle. He yanks, and I splat flat on my back. My heart pitches so fast, I go dizzy.

When I try to sit up, he pushes me down. His harsh gaze caresses me like molten sandpaper, and I can't deny—I never want him to look away. He dips closer. "You call this a fight?"

I shove him harder, and he snatches my arms like I'm a paper doll. We're bare. Just hot skin and heavy breaths. The latter are mostly from me.

"Fuck you," I curse out.

"Tell me to go fuck myself," he whispers against my ear. "Tell me to fuck off. Use your dirty *fucking* mouth because you know you'll never be physically stronger than me."

I breathe like I'm running up a ninety-degree incline. I feel myself get wetter, and I can barely figure out why this is turning me on right now. It's not because we're naked wrestling. Or because I'm losing.

I wriggle my legs under him, kicking frantically, but he roots me to the bed with such lazy effort, whereas I'm exerting every ounce of force in me. Growling out, I try to reclaim my arms, but he has sufficiently pinned me.

I squirm.

He grips and imprisons.

Our eyes are impaling each other.

I writhe beneath him. "I won't stop," I rasp.

"I know," he breathes. "Because I know who you fucking are."

Then, with his knees, he spreads me wide open. *Yes, yes.* Rocky is so hard, and in these next seconds, which become blissful minutes, he fucks me with absolute aggression. *Possession.* As if he needs to reach the deepest parts of me, and that's it—that's why I'm overcome so fully, so suddenly.

The connection.

The feeling that he's pulling me into him, and I'm pulling him down into me. That we could be chained and padlocked together and it still wouldn't be close enough.

His eyes excavate mine, and my struggle is weak under an onslaught of raw pleasure and emotion. I want deeper, too.

I want to dig my claws in him. I want to etch my chosen name on his back. I want him to carve his chosen name on mine. Blood dripping down our bodies. Kissing through the crimson mess of each other.

Never letting go.

"Deeper," I grit, and it becomes a tiny cry.

He presses his forehead to mine. *"Phoebe."*

"Rocky. *Rocky.*" I'm going to come.

And when I do, hot tears spill out of the corners of my eyes. He holds me tightly, securely, firmly against his body while he thrusts. He's warm inside me without a condom. When he pulls out, he's knelt over me, and he pumps himself a few times.

He comes on my abdomen with a coarse, guttural noise.

That visual. A strange whimpering noise escapes me. Fuuuck. I roll my face into the pillow. "You didn't hear that."

"You mean the sound of you loving a cumshot?" He's off the bed. Already making another sexy naked trek. Déjà vu. How many times can we do this?

My face is on fire. "I've *never* loved being comed on."

"Because I haven't come on you until today." He grabs a hand towel out of his closet. "And whoever came on you before me is a fucking loser and has to die now." He flashes a cold smile.

It makes me actually smile.

He returns to the bed, and while I'm leaning back on my elbows, I let him wipe my abdomen. He asks if it was too rough for me, and I say, "No, I liked it." Tension ramps up between us, a sexual and emotional desire all wrapped in one deadly bow.

His narrowed eyes flit up to mine. "Don't look at me like that."

"Like what?"

"Like you want to fuck again."

"I know you have to go meet Trent." I cringe even surfacing Jake's brother again. "And anyway, I need to leave for work soon. It's a mutual smash-and-dash."

He grimaces. "Don't say it like that."

"Fine," I say. "Hit-it-and-quit-it."

He rolls his eyes and stands up, throwing the dirty towel into the wicker basket.

"What? *Rocky*." I frown and slide off the bed. "I'm *joking*. Probably not my best one, but a joke nonetheless."

He chucks his charcoal sweatpants to me with no animosity on his face. I catch and step into them as he says, "Being around Jake's brother is stirring things in me that I can't fucking explain, Phebs. He's not a special breed of evil. I've been around so many Trents before. I've pretended to be them all my life. But I've never *really* been with *you*. Not in this way. Not while doing a job like this."

"It's making it harder?" I pull on his plain black tee. It hangs loose around my frame.

"I'm on an edge . . . like right at the precipice, and the only thing keeping me sane is knowing I have you. Physically. Sexually. Emotionally. Every way, inside and out."

I understand him, I think more than he realizes. "And here," I say softly, "I thought I was the needy, greedy bitch." When his smile appears after mine, I walk into his arms.

He wraps them fiercely around me. Resting his chin on my

head, he murmurs so quietly, I almost miss the words. "I'm falling more in love with you."

Tears prick my eyes as the sentiments overwhelm me.

I didn't think I could love Rocky any deeper than I did, but if there was a way to slip into someone's body, I think we'd both choose to do it in these intimate moments we have together. Because they aren't always frequent or guaranteed. They're fought for every day.

Even now, I'm risking being at his boathouse when I'm dating Jake, but my brothers live with Rocky. It's a decent reason as to why I'd crash here one night or two. But not every night of the week.

We separate with more reluctance and strain. Rocky hustles to the shower, and I text Hailey:

Picking you up in a bit for The Hunt! Be ready by 9?

She's quick to respond with two thumbs-up and confetti-cannon emojis. I smile, happy that these quirky town events have been A-plus mental distractions for Hails.

Like the pumpkin-pie contest. Ugly Sweater Run. Winter Wonderland Festival—where we busted our asses on an ice-skating rink and sat on bags of frozen peas the next day.

They've powered her through the past three months. She's laid off the cyber searches and late-night book obsessions . . . for a moment, at least.

Small wins are *big* wins in my book.

We're working The Hunt together today, and I'm crossing my fingers Victoria's most anticipated February event will be another good anxiety-reducing distraction. So maybe she won't stake out the postman all day.

Even if today is *the* day, the mail doesn't get delivered until tonight.

I pocket my phone and grab a bite to eat in the kitchen. "Morning," I tell my brothers. "Happy DNA Results Day." I hop on a barstool beside Nova. He's flipping a page of a comic book and drinking OJ.

"Happy Triplet Day," Oliver says, convinced we are, in fact, triplets. He's doing the hard task of cooking a French omelet, but he slips me a clandestine smile—one full of amusement and *knowing*.

Like he's well aware I just had my world rocked all night by his roommate. Hopefully he's concluded this because I'm wearing Rocky's clothes. And not because he heard us through the walls.

No way were we that loud.

Nova scrapes a hand back and forth over his buzz cut, barely glancing up from the Marvel comic. "You smell like Rocky."

"If you raise your eyes a little higher, you'd see that I'm wearing his shirt."

"That's not what I meant."

"Oh." I cringe and sniff beneath the tee. Okay, I unfortunately smell like sex. Not my proudest morning-after moment. I definitely need a shower.

Oliver laughs and nudges the wet eggs with his spatula.

"It's not funny," Nova says sternly.

Oliver is hardly put off by our brother's normal grouchy disposition. "*Bad, Phoebe.*" He waves the spatula like a teacher swinging a ruler. "How dare you have a wild night to remember—that is *against* corporate policy. No raunchy acts of indiscretion. You must be celibate."

"And miserable," I add.

"At all times."

We share a smile.

Nova isn't swept into our banter. He puts the OJ down. "Is it a relationship or just sex?" he asks point-blank.

"A relationship *with* sex." I reach forward and snag a grape out of the fruit bowl. "But right now, we are having a lot of sex."

Nova stares at me with enough caution tape to mummify me.

How do I even describe the severe need to be close to Rocky? When we're together, not having sex feels more painful.

"Sex is the foundation," Oliver tells him with a spatula jab.

"*Sex is the foundation*," I parrot to Nova.

"Of what? A booty call?" he retorts.

I toss a grape at him. It hits his cheek and bounces across the counter.

He never flinches. "I'm serious," he tells me.

I steal a piece of honeydew. "I know, because you're always serious."

Oliver plates the omelet and slides it to Nova. "And you sound exactly like someone who's not getting any."

He picks up a fork. "You two fuck enough for the rest of us."

"Categorically untrue," Oliver says. "We couldn't sustain the entire population with our fornicating habits." His brown eyes shift to me. "Three eggs, hard scrambled?" *My favorite.*

"Yes, please." I glance over at Nova. "Are you going to The Hunt?"

He stabs the omelet. "It's not part of the job."

I frown. "But you can attend . . . for fun."

He's quiet, and Oliver peers up at me while cracking eggs in a bowl. "He's never heard of that word."

Clearly.

I swivel on the barstool to Nova. "The point of staying here is to also have a life outside of the job."

Nova is mutilating his omelet. "Not for me."

He can't rest until the job is done. That is also painfully clear.

Infiltrate Jake's family. It's step one in the ultimate plan of deception, and we all have specific parts to play.

For Nova, he isn't supposed to cozy up to any influential townspeople. His role is to aid us if shit takes a wrong, *horrific* turn.

If he's not at the art museum, then he's spending all of his time on Oliver's liveaboard speedboat. Courtesy of Meara O'Neil. The elderly lady simply *gifted* the boat to Oliver for being "the best listener" she's ever met. She's not even his client! *I've* spent more time serving her soda and crab cakes and listening to her yap about being three degrees from some billion-dollar family who owns Fizzle. Where is my boat?

Yes, I am jealous.

Nova, I hope, loves the speedboat, since he spends every day on it. He'll moor the vessel out in the calm water alongside a few other sailing yachts.

Right in view of the Koning estate.

Whenever Rocky, Oliver, or I am invited to the estate as guests, it's not suspicious that Nova is one dinghy ride away from the shore because he's *always* there.

"Just promise me you won't become a recluse," I say to Nova. There've been times where we haven't seen each other for three months or four while pretending to be other people, and I've started loving the idea of not being torn apart.

He stares faraway at the plate while he says, "I couldn't be away from you two for that long."

Good.

Oliver whisks the eggs. "The grim-faced art curator who lives in solitude on the sea. Women love it. You've shot up on the list of Most Eligible Bachelors in Victoria."

I scowl since Rocky is *firmly* on that list. Jake is off it since he's taken by me.

"I'm not looking for anything with anyone." Nova washes down his food with a rougher swig of OJ. "It'll get in the way."

Of the job.

It's strange to be the one to protest. I've always been "for the job" first and foremost. Now . . . being here, being with *Rocky*, it feels like we're paddling toward a new future we've never even seen before.

I want that for my brothers, too.

"Ol," Nova says tensely, causing me to follow his pinpointed gaze to Oliver. "You're bleeding."

A crimson river flows out of his nose. Oliver quickly smears the blood with the side of his hand. "Shit," he mutters.

I rip off a paper towel from the roll and toss it at him.

Squeezing his nose with it, he staunches the bleeding. None of us say a thing. The silence is heavy, and my stomach won't settle. Even a bite of melon sits like peanut butter in my throat.

"How much coke are you snorting?" Nova asks with the grinding of his teeth. "Is it that necessary?"

"I can't say *no*." He sounds nasally. "Collin Falcone likes to party, therefore Oliver Smith likes to party. He loves that I keep up with him, and we all love that he's no longer Trent's closest friend."

Oliver spends less time conducting therapy sessions and more time integrating himself into Trent's social circle. He's quickly separated Collin from Trent—which gave Rocky the perfect path to becoming Trent's Number One Guy in the Group.

"I'm fine, Nov," Oliver says gently, tossing the bloodied wad of paper towel in the trash. "See?"

"You're going too far," Nova warns. "Use sleight of hand. Act like you're snorting it."

"He'll notice. I'm okay. *I'm okay*," he emphasizes. "Phoebe, tell him."

"He's okay," I chime in. I know most of what Oliver has done for jobs. This isn't even the half of it.

Rocky, Oliver, and I are more trained in face-to-face manipulation than the others, and sometimes we'll go to extremes to complete a job. Oliver has been known to take things too far, but I trust he's profiled Collin.

"If he thinks joining in the drug use is necessary, then maybe it is," I reason.

Nova is pissed. "You're only saying that because you'd do the same thing in his position."

"I mean . . ." He's not wrong. "Let's change the subject."

Oliver washes his hands. "You want to join the quatro, Nov? I can get you in Trent's friend group."

"Hard pass."

"What do you mean?" Oliver mock gasps. "You don't want the Fortunate Four to become the Foxy Five?"

I internally gag at the nickname the town has adoringly begun calling Trent, Rocky, Oliver, and Collin. When they enter a venue together, people act like gods have dropped from the sky and chosen to grace us mere mortals.

I'm not charmed.

"Fortunate Four," I seethe. "The irony. Considering every encounter with Trent feels like one big, ugly misfortune." My nose flares as emotion burrows too deep.

Don't think about it.

Don't remember it.

"What happened in the Alps?" Nova asks me, then Oliver. We spent the holidays apart from him, Hailey, and Trevor. While they stayed in Victoria, the rest of us wintered in the Alps with the Koning boys.

"It doesn't matter," I say under my breath, my stomach doing a vicious gymnastics routine.

Oliver has an all too concerned and empathetic look.

Nova sees and shoves his omelet away. "You know I asked Rocky the same thing—*what happened in the Alps?* And he threw his luggage on the floor, stormed in his room, and slammed the door like he was back to being *eighteen.* So I would appreciate if either of you clued me in to what the fuck went down."

"Trent is a dick," I say plainly.

Nova zeroes in on Oliver. "That can't be all."

"You don't need to worry about me," I say before Oliver can speak. "I'm *fine.*"

"You're *shaking,*" Nova retorts.

"In anger. I'm pissed." *I want Rocky.* It's such a sudden, involuntary response that I immediately glance over at the hall that leads to the bathroom.

"First Carlsbad, now this—"

"Stop," I groan into my hands.

"Let's all take a breath here," Oliver says to us. "She's okay. You're okay. We're all okay."

We're not okay.

I haven't been able to tell my brothers about my bad experience in Carlsbad, and purging the nitty-gritty details from the Alps isn't any easier. There are memories I want to tear out of my brain and set on fire.

I might be attracted to drama, but I prefer the *fun* variety. Which is why I shift my focus to The Hunt.

It's a slice of chaotic normal inside our bizarre pie.

EIGHTEEN

Phoebe

Jake: I thought Katherine told you what you'd be doing and everything The Hunt entails. I'm so sorry. I would've given you a heads-up.

I want to groan at the phone in my hand. My boss didn't inform me or Hailey what our roles would be during The Hunt. It probably slipped Katherine's mind, but that doesn't explain why other servers and bartenders also withheld certain details from us.

I thought I'd grown a decent workplace friendship with Chelsea Noknoi, but the longer I date Jake, the more she distances herself from me, like I could rat her out to the Powers That Be just for serving a lukewarm latte.

Hailey isn't faring much better.

When we first came to town, she started a fling with Erik the Bartender. She's been too preoccupied for him as of late. Understandably. But ending things before the holidays did not go so smoothly.

My run-in with him while working last month's New Year's Bash was not spectacular, to say the least.

His face visibly turned squeamish like the sight of me caused gastrointestinal distress. "I'm busy," he told me, rolling up the sleeves to his button-down. Tattoos glided up his forearms and disappeared underneath his shirt.

"Too busy to make a negroni?" I asked. "One of the widowers wants one."

Erik worked his jaw.

I groaned. "Come on. You can't be that upset over Hailey breaking things off. You guys barely dated—"

"It was how she did it, Phoebe," Erik growled. "She said, *This was fun, but I'm done.* Who says shit like that?"

Straight and to the point. Sounds like my girl Hailey Tinrock. Maybe she wouldn't have been so curt if she could have French exited and left town without confronting Erik, but that option doesn't exist anymore.

"So she was blunt," I defended my best friend. "Some people don't sugarcoat things. Would you have rather she kissed your ass and left you thinking there was hope in the future?"

He scooped ice into a cocktail shaker with a stink face. "I would rather she have been nice—"

"She is nice," I argued.

She just doesn't have breakup experience. Neither do I. I'm sure I would have flubbed a breakup just as hard. I haven't even broken up with my *fake* boyfriend! And that was in the works for how long before we shelved it? If Erik knew Hailey well at all, he wouldn't have taken her tone that badly.

And if he cared about her—maybe he would've seen she's not doing so fucking great. That she has little time for his emotional state because she's more concerned with her own.

So *there*.

Erik shook his head like I was wrong.

"You know what," I said coldly. "I'm going to make the negroni myself—"

"You're not allowed to mix drinks."

"Since when?" I've made plenty of mimosas and helped behind the bar.

"It's in the handbook."

"Fine. I'll go find Lola. She makes better drinks than you anyway." I strutted off without a second glance and tossed my maturity in the trash can. Replaying that scenario literally sends thick wrinkles to my forehead in an ugly grimace. Lasting impressions are new for me, and some not in a good way.

Erik responded to that confrontation by gossiping about my best friend to the other servers, the sous chefs, the lifeguards—basically *anyone* who would listen.

It came out that Hailey also slept with Peter the Valet and Lewis the Golf Instructor before Halloween.

Her reputation as being an "easy lay" has been cemented.

There's nothing wrong with one-night stands or wanting to keep things casual. It's basically the grifter norm. *Nothing serious. Sex only.*

But the staff have taken Erik's side and branded my best friend with a scarlet A. I feel at fault. Like if I didn't provoke Erik, he wouldn't have spiraled. (He also is *majorly* to blame, too.)

Hailey said she doesn't care about him or the gossip, but I think she's been too invested elsewhere and hasn't seriously contemplated what this means.

The longer we stay in this town, the more we have to deal with the consequences of our actions and the ruin we leave behind. We're not just kicking up dust. We're supposed to be here when it settles.

That time . . . is not now, but I hope peace isn't an illusion. I hope it's a real outcome we're working toward.

My phone buzzes.

Jake: She did explain The Hunt to you?

I sigh and send him a quick **yes**.

This annual event isn't like *The Hunger Games* or *The Purge*. Citizens aren't armed to shoot the weak and poor. Packs of men aren't tracking Bambi with rifles slung on their backs either.

It's a scavenger hunt.

An innocent, simple, *fun* time where locals gather together and act like sleuths for the day.

Or so I thought.

"You're Clue Girls," Katherine told us when we were one foot into the country club. I thought we'd be assigned to a refreshment table. Serve nonalcoholic beverages, maybe the occasional Bloody Mary. Or we'd pass out VCC pamphlets, enticing locals to join and pay the astronomical club dues.

But no.

We're *Clue Girls*.

It has nothing to do with the board game Clue. I already asked.

Katherine Rhodes and her clipboard make their rounds in the country club's atrium garden. Wearing the tightest, most unwalkable pencil skirt—that she somehow manages to move in—she appraises me and twenty other "handpicked" girls.

Some are servers.

Others are rich caufers and locals.

No one is older than mid-thirties.

We stand among the boxed greenery and sticky humidity. "Why are we doing this again?" I whisper to Hailey, who snaps off a honeysuckle flower and slips it behind her ear. There is most definitely a rule about not picking the foliage.

She's humming to herself, then stops to say, "It'd be a crime to live here and skip the annual scavenger hunt."

I raise my brows. "Call me a criminal—"

"Never." She untucks a rolled newspaper from the waistband of her cargo pants. Her black long-sleeved shirt says BIG WITCH ENERGY, but the words are slightly hidden behind a brown tartan sash with CLUE GIRL embroidered in gold thread.

The same sash accompanies my baby-blue sweater, which has ruffled sleeves.

"And you know it's going to be fun. I've always wanted to be a Clue Girl." She opens the paper, beginning to speed-read.

I give her a look. "You learned what a Clue Girl is twenty minutes ago." The same time Katherine roped us into this tradition.

Hailey smiles deviously with her eyes still glued to the newspaper.

She's been reading the local paper religiously for the past three months. I'm not sure how she doesn't fall asleep.

I've glazed over the paper, and it's mostly posturing from local city council. *New trees planted in the square! Great turnout for the 10K! Sign up for the weekly handmade market!* And don't forget the advertisements in the back for the gutter-repair and window-cleaning companies. Truly riveting material.

I glance around the atrium and notice three more girls

reading *Victoria Weekly*. My brain physically record-scratches. There isn't any way I'm seeing what I'm seeing.

"Did they put smut in the *Weekly*?" I ask Hailey.

She frowns. "What?"

I wave a hand toward Julia Kelsey, who has her nose glued to the newspaper. Her friend reads over her shoulder, and they're whispering like they've somehow acquired Regina George's Burn Book.

To Hailey, I say, "Because if there's some spicy articles in this paper, I'm kind of pissed you wouldn't tell me." I'm not a voracious reader like Hailey, but I will devour a good fanfic. "You know how much I love *Underworld* smut."

She glances at me like I'm out of my mind. "You think they would print vampire fanfic in the town's newspaper?"

I stand my ground. "We're about to go on a scavenger hunt, Hails. Dressed like we're starring in a crossover of *Clue* and *Troop Beverly Hills*. Anything is possible."

She takes this in for a second before nodding. "Valid." She flips another page. "And it's not smut. It's a new column about the happenings around town."

My brain buzzes like a fly trapped underneath a glass. "Happenings?" I let out a sudden gasp. "Hailey Thornhall, are you reading gossip?" She hates tabloids.

"These are *facts*, Phoebe Smith."

"Some gossip is factual," I point out.

She smiles, but it's stolen too fast by her hyperfixation. She's consumed by the *Weekly*. I try to read over her shoulder, but she flips another page.

Katherine struts right in front of us and smiles warmly at the paper in Hailey's hands.

Very odd.

"I'm just so proud of Sidney," Katherine says with the affection of a mother hen to a tiny chick. Even knowing she was Jake's nanny, I really did not think Katherine possessed a soft maternal bone in her body. More like an iron rod in her butt. "She's really blossomed with this new internship at the *Weekly*. Isn't her column so engaging? Claudia Waterford even called it a delight."

I feel so far behind.

All because I don't read the damn newspaper. Sidney Burke stands twenty feet away near the orchids, but I only see her blonde hair and blue velvet Blair Waldorf–esque headband since girls cluster around her.

"It's an intriguing column," Hailey says. "I didn't know that Archer Fitzpatrick adopted a three-legged dog."

"Wait, *that's* the happenings around town? Archer's new dog?" I say in disbelief. I just can't believe this information has the rest of the Clue Girls fawning over black-and-white print.

"He also volunteered at the blood bank," Katherine snaps at me, like I should be praising his very good deeds. "He's not even thirty yet, but he's already up for tenure at Caufield University." She peers at the newspaper in Hailey's hands. "It's such a mystery how that man is still single."

"You could always ask him out yourself," I suggest.

Katherine blanches. "I'm nearing fifty."

"And?" I shrug. "You're hot, and he might like women with good balance in pencil skirts."

She sucks in her cheeks. Maybe she thinks they're back-handed compliments—which they aren't. I admire her ability to dart around in corporate attire. "You'd do well to mind your own business, Phoebe."

"Like how everyone's minding theirs?" I mutter at the newspaper.

Katherine huffs like I am a pain, bother, and nuisance she's forced to suffer with. She digs out two envelopes from her tote bag. "Here."

Hailey and I take our envelopes, and Katherine struts out of earshot to fix Chelsea's torn sash. I run my finger over the red wax seal with Victoria Country Club's mountain-laurel crest.

From what I've been told, the country club hosts The Hunt, but the entire town is invited to *bid* on Clue Girls.

We're being auctioned off.

"For your clues," Katherine emphasized, but the way she described it, people are paying to spend the afternoon with us.

"Grey is picking me," Sidney Burke says so loudly, I instinctively twist around and catch her smug smile. Her chin lifts. "I'm his first choice. He's already told me."

Liar.

I bristle. "He's not going to The Hunt." I raise my voice so she can hear.

"How would you know?" Sidney retorts, causing the atrium to fall more hushed. Clue Girls are staring uneasily between me and her.

"Hailey told me," I snap back. "*His sister.* Right here." I point at her platinum-dyed hair. "My best friend."

Hailey waves, not looking up from the newspaper. "He did tell me."

"See."

Sidney coils a blonde tendril around her finger. "I think he'll be there, and he *will* bid on me."

"You're *nineteen*. He wouldn't."

"You have the maturity of a fourteen-year-old, and he married you."

Ouch. Direct hit.

Girls snicker, some wince, and Hailey sends a harsh look

Sidney's way. I breathe in toxic fumes to say, "He's *not* interested in you." I sound too territorial, but the concept of Rocky with *anyone* sends poisonous darts out of my mouth.

I want her dead.

Sidney prickles. "Why do you care? You're with *Jake*."

I'm with Rocky.

He's my Rocky.

Mine.

I take a breath. "Grey is still my ex-husband. Maybe I think he can do better than you."

The atrium is uncomfortably quiet. Some girls giggle at Sidney's expense, and guilt knots my insides for a blip.

Sidney goes red. "At least I'm a step up from you."

Back off, Phoebe.

I'm trying to retract my claws. She's nineteen. I'm twenty-four. Be mature. I force a pained smile, and I'm happy to hear Katherine's strict tone.

"It's time," she snaps. "Get yourselves together."

Sidney fixes her Clue Girl sash on her shoulder. I adjust mine, and my face contorts in an ugly scowl like I'm shape-shifting into a grotesque monster. It's hard to hide my sweltering disdain toward anyone who's eyeing Rocky. I wish I could scream that he's taken.

By me.

But I didn't come this far to blow up our spot because of Sidney fucking Burke.

Pink garlands hang from lampposts, and the fountain on Main Street has been drained for the winter. Heart-shaped chocolates, stuffed bears, and red roses are displayed in various shops like Hidden Treasures and Petals & Pearls.

No one in this town will let you forget Valentine's Day is right around the corner.

I've never been a sucker for the holiday.

It's just another way for corporations to dig their hands in people's pockets with the pressure to *buy buy buy!* The balloons, the candy, the cards, the flowers, the expensive dinner out—it's a capitalist's wet dream. It's kind of one big scam.

It really does feel like you're getting ripped off.

And okay, maybe I have been played before and bought my fair share of heart-shaped Reese's cups. But I've never dreamed of having a Valentine's date.

I've been more than happy spending February fourteenth watching movies with Hailey, both of us gorging ourselves with Sweethearts candies that give positive affirmations like *Cutie Pie* and *Ur Hot.*

Except this year is different.

This year I'm bummed that I can't go on a Valentine's date with Rocky, and I'm a little worried if Jake and I aren't seen out together, people will think we're "taking a break" when that's not exactly true.

Wind assaults my skin as I stand on the steps of town hall with twenty other Clue Girls. Goosebumps are mountains on my forearms, and I hug myself to try to contain the warmth from my thin blue sweater.

I'm the only one who didn't bring a jacket. I blame my hostility toward Sidney, which made me pretty warm up until two minutes ago.

Everyone else is bundled with mittens and hats. Even Hailey slipped on a pair of black leather gloves when we walked outside.

The town square is packed.

Bodies everywhere, none shivering from the cold. Tall

gas-lamp heaters have been placed around the cobblestone square to warm the residents, and the richest stay huddled beneath a tent reserved for country club members.

Claudia Waterford included.

I wave my fingers like she's my mother-in-law to be.

She noticeably cringes, then whispers to her best friend, Stella Fitzpatrick.

I hope you hate my guts. I hope you show me who you really are.

Katherine approaches a microphone in front of us. Clutching a clipboard with gloved hands, she scans the audience with a quiet reverence. She's spent her entire life in this town. Grown up around the three founding families. Unless you're a caufer studying at Caufield University or a skunk who's passing through, she most likely knows you by name.

Not quite royalty but not quite among the middle class, she thinks of herself as the glue, I've realized, holding the ill-fitted pieces of Victoria together.

She leans down to the microphone. "Welcome to the eighty-eighth Hunt!"

A round of applause booms from the crowd with a few hoots. Beside me, Hailey's grin expands, and for a moment, I'm swept into the infectious energy.

Katherine explains the rules of the event. "Twenty girls behind me are in possession of envelopes filled with five clues. These clues will lead you to five golden geese hidden around the town. The first person to bring back all five golden geese will win the coveted Victoria Hunt Trophy and be named this year's Huntsman. But not everyone can participate in this event. To play, you'll need to bid and win a Clue Girl." She outstretches a hand to display us.

Girls give pageant waves. Julia has a sheepish smile.

Hailey is fidgeting.

I scowl and search for Jake.

With an incoming chilly gust, the cold annihilates every inch of exposed skin. I tremble.

"Without further ado—" Katherine's voice cuts off suddenly as the crowd shifts and parts, letting someone through.

I see the muscled, never-ending limbs and the serious, ocean-blue eyes of my fake boyfriend.

"Sorry, Katherine," Jake apologizes as he approaches. His long legs practically skip the five steps up to where I'm standing.

He shrugs off his long black overcoat. A chorus of *awww*s echoes from the crowd as he gallantly fits the coat over my shoulders. I eagerly snuggle inside the warm wool. He bends down to my ear and whispers, "Your boyfriend says *hi*."

Rocky.

"Is he here?" I whisper back, my heart flipping, melting, and panging all at once.

Jake just nods.

Do not look for Rocky. The desire to find him tears at my insides, and I force myself to nestle in the woolen fabric. "Thanks, Jake," I say louder.

"Anytime, baby." His head slants, and there's no lingering hesitation. He kisses my cheek.

It's warm but perfunctory.

A boyfriend would likely kiss his girlfriend in this scenario, and despite some love triangle rumors, Jake and I have established ourselves as a normal, modest couple. PDA is not for us, and no one questions it.

Jake is Polite Panda, after all. He's not the groping type.

I hear the second wave of *awww*s from the audience before Jake backs away and descends the steps into the gathering throngs.

Katherine returns to the microphone. "Well, we all know who will be bidding on Ms. Phoebe Smith." It draws a wave of chuckles from everyone. My cheeks roast, and they burn a thousand degrees hotter when I catch sight of him.

Rocky.

My pulse spikes unsteadily.

Why is he even here? The question withers inside the raw craving of him. Of hoping he will stay.

I do everything to not show the emotion assaulting me.

Rocky stands darkly beside a lamppost, wearing a white button-down beneath a leather jacket and a casual, consistent glare. Arms crossed over his chest and gray eyes shadowed with tormented irritation.

When his gaze latches on to mine, it doesn't soften. It's penetrating. Excavating. Digging so damn deep, I'm unsure if anyone else can see the love on the other side.

NINETEEN

Rocky

Witnessing Jake and Phoebe become an "it couple" has been like adding a pound of rock salt to my daily breakfast. Yet, I'd rather be here and watch it happen than be stuck anywhere *fucking* else.

So as soon as breakfast ended with Trent, I decided to join The Hunt.

I lean an arm against a pink garland–wrapped lamppost, and Jake sidles close, sans overcoat, but he dressed warm in a thick cable-knit sweater. Giving Phoebe his extra layer wasn't a setup to add credibility to their fake relationship.

I saw her trembling.

I whispered to him, "She's freezing."

And he did something about it because I couldn't. Part of me likes having Jake at my side—the other part is just *very* aggravated.

"Knight in shining armor," I say coarsely. "So brave. So bold."

He gives me a concerned look like a big brother worried

about his kid brother's mental state. "You really want to be here? At *this* event?"

Where he's about to bid on my girlfriend.

Yeah.

"That's exactly *why* I want to be here," I whisper between my teeth. I can't let her go. The idea that she's being purchased by someone else—been there, done that for a Pay Up or Be Arrested job.

The idea that I'm not in reach?

Never happened. It's not happening now.

Jake still studies me with worry. I should've known he wouldn't morph this into a dick-measuring contest (*that*, I'd win). Instead, the monthslong fake-dating ploy has only turned his soft heart softer. He's a marshmallow that has been standing too close to my burning irritation. Now he's just goo that's stuck all over me.

We're inextricably intertwined these long, *long* days.

After I give him a harsher glare, he averts his attention to Katherine, who's introducing last year's Huntsman: Raul Garcia.

Jake surveys the masses and whispers, "I think you should be more concerned about who's going to bid on your sister since we know I'm bidding on your ex-wife."

Is he *often* more concerned about Hailey? If I had a Magic 8 Ball, it would say, *Signs point to yes.*

"Carter is bidding on her," I tell him. "That's what he told me when I found out about the auction portion of this silly shit." I wasn't shocked he'd pay money for Hailey. They have biweekly meetups at eight a.m., and whatever intel they've gathered about our parents, they don't casually share.

Maybe he wants extra time with her to solve this mystery.

Maybe he wants extra time with her for other things, but

you know what? I'm not going to go there in my brain. There's not enough bleach in the world.

"Carter had to leave a half hour ago. His grannie needed a ride to the post office."

I blink hard.

Great. Last thing I need is for Weston Burke, the worst widower and Sidney Burke's father, to bid on my sister to spite me. Now that I'm rising in the social ranks, he despises me even more.

I send Oliver and Nova a group text.

Need one of you to bid on Hailey at The Hunt.
Nova: I'm not there. On the Salty Miss.

The speedboat.

I don't wait long for another response.

Oliver: I can be there in twenty. At gym with Collin.

I pocket my phone. "Oliver will bid on her."

"Oliver?" Jake does a harsh double take.

I cock my head, reading his tensed reaction. *He doesn't trust Oliver? He dislikes Oliver? He's jealous of Oliver?* "What'd Oliver do to you?" I ask.

"Nothing," Jake says fast—too fast. He combs a hand through his hair. "I just didn't think he'd want to bid on Hailey."

I lower my voice and stare ahead. "You didn't think he'd bid on her or you don't want him to? Because you do know they're close—"

"Phoebe said they're not together." He's careful to whisper the next part. "Not even in a grifter sense."

"Okay, how about you don't utter that word in public,

ever," I grit out under my breath and try not to see who's watching, avoiding appearing cagey as fuck.

"Sorry," he apologizes with a frustrated sigh.

My temple pounds. "You're okay with Carter bidding on my sister but not okay with Oliver?"

"Carter is my friend. Oliver, I hardly know."

"She knows Oliver."

"She knows Carter. They've even . . ." He cuts himself short, as if remembering I'm Hailey's brother.

I roll my eyes into a sharp glare at him. He's to blame for my next question. "They've hooked up?"

"Yeah. He said it was in the past. They're just good friends now."

I'd like to rewind to the part where I never knew my sister slept with Stuart Cartwright. But sadly I'm not a fucking TV.

I stare straight ahead again. "You're jealous of Oliver."

"I'm *not* jealous," he says with the heat of someone trying to convince themselves.

Onlookers are journaling our frigid interactions in their heads for their next watercooler session at work. *Jake Waterford and Grey Thornhall were bickering at the scavenger hunt!* The town believes we only tolerate each other because I'm close with my ex-wife and he's dating her.

Really, it feels more like a partial truth than an outright lie.

My phone buzzes.

Oliver: Car isn't starting. I'm on the phone with Nova to fix it, but I'm almost positive someone stole the catalytic converter. It's DOA. It might be an hour before I can make it there.

That's not soon enough.

Jake sees my frown deepen. "What's wrong?"

"Oliver can't make it." I slip my phone in my leather jacket. "I'll bid on Hailey."

My jaw hurts from clenching my teeth so hard, and when I look at Phoebe, I see her blue hair blowing in the wind and how she hides her chin deeper in the collar of Jake's coat. Her cheeks are pink, and she laughs at a joke Raul Garcia makes about golden geese.

Watching her, I can *almost* breathe.

Raul raises a large golden trophy shaped like a goose taking off for flight, and my sister eyes the gaudy thing like a predator who's found its prey.

Hailey loves any random competition, and I'm glad my sister has found something other than our family tree to obsess over. But she knows I'm about as likely to take this scavenger hunt seriously as I am to climb the Andes.

She's not going to want me to be her partner in this.

She can be mad at me later. It'll be good to show the widowers they can't steamroll me and get everything they want.

"We'll start the bidding with Miss Sidney Burke." Katherine speaks into the mic. "A studious sophomore at Caufield University, Sidney was named Miss Victoria's Sweetheart two years in a row . . ."

Sidney's gaze veers to me, and I look in the opposite direction.

Jake sighs heavily. "I'll talk to her again."

I straighten up against the lamppost. "And say what? *Grey's not interested? Grey's too old for you?* She knows this, man. I have given her *every* hint that exists."

"You didn't know Sidney before Kate died," he whispers. "She never even dated. She was more interested in getting straight A's. I think she's just having a hard time now that her best friend is gone. She's rebelling."

Jake is feeling a sense of guilt for Sidney's grief. Because Kate isn't actually dead.

"Just because she's grieving your sister—it doesn't make her entitled to anything she wants. Stop coddling her."

He's not taking that well, so I realize I need to be more honest.

"She's tried to cop a feel of my cock *multiple* times now. Last instance was the party on a superyacht with Trent and his friends. I'm done with her."

Jake goes still, concern in his gaze. "Does Phoebe know?"

"No, because she'd probably strangle Sidney."

"I'll talk to Sidney about boundaries." He seems horrified.

"Yeah, you do that. Maybe throw in a sexual harassment class while you're at it."

"Just try not to be a dick," he says matter-of-factly. "It's obviously attracting her."

"Oh wow, I hadn't thought of that."

"Five thousand!" The bidding begins, and I barely acknowledge the Caufield student who raises a hand to bid on Sidney.

"Six thousand."

My head whips over to the familiar flat voice of my brother. Trevor is hanging around other students his age. He's enrolled in college, which he doesn't love since he's graduated about two times before, but everyone knows he's nineteen. It'd be stranger if he didn't attend Caufield.

"Why is he bidding on her?" Jake whispers to me. "Is there a setup?"

"No." We didn't plan this, but I did unfortunately share with Trevor that Sidney was handsy on the yacht. I shut my eyes tightly and open them up with a sharp breath and a wince.

"What?" Jake frowns.

"I think he's trying to protect me."

"Seven thousand!" the other student counters.

Jake crosses his arms, assessing this situation like a Boy Scout. "Should we intervene?"

"I don't know." *I can't.*

I won't bid on Sidney. My stomach roils, and I refuse to even look at Phoebe, or else it'll inflict more pain.

"Eight thousand," Trevor bids.

"Will he hurt her?" Jake asks very, very quietly.

I slowly shake my head, then whisper back to him, "I'm more afraid she's going to sexually assault my brother. But if I interfere, he'll think I'm babying him like our parents. So it's going to happen."

"I'll talk to her," Jake assures me.

I nod harsh, neck-aching nods. "Yeah. You better."

Trevor wins Sidney, and when he whisks her off the steps of town hall, she immediately checks for her dad's reaction. Steam is jetting out of Weston's ears. He likely had envisioned an Ivy League quarterback winning his daughter for the afternoon.

Now he's stuck with his worst nightmare's little brother. Sidney couldn't be more pleased to stick it to her dad.

She practically skips down the stairs with Trevor.

Maybe that will work out in my favor.

While Rachel Rawlings is next, I tune out the auction, open a game on my phone, connect two candy pieces together.

"There should be Clue Guys," Jake says like it's been a point of contention.

I glance over. "Too hetero for you?"

He cracks a smile. "I'd take a Chris Evans. With tattoos."

"With tattoos?" My brows jump.

"You wouldn't?" he volleys.

"No." I go back to the app. "I'd only bid on Phoebe." It's practically said under my breath, but he's standing at my side and hears.

His smile softens on me like I'm sitting at his fucking Round Table with other Arthurian knights. I don't want to be there.

"Christian Slater circa *Heathers*," I tell him quickly.

"That's your type?"

"One of them."

"So you'd fuck yourself?"

"Well, I don't think I'm ugly."

He laughs.

I hate that I want to smile, and when I meet Phoebe's gaze, her happiness is what really gets me. She brightens seeing I'm getting along with Jake. He's getting along with me. We're not about to slit each other's throats when we've been taking the world's greatest trust falls with one another.

"Next up is a fairly new server from our very beloved Victoria Country Club," Katherine announces, and Phoebe's smile plummets from the ozone. "Phoebe Smith."

I shove my phone in my jacket, and Jake focuses on his fake girlfriend. She gives a polite wave, then hugs the overcoat tighter to her frame. It's easy to hear the whispered words around us—and not just from nosy ladies at the country club.

These are college students.

"Grey will win her."

"Grey doesn't care that she's with Jake. Just watch."

"God, Jake is *so much* better for her. Grey is a giant red flag."

"I know. Watersmith is everything."

Watersmith. They have a couple name. This is new. Kill me later. (Or not.) I rake a hand through my hair. I wish everyone would say Jake isn't good enough for Phoebe.

That I am.

Hailey said it's obvious why interest in the new happy couple has extended beyond socialites and now to caufers—that Phoebe and Jake are the "Peyton and Lucas" of Victoria.

"They're from *One Tree Hill*," my sister reminded me when I gave her a look.

"I know the TV reference," I said. "I also know that Lucas is a cheating wet blanket."

"Jake isn't a cheater," Hailey replied definitively, like she knew him too well. They've spent a handful of hours together at a thriller/mystery book club that meets at Baubles & Bookends.

"Yeah? Did he just offer that fun opinion over a deep-dive analysis of *The Girl with the Dragon Tattoo*?" I asked her.

"He didn't blatantly say he wasn't a cheater. I've just gotten the sense he's very loyal."

I flashed a smile. "A regular golden retriever."

"At least Phoebe prefers German shepherds," she said. "Protective, faithful, way more like you."

My lips almost lifted. *Almost.* Because Hailey didn't look into my eyes when she said it or even afterward. She's shied away from talking much about my love of her best friend.

I've picked up that she's hiding something.

Call it a hunch. (Usually mine aren't that far off.)

"Watersmith is *so* cute," I hear by the fountain, and I grimace. *Phake* was right there, and that's what they are. Fake.

That's also the foundation of my relationship with Phoebe. The two of us—playing pretend. Could he really fill my role in her life? *No.* Still, I'm wading in a vat of jealousy watching him try. And knowing it's better if he doesn't fail.

Katherine gestures to my girlfriend/wife/*everything*. "We'll start Phoebe and her clues at two thousand dollars."

Without falter, Jake says loudly, "Two thousand!"

My teeth ache as I grind down. *Don't bid on her.*

I can't.

Phoebe produces a phony warm smile at Jake that likely only I can pinpoint as insincere. Then her brown eyes so very subtly shift to me. My chest rises.

I love when I stare at Phoebe across a crowd of people—it's like we're in a dreamscape of our own making. One that only we can see.

This is what I've always shared with her. A great, unyielding truth beneath hundreds of lies.

Phoebe's cheeks go rosy, and she drags her gaze to the ground.

My lips tic upward.

"Two thousand," Katherine says. "Do I hear three?"

"Five!" Weston interjects loudly. His smug smirk meets my pissed glare. I didn't anticipate him bidding on Phoebe. That irritates me.

"Six!" Jake shouts, then he sends Weston a lukewarm threatening look. It wouldn't burn a baby.

"Seven," Weston counters without much pause. He's still staring at me.

I'm not acknowledging this prick anymore. I hope he thinks about me so much, I give him a brain clot.

Jake makes a confused face at Weston. "You do know you're bidding on my girlfriend?"

Weston takes a perfunctory sip from his thermos. Sure, he has all the time in the world. We can wait on him. He smacks his lips. "I'm not bidding on the *girl*, Jake. I have a gut feeling she holds the best clues." He raises his voice to ask me, "What about you, Grey? Too rich for your blood?"

He's saying I can't afford my ex-wife.

Phoebe crosses her arms haughtily, and as she mutters something, I read her lips as they form the word *asshole*. She needs to be careful.

We all do.

"I'm saving for someone else," I tell him, like this childish shit is beneath me. "Have fun with Jake."

Whispers and commotion thunder around us, along with a wave of gasps and speculations.

"Who is he bidding on?"

"It has to be Valentina de la Vega, right? Isn't she friends with Grey?"

Weston grows red in the face.

"Eight thousand," Jake bids quickly.

Weston quietly shrinks back.

"We have eight. Do I hear a nine?" Katherine asks, and a wedge of silence eases tension in my muscles. It's going to end soon. It'll all be over.

"Going once. Going twice—"

"Nine!" All heads swerve to the new bidder, and I must be hallucinating. I have a mental Rolodex of townspeople here in Victoria.

I know all the main players.

All the people who'd have enough loose cash to throw nine grand on a fucking scavenger hunt to win a cheap trophy.

I've memorized names and faces and more information about this town and its inhabitants that would exceed a Wikipedia page.

And yet, the man who just bid on my girlfriend . . .

I don't recognize him.

TWENTY

Rocky

He's back." The hushed phrase has traveled from ear to ear, and I don't need to ask Jake who the hell has caught everyone's attention like the Queen of England dismounting from a Thoroughbred.

People whisper his nickname, one that was formed after Emilia's death.

"The Lone Wolfe," a lady says behind me.

"Is that really him?" her friend asks.

Jake shares a hesitant look with me. He leans in to whisper, "That's Varrick."

"I figured."

"I can't believe he left Stonehaven," Jake says in a labored breath like he's running a 5k. "Twelve thousand!" he shouts over the commotion, and I hope that's the gavel. The end note.

"Twenty-one," Varrick Wolfe says, too casually.

People shuffle away from him. His self-assured stance reminds me of every Wall Street broker I've ever met. His shit doesn't stink. He could buy half the street. Nothing here fazes him.

He's next to a marble planter filled with reddish-orange poppies, and a gaping path opens from him all the way to Jake, who's beside me and the lamppost.

Everyone has a better view of this face-off.

Unlike Weston, Varrick has trained his focus solely on Phoebe.

My instincts buzz, and my blood boils. I do my best not to tense while I scan the length of him.

He's white. Likely between forty-five and forty-eight. Fit, as if he wakes obsessively at five a.m. for a treadmill sprint and barbell presses. Clean-shaven. He's well groomed with wavy, dark brown hair and moisturized, fair skin. Everything about him screams *rich*.

The fitted blue sports coat is designer. The matching slacks look tailor-made. But his wealth isn't just in his custom wardrobe or the Patek Philippe watch on his wrist—one that reminds me of my father.

It's the superiority he exudes—the calm arrogance as the commotion never disturbs his desires—and it has the town collectively holding their breath.

He is as magnanimous as they fucking envisioned him to be.

"Twenty-two!" Jake calls out.

"Twenty-three," he states. He's closer to the country-club tent, and in the shade, I see Claudia. I see Stella Fitzpatrick and a handful of other ladies huddled and sipping proseccos with newfound interest.

"Twenty-four," Jake counters.

"Twenty-five."

"You do know you're bidding on my girlfriend?!" Jake shouts with bubbling ire across the square. He's trying to protect Phoebe.

Varrick pretends not to hear.

I swear he's fucking smiling.

My muscles are on fire as I root myself in place. I've stuffed my white-knuckled fists in my leather jacket.

Jake twists to me, and fear is ejecting from his gaze. He only shows me. Jake isn't half bad at being secretive, and if he weren't so in touch with his morals, he'd make a great lifelong con artist.

I'll give him that.

Fear—he feels it because it's not just the Konings who hold power in Victoria. It's the Wolfes, and up until this moment, I doubt there was any person that could rival a Koning boy.

I slip him back a hardened look. We're not letting this prick win Phoebe.

She looks *disturbed* on the steps of town hall. She's avoiding Varrick's intense eye contact and whispering to Hailey beside her.

"Is there another bid?" Katherine asks, eagle-eyeing her godson, Jake, for a response. She's encouraging him to not give up, despite not being fond of Phoebe herself. Katherine genuinely loves him, maybe more than his own mother does.

"Twenty-six!" Jake shouts.

"Twenty-seven thousand," Varrick counters. The low hum of whispers roars louder.

Leaning into Jake, I whisper, "Did you tick this guy off?" It feels personal somehow. Like a vendetta.

"I've never spoken to him in my life," Jake says with a cautious side-eye. "Twenty-eight!"

"Twenty-nine."

"Thirty!" Jake calls out, and as Varrick continues to stare down Phoebe, more unease crawls beneath my skin.

"Thirty-five thousand." Varrick hikes up the price. It's higher than anticipated, and Jake's funds are tied up to the point where he couldn't buy his sister's horse.

Jake tries not to act flummoxed or panicked. He's just vexed. "Thirty-six!"

"Forty-one thousand." Varrick surges the bid like it's nothing, and the volume in the square amplifies. I can't even hear myself think. Words muffle together, and Varrick slowly begins to smile again.

My eyes sear inside out. I can't quit glaring. My mind is reeling at theories behind his motives. This forty-something arrogant prick thinks he can take a girl half his age from a Koning. As a power move—a Wolfe showing up to put the Konings in their place. Phoebe is a pawn in a rich man's game—and I fucking *hate it*. I can't stand it, and yet, I've entered the arena far too many times to count.

Or he might just think she's the most attractive Clue Girl. He wants to fuck her.

I don't care which one is worse. It's all emotional. Unhelpful. Pain.

Phoebe is cringing. She threads her arms hotly over her chest.

"Quiet down! Quiet down!" Katherine calls out into the microphone.

Over the noise, I pull Jake closer to whisper, "Stop bidding on her."

"What?" His blue eyes narrow back at me. "*No.*"

"He's doing this for a reason," I say roughly under my breath. "We need to figure out why."

"Grey—"

"We're a team," I remind him just as quietly. Flashes of my brother, my sister, Nova, Oliver, Phoebe race through my head at the word *team*. I can't believe I'd also include Jake in it, but we are so permanently, doggedly on the same side. I think we'd die here together before stepping even a hundred feet closer to the warring position.

Katherine speaks into the mic. "Do I hear forty-two thousand?" She gives Jake ample time to respond.

All eyes are on the third-born heir.

My pulse breaks every speed limit, and I wait for Jake to relent. He slips me a look that says, *I'm with you*. But also, *This better work*.

He trusts me. Scarily enough, I've been slowly learning to trust him, too.

"Going once," Katherine says, worry straining her voice.

Then I step in front of Jake. "Forty-two thousand," I call out.

There's no thunder of noise. No buzzing chatter. Silence falls on the square in certified shock. It's been three months.

Three whole months where I've never protested or fought for Phoebe. I've let her be with Jake as if I'm the bitter ex-husband with an *L* on his forehead.

Until today.

When I bid on her.

Heads swing to Varrick. And for the first time, he pries his fixed attention off Phebs. And he sets these glimmering, strange, bluish eyes on me. They're boring. Like a drill into the eye sockets. It's uncomfortable, and I know why Phoebe would avoid his face.

I also know I've used this look on others before. To intimidate them.

I say nothing. I just meet his challenge head-on. Never

breaking our gaze. He thinks he's a jackhammer? I'm an entire fucking wrecking ball.

His lips hike up.

Yeah.

He likes this. Competing. Is he just bored then? Is this what gets him off? He's tired of holing up in his mansion on a lonesome island, so he came out for some afternoon entertainment.

I can't see the truth, but I'm accustomed to living among lies. Varrick Wolfe doesn't scare me.

He sees, and his smile seems to brighten.

As Katherine says, "Do I hear forty-three thousand?" Varrick is already casually strolling out of the masses and down the street. As if The Hunt means next to nothing to him.

"Going once," Katherine says. He's gone, but my ribs have caged my lungs. "Going twice." Noise suddenly picks up around me. Katherine leans into the microphone, disappointment etched in her voice. "Phoebe Smith and her clues. Sold to Grey Thornhall."

TWENTY-ONE

Phoebe

What the fuck was that?" I whisper in slight panic. Okay, maybe more than *slight*. I can't catch my breath, and partly, it's because we practically *ran* into the bathroom together.

A graffitied single-toilet bathroom.

Rocky locks the door. McIntire's, the local Irish pub, was near dead when we entered, but it wouldn't even matter if someone saw us slip in here together. He just publicly won me in an *auction*. Now we're paired up for The Hunt, and this is the only source of privacy we could find in such a short amount of time.

"I don't know," Rocky growls out, a rough hand skating through his black hair.

"The job," I whisper. "We just risked *the job*. It's not what we do. We're very, very good at this, Rocky." We can set aside our emotions to do the hard thing.

So why did he win me?

He's too quiet.

Concern flares. "Rocky?"

His eyes hit mine, and the emotion penetrating his gray irises takes my breath away. "I had to."

My chest rises and falls.

"I wasn't going to let him have you, Phoebe."

I just collapse into him like a book closing its pages. His arms fit so snugly around me. His chin settles at the top of my head.

I grip him. He grips me.

Leather and pine smell stronger against the crook of his neck than Jake's cedar-scented cologne on the overcoat. It's not that often we can steal time together outside of the loft or the boathouse. I'm already craving to pause this moment. So I can sit inside of it for hours.

While we're still holding each other, he tells me, "Varrick Wolfe wasn't going to stop outbidding Jake. I thought there was a chance that if I bid on you, he might back out."

"Which he did. So what does that mean?"

"Three guesses," Rocky says. "One. He hates Jake and was just trying to bleed him of money." The way he speaks, it seems like he believes this option less. "Two. He wanted to show the town that he holds more power than the Konings."

"Probable," I say. "And three?"

Rocky goes silent again, and I step away to see the apprehension warp his face. Especially as he says, "He was toying with me."

"What?"

"He got off on it. On the game."

"But he *lost*."

"I don't know, Phebs. Something isn't right." Rocky stares

right at me, but there is a haunted tunnel inside his grays that pulls him farther away. "It's almost like he sees me, like he knows what I am, and he . . ."

"He what?" I'm caging breath.

"He respects it." He crawls through his thoughts. "That smile he gave me—before he lost. It was *pride*."

I tug the Clue Girl sash away from my neck, feeling choked. "Hailey said we need to look deeper into the Wolfe family."

"No shit." He rests his ass on the silver bar that helps people lower onto and rise off the toilet. The bathroom is tiny, but I press my back to the graffitied door, letting a few feet of space separate us.

With the intimate way he's looking at me, it still feels like he's right up against my body.

"What now?" I ask him.

He removes his hands from his jacket, then flicks this stupid gold coin at me with his thumb.

I catch it. "Trying to pay me to go away?"

"Yeah. That's what I'm doing when I just paid forty-two grand for you to stay."

"Burning all your cash on me. I'm flattered."

"Not all of it."

"Cheapo depot."

He begins to smile, and my heart rate elevates. As he glances at the coin in my hand, I inspect the foil.

My head snaps to him. "This is fake." It's obvious by the weight.

"It's definitely not real."

I peel at the foiled edge, and I tear the gold film off to find chocolate underneath. The center is pressed with a pink heart and arrow.

Valentine's chocolate. Smoothing my lips together, I battle

the surge of an overwhelming smile. He tilts his head, a little more than just satisfied at my reaction. He's devouring every piece of me.

"How much did this cost you? Like fifty cents?"

"I bought a whole bag at the gift shop. More like three bucks."

"Wowww," I draw out. "You know how to woo a girl."

"I know how to woo you," he says. "Fake coins and strawberry things." Is it strawberry flavored? I can't even ask. My throat swells with more sentimental emotion.

I look up at Rocky. It's simple. The act of being remembered while you're passing a store. For as complex and twisted as our lives are, the simplicity of love strikes me to the core. Love doesn't have to always be pain.

"Fair warning," he says, "I ate one, and the chocolate is fucking gross."

"That's probably because you're a chocolate snob."

He doesn't deny it. Truth be told, Rocky just loves chocolate, so he can tell what's bottom of the barrel.

He watches me peel off more foil so the entire heart comes into view. My eyes well over a basic thing.

Rocky knows I have an admiration for the counterfeit, and maybe that's why the reality of what we are together is as compelling as the many layers we've created on top of it.

"Thanks for spending three bucks on me," I say, meaning to be sarcastic, but my emotion softens my voice.

A smile reaches the darkness of his gaze. "You're not going to thank me for the forty-two grand?"

"Oh no, that's on you, buddy."

His laughter causes mine to rise out of me, and I could bathe in the bright sound we create together.

Literal warm fuzzies—that's what he just gave me. It's so

strangely comforting, I wish this feeling could be bottled and purchased through a vending machine.

He scrutinizes the door behind me. The idea of leaving isn't as enticing as staying here.

We linger together. It's what we've always done.

"How badly do you want to win this scavenger hunt thing?" I wonder after I wrap the coin carefully back in the foil and slip it into Jake's coat pocket. *I won't forget it.*

He raises his brows. "You really have to ask?"

I shrug, starting to smile. "I thought being dubbed the Huntsman might do it for you—it's pretty in line with your MO."

"My MO?" He nods to me. "Which is?"

"Hunting prey. Being the predator."

"Maybe if we were hunting something worthy of being caught. Fake geese don't do it for me. But for you . . ."

"Oh, I love a goose replica."

"Knew it. Fake wife." He holds my gaze for so long that we're both smiling again.

"Fake *ex*-wife," I correct. "Married only a year, remember?"

"Worst year of my life, apparently."

"Worst year of mine, too."

We can't stop staring at each other. My heartbeat outpaces my thoughts.

Rocky pushes off the metal bar. Coming closer, he plucks the envelope from my fingers and spins the first clue to me. It sent us to this Irish pub.

Find me where the luck never runs dry.

He opens my coat with a slow seduction that feels too natural. My breath hitches as his knuckles brush along my collar, down my nipples, before he slips the envelope in the inside pocket.

Blazing, I try to collect my bearings by gathering my hair into a claw clip. "I give you a four point five."

His lip quirks before a shadowy glare takes hold. "For what?"

"Seduction. Actually, four point three. You're decreasing by the second."

He doesn't take his eyes off me. It's unnerving, but I love how the intensity of him pumps adrenaline into my veins.

"You think you can do a better job?" he asks.

I place two hands on my chest. "Seductress." I put the same palms on his. "Silver-tongue. One is light-years better at *temptation*. And that would be me—" My voice catches as he pushes me up against the graffitied door. Breath ejects, and he encases my cheek with one commanding hand while he slides his leg between mine.

Holy shit. My nerve endings light up. Shock waves ripple down my limbs. Instead of sweet, caressing eye-batting, we're staking deep, penetrative glares into one another. Knives and ripping and cutting over featherlight caresses and soft little pats.

My thrumming body is screaming *yes!*

His breath is hot against my lips. "I give you a two."

"Fuck you." I try to move forward.

He pins me with his forearm to my breastbone. "One point five. Decreasing by the millisecond."

I pulsate, aching for him between my legs, and I arch my hips against his muscular build, feeling him hardening. "You want me," I rasp with desire soaking my eyes.

He stares down at me darkly. "You remember when you were twenty?"

I'm captivated by the unknown, dangerous path he's suddenly leading me down. I hear my shortened breath in my ears. "Sure," I try to say with heat.

"We were in Sedona."

My face burns. "It's barely ringing a bell."

"Barely ringing a bell," he repeats like I'm full of shit. "What about the hotel room we shared? Or the part where you watched me take a shower?"

I bake alive. "I didn't watch you." I push forward.

He shoves me back again. More breath jettisons from my lungs, and huskily, he says, "You didn't watch me jack off?" He bears too much of his weight on me, to where I can't budge, and I love the feeling of Rocky shielding my whole body with his. I love how his right hand clutches my face and his left unbuttons my jeans.

"You jacked off?" I try to play dumb—which is *dumb*, honestly.

His breath is hot as he whispers, "I saw you. I saw you watching me grip my cock."

Oh . . . fuck. The vivid memory of seeing Rocky masturbate in a hotel shower—it floods me. So does the hot wave of guilt for not turning away sooner. We've never verbally acknowledged that moment . . . *ever.*

"You watched me stroke myself up and down." He slides his hand down the front of my jeans, beneath my panties. *Oh God, yes, yes.* "You watched my muscles contract." *Yes.* "You watched my dick jerk forward." My lips break apart with a sharp breath. "You saw me spill my cum down the drain." He thumbs my clit in perfect circles. I shudder and clutch his wrist, feeling the strength in his hand between my legs.

"You left the door wide open," I rasp with not enough bite.

"Maybe I wanted you to see me." He drills his gaze into me. My body blazes with arousal, especially as he says, "Maybe I wanted to see what you'd do."

I didn't join him in the shower, that's for damn sure. "I had so much fun without you," I taunt, aching for him, but I push forward with the same sensual, devilish needling. "The whole bed to myself." I nearly grin when he pins me back to the door with hotter force, his cock pressing hard against me.

I lift my chin like I'm the victor, but we're both suffering under our own carnal spells. "Then I took off my panties," I say off my tongue, the sound oozing like sex. "And I slipped my fingers in—" My voice catches on a slight moan when his finger fills me. The fullness, the sensitivity. *Holy* . . .

He's not slow.

He pumps his finger in me with a dizzying aggression. The sexy pace is *annihilating* me. My knees tremble, my breath trapped, and he's whispering exactly what he pictured when he was jacking off years ago.

Me.

He was picturing taking me in the shower. "My cock, *ramming* inside your pussy," he breathes against my ear, "until you couldn't stand up without me holding you."

I'm so wet. He knows how wet.

He slips another finger into me. I swallow a moan and shut my eyes, then open them while the sensations ride me way too hard. He's pumping two fingers in my pussy, and I never want this closeness with Rocky to end.

I clench around his fingers in the start of a climax, but it's not enough. It's never really enough.

We both want more.

And we detonate together. Colliding into lethal, fiery kisses that steal thoughts and imprison breath. The headiness makes me lose sense of place and time, but instinct is brutal.

We know to be quiet.

Very, *very* quiet, and I find out in these sweltering seconds, where he has me in his arms, where his cock is deep inside me, what it's like to make diabolical, furious love in silence.

My ears are ringing as we shelter breath. Heat licks us. Tears seep from the corners of my eyes and his eyes. His muscles flex. Veins protrude in his neck, and my body torches to a million degrees as we resist and succumb all at once.

It feels like being ripped alive.

Don't stop, I want to rasp against his lips as he holds me, as he arches into me. We're consuming each other. Gorging from the inside out.

When we come together, spots dance in my vision, and I black out for a second. "Breathe, *breathe*," Rocky says against my ear.

Okay, it might've been more than a second. He has me propped against the wall, his hands on my hips, and I grab on to the metal rod for balance.

I blink a few times, seeing the ripped foil wrapper to the condom on the tile. At least in the heat of the moment, we're still careful.

Rocky isn't happy. "You need water?" he's asking while he lowers me to my feet and helps me step into my panties and jeans.

"No." I intake big gulps of air. "I'm fine." I pull my waistband higher on my hips. He tucks his black button-down back into his slacks, zips his pants, and I fix my hair in the claw clip, trying to decipher his expression. "What's that look?"

"You would pass out before getting caught." He's not surprised I'd go to great lengths for the job, but I detect notes of concern.

"Wouldn't you?" I shoot back.

"No." He throws the ripped wrapper in the trash by the sink, then washes and dries his hands. "Because then I couldn't take care of you."

My brows crinkle. "You don't trust I can take care of you?"

"That's not it." He scrapes his hands through his hair, taming the messy strands. "I don't like being out of control—not with my body, not like that, not with anyone."

"I get it," I breathe. "Mostly when it comes to being drugged." It's happened to me before. My worst nightmare growing up was getting roofied, and I crossed that one off the list of fears during a short con in Nashville.

I was twenty-one.

I've been so careful never to let it happen again, and due to determination and savvy, it hasn't.

Rocky pulls me into his arms. Right when we embrace, a fist bangs on the bathroom door.

I freeze. He's just as motionless.

"I gotta piss, man! How long are you gonna be in there?!"

Shit. Only the bartender was at the pub when we first arrived.

Rocky stares at me while he yells, "I'm busy! Fuck off!"

The guy grumbles from outside the door, but Rocky isn't concerned. He kisses me, and my uneven breathing levels again. I kiss him back with more certainty.

Until he presses his forehead to mine and says in an aching, rough whisper, "You need to yell at me."

I don't ask why. It's obvious if we walk out together, it'll look like we just had raunchy bathroom sex.

Which . . . we did.

I cling tighter to him. We've been in this situation before—okay, not *this* exact situation. But one where we needed to improvise on the fly.

With his arms around me, I yell, "You're such a jackass, you know that?!"

"Yeah?!" He raises his voice to the same octave as mine. He's staring at my lips. "Say it a little fucking louder! I couldn't hear you the first time!"

"YOU'RE A FUCKING JACKASS!!"

He kisses me deeper, rougher. *I love him.* My heart hammers into those syllables.

I.

Love.

Him.

I feel the heavy thump of his pulse as we meld together. As my arms weave up around his neck. He's snapped the claw clip out of my hair again. Just to clutch a fistful of the dark blue strands.

I almost moan. "Screw you," I grit out.

The heat of his body, the strength of his hands—it murders me into a blissful death I want. I crave. Forever with him.

"Screw me?!" He shoves me hard against the wall again, and the bang should be audible to whoever's on the other side. Our lips ache over each other. Toying, possessing with the need to capture and keep. "Jake didn't have the money for you! You ever think of that?!"

"UGHHH!" I growl out while fisting his leather jacket. *I love you. I love you.* Our foreheads touch again, our bodies searing against each other.

"Keep fucking complaining!" he yells. "Or how about you appreciate what I just fucking did for you?!"

I do.

I always do.

I cup the back of his neck. This is too deep. Too much. I'm

being figuratively slammed into him in visceral, tightly wound ways. "I fucking hate you!" I scream.

"Then hate me!!"

I've never loved someone more in my whole life.

He holds my face. "Slap me."

My stomach drops. "*No*," I whisper-hiss.

"It wouldn't be the first time," he says like it's nothing. Like it'd mean *nothing* to do it again.

I have had to slap him before. For the job. But this is different. "I'm not getting the reputation of being physically abusive toward an ex—so don't you *dare* slap yourself either."

"Yeah, I'm not your brother."

Oliver has one hundred percent gone the extra mile by giving himself a bloodied lip, a bruised cheekbone—and not with makeup.

"I didn't say you were," I snap back. If this was his plan to deplete the sexual tension, it's working.

Our limbs unravel from each other. The last thing he does is kiss the outside of my lips. It's a hot kiss, meant to stoke, and it singes my emotions in the best way.

Rocky has a hand on the doorknob. He turns back to me. "You first. Ready?"

And I just think, *It's me and Rocky.*

It's always been me and Rocky. From the beginning. Until the end. No one else could ever take his place. I've told Rocky this so many times, it might as well be a nightly prayer.

TWENTY-TWO

Phoebe

Wearing a semidecent pissed face, I exit the bathroom and head to the bar. Only a handful of people are here, and three heads instantly twist toward me, then toward Rocky as he trails behind with frustration.

It's like a court liaison announced our royal arrival. *Hear ye, hear ye, here are the messy town divorcés!*

As soon as I see who's at a barstool and drinking a whiskey on ice, I force myself not to stagger back.

The urge to quit the scavenger hunt plows into me.

Maybe I can just watch *Wrong Turn* in the loft with Rocky. He hasn't seen that backwoods cannibal horror flick since we were teenagers.

Watching people feast on other people is ten times better than enduring three minutes with Trent Koning Waterford.

I can't believe he's here right now.

The thirty-two-year-old jumps up from the barstool with a pompous grin. Arms spread like he's meeting his long-lost friend. "Grey!"

Puke.

I don't conceal my true feelings. I don't need to. Disgust is all over my face as Rocky bro-hugs the spawn of Claudia Waterford.

Which must be worse than the devil's sperm, because I'd rather hang out with *Satan*.

Trent is dressed like he just finished playing eighteen holes of golf. A super boring activity he did last week. With Rocky. He's in a white linen shirt and navy slacks. Oliver Peoples sunglasses are hooked around his neck. His hair is two shades darker than Jake's. All the Koning boys have a similar athletic build—fit to play polo and to pose for cologne campaigns in Ibiza. He's handsome in a generic sense.

My body physically shrivels like a prune being ten feet from him, so I seek out a vacant barstool against the wall.

"I heard the auction was wild," Trent says to Rocky. "They said my little brother was almost out fifty g's until you stepped in." He pats him on the bicep in pride, then he cuts his gaze to me. "Admit it, Phoebe, you're cute, but you're not worth that much."

I settle a glare on him. "I think I'm worth more than whatever cheap carbon atoms you're made of, Trent."

"Oof." He grins, then glances at Rocky's nonreaction and nods toward the bathroom. "You two sounded like cats and dogs in there." At this, his sleazy gaze drips ever so slowly down my body. "Our Phoebe, always so *feisty*."

Rocky is standing behind Trent and doing his best not to have a face full of venom. His jaw tics more than it should.

"Don't you think, Grey?" Trent asks Rocky, wanting him to pipe in about me.

"She's not feisty. She's *unpleasant*," Rocky says, glaring at me.

I glare back. "Pot, meet kettle."

"Unpleasant little Phoebe," Trent tsks while appraising me again.

"The only thing *unpleasant and little* is your . . ." I swallow the biting retort. Rocky is smearing a hand over his mouth, fighting a look of rage, but it's not toward me. My stomach is in vicious knots.

Trent is grinning. "Go on. Say what you mean."

No.

I'm trying so fucking hard not to make this harder for Rocky.

He's warned me ad nauseam that insulting Trent only provokes him—that Trent gets off on the hunt, on taking whatever he can't have, and that also includes anything that remotely belongs to his youngest brother.

And to Trent, I'm basically considered Jake's property.

He wants *me*.

I want to deck *him*. But I can't even try, because Rocky will break character to protect me, and we all need him to maintain this friendship.

Disgruntled, I face the bar and do my best to ignore Trent. It's safe to say that most of the rumors at VCC about the firstborn Koning heir being a grieving widower are bullshit.

He's not a tortured, lovesick soul.

He does, in fact, have eyes for other women.

Wintering at the Alps with him, I saw Trent openly checking out ski bunnies on the slopes. Later, he bragged to Rocky about the threesome he had with the girls. It's not like the holiday trip consisted of any servers or club members who'd pick apart the tender story about the death of Trent's wife.

It was a Koning family and closest (most-trusted) friends vacay. One I'm pushing so far down, I actually might puke.

While Trent collects his whiskey off the counter, I ask the bartender for a Guinness, and Trent moves toward me, about to approach.

I stiffen.

"I should be the one offended." Trent speaks to me. "You still haven't called me TK when it's the *very* thing I only allow my nearest and dearest friends." He raises his whiskey to me. "That's you, Phoebe."

"I'm touched," I mutter.

"I bet," Rocky interjects, outpacing Trent to reach me. My heart pitter-patters at his sudden closeness, and while I'm smushed against the green paisley wall, Rocky towers and presses a hand to the plaster, high over my head. He traps me with his build.

Hairs rise on my arms. The adrenaline rush—the static electricity of him—dizzies me.

I hear whispering from the bar.

No one tries to protect me from what looks like an uncomfortable situation between me and my ex-husband, but I am . . . really, *really* turned on. I cross my legs while my pussy thumps, still sore from the bathroom.

Rocky drops his head down to whisper against my ear. "He's a little prick."

I fight off a smile.

Yes, he is.

The bartender clears his throat as he attempts to slide me the Guinness. And Rocky pulls away from me, just to claim the sole barstool at my side.

Trent whistles lowly and takes a seat next to Rocky. "Grey, you are intense, man. Give the girl some space."

"Long day, TK," Rocky says with a heavy noise, like he's blowing off steam.

Trent squeezes his shoulder. "Here, take mine." He gives him the glass of whiskey, then asks the bartender for another.

Rocky subtly blocks Trent from ogling me. He's hunched forward, arms on the wooden counter, taking strong sips of the amber liquor.

His quiet, simmering rage isn't that hidden, but he has reason to be publicly upset. He just had a fight with me. Jake is dating me. I think it'd be worse if he had to conceal these real feelings, too.

I ease some.

And I wonder if it's been harder on Rocky, not just because we're truthfully together now, but maybe it's also because I'm more myself in Victoria. This is my personality with my real, chosen name.

I'm not playing much of a character here.

The fakest thing about me are my ties to Jake.

"Don't be upset with me, Phoebe," Trent says, trying to capture my attention from behind Rocky.

"I'm not upset." I lick beer froth off my lips and take out the envelope from the coat.

"I know you're soft, though," Trent says, elbow on the bar and head perched in his palm. "It's Jake's type. *Soft girls.* Little duckling types." He walks two fingers across the bar counter toward me.

Rocky sets down his glass in Trent's finger-walking path and acts oblivious to the move. Trent doesn't notice his new BFF is actively cockblocking him.

I don't give Trent the pleasure of a retort. His ego is the size of Mount Rainier, and after what happened in the Alps, I really couldn't care less if he fell five hundred feet off a ski lift and broke every bone in his body.

I remember when we first met, he pulled me into an overly

friendly hug and picked me up a foot off the ground to spin me around like we were seeing each other for the thousandth time and not meeting for the first.

He said, "Well if it isn't my little brother's skunky girlfriend. Jake's told me absolutely nothing about you." His blue eyes were soaked in charisma. "Gotta be honest, we were all shocked he's even with someone. It's been so long, Jordan and I were convinced he might have ED."

First impressions were made, and I absolutely did not give him the benefit of the doubt. Not that I needed to.

He's a tool. Among other things.

Rocky strikes up a friendly conversation with Trent that I eliminate myself from. I attempt to flag down the bartender again, but he's busy chatting with a gray-haired woman in a Columbia puffer vest.

She clutches a stout and hovers over a copy of the *Weekly*.

Beckham North, the wiry bartender in his mid-twenties, gives me a nod of acknowledgement but returns to chatting with her. Wow, I thought we had a slight moment earlier— when he interrupted Rocky being a jerk with a quiet beer slide.

This sudden brush-off feels personal. He's filled in a handful of times at the country club, and I might have commented on his weak mojitos.

Or maybe he's just really great friends with Erik.

Ugh. *Reputations.* Hailey might have one as an easy fling, but I'm getting the feeling I'm the bitchy one. I rub the creases of my eyes.

"You didn't want to bid on a Clue Girl?" Rocky asks Trent.

"You know me. The town traditions are Jake's thing." He sips his new whiskey. "I'm too busy for this trivial shit."

Translation: *I'm more important than my brother.*

Maybe it's fake-girlfriend defense mode, but I lean over the bar to get a good look at Trent. "Jake's far busier than you, I can assure you." I hear my rising anger.

Rocky cocks his head at me and sips his whiskey. His sharp, warning look says, *You're digging a fucking hole. Be careful.*

I know I'm falling into Trent's ego trap, but I have decent enough upper-body strength. Trying to pull myself out— worth it.

Trent laughs, spinning on the stool to face me. "What is my brother up to these days? Mopping the floors of the club? Replacing broken lightbulbs in the rentals?"

"I can tell you what he's not doing," I retort. "He's not drinking Macallan in the middle of the afternoon alone like a sad little—"

"Pest?" Rocky says to me.

Why does that almost make me smile? I scrunch my face and battle the bright feeling away with a deep sigh. Do not look smitten by Rocky. Do. Not.

"Let her finish." Trent waves him off, then rests his chin on his fist, mockingly attentive. "I'm all ears."

Whatever I say will only fuel his ego engine. Steam leaves me all at once, and I slump back on my stool.

Trent drops his hand back to his liquor. "Can't volley with the big men, Phoebe?"

When I don't respond, his interest begins to deplete.

He won't risk appearing too needy for my attention, so I'm not surprised when he twists to Rocky. "Like I was saying about Hank. He thinks he's a better doubles partner than you are, but he serves like he's a ten-year-old wearing drunk goggles. I'd be better off getting Val to play mixed doubles, and she can't even hit the ball over the net." He laughs, lifting his drink to his mouth. "But at least she has a better ass to look at."

Beckham overhears and barks out a laugh. "Girl's a flirt, but she won't put out."

I glare. Okay, he's not getting a tip from me.

Trent motions his drink toward him. "That's what you think."

Rocky takes a stiff swig and smiles when Trent looks at him.

Acid burns my throat, and I wave the envelope at Beckham. Finally, he notices. "Ah, the first Clue Girl of the day. Hold on a sec. I left the geese in the back." He wipes his hands on a dishcloth and disappears.

Rocky glances at me. "I'm chilling with TK. Go hunt for the geese without me."

"Really?" I frown.

"I'm busy." He holds up his glass and flashes an assholish smile.

Trent slings his arm around Rocky like his best friend just stated, *Bros before hoes, bitch.*

My scowl hurts my jaw.

I don't want to leave him here with this insufferable dickhead. Yes, he's giving me an out to sail *far* away from Trent's presence, which is the equivalent of tossing me a life ring in an open ocean. But if Rocky's drowning, I don't want saving.

I'm prepared to drown with him as his coconspirator. His partner in crime. His girlfriend. His pretend wife. All the fucking things.

I use the envelope as a coaster under my pint. "I have a beer to finish, too."

Trent smirks. "Can't stay away from us, can you?"

Ignore.

I take an angry sip of beer. Rocky shakes his head at me,

pissed. Fine. He can be mad, but I'm not ditching him just because Trent nauseates me.

He hasn't abandoned me when I've kissed Jake on the cheek. I won't abandon him when he kisses Trent's ass.

Beckham returns, placing a gold-plated goose beside my Guinness. I like the occasional beer, but I'm more of a wine drinker. Still, I find myself taking big gulps to stop myself from telling Trent he's a douchebag.

Trent switches his conversation with Rocky to the stock market. It reminds me of being teenagers and Addison crash-coursing us through Nasdaq and the S&P 500. I had such a difficult time picking up call options, whereas Hailey breezed through it like she was birthed on Wall Street.

I finish my pint and order another. Rocky is at the bottom of his whiskey glass and in a full-bellied laugh over some inside joke I'm not privy to.

Then the pub door bursts open.

A flurry of platinum-blonde hair follows. Hailey barrels to the bar, landing between me and her brother.

"Whoa," Trent laughs.

"I'd like a golden goose," Hailey says to the bartender, half out of breath, like she's ordering a drink and not a cheap paperweight. Her angelic goth spirit lifts my morale, and I instantly smile.

We side-squeeze hug in greeting.

"Hey, Rocky," she says quickly to her brother.

He up-nods, acting indifferent to Hailey. He has to in front of Trent.

"No time to talk," she says in a rush to me. "I have a trophy to win." She takes the goose from Beckham. Chains jingle on the belt loops of her black cargo pants.

Spinning around, she runs smack into Jake Waterford's

chest. "Umph," she grunts, and he places his hands on her shoulders, steadying her.

"Sorry," they say in unison.

It's no surprise Jake was tailing her, seeing as how he bid for and won Hailey in the auction. She must be outrunning him from clue stop to clue stop.

"I'll hold that for you." He's already football gripping a golden goose, and Hailey is quick to hand him the second one.

"There's my little brother." Trent rises with wide-open arms.

Jake freezes in the middle of the pub, fisting the paperweights. The gray-haired woman at the bar deserts the *Victoria Weekly* for the new drama rolling in.

Hailey is piecing together the puzzle since I keep her freshly up to date on all things Koning boys. Her brown eyebrows lift to me, and she mouths, *Backup?*

I shake my head. "Go win that trophy, Hails." This is the brightest, bubbliest I've seen her in so very long.

Jake even tells her, "I'll be a minute. Text me if you need help solving the clues."

"You sure?" She hesitates.

"Yeah, I'm sure." He's staking his brother with a deeper glare. "Really, go." He sounds serious, almost pleading—like he's a half second from picking her up and carrying her outside because the bar is on fire.

If we're all going up in flames, Jake is okay with me being singed, but I think he classifies me as someone who is meant to light the bomb and withstand the fire. We're all a little more protective of Hailey.

I remember, though, how she orchestrated our move here . . . just to protect me.

She tries to unglue her feet. "Okay . . . okay, thanks." At

this, she walks backward to the door, ensuring this spaghetti Western won't end with a shootout.

Then she leaves.

Jake refuses to step into Trent's arms. "I told you not to talk to Phoebe." His voice is cold and ice-chipped.

Time to leave. I guzzle the rest of my beer.

Rocky is taking cool, casual sips of whiskey.

Trent lets out a sharp laugh and drops his arms. "That's what you're pissed about?"

"Stay away from her," Jake warns.

I rush to his side and feel the strain of leaving Rocky's. I wish beyond anything he could just . . . follow me.

But he stays close to his new friend. His narrowed gaze shoots daggers every which way, but the real target is the one he can't hit. Not yet, anyway.

Every job has a setup. Because when we pull the rope, we want to ensure the mark will be drawn so close they won't realize they're in a vise they can't get out of. There's no room for failure.

I won't screw up.

Trent raises his whiskey glass. "There my baby brother goes again. Jake Koning Waterford. Creating drama out of *nothing.* His only real talent."

At least he has one. I bottle the retort and start to leave the pub, forcing Jake to follow me.

Trent waves a couple fingers at me. "See you later, Phoebe." He says it just to dig under Jake's skin.

It's working on him.

And on Rocky.

TWENTY-THREE

Phoebe

My spine is stiff and my body pale, find me where I tell my tales.

It's not a graveyard like I thought. It's a bookstore.

Jake solves my next clue in under two seconds, and once we're inside Baubles & Bookends, we seclude ourselves in the least visited section. Bird-watching. I don't dust off a guide to spotting warblers, not when Jake is forcing himself from pacing by death gripping a shelf.

The *top* of the shelf to be exact.

He is the tallest Koning boy.

By now, I'm used to craning my neck to meet his eyes, especially when we're standing only inches apart. He said he's just shy of six-three. I think it's more likely he's six-four. An inch taller than my brother Oliver. If anything smells like a boast or success, Jake undercuts it. He's not even a humble-bragger.

He's just plain humble.

I've never met someone with his affluence who would

actively downplay all their accolades—everything they've done and everything they can do. Like how they were recruited for a top-three US polo club but declined, or how they were Mr. Victoria's Sweetheart five years—five freaking years!—in a row.

It makes what Trent said even more infuriating.

Jake has talents. *Plural.* His lack of patting himself on the back is making me want to take out a *Jake's Awesome* ad. Hoist it in the air, pass around flyers, buy a billboard, print it in the *Weekly.*

"Are you okay?" I ask him, more concerned as his breathing sounds arduous and his eyes hold a steady glare. It pushes me to say more. "Trent was wrong. You're not talentless. Really, I think he's jealous of everything you have going for you, which is a lot."

Jake tries to calm down. "I don't really care what my brother says about me. It's like a fart in the wind."

I let out a surprised laugh. "Did you just make a joke?"

"A small one." His lips begin to rise, too.

I share his smile.

Jake is very secure about who he is. It's admirable . . . and it reminds me of Rocky. No one can tell them who they are.

Jake peeks out the store window. As if half anticipating Rocky will rush out of McIntire's to find me. I'm fully anticipating his arrival, and I'm trying not to be disappointed if it doesn't happen.

Then we check to see if any bookstore browsers are around. Coast is clear.

"How long were you at the bar with Trent?" Jake asks, hushed.

"I don't know," I say truthfully. "It's not like Rocky and I knew he'd be there."

He can't stop shaking his head. "You shouldn't be in a room alone with him."

"*Rocky was there*," I emphasize. Did he not see him?

"He can only do so much, Phoebe," Jake whispers with a type of raw concern that tries to cut me open. "This is torturing him . . . and you."

"It's always been a little bit of torture," I murmur with slight heat. "It's what we're used to. It's what we're good at."

Jake swallows, then shakes his head again, staring at a kid's stuffed pelican. His eyes glass and become bloodshot before they reach me. "Your parents abused you—after what they did to you six, I feel like a *monster* for using what they taught you for my gain."

"Don't," I choke out. "My mom was kind to me. I loved her. They gave us so much—"

"They took so much more from you, Phoebe."

I know they did. I sit with this for a beat. "I think Rocky could always see that in a way we couldn't. We were so blinded by love, but they couldn't shine a light bright enough at him." I choke on a strange laugh. "And he could've left us, you know? He could've walked away, but he never did. He stayed for us even though he hated them." I stare dazedly around the bookshelves. "Now we all hate them . . . and we're still working with them."

Addison and Elizabeth have remained in New York, with the occasional pop-in to spend a lunch or two with Claudia. They've been giving Claudia reasons to think I'm low-class trash and not worthy of Jake or the Koning name. Even going as far as making her paranoid that we might be getting engaged.

His mom's distaste for me is helpful. She's become ruder,

and I hope she continues losing tact. It means she's more likely to do something awful.

Everett has stayed in Connecticut, strangely. He's slithered his way into the Koning estate. Jake's father hired Everett as staff manager for the housekeepers, groundskeepers, pool boys, private chef, etc.

"It's hard to see whether we could do this by ourselves," I whisper to Jake. "I'm more scared of trying to do it without them and failing, because failing means . . ." *Death*. It feels like death, at least.

He reaches out and holds my hand. Not in a romantic way. It's just pure comfort, purely consoling. "I'm not going anywhere, even if it does fail. This is my home, and some things are worth sticking around for."

I nod robustly. I think of Hailey racing around for The Hunt. I think of Nova out on the *Salty Miss* staring up at twinkling constellations in the night sky. I think of Oliver grinning as he picks out tacky sweater-vests for the Ugly Sweater Run. I think of Trevor trying to be involved in everything. I think of Rocky . . .

Of his laughter when I fell on the ice rink during the Winter Wonderland Festival. Of how he skated effortlessly closer and helped his sister up—and then teased me.

It's not about the quirky events. We've all been more ourselves here than anywhere else. Our relationships to each other have never been this real in one place, one city, one town. Not until now.

"I think I know what you mean," I say so quietly.

His gaze drops to me. "I'm glad you're here. I'm glad he's here with you, too. That you all are hoping to create something for yourselves. And the only peace I really have is knowing I can fight for it with you."

It feels comforting knowing he will. "You're a good guy, Jake."

"You're a good person, too."

I snort.

"I'm serious, baby. I think I've gotten to know you pretty well so far." His eyes move over a bookshelf, and I'm sensing he sees a bystander-turned-eavesdropper.

I'm careful not to act suspicious, so I just stay in tune with Jake as he says, "Like how you love teatime, only for the finger sandwiches and petit fours."

True. I smile. "Who doesn't love a tiny bite-sized cake?"

"You're very familiar with etiquette. But you prefer when there are less forks set out, purely because they take up space on the table."

Also true.

"It's not practical," I note.

"You love the sand. Most people hate when it gets in their toes and ends up everywhere in their house, but you love the remnants of a place. You love taking pieces of *somewhere* with you."

Chills slip down my arms from being seen. It's not uncomfortable like I'm standing naked in front of Jake.

I realize I like that he sees me.

His eyes flit from me to the bystander, then back down to me. "And you're damn near proficient at beating me at poker. You've never lost on purpose, which I appreciate."

"Hailey taught me, you know. She's way better than I am. You should ask her to play sometime."

"And that right there—it's not self-deprecation as much as it is your love of her." He reads me. "You ride hard for others more than you ride for yourself."

"All likely true." I motion back to him. "You absolutely

adore animals, but you don't have any pets of your own. It's not that it's too much work, because you're used to juggling a thousand and one errands and tasks. You just don't want them to be lonely when you're not around."

He seems impressed, but then says, "You're the second to notice."

I'm interested. "Who's the first?"

"Who do you think?" Must be someone I know by the way he's speaking.

I squint at him. "Hailey?"

"Yeah. Hailey." He has a soft smile, and I love that he's grown fond of her. Who wouldn't? She's *amazing*.

"She would solve the mystery of Jake Waterford before me." *That's my best friend!* I could shout it from the rooftops of the world. "But you weren't that hard to crack."

"A little hard, come on." We share a smile.

"You hold people at arm's length," I mention. "You're scared to let them into your world, but you've let us in."

He nods. "Yeah, I have."

I nod back, too, because we've done the same for him. Then I point out, "And you hate cilantro."

He opens his hand like it's obvious why. "It tastes like soap."

"It's *delicious*, and you're not the only one who thinks it's soap."

"Grey," he nods, already knowing. We really have spent too much time with each other. Unlike Jake, Rocky will eat anything with cilantro, despite being repulsed by the flavor, and Jake will pick out every speck of green leaf with his fork.

I smile bigger, just thinking about Rocky, and Jake is witnessing my mushy, too lovey-dovey reaction.

I scrunch my face.

He just says, "He's your forever person."

It's not even a question. "I can't lose him." It'd feel really catastrophic now, but likely, it always would've.

I think about how Jake has never wanted to bring a date home to his family, and he's lived a life trying to protect everyone around him, much like Rocky. Only, Rocky has finally let himself chase after love and be with me, despite the risks around us.

Jake isn't willing to take those kinds of risks for love. Not until he's usurped his family.

"Maybe one day, you'll be able to have a forever person, too," I tell him.

"Maybe," he breathes, then his brows furrow at the window. "He's jogging over here."

Sure enough, Rocky is jaywalking across the street to reach the bookstore. I press my lips together to keep the enthusiasm at bay.

Once on the sidewalk, Rocky forces a smile at Jake through the shop window. It looks like a *fuck you* smile, and Jake side-eyes me. "Your ex."

"You mean, you didn't sign us up for a couple's date with the devil?" I mouth, *My favorite.*

He laughs.

I hear the chime of the door as Rocky enters Baubles & Bookends.

My real boyfriend finds me with my fake one in the back. He pretends to examine the many shelves, but really, he's taking stock of potential eavesdroppers. "So your brother is a real sack of shit," Rocky states quietly enough.

"He's getting worse with Phoebe, isn't he?" Jake asks, concern and anger hardening his face.

Rocky speaks in a harsh whisper. "The longer you're with her, the more he wants her. It's that *painfully* simple, unfortunately."

Jake rubs the bridge of his nose, and when they both stare down at me like I'm the fragile doll threatening to crack, I'm offended. I've worked *so hard* not to be the one to compromise a job.

I can't be the reason they start backing out now.

I spot a flash of blonde hair behind a bookshelf. Relief washes over me when Hailey rounds the corner.

"I've got them all," Hailey pants, her hands on her knees and her tote bag of golden geese thumping to the ground. "We . . . just . . . need . . . to go . . ." She motions toward the town square. "To win."

Pride swells so strong. "That Huntswoman title is yours, Hails. Go get it."

"She doesn't get the title, technically," Jake tells me.

"Jake does." Rocky raises and lowers his brows with bitterness.

I'm pissed. "So Hailey did all the work and you get to be Huntsman?"

"I can forfeit it," Jake says, "but they won't give the title to her. She didn't pay to participate."

"I'm just a Clue Girl." Hailey catches her breath and shrugs at me like *you know how it is.*

Yeah, it's bullshit, and if we were here in positions of power like Rocky, Hailey could've played this game from the other side and been dubbed Eighty-Eighth Huntswoman. But she's been a broke server at a country club for me.

"We'll meet up in five?" Jake asks me and Rocky. *Somewhere more private* is an unsaid note. We agree, and Hailey reminds us about the DNA results tonight—where me, my brothers, and the Tinrock siblings are planning to read them together, also in private.

I have a feeling half her chipper spirit is knowing answers are on the horizon.

Hailey picks up the tote bag of golden geese, but Jake reaches out a hand and slips his fingers in the canvas straps. She blushes a little when he slings it on his shoulder like it's a rucksack. "Thanks," she says with a rising smile.

"It's what I'm here for."

Hailey nods a ton, and he nods back, their lips lifting higher and higher. They're locked into each other like we've completely disappeared from the bookstore.

They're just friends . . . right? I haven't really picked Hailey's brain about her current crushes, one being Carter, because when I do bring up guys, she switches the subject to *research*. I figure I'm just causing her unnecessary stress, and that's the last thing I want to do.

My eyes ping between them, then to Rocky.

He has an expression like he'd prefer to teleport to a remote island and dive into the abyss.

"Let's go get your trophy," Jake says.

"My trophy?" Hailey smiles even more up at him. I think I like this for her. Is she glowing?

"It belongs to you, if you want it."

Her smile touches her eyes. "I have a perfect spot for it. Now we just have to run." She takes his hand and literally sprints, tugging him along on her chase for first.

Jake, Rocky, and I are alone in my bedroom above the bookstore later that night. Tension from Baubles & Bookends has most definitely returned since Hailey isn't here to cut through it. I'm sitting cross-legged on my bed while Rocky leans a hip against my dresser, and Jake sits on my vanity ottoman like we're about to have a therapy session.

Which I, frankly, don't know if I'm going to be good at. Maybe I suck at therapy. Maybe it isn't for me.

I raise my palms. "I know you both care about my well-being, but you don't need that to affect the outcome of this job. This isn't *anything* out of the norm."

"What's the norm?" Jake asks.

"Our norm was fucked up," Rocky says.

"So is Trent." I give him a haughty smile.

He returns one with a little more acid. "Cute."

"The *cutest*." I lean back on my hands, and I reflexively spread my legs open. Jake is right *there*, and I didn't . . . I didn't even think about him.

I go numb, and I swing my legs closed. My feet thump to the floor. Their concern is asphyxiating.

Jake is hunched forward with his fingers steepled to his lips.

"Phebs?" Rocky pushes off the dresser.

"That wasn't for you . . . I mean, I wasn't trying to seduce you. I was on autopilot." My face burns.

"It's fine," Rocky assures me. He keeps his distance, probably because I'm shooting him looks to stay five feet away. I simultaneously do and don't feel like being touched.

I tuck a strand of hair behind my ear. "Let's just stay the course. Let's not nuke any plans because you think I can't cope with an asshole."

"He's a little more than an asshole," Jake says, his strong jaw tensing.

"But sure, let's downplay it," Rocky says with the tip of his head at me. I take it all back—I don't like their amity. Maybe it was better when they were at war with each other.

I think I fucking hate this.

"We know what he is," I say more angrily. "When it comes to Trent, you don't need to think about my feelings."

Rocky looks at me like I've driven off a cliff without him. "Yeah, that's not possible."

"We can try," I protest.

He shifts his stance with heat. "I'm no better than my fucking father if I don't think about your feelings. So no, I'm not trying that out like it's a new sports car."

"Don't make this about me," I say with pain in my lungs. "This is about the two of you being scared for me, when you don't need to be."

"Phoebe," Jake says gently. "We have *reason* to be. The Alps—"

"I know," I cut in fast, not wanting to crack open that dingy closet. I swallow a lodged lump. "I can handle Trent."

"I can *barely* handle him," Rocky confesses, bowing toward me with his hands on his thighs. He's not touching me, but it feels like he's reaching inside of me and fisting my heart. "You're not taking one for the team."

Carlsbad. What I did. It crashes into me. My eyes sting. "But you'll take the one?" I point out as he straightens up. "And then the second, the third."

"You've taken *enough*, Phoebe."

"And you haven't?" I counter.

"It's not a competition to see who can suffer the fucking most."

"You're right." I cross my arms, holding my elbows. "None of us should be suffering, but it's kind of the consequence of scamming people. It's not all sunshine and rainbows with pots of gold at the end."

Rocky has his hands threaded on the back of his neck. He's

just staring at me like I'm volleying off a wall he wants to tear down.

I want to be of use, but it feels like I'm warring with myself just trying to be.

"Jake, you wanted me to handle this, didn't you?" It's why he believed I could be his fake girlfriend in the first place.

"I meant more for you to handle my mother, who pressured one of my girlfriends to eat *dog food*—this isn't the same as that."

God, Claudia.

I let go of my arms.

Jake rests his elbow on my makeup vanity, but he looks far from relaxed. His whole body is as tightly coiled as Rocky's. "Can you be honest with yourself?" Jake asks me.

"I usually am."

"Then really, would you be okay in a situation where neither of us could get to you, and you were alone with my brother? Because we wouldn't be okay."

I'm *angry* that this is even a problem we're dealing with.

Rocky can tell, because he says, "This isn't your fault, Phebs. This is how these fucking pea-brain men are."

"I know," I say hotly. "I've dealt with them since I hit puberty and grew tits. I *get it*."

I hate it.

I want Trent to suffer. Horrible, *horrible* pain. Blood simmers underneath my skin, and I breathe hot breath through my nose. "We're hoping to get dirt on Claudia and Trent, something that could ruin their reputation with the board. Get them axed. Tarnish their social standings in Victoria. Well, Trent is *right there*. We've seen it—"

"No," Rocky cuts in.

Jake has a confused wrinkle between his brows. "What are

you talking about?" he asks, then glances at Rocky, who is tunnel visioned on me.

"It's what our parents would suggest," I say, more to Rocky. "You can't even deny they wouldn't. Everett would tell me to pretend to be drunk and lie there as he tries to—"

"It's not happening," Rocky says so softly, in a tone meant to cradle me. "It's *not* happening."

I take short, choppy breaths, uncertain of what I feel. Because I want to say, *I can do it*. I've learned to be numb to it. I can do anything, but I've stopped wanting to put myself in those situations. To put Rocky in that position where he has to be on time.

Right. On. Time.

Because if he's too late . . .

I squeeze my eyes shut. "It's the easiest . . ." I trail off because it *is* the easiest way to trap Mr. Firstborn Fuckbag in his own misdeeds. But it's also the hardest on us. "I was wrong— this isn't a normal job. If it were the norm, one of us would record him trying to get with me. Then Trent would pay another one of us off to either clean up the mess or to keep quiet. After that, we'd be gone, and he'd *still be there*. Do you know how infuriating it is?" I breathe fire into my lungs. "To walk away with money that's like *pennies* to them while they get to just . . . go on?" I let out a shrill laugh. "The sting of shame fades in time, and they've learned *nothing*."

They're both listening, and I can't tell if I'm speaking to them or to the walls or to a higher power I've never believed in before.

But it just pours out of me. "I've loved what we do, not for the cash grab, but for the high of the victory. Of the retribution. But the lows are so low because we can never cut deep enough, and I'm . . . so . . . *angry*." I force out the words. "I'm mad that guys like Trent think they can get away with murder, and maybe they really can. I'm mad about the Alps." My chin tries to quake. "Because that *so easily* could've been another girl, if not me. And I just keep thinking, that girl wouldn't have had a Rocky, and . . . she shouldn't have to *need* one."

I blink past the scalding tears to try to see Rocky, but I can barely make him out clearly through the glassy film. "I shouldn't have had to need you, but our moms knew in this stupid fucking world, a *man* is what protects me from another man. I am a *thing.*" I press my hands angrily to my chest. "To people like him, that's what I'll always be." I blink a few more times, and tears stream down my cheeks.

I wipe them roughly away.

Rocky is close.

He drops to his knees in front of me. While I'm still on the edge of the bed, his hands hover around my elbows. "You burn at the same temperature as me," he breathes fiercely. "So when you say you're *angry*, I fucking know." His voice is hoarse. "*I know.*"

He's been there.

He's always been there.

Our rage brews together. Visceral, unyielding, controlled fury. Our love is just as volcanic, and there is an undercurrent, a need inside of us, to just explode.

My eyes sear. "Then you know, here, in this town . . . it's a chance for us to do more, Rocky. To really make someone pay."

Trying to help Jake claim the Koning crown—it takes bad people out of power. People who are diseased by it, who should've never had it in the first place.

I take a breath, adding, "And what if there's not another way than to use me? What if he does this to another girl?"

"That doesn't mean you should be that girl."

"But I could be the last one," I say, sounding hopeful. "It could end with me."

Rocky never shies from me. "Ask yourself, Phebs, what do you really want? I know you can get through this job. I know you can take it—like you always fucking have. But after Carlsbad—"

"I don't want the Fiddle Game to change anything." I wince because I know, deep down, it already has.

"It's okay if it did," Rocky says. "Really, it should probably change how you look at the job." He edges forward just a little but doesn't touch me. "My sister brought you here because she saw how Carlsbad affected you, and you can try to keep running away from it—but it's here again. In this job." His gaze grips mine. "You said this is our chance to do more. It's also our chance to do things *our way*. Your choice, not theirs. What do you want to do, Phoebe? *You.* Not me, not them. But you."

I intake slow, cavernous breaths, and I careen forward, my forehead pressing to his. Lifting his hands to my cheeks, I place them there and hold them against my face.

His large palms encase me. They're warm. Safety. Devotion. Power.

He's breathing harder. "Phoebe." He's scared of my answer, but he would do anything for me. He already has.

"If there's a way where I don't have to be in that position with him, then I think . . . I know I'd choose not to be. You take Trent. I take Claudia. I can handle her."

His hand slides into my hair, clutching. He presses a hot kiss against my lips. It beckons me forward, and when it breaks, it's not enough.

I want to be wrapped up in him. "Can you hold me?" I ask in a whisper.

He casts a look over his shoulder while he lifts me in his arms. "This has been fun and all, Jake, but you're going to need to get the fuck out."

I swear Jake is smiling. "Bye, *Phoebe*," he says pointedly at the door, not offering that same farewell to my real boyfriend.

"Bye, Jake." I'm entrapped by the man who has me so completely. In every way that matters, I am Rocky's.

TWENTY-FOUR

Rocky

TWO MONTHS AGO
THE ALPS
Northwestern Italy

On the foothills of the Matterhorn, overlooking a prestigious Italian ski town, the Konings' chalet stands like a beacon of wealth. It screams *look at me!* with its six floors, three-sixty-degree views of the snow-peaked mountain, an indoor pool, spa and sauna, fully outfitted gym, and state-of-the-art wine cellar.

Oliver was the one who looked around and casually said to me, "Some people have too much."

I know this is why he's a grifter. Not for the power, like me.

He does it because he truly believes there should be a limit to wealth. That billionaires shouldn't be able to hoard more than they need and create generations of lazy, entitled spawn. So he takes from them.

Being here, under the guise of Trent Waterford's best friend, I've never felt more of a hunger to *take*. And it has nothing to do with the fucking Ferrari in his garage.

As Trent's plus-one, I'm silently expected to stay by his side like a Pomeranian. Be engaging enough to be a good time without overstepping and taking the spotlight for myself. Never be too boring or dull as that will get my plus-one invite revoked on the spot.

Never say *no*.

I am a yes-man in his presence.

Yes, I will surely take the shot ski with you.

Yes, I think that snowboarder looks hot.

Yes, we can go on the black diamond again . . . and again.

Yes, you should definitely ask out the ski-lift operator and her friend.

Yes, I'll watch the threesome.

My brain is on fire. Trent's head only has room for three thoughts. Drinking. Fucking. Money. And let's be clear, it's not how to *make* money. He's just finding new and creative ways to spend it.

My muscles ache from the slopes as I shed my winter coat and toss it on the king-sized bed. Clock on the bedside table reads one a.m., and my brain thumps from the Macallan that Trent likes to drink before lights-out. *Yes*, I'll have a nightcap with you.

I groan as I kick off my boots. I've barely seen Phoebe since we arrived five days ago. Trent took a different private jet, stating he needed some peace and quiet for the ride to concentrate on "work," but he invited only me.

He slept the whole flight.

Customs was a breeze. It always is, but I still hated that Phoebe had to go through it without me.

Oliver was there, though. Along with Collin Falcone—Trent's former best friend who would've been invited on his jet, had I not taken his place. Collin is still living his frat-house glory days, which Trent thinks is both amusing and pathetic.

Collin is too coked up most of the time to really give a shit.

When I told Oliver to look out for Phoebe, he said, "She's my sister. What else would I do?" I was still holding my breath.

He saw and said, "I'll be careful." Oliver's go-to phrase holds about as much weight as a paper airplane.

He makes *me* nervous when we fly. He's a showman, and you don't want to be anything but invisible in a fucking international terminal.

Even if we're led to a private jet on a private runway.

At least she was with Jake. I grimace at my own thoughts. Does he count as part of the team?

Maybe.

I roll my eyes and take out my phone, wondering if she's even awake. Jake and Phoebe spend most of their time hanging around the chalet and reading books like this is a rest-and-relaxation retreat.

I'm not lying to myself—I am jealous.

I'd rather be doing anything else on my holiday than entertaining Trent Waterford, but I'd also be kicking myself if I brushed off his invite. I have to be here. Close enough to protect Phoebe and close enough to keep myself in Trent's good graces. I have to do the hard fucking thing.

It's Christmas Eve.

This can't be all bad. Maybe I can sneak into Phoebe's room. Kick Jake out. It all makes sense in my head as I send her a text. **You awake?**

She's quick to reply.

Phoebe: Outside. Hot tub.

I want to ask if she's alone. But I don't. It wouldn't matter. Every ounce of my body wants to go to her. Be with her.

I put my boots back on, quickly tying the laces, and when I'm down on the first floor, I realize I forgot my coat. The cold winter air chills my exposed flesh, and I follow the gray slated walkway to the back of the chalet.

Lights twinkle in the distance, down the ridgeline where hundreds of smaller chalets nestle close together by the village. Up here, we're alone. Wind howls through the foothills, and I avoid deep breaths, not wanting to wake tomorrow with a sandpapered throat from the dry, frigid air.

Three more steps, and I hear soft, muffled voices.

My disposition plummets down the fucking mountain. *Great.* She's not alone. Another night third wheeling to Phoebe and her fake boyfriend. Love this for me.

Two more steps, and I stop suddenly, her voice now crystal clear.

"You should really go inside," Phoebe snaps. "Your brother will hate that you're out here."

Laughter. He's laughing. And I know it's not Jake. I know it before I even hear Trent's smarmy voice. "See, Phoebe, brothers are a special breed. Jake knows what's his is mine. It's been that way since we were kids playing with Hot Wheels."

Razor-sharp adrenaline slices through my veins as I high-tail it around the corner. I stumble into view like I'm tipsy from the Macallan just as Phoebe says, "I'm not a fuck-ing *toy.*"

Heat gathers in her brown eyes. Heat that smolders like a furnace inside me. Stoking my frustrations and anger.

Trent swings his head in my direction, and I push it all down . . . and down . . . and down.

I'm drunk. *So it appears.* I hang on to the nearest object, which happens to be a gas-lantern lamppost. "Grey." Trent smiles, but it's tighter than usual. He's annoyed at me.

I haven't been invited into this moment. I am *unwelcome*.

That gnaws at me in a deeper way, especially as I see Phoebe's back glued to the edge of the hot tub, like she's physically repulsed by him.

"TK, that whiskey, man . . ." I let out a chortle. "I can't find my room. This place is a fucking maze."

Trent laughs, and this time it's more genuine. "It really is." He props his arms on the stone edge. "Second floor. Third door on the right."

I narrow my gaze at him like I'm just piecing together where he is. "Why—why are you in a hot tub with Phoebe?" I ask.

"That's a fantastic question," Phoebe snaps at him. "What are you doing here, Trent? And why are you naked?"

"Naked?" My brows cinch together, and I try to smother my fury. *Confusion. I'm confused*, I tell myself. Definitely shouldn't look like I want to snap his fucking neck.

Trent glances between us. "This is a Jacuzzi. What—are you *both* prudes?" He laughs at that. I don't say anything. My blood is on fire.

He stepped into a hot tub with her.

Naked.

Nude.

His dick out?

Does he have an erection?

I want to break his cock in half.

He's cornering her. To make her feel small. To do something to her? Phoebe was alone. Even I know that's not right. Not okay. Not in a million *fucking* years.

Trent's gauging my reaction. Even though we're "friends,"

Phoebe is still my ex-wife. "She's not like that," I tell him. "She won't even take her clothes off for a massage."

Her cheeks are red. Flushed at the lie.

She'd go naked for a lot less. Hell, she's been nearly naked, sometimes fully nude, during cons before. I think back to the job Phoebe never names. Where we simulated having sex. She had no clothes on at one point. It would've been better if our parents weren't behind it. If it really felt like her choice.

Trent looks Phoebe over again like I gave him permission to appraise her. "I doubt that."

"Fuck off," Phoebe growls.

He smiles, and I can tell her resistance is a game to him. It turns him on. But he must also know this isn't a good time. Maybe it was before I showed up, but now, now he's standing up and letting the water drip off his body.

Phoebe was right. He's *naked*.

His semihard dick hangs at her eye level, and I watch Phoebe crane her neck to stare at me. "Collect your friend, Rocky," she says.

He's not my friend.

"No need," Trent says, hopping out of the hot tub. He grabs a towel and throws it over his shoulder. "I'll see you tomorrow, Phoebe," he calls out. He passes me and gives me a sly wink like we're in on a secret. *The* game.

He wants to fuck her.

Three seconds go by as he passes my body. Three seconds of opportunity to slam him against the wall, break his fucking nose, and bury his head in the snow.

I let those three seconds slip between my fingers.

I can't. *I can't.*

Being his friend is more important than defending her.

Even thinking those words sends brittle air into my lungs. When he's inside, I make my way to the hot tub, housing regret in my core with each step.

Phoebe shoots a glare at the shadow he left behind. "He's vile," she says softly. Too softly.

I sit on the stone ridge of the hot tub and shed my boots. "Are you okay?" I ask her.

Her jaw sets. "He wanted . . ." Her voice drifts off.

"I know what he wanted, Phebs." I dip my bare feet into the bubbling water as her eyes shift to mine.

Fear. She's scared. "He would have taken it, if you hadn't shown up."

My stomach roils. I want to tell her, *He's not going to get away with this.* But we're not fleecing Trent yet. Tonight isn't about pulling the rope, and so he doesn't get punished. He doesn't get broken. He gets to walk away.

Nova would say we're just surviving at this point.

"I should've filmed him, or at least gotten an audio recording," she says, cringing like she failed to bubble in an answer on a Scantron sheet.

"He's in his own private hot tub naked. People would say you could've gotten out. They'd say he was just being charming. What that was"—I point back to the chalet—"it wasn't enough dirt to bury him, let alone make him cough. You know that, Phebs. It wouldn't have been worth the risk to do it."

She's blinking a lot. "Yeah . . . yeah."

"That's not the plan either. He's not your mark," I remind her under my breath. "You shouldn't be alone around him."

She lets out a hotter breath. "Jake told me the same thing. It's not like I invited him to the hot tub."

"Where is Jake?" I ask.

"In bed," she mutters. "We spent all night at the clinic. Even after he asked, there were still peanuts in his salad dressing. I had to inject him with his EpiPen."

Trent must've known that. It's why he took the opportunity to corner her tonight. I let out a long sigh and run a hand through my hair, the wind tousling it. My skin feels colder with my feet in the scalding-hot water. Phoebe dips her chin under the liquid, and she stares off.

She's always been a hard book to read.

Closed off.

It's what we're taught to do. It's hard to open up, even to the people you trust, when you spend most of your life hiding not just your secrets but your truths.

"You're really okay?" I ask her. After Carlsbad, this can't be an easy situation to brush aside. If she thinks *I'm* the only reason she was able to be safe from Trent tonight, that's not an uplifting thought. She usually has all the confidence in herself to get out of bad situations.

She tilts her head side to side before she shakes it in a *no*. Her face breaks for a split second, and I jump into the hot tub with my clothes on, grabbing her just as she starts to cry. She buries her face in my chest, and my fingers tangle in the back of her blue hair.

I tell myself I'm her ex-husband.

I can talk this away if any of the staff see. If any of Jake's family comes out.

She needs me, and I'm not pulling away. Not for anything. I hold her, cupping the back of her head for another few seconds before she gathers herself like she's a windup doll and being spun into the upright position. It's a trained move. Something I recognize.

Her tears are gone. Dry.

Her shuddering has stopped. She pulls away, and her eyes flit to my lips. Christ, I want to kiss her. To reassure her.

"We can't," she whispers and rubs at her eyes. "Rocky." She looks me over, realizing I'm drenched in my clothes. "We can't."

The pain grips my muscles, and I release her from my arms. She floats back to the edge of the tub. The strap of her pale pink bikini slipped off her shoulder, and I stare at her bare skin. Her eyes graze my chest, my shirt suctioned against my muscles.

Attraction teems around us with a longing ache, billowing with the steam from the water. Emotion tunnels from her to me. Our eyes meet, and in the dead of night on Christmas Eve in the Italian Alps, I make her a promise. "If he tries that again, Phoebe, I'll kill him."

TWENTY-FIVE

Phoebe

NOW

I wiggle my toes in the darkened sand and look out at the murky black ocean water. Moonlight is scarce, and I hear the waves lap more than I see them in the night.

Wind pierces my pink strawberry sweater, and I squeeze my arms against my body as I trek closer to the meetup spot. I quickly realize I'm not the first one to the beach.

Trevor.

Ugh. He wouldn't be at the top of my list to spend one-on-one time with, but I'm hoping everyone else shows up soon.

He tosses wood into a firepit. The hood of his dark maroon windbreaker shadows his angular face. My toes sink deeper in the soft sand, and I hold a pair of black Louis Vuitton heels by the straps. They were an "I love you" gift from Jake that I opened in front of his family during a Waterford brunch.

Claudia nearly choked on her mimosa. Trent told me that Jake hardly ever gave his past girlfriends presents, so I must be different. The implied wink and smirk let me know he meant *different* in a sexual way. A shiver of revulsion skates down my back.

Regardless, I like the heels. I think after we make Jake heir, I'll keep them.

Trevor groans when he sees me land on the opposite side of the unlit firepit. "You're early," he says with edge. "Hailey said to be here at three." *Three in the morning.* A fact that Rocky disliked since it's considered the witching hour.

"It's fifteen till, and you're early, too," I shoot back.

"So I could sit with my thoughts." He takes out a box of matches from his jacket and strikes one. *"Alone."* He tosses the matchstick into the pit. There must already be kerosene on the wood, because it lights in a fiery plume.

"Did things go that poorly with Sidney?" He won her earlier at the auction, and I'm wondering if some of his angst is from spending the afternoon with Victoria's *Sweetheart.*

He says nothing.

Fine.

But I frown more, finding the silence too disconcerting, so I try again. "I thought you were tired of being the loner," I say. "Haven't you been begging to be a part of the team since you were ten?"

He glares into the flames. "Yeah, and you're the reason I'm not."

"What?" I shift my weight, confused.

He pulls a flask out of his windbreaker. "Don't act surprised. You're not dumb."

I rock back a little. It's a strange compliment from him. Because Trevor is certifiably a genius like Hailey, and I am not the brainiac. I've felt leagues behind in that way.

My face falls more. He is right, though—I had an itching

feeling he blamed me when we were growing up, but hearing him confirm it out loud gnaws at my insides.

My grip tightens on my heels. "I'm not barring you from being on the team. You're here, aren't you?"

"Yeah, I'm here," he says flatly. "Background character in this play." He takes a long swig from his flask.

"No one thinks of you like that. Everyone has their roles."

His nose flares, and he drops his hand with the flask, letting it hang loosely at his side. "Yeah, well, you're in *my* role. If it weren't for you, I would've been paired with Rocky during jobs. I would've mattered."

The casual honesty from him catches me off guard. I'm used to the snarky jabs and caustic, immature banter.

"Trevor." I walk around the firepit to his side. Nineteen. He's nineteen. Which isn't that young anymore—but he will always be the youngest. There's a part of each of us that feels a responsibility toward protecting him. Maybe we butt heads and annoy each other like a brother and sister would, but I never thought he didn't matter. Not to me. "You matter—"

"Stop," he deadpans. "See, this is why we don't have heart-to-hearts, PG. As soon as you see a problem with any of us, you jump in front of a train, thinking you can fix it."

My stomach coils. "So I'm not a person who stands by and watches the people I love sulk in their own misery. Is that so bad?"

"It is when *you're* the problem. Your existence is the fucking problem. And unfortunately, you're one of five people on my Do Not Kill list."

The fact that he even has a list . . . ooh, *scary*. I swear he tries to be tough—maybe to live up to his moniker.

"Thank you?" I say half-heartedly.

Heat has been extinguished from his gaze. "It's only by association to Rocky. Otherwise . . ."

"You'd off me?"

"Maybe."

Gremlins are more terrifying than him, and I think those balls of fur are pretty fucking cute. I try not to poke fun at his weak sinister demeanor when he's being serious with me.

"So I'm in the spot you want," I say, testing out this heart-to-heart thing. Maybe I can't fix it, but I can understand him better.

He kicks an exposed log with his sneaker. "I just want to work with my brother." Okay, that's actually sweet, and seeing as how I love working with Rocky, I do relate to that feeling.

"I don't choose the roles, Trevor. And even if I did get offed, you realize that Oliver would most likely replace me?"

He nods slowly. "Yeah, I know. But that'll change, right? When it's just us six? We can decide our roles ourselves." His darkened gaze meets mine with a glimmer in it. It's hope.

I see what Victoria means for him. A chance to obtain what he's always really wanted without the control of our parents.

"Yeah, that's the idea," I whisper softly, letting that hope reside in the air. A tether between us.

He offers me his flask, and when I take a sip, our siblings approach the rising flames.

Hailey has a thick manila envelope in her fingers. Dark crescent moons still shadow her eyes, but she raises the envelope of DNA results like it's a gold medal, bounding closer to me. Her excited energy makes me smile.

I meet her halfway, then we trek back to the firepit together, and Oliver isn't far behind Hails. He sneaks up on her and bear-hugs her from behind like they're fifteen again. She holds his arm, maybe so she doesn't trip and fall. Then he steals the flask from my grip. "Midnight beverage for the wicked," he says and tips it into his mouth. "What about you, Hailstorm? You've been bad or good?"

"Good, mostly."

Oliver pouts.

Hailey doesn't even look, but it's like she knows he's teasing her. She smiles at the sand, and his smile stretches wider and wider at her.

"And you, Phoebe?" Oliver asks. "Good or bad?"

"It's a matter of perspective," I point out.

"Ah, yes. It's all in the eye of the beholder."

Oliver squeezes between me and her, then he slings his arms over our shoulders, pulling us against his sides like we're at college again, or boarding school. Secret societies. Clandestine meetups in cemeteries. Our mysteries.

Our codes.

Our truths.

Hailey laughs at a joke Oliver makes, and my smile brightens from within. For a moment, it does feel nostalgic. Happiness isn't in short supply when we're all together. It's one of the few times where it feels abundant.

Nova is already at the firepit. He tosses another piece of wood in the circle. Flames spark and crackle. He holds out a hand to Oliver, who silently passes him the flask.

I peel away from my brothers, just as Rocky emerges from the darkness of the dune grass. He immediately joins me. And he slips his hand in mine.

His lip tics upward. "Hi," he says. I'm not pulled into our messy past, as much as I'm relishing this moment—*us together*.

"Hi," I reply, falling into the depths of his gray eyes.

Trevor has gray eyes.

Hailey has gray eyes.

And the envelope in her hand will finally bear the truth with real, concrete proof. I intake a deep breath of anticipation.

We all face the fire.

Rocky appraises each of us in a slow sweep. "Before we read the results, I have something to say."

"Say it fast," Nova says, tightening his utility jacket around his body. "It's fucking cold out here."

Light flickers from the bonfire, and I stare at the glowing embers while Rocky speaks.

"They raised us," he says. "For better or worse, they've molded our lives into what they are, and there's no going back from what we've done. But *who* we are—a piece of paper isn't going to tell me that. I already know who I am. I've *always* known who I am." Flames flicker against the darkness of his eyes. He touches a hand to his chest. "Spider." He points to Trevor. "I'm your brother." Then he looks to Hailey. "I'm your brother." Then to Oliver. "I'm your family." Then Nova. "I'm *your* family." His gaze lands on me and the intensity tunnels through me in a long beat. "I'm yours," he says in a sheltered breath. The unsaid words cling to the air: *I've always been yours*.

Rocky unfixes his gaze to stare at each of us, emotion circling around like a spinning coin. "My purpose in life isn't to bag millions. It's not to tear down miscreants or fuck over rich pricks. It has been, and always will be, to protect the five of you. So I don't care what that paper says. It's not going to change *this*. Us." He takes a deep, readying breath. "That's it."

Nova sways on the balls of his feet. "I'd clap but my hands are too cold to take out of my fucking coat."

Oliver wears a lopsided smile. "What Nova is trying to say is you're our family, too, Rock."

"Same," I agree.

He glances down at me, the heat of his gaze warming me more than the bonfire.

"Let's just hope this isn't a Luke and Leia situation," Trevor pipes in from the other side of the firepit.

My head whips to him. *Ew.* The *Star Wars* reference is not lost on me, and I can't even imagine Rocky being my actual brother. We're one hundred percent not related. I'd know.

I scowl. "That's impossible."

"Not impossible," Hailey mentions next to me, and my heart shoots out of my rib cage. "Improbable."

"Highly improbable," Rocky clarifies. "Elizabeth, Addison, and Everett have been pushing us together since puberty. They're fucked-up, sure, but that'd be on a different, disgusting level of fucked."

"Agreed," I say.

Oliver sets a hand on Trevor's head. "Demented."

Trevor whacks his hand off. "I'm just putting it out there so you all aren't shocked if the *highly* improbable comes to fruition."

"It's out there, all right," Nova grumbles with a harsher swig from the flask.

"Hailey," Rocky says, rubbing at his eyes. "Please get this over with."

"Okay . . ." She rips open the envelope with shaking hands. "There'll be many different results in here. All of our DNA has been tested against Elizabeth, Addison, Everett, and also each other." She leans closer to the firelight, her widened eyes skimming the results quickly. "Trevor . . ."

"First up," he says and swipes his flask back from Nova.

Hailey's bugged, unblinking eyes reveal the answer before her words do, so I'm not surprised when she says, "You're not related to any of us."

"Shocker." Trevor lifts his flask up to the sky in cheers. Then downs the alcohol for longer than a couple seconds.

"Whoa, save some for the thirsty." Oliver captures the flask before Trevor can chug it all, and as Oliver takes a casual sip, he exchanges a brief, protective look with Rocky.

Hailey rapidly, frantically sifts through the next three pages. Her eyes dance a mile a minute.

"What is it?" I ask, worry seizing my lungs.

"I-I . . ." Her eyes grow wider with confusion and another emotion as they ping from me, to Nova, and then stay on Oliver. It takes me a second before I realize she's happy. "You're triplets—fraternal triplets. It's real."

"What?" I squeak out. My hand flies to my mouth, and a rush of relief surges through me in a tidal wave. Not just siblings. *Triplets*.

Oliver and Nova come to my side in a quick flash and scoop me up into a brotherly hug. "I knew," Oliver declares. "I fucking knew it. What'd I say, Nov?"

"You knew it." Nova grins and lets Oliver skate a hand over his head in affection. I cry into Oliver's preppy trench coat, and Nova hugs me tighter. I didn't know how much this would mean to me until right now. My brothers.

My brothers.

"Phoebe," Hailey says quietly, breaking me from my reverie. "Y-you're her daughter."

My ears ring. "Wait . . . ?" I whisper, and Oliver's and Nova's arms slowly drop off me as Hailey delivers the news.

She gives me a sad, pained smile. "Elizabeth is your mom, and that makes her Nova and Oliver's mom, too."

The world rotates around me. She didn't lie. She *hasn't* lied. I twist to Rocky, and his jaw is set in a hardened line. I've hated her for the deception, but has she even deceived me?

Hailey flips another page, and her chin trembles before the papers slip from her fingers. "Shit," she curses. "Shitshitshit." Rocky drops to his knees, and I follow suit, quick to gather up the pages from the sand before the wind carries them into the fire.

I pause on the paper that Hailey must've just read. It's *her* results. "Hails," I breathe out, my insides kneading. Rocky leans into my shoulder to read it.

"What does it say?" Trevor asks.

Hailey swipes the tears under her eyes. "I'm not related to anyone."

Oliver squints in confusion. "Not even Addison?"

Hailey shakes her head. "No one." The way she says it sounds so tortured, like she appeared out of thin air.

"You're related to *someone*," Rocky tells her, his voice edged. "You're not an immaculate conception, Hails."

"She is pretty divine, though," I offer with a friendly nudge to her shoulder as I rise to my feet. It doesn't draw a smile. Her gaze is lost in the fire. We've all known the only way to break her obsession over this is to find answers, and I wish our positions were reversed. I wish Addison was her mom—if only to splinter her hyperfixation.

"What about you?" Trevor asks Rocky.

I shuffle through the papers in my hand, but I don't have Rocky's results. They must be on one that he pried off the sand. Sure enough, when I turn to him, he's reading a page. His eyes carry nothing. No pain. No lament. No happiness.

They're just void.

"It seems like us Tinrocks are all the same," Rocky says and hands it off to Nova.

My brother reads it with furrowed brows. "You're not related to anyone," he confirms. "So what does this mean?"

"It means Elizabeth lied to my face," Rocky says, then looks to me. "To yours. She told us that Hailey and I were biologically Addison and Everett's."

"Why would she do that?" I say, pained again. "She knew we were already questioning Trevor's paternity."

"She thought we wouldn't go this far," Rocky says, scratching at the tag at the back collar of his shirt. He rips it off.

Nova crumples up the paper into a ball. "I don't think any of them thought we'd ever go this far."

"The triplets," Hailey whispers in a haunted daze. "The perfect shills."

Her words hang in the air agonizingly. She's right. Why would we question Rocky's and Hailey's identities if Nova, Oliver, and I are so clearly related?

"So are we all adopted?" Trevor asks.

Rocky raises and lowers his shoulders. "Who the hell knows? But if we ask them, they're going to feed us another round of bullshit."

"I can dig harder for answers," Hailey says with a determined, anxious nod.

We all share a collective worry. "I think you've been digging hard enough, Hails," I tell her. "Maybe let go of the reins a little on this one?"

She slips a blonde hair behind her ear, the lobe and cartilage covered in studs. "No," she says. "I'm in charge of being five steps ahead. My role. My responsibility." She spins around on her boots and heads back for the street.

"Hailey!" Rocky calls out. *"Fuck."* He's the first one who chases after her, and Trevor follows behind, careful not to stumble in the sand. The Tinrocks disappear in the night together.

Nova balls up all the results and chucks the papers in the fire. My brothers and I watch them burn.

TWENTY-SIX

Rocky

Passing through. It's what we've been doing the past couple of weeks. Hopping from motel to campsite to budget inn like vagabonds. I yearn for a mattress not covered in piss stains. AC that works. A smell other than sewer or mold. Simple fucking things I always take for granted between jobs.

Sometimes I wonder if our parents eke out these "between" days as a grisly, sordid reminder of what our lives would be like without conning. If I asked, my mom would just tell me we can't rush the planning process.

I'm not even sure what our next job entails. Hailey and Trevor have been in Athens, Georgia, hanging around the university's campus while they help the godmothers construct the con. If I had to guess, we're ripping off either a rich college student or a tenured professor.

"Two hundred it's a professor," Oliver tells me after I express the theory.

"Not taking that bet." I stuff my jacket in a duffel bag, then check my burner phone again. "The odds are too even."

No missed calls. No texts.

The yurt stinks of dog piss, so the faster we can get on the road, the better. Oliver's long legs stretch across a cot. It's not terrible accommodations for a state park, but I'd rather be at a five-star hotel right now than breathing in the warm, stale air that's barely circulating from a box fan.

A two-person table and camping chairs are pushed up next to the tarped wall, and the microwave and coffeepot might as well have been teleported from the early nineties.

Oliver is still in his underwear. He's flipping through a *GQ* catalog he picked up at the last gas station and rubbing expensive cream on his forehead. "Get dressed," I tell him. "I'm going to tell your sister we're hitting the road."

Phoebe slept in the yurt across from ours. *Alone.* Hers has a full-sized bed, not two cots, and I offered to crash on the floor so she wouldn't be by herself, but she acted like I was sacrificing oxygen.

"I'll tell her." Oliver hops off the bunk and practically pole vaults into his pants.

Oliver Graves is a fantastic liar, but I know him too well.

And I can count on one hand the number of times he's rushed his morning routine. He's three steps from the exit just as I casually slip in front of the yurt's wooden door. Blocking him.

Oliver zips up his pants, then runs a hand through his hair, trying to brush back the golden-blond strands without a comb. He's been a blond for half a year, mostly posing as a surfer from sunny California or the beaches of Florida.

He waits for me to move. I don't. "Why can't I tell her?" I ask him.

"Because you know Phoebe," he says. "Grumpy in the morning. Doesn't become a ball of sunshine until her second or third cup of coffee. Let me save you from her attitude."

I like her attitude.

But that's the last thing Oliver needs to know.

I flash a dry smile. "Thanks for the offer, but I don't need saving. Especially not from your grumpy little sister." I spin around to grab the doorknob, but Oliver puts a hand to my shoulder.

"Wait." He tries again. "She probably wants to sleep in." He's hiding something. It's becoming more obvious, and concern skates through me like a shotgun blast.

"Too bad for her." I shake off his grip and tear open the door.

Oliver reaches past my arm and pries me off the door. He's holding the knob hostage in a tight fist, and I twist my head over my shoulder. He's physically blocking *my* exit now. Our eyes meet, and I realize I'm the only irritated one. He's more . . . desperate.

"Oliver—"

"I promised I wouldn't say anything to you." He folds like a plastic chair. Maybe he realizes I'd yank out the truth from him sooner rather than later, and he's just defaulting to *sooner.*

"Say what to me?" I ask.

"*Phoebe* made me promise. You know, my triplet. Do me a solid and let me keep my promises to my *sister.*"

Like hell.

He emphasized *sister* because I have a sister the same age. It's a commonality between us. He wants me to relate and be sentimental over promises I've made to Hailey, so that I'll back off here.

If I were a better person, maybe I would respect that, but I fully expect people to try and rip secrets out of me. Maybe he should've, too.

"Do me a solid and move your hand," I tell him.

Oliver groans. "Rocky. She's *fine*."

Phoebe might not overshare her life with me like she does Hailey, but I didn't think she'd actively keep important shit from me. We've been wound up in too many jobs, too many situations, to be that closed off to one another.

So I can't conceptualize what she's hiding. Other than she's hurt. Did I do something? Is she pissed at me? I'd rather talk it out. Figure it out. I can't just *stand here*. Idle.

"How am I supposed to know she's okay?" I ask. "I haven't seen her this morning. Neither have you. But you two are keeping secrets, and I'm supposed to what . . . sit here and twiddle my thumbs? No thanks."

He doesn't let go of the doorknob, but after a short breath, his resolve fractures. "You really want to know?"

"No, I'm just playing mind games," I retort.

Oliver raises his brows. "It wouldn't be the first time."

"It would be with you," I tell him.

"Yo también te amo." He winks, and from my well-endowed Spanish knowledge, I know he said, *I love you, too.*

I stare deeper into him. *"Oliver."*

His fingers loosen on the knob, and he confesses, "She's with someone."

My stomach knots. "Come again?"

"The park ranger from yesterday—"

"The guy who didn't rub in his sunscreen?" I grimace. He had white splotches all over his nose and chin, and he'd been restocking pamphlets at the visitor center when we arrived yesterday evening.

Oliver gives me an intrusive once-over. "Yeah, him. He

spent the night in her yurt. She told me not to tell you because she thought you'd freak out, and she's not wrong. Is she?"

No.

She isn't wrong.

Oliver sees through me. He sees I care about his sister on a level that shouldn't be advertised to anyone.

"Let go of the door," I tell him.

He still doesn't. "She was going to sleep with someone eventually, Rocky. We've all had sex. We all lost our virginities years ago. One-night stands are our norm. This isn't any different, but if you wanted it to be, maybe you should've done something."

I glare. "You wanted me to fuck your sister?"

He's rattled by nothing, so I don't know why I even tried to throw him. Oliver volleys back, "You want me to fuck yours?"

I grind my teeth. "Don't fuck with Hailey."

His eyes sweep my face. "You don't think Hailey would fuck with me first?" Honestly, I try not to dive too deep into their psyches, so this is making my head throb. He's quick to continue, "Whatever Phoebe wants, that's what I support."

"And you think Phoebe wanted to sleep with me?"

He shrugs. "You said it."

Want is a desire. One I share with her.

Can't is where I've been. I can't have sex with Phoebe. I can't be with Phoebe like that, and possibly Oliver believes she's been saving it for me. That I could've been her first. That I could've satiated all her *dying* needs—that she didn't need to go run after a gangly, sunscreen-splotched park ranger to fulfill anything.

Like everything in our lives, it's not that simple. She wasn't waiting to have sex just so she could have sex with me. I'm almost positive about that.

I comb a hot hand through my hair. She's alone, vulnerable, with a guy I barely even said two words to.

And Hailey is miles away. Phoebe's best friend, who she relies on and confesses secrets to, isn't even around. Just Oliver, who's so laissez-faire about this that it's driving me insane.

"Just move," I say.

Finally, he releases the knob, giving me enough room to whip the door open and push through. I don't expect him to follow me. He doesn't. Because if someone is going to wear the badge of a certified asshole, it's going to be me.

I have no change of heart when I cross the graveled road to her yurt. None when I put a fist to the wooden door. "It's me!" I call out, not saying her name. Not knowing what alias she slipped the park ranger.

In the thirty seconds that I don't hear a reply, I fight within myself not to break the door down. *She's fine*. I repeat Oliver's words in my head.

But countless times, I've seen men gawk at her, salivate over her. I've borne witness to marks putting their hands on her.

He's not a mark, I remind myself.

A park ranger. A guy. She chose. She chose him. Those are the last three words in my head before the door swings open.

Phoebe doesn't allow me room to peer into the yurt. She slips through the crack of the door and shuts it behind her. An oversized pink Strawberry Shortcake T-shirt stops at her thighs. I bought that shirt for her two years ago. It'd been her seventeenth birthday. She acted like it was just *okay*, then proceeded to wear it every night between jobs.

Did she have sex in it?

"Nice shirt," I say.

She keeps her eyes on mine. "Nice abs." I'm not wearing a

shirt. The hot morning air feels thick and sticky against my bare chest. "Or lack thereof."

I have defined muscles. A fucking six-pack.

She's not wearing a bra. I can only tell when she crosses her arms and the fabric tightens over her tits. Her nipples are pebbled mounds like it's below thirty outside, and for some agonizing reason, I can smell her. Not him on her. Just Phoebe—a pungent, intoxicating, *sweet* odor that I want to bury my face in.

I'd say she's on her period if it weren't for the fact that she just had sex. I doubt she'd want to lose it while she's bleeding. She must be ovulating, and my senses are going fucking feral for her.

I flex to force down this primal urge. My body needs to get a grip. We're not the last two people on earth. We don't need to procreate to sustain the human race.

I don't cast a quip back in her direction.

We're both standing in a crater of tension and a vat of pheromones. Our eyes never shifting off each other.

Her lips pull in a deep frown. "Oliver told you?"

"To his credit, he tried hard not to." I stare past her, at the door. There are too many things I want to ask her. *Are you okay? Why him? Why now?* Oliver was right—all of us, except Phoebe, lost our virginities ages ago, a fact we all learned through truth or dare one bored night at a Four Seasons.

Which was recent. Maybe recent enough that it'd been on her mind. Maybe she was irritated that Trevor had sex already. He lost it at thirteen. He said to a lifeguard at the hotel pool. Thankfully she was around his age.

Hailey had been fourteen. Oliver, fourteen. Me, fifteen. Nova, fifteen.

Sex has never been something to protect. It's a way to blow

off steam. A way to release pent-up emotions. We fuck and move on.

Except . . . Phoebe.

She's *nineteen*. Nineteen. And she's never had sex. She explicitly told me it's because of her mom. That her mom likes to know everything about her crushes and love life, and she figured it'd be better to wait to open that can of worms.

I always thought maybe, deep down, she's worried for the same reason I am.

Now that she's had sex, our parents will put her in worse positions in cons. More sexual. Lewder. I've never brought up my fears. Never wanted to instill my worries in anyone else. As if saying them out loud will manifest them somehow.

But here, outside the yurt, knowing things have changed, I just go with one of my million questions. "Why him?" I ask.

She uncrosses her arms in a huff, caught off guard. "I don't know, Rocky."

"You don't know why you slept with him?"

"He's *nice*." She glares.

I cringe. "Nice?" My cinched brows rise higher. Have I read her wrong? For this many years? Since when does she like *nice*? Maybe she wouldn't like me in bed. Maybe she'd be turned off if I pulled her hair and pinned her down. Maybe it doesn't fucking matter—because I'm never coming inside Phoebe Graves.

She grows hotter. "Is that why you barged over here? To quiz me on my hookup? It was an A-plus, stellar, over-the-moon event. Practically God-tier worthy."

"Wow," I deadpan. "Hit me with more of those overbaked platitudes. Tell me more lies."

She scowls. "I don't need this overprotective routine. I already have two older brothers."

I roll my eyes at the word *older* when it's by *minutes*. Emotions are gnawing on my insides. "I'm not trying to be your brother." Those words are almost a growl.

"Then what is this?" Phoebe asks.

I let out an angry breath. "Hailey isn't here. I'm just trying to be your friend . . . I guess." Is that what this is? *Doubtful.* Because I really feel like storming into the yurt and dragging the park ranger out by his ugly hat. And yeah, in my mind he looks like Smokey Bear.

Her brown eyes carry less heat. "Just because this is my first time doesn't mean I haven't done things. I'm not so different from you." She sizes me up for a slow beat. "We've both sucked cock. We've both eaten pussy—"

"It's not a competition," I cut her off. Knowing we're alike in a lot of fucking ways. We both feel attraction on a wide scale. We both have a sexual appetite. But only one of us has been safekeeping their virginity like it means something.

Like it *meant* something.

Her cheeks turn a deeper shade of red.

"Piper?!" the park ranger calls out from inside her yurt.

"One second!" she shouts back, not opening the door. I'm a little surprised she's brushing him off and not me. She rotates back to me. "Hailey's not here, but I plan to call her before we leave. So if you're trying to be her stand-in, you're dismissed." She shoos me away like a fly.

I don't move. "We're heading out on the road in five. So how are you going to ditch the park ranger?"

"I'll give him a fake number." She gathers her hair in a pony and twists a scrunchie around the brown strands. It lifts the bottom of her tee, flashing her lacy blue panties, and my eyes flit down to her pussy, then up to her.

Phoebe looks dizzy at either my expression or closeness.

Resting her shoulders against the door, she takes measured breaths through her nose. "You never said if you liked it."

"Liked what?" I ask.

"Your first time. Was it everything you hoped for?"

"It was okay, C-minus, unimaginative, uneventful, border-line boring." I watch her eyes fall to her toes, and I can't read her fast enough.

Her eyes slowly rise to me again. "Your first fuck is never supposed to be the best, right?"

Is she talking about me or her or us? My pulse hammers in my veins. I stare at the door again. "Did he hurt you?"

"No," she forces out. "He was nice. Remember?" She's not lying.

I push my hand through my hair. "So you're giving him a fake number, then what?"

"Then I'll tell him to call me later, but he won't ever reach me."

"You think that'll work?" I ask her. "If this was an A-plus, stellar, out-of-this-world, God-tier-worthy experience for him, do you think he's going to just let you go that easily?"

She thinks about it for a second. "If you were Hailey, you'd be telling me to dine and ditch."

I cringe.

Jesus, I can practically hear my sister in my head. Did I already know that's Hailey's MO with hookups? Yes. And I'm happy she chooses to ghost her one-night stands rather than give them a chance to be clingy shitbags.

I'd say I want the same for Phoebe. But really, I don't know *what* I want for Phoebe other than for her to be . . . mine? No, not mine. I can't have her.

I don't fucking know.

I don't.

She's digging her shoulders farther into the door, but her hips are angled out toward me. It's unconscious, I think, how much she's splitting her knees apart. How much she's opening herself to me.

My cock is aching in my cotton track pants, and I'm trying not to get a fucking hard-on. We're both aroused. We're stoking each other's arousal just in these silent seconds, *staring*, and I hate the idea of her going back in the yurt and the park ranger smelling her.

I know nothing about him.

He's nice.

That assessment isn't good enough for me.

I edge closer to Phoebe, and her breath catches.

My muscles contract. "So this is the part where you ditch," I tell her.

She peers back, but the door is still shut. "My bag . . ."

"I'll grab it," I say.

She frowns and straightens up. "You sure?" She's not worried about the park ranger. Not concerned about what I'll do or say to him when I get in there.

It makes me feel better that she doesn't give a shit about this guy. Makes me feel worse that her first time was as meaningless as mine.

I nod. "Yeah, just start the car for me."

"Can I borrow your phone?" she wonders.

I dig in my pocket, then place my cell in her outstretched hand. She smiles, the first one I've seen all morning, and I know she's excited to dish to my sister. Not to me.

We're not best friends.

We're something else.

She steps onto the graveled street, and I head into the yurt. The park ranger is lying naked on the full-sized flimsy mattress. He immediately jolts when I enter, then he reaches for the thin sheet to cover his dick.

"Don't bother, I'm not looking," I tell him.

"Who the hell are you?" he panics.

"No one." I reach down for Phoebe's duffel bag by the door. It's already packed like I knew it would be. Quick exits are a thing we do.

"Hey!" he barks. "That's not yours!" He's not even moving a pinky toe off the mattress. Maybe he is *nice*.

"It's not yours either." I try not to get a good look at him. Don't want the mental image of Phoebe's first in my brain. I will die happy just picturing Smokey the fucking Bear. "Have a nice life." I leave the way I came.

He doesn't put up a fight, which is a little disappointing. I would've loved to punch him in the face.

Two steps away from her yurt, I feel a vibration in the duffel. I pull Phoebe's burner out of her bag. *She did not give that wet noodle her number.* Phoebe's not dumb.

I flip open the phone and put it to my ear. "Hello?"

"Rocky?" Elizabeth's honey-coated voice is unmistakable. "Is my bug with you?"

"She's around. I can get her." I walk toward the car, but stop short when I see Phoebe crouched on the ground behind the silver Chevy Impala. With her phone to her ear, she presses her other hand to her forehead.

She's crying.

Fuck. My stomach clenches.

I wait and hear her. "It just kind of sucked, Hails. He made me do all the work, then he lasted like five minutes. If that. He came so hard, thanked me, and fucking rolled over . . . yes, away from me. It made me feel like a glorified sex toy . . . hell,

I bet sex dolls get more affection than that." Her voice cracks, and I back away before she can catch a glimpse of me.

Fire blazes in my lungs. I'm breathing out toxic fumes. It's taking too much control to not storm her yurt and sock that fucker. Remorse, guilt, balls up in my chest just as fast, and I wonder if Oliver was right. If I should've just slept with Phoebe.

I can't.

We can't.

I feel like I'm physically being ripped in half. Pulled in two directions so forcefully, the pain down my core is visceral.

"Rocky? You still there?" Her mom is still on the phone.

"She's actually busy," I tell Elizabeth.

"That's all right. We have an issue all of us need to go over."

I go still. "Everyone?"

"Yep," she says casually, like we're dealing with a missing set of keys. But no *issue* is that small if it means a group meeting with all nine of us. "I'll call you with coordinates in about an hour. Just head due west until then."

"Anything you can tell me over the phone?" I wonder.

"MySpace isn't the only thing blowing up," she says. "Facebook is gaining legs. Especially out here in the colleges."

"Shit," I curse. Social media. My mom has been warning all of us that we need *new strategies* to combat the rising popularity of posting pictures online. Guess it's that time.

Not looking forward to ditching a job in favor of a family grifter seminar.

But our parents haven't made it this far without being smart, and I want to learn everything I possibly can from them. It's the only way to stay ahead of their own game.

TWENTY-SEVEN

Phoebe

J esus fuck," Rocky groans, staring at his phone in the middle of the grocery store aisle. I halt my shopping cart next to the dairy fridge. It's twenty minutes until closing, and besides the cashier, no one is in the grocery store. Except for Hailey and Oliver one aisle over.

We've been talking more freely than we normally would, but it feels like a measured risk since this store is on the edge of town. Hardly the one favored by locals.

"What is it?" Jake holds a bottle of Bordeaux by the neck.

"Your needy bitch of a brother," Rocky says, those words coming out so casually it even takes me aback.

My brows shoot up. "Okay, that was nasty, even for you."

He runs a hand through his hair. "I can't help it. Trent's a parasitic leech." He reaches absentmindedly for a carton of milk while texting with his other hand. "He wants me to come over for poker night."

I wince. Poker night for Rocky is an art of restraint. He

could clean out the entire group without blinking, but he has to actively try to be average.

Rocky sees he grabbed the skim milk and puts it back with a scowl. I reach for the chocolate milk and pass it to him. His gray eyes soften at the gesture, but we're in public. Can't kiss. Can't hold hands. It's not as painful as I thought it'd be, because a deep look at his gaze says, *Later.* And our *later*s tend to bring the most sweltering heat.

Jake watches us carefully before his eyes roam around the empty grocery store aisle. Both Jake and Rocky wear dapper suits like they stepped out of a board meeting an hour ago, but really, they attended a wine-tasting evening at the country club.

I served guests New Zealand whites from the region of Adelaide Hills and did my very best to annoy Claudia. I kept offering her a taste, and her lip curled higher and higher.

She wants nothing to do with me, and even when she commanded "Go" and swatted the air, I acted dumb and came back around. I just won't go away.

I won't listen.

I won't obey.

It's been fun trying to unzip the monster inside, but unfortunately, Rocky is dealing with a different species of beast.

"What if you brush him off once?" I ask Rocky. "Would it really ruin everything?"

"It'd piss him off. He likes his friends on a leash."

"I'll go with you," Jake says, passing me the bottle of Bordeaux. "Without Phoebe." It's been clearer these days that Jake is trying to "big brother" Rocky—who has *never* had anyone outside of our two families outright, and genuinely, care about him.

I don't think Rocky knows what to do with it yet. Other

than be peeved. "You weren't invited, sweetheart." He flashes a dry smile.

"I'm a Koning," he says with ironclad confidence. "I don't need an invitation."

Rocky lifts his brows, almost impressed. "Truth . . . I do like watching you go toe-to-toe with your brother, but you say about fifty percent of what I *actually* want to say to him."

"You want to write a script? I'll memorize it?"

I make a face. "Are you being serious?"

"I'd do *anything*," Jake emphasizes with brimming anger. "Short of murder."

"That shouldn't even have to be stated," I tell him, placing the wine gently next to a frozen pizza in the cart. "We're trained to deceive, not to kill."

Jake exhales a long, powerful breath, his gaze on Rocky. "What more do you want me to tell Trent? I'll say it if you can't."

"Forget it." Rocky texts again.

"*Grey*," Jake forces out. "Let me. Help you."

Rocky lifts his eyes off the screen. "You don't want to become me, man. You don't want to know what's *writhing* in my head."

"Maybe I do."

"No. It's good you're only fifty percent acid, because if you go a hundred percent, you'll only burn yourself." He pats Jake's firm chest. "Let it go, Prince Arthur."

"You mean King Arthur."

"You're not a real king yet."

Rocky cares about Jake, too.

He's already giving me a hot *fuck off* look, since I am smug and happily drawing hearts around this newfound friendship. Despite the annoying aspects when it's two v. one against me.

The longer I gloat, the more Rocky stares me down like he's a second from throwing me over his shoulder.

I'd like to see him try.

He yanks the cart forward, since I'm stalling for this conversation, and it slips out of my hands.

I give him a middle finger. Soon, we're in a seasonal aisle, and with Easter approaching, the mountain of pastels and bunnies makes me feel like we've landed in the very trippy children's video *Wee Sing in the Big Rock Candy Mountains*—which I *loved* growing up.

Nova says it's deranged.

Jake turns to me. "About brunch tomorrow."

"What about it?" I ask.

His family brunches have become a staple, and usually they're boring affairs filled with talk of the weather. My presence is always mandatory as a reminder to Claudia that I'm not a one-off girlfriend for Jake.

He slips off his suit jacket and splays it over the cart. "You don't have to go tomorrow morning."

"Did it get canceled?" I watch him roll his sleeves to his forearms, something he does very often. I thought it was a nervous tell.

Rocky said Jake isn't nervous. He's being protective. Like he's shedding the extra weight to fight for someone or something.

"No, it's still happening," Jake says. "But you've both been dealing with my family almost every day for months. No stopping. Not to decompress or even really take in what you learned about your parents weeks ago. You can pause—"

"There's no pausing," Rocky cuts in sharply. "This isn't a game you can hit a button on."

"Rocky's right," I say. "Our job isn't one you can call out sick for. It's an all-in or cash-out kind of thing."

Jake rubs the back of his skull, then sets his hand on the metal frame of the cart. "I'm just worried about all of you, I guess. It's not a small thing."

Our parentage. The DNA.

But my world hasn't been throttled as roughly as the Tinrocks'.

Rocky, Hailey, Trevor.

It's hard to really mope or complain that I'm Elizabeth's daughter since it's what I've believed my entire life. But Rocky—he's taking it all in stride. I think, maybe, he's a little relieved he's not biologically Addison and Everett's. Maybe it makes hating them easier on his soul.

"Redirect your worry elsewhere," Rocky advises. "We're all fine . . ." His voice tapers off as wheels to a grocery cart squeak.

Coming down our aisle, Hailey pushes her cart unhurriedly. I tried to comb her hair yesterday while she was on her laptop, but tonight, the platinum strands are matted and frizzed like she rolled out of bed.

But I'm not even sure she's really been sleeping. She's skipped so many days of work ever since we read the DNA results on the beach, and whatever rabbit hole she's descending, I wish she'd bring me down with her.

I told her, "Please, Hails. Just talk to me."

"I don't know what's real . . . Phoebe, I don't. There's so much . . . that isn't adding up, and it's a lot of assumptions . . . I-I can't, I can't." She tucked into herself, clawing at her head, and I wrapped my arms around her until she took deeper breaths.

In the grocery store, Oliver stands on the front of her cart.

"Pink or yellow?" He's holding two packages of marshmallow chicks.

"Yellow," Hailey says with a faraway, glazed look.

"Classic." He bops her nose with the package, and her lip tics in a fleeting smile. Then he chucks the Peeps in the cart.

She's muttering something inaudible. Oliver either pretends to understand or he's learned her garbled language, because he's nodding along.

All week, she's forgone her usual smoky makeup. No black eyeliner. No shadow. Not even a lip gloss. She looks younger than twenty-four.

Rocky has a dark expression as he restrains a tidal wave of worry for his sister's health and mental state.

If we were regular people, we would have told her to talk to someone by now. A counselor. A psychiatrist. And not just Oliver, who might be this town's charming part-time therapist, but has zero qualifying degrees to back it up.

Jake runs his fingers against his strong jaw. He twists back to Rocky with a pointed look. "You were saying? About everyone being fine?"

Rocky sucks in a sharp breath through his nose. "We're working on it."

"She'll be okay." I nod a lot, because I can't fathom a scenario where this gets worse. It can't get worse.

The *only* solution will be figuring out the origins of the Tinrocks, but every time Rocky and I try to insert ourselves into the research, she's adamant that she has it handled. That Carter and Jake are helping her piece things together.

That we need to focus on the Konings.

Her cart screeches louder as it nears ours, and I see it's full of Easter baskets, chocolate bunnies, and a floppy stuffed rabbit with lavender fur. It's missing an *eye*.

"That ugly bunny should be on clearance," I say.

Rocky doesn't look up from his phone. "Phoebe is a full-fledged frugal princess now."

"Well at least I know how to budget." *Sort of.*

He almost smiles, but he's rage typing.

"I like the ugly bunny," Hailey says to me, and I grow a million feet tall. She was listening to us! She's here.

"It's definitely worth getting, Hails. Every ugly bunny needs a home."

Oliver checks the tag on its floppy ear. "No markdown, but I'll work my magic with the cashier. Full price discount." He winks at Jake. "Learn how it's done, Koning boy."

"Or I can just pay for it," Jake offers.

"Or you could follow my lead. Every spider needs to stretch its legs," he whispers furtively, his smile infectious. It draws me in and makes me want to be what he is, too. A spider. Devious. Cunning and shrewd. I'm grinning. He hops off the cart and practically glides around Jake, just to pluck white bunny ears off the highest shelf. He slips them on his own head. "I'll give you tips and tricks—"

"Don't corrupt him," Rocky warns.

"I'm just bringing him into the fold." Oliver perches against the shelf of egg-dyeing kits. Jake doesn't shift to make room for him, so their shoulders brush, but Oliver isn't one to be intimidated, ever. His smile softens on Jake. "It's enticing. Our lives. You want to know all about us."

Jake lifts his brows. "I'm not going to lie and say I don't."

Oliver gasps at me like a scandal has occurred. "He's not going to *lie.*"

I snort. He grins, then tells Jake more seriously, "Don't dig too deep. You might not like what you find."

"Ominous," I say to my brother. He wags his bunny ear at me.

Jake doesn't seem afraid. He's already bitten the forbidden fruit. There's no going back anyway.

I check the price of a bunny-shaped night-light. Between its paws is a strawberry. Twenty bucks? Are they out of their minds?? It's suddenly ripped right out of my loose grip, and I spin around.

"Rocky," I accuse.

"I'll buy it for you." He's half focused on me, half frustrated at his phone.

He'll buy it for me? "I have the money."

I've been able to form a meager savings. All because Hailey and I caved and let Jake waive our rent when he offered. Maybe we could've swung the cost, but not with how many unpaid days she's taken.

Her time *is* better spent solving this mystery rather than being barked at by Katherine. We need her, but I also just need her to be healthy.

With Jake's payout at the end of the job, money shouldn't be much of an issue anymore anyway. It's a little freeing. And do I feel bad that I couldn't really hack it without returning to a con? Maybe . . . maybe not.

This is what I'm good at. At times, it's even what I love. It's like telling an Olympic swimmer to stay out of a pool.

"I know you have the money," Rocky says, his eyes meeting mine like *I'm your fucking boyfriend, Phebs. I can get this for you.*

My heart flip-flops. I press my lips together. "Yeah, okay," I say nonchalantly. "You can buy it."

"Don't sound so enthused."

"Ohh, *thank you so much, Rocky.*" I flail against the shelf and put my hand to my forehead. "What would I ever do without you?" I stake a glare on him. "Better?"

"You're such a—"

"Wonderful, kindhearted, gracious soul."

"Drama queen."

I scoff. "Take it back."

He's smirking now. "No." He's walking backward down the aisle with the night-light.

Oliver chucks a box of Cadbury Creme Eggs at him. "For the sweet tooth."

He catches it. "Thanks, man."

My smile fades into a deeper frown. "You're leaving?" I call out, trying to mask my disappointment. *You can go five seconds without him. He's not gone forever.*

"I have to," Rocky says, then asks Jake, "You coming to poker night or not?"

Jake hesitates, his blue eyes lingering on Hailey. Like his main regret is leaving her behind. I want to ask—I *need* to ask about this. "Yeah, I'm coming," Jake says. "Hailey?"

Her eyes slowly rise to his.

"I'll catch up with you later?"

"Yeah." She nods quicker. "For sure. We need to share notes on *Treachery in Death.*" Must be a book. Maybe for their book club?

Oliver is sifting through the groceries, checking the nutrition labels, and when Jake passes, my brother tells my fake boyfriend something in Dutch. But I can't make out the words.

"I already told you," Jake says, "I don't know Dutch."

"Look it up," Oliver says breezily, but Hailey must know it. Her face is fire-engine red, and she's suddenly very preoccupied with her phone.

I zero in on Rocky, but he's not catching these signals. He's checking the time on his watch.

Jake has an authoritative stride as he follows Rocky out, but Rocky is still walking backward, our eyes lassoed in a vise. His scarily attractive, confident gait has a way of pulling me in. No kiss or hug goodbye.

He's going to buy me a strawberry bunny night-light.

He's going to see me soon.

He better.

Because I can't have anything happen to him either.

When he faces forward again, disappearing from sight, I intake a big breath, and then I see Oliver placing his bunny ears back on the shelf.

Hailey sees as well. "You're leaving, too?" She frowns.

"I've also been beckoned to poker night with the boys." He hugs me goodbye, then he squeezes Hailey in a bigger one. Her smile peeks out when he shakes her. Then he sets her on her feet.

"Olly," she says, but her thought is caught or lost.

"Be terrible and get some sleep." He kisses her cheeks, then her forehead. "Do it for yourself, Hailstorm. And if not that, then for Phoebe. My sister is losing her hair over you."

"Am not." I cross my arms.

Oliver just smiles, then lifts a hand in a farewell as he strolls out of the grocery store. Leaving me with my best friend.

It shouldn't be tense. Or awkward, but Hailey is staring more at her combat boots than at me. The grocery cart lies between us.

"We don't have to talk about it," I say. "Whatever's bothering you." Maybe I shouldn't give her an escape hatch, but can I really prod her right now? "Let's just check out." I'm about to push the cart, but she grabs on to the handle to stop me.

"It's just . . . I've . . ." Her gray eyes flash up to me nervously. "There's a lot going on with . . ." She takes a breath. "You know I've always liked Carter." Even saying his name, blush creeps up her neck. "I crushed on him *so hard* when I first met him at seventeen. Like *immediately*. It's not just that he's really talented. He lights up a room, and I-I don't know, it felt like he lit me up, too."

My lips lift higher, then I realize she said *felt*. Past tense. "Has that changed?"

"I thought we'd be like my parents. Me and him. You know that."

"Yeah." Of course I remember Hailey fantasizing about this epic grifter romance between her and the master forger. But that was well before our lives were overturned. "Do you not want that anymore because you see Addison and Everett differently?" They lied to Hailey, to all of us. It wouldn't be easy to idolize them anymore.

"I don't know if I want to be anything like my mom," Hailey admits, her voice cracking. "Carter hates being stuck in one place for so long, and I thought I did, too. I thought I'd hate this, Phebs, but I-I don't want to go. I know gossip is everywhere, even about us, but I like being in a small town. I love the festivals and the way people recognize me and smile— even if I look *moody*, they smile. Because they've seen me around, they know of me, and it makes me feel like . . . like maybe I belong somewhere." Her face scrunches in an ugly cry.

I come forward, my stomach in knots, but she squeaks out, "Wait."

Pulling back, I stay on the other side of the cart.

"He's going to leave," Hailey says, wiping at her eyes. "Carter told me up front and said that it's better if we don't hook up while he's here. He could tell I'm not doing well, and he didn't want to add to it by having sex and then taking off." She sniffs, controlling the waterworks. "We've slept together when I was younger, you know, but I-I agreed with him because I don't think I can handle him leaving after restarting something. Not now." She grips the handlebar again. "It's already hard enough knowing he's going back to England."

I mull this over. "It's okay to envision something different for yourself, Hails. It's okay to feel like what you wanted in the past might not be what you need now."

"Is that how you feel with my brother?" she asks quietly.

Have I always wanted Rocky? *Yes.* Is he what I need now? *He's all I need.*

But I also never thought I'd be with him this honestly. "I think in my case, I just never let myself envision anything. Not a relationship, not a real future together, *nothing.* I didn't want to need him as much as I do."

Hailey seems understanding, but she gets in her head, and tears squeeze out of the corners of her cinched eyes. "It shouldn't be this complicated."

"What shouldn't?"

"Emotions. *Sex.*" Her nose reddens as she restrains another onslaught of tears.

"I feel like you're still not telling me something," I breathe.

Her gaze is on mine, but she picks at her chipped black polish, nervous again.

"Is it about Jake?" I wonder, since my flirty senses have been tingling. "It's okay if you like him. It's not like I'm *actually* with him—it wouldn't bother me."

She's quiet.

"And what's not to like, right?" I go on. "He's handsome

and he's sweet to you, and he'll be here. He's not leaving Victoria. I honestly think he might have feelings for you, too. But I haven't asked him . . . and I'm rambling."

"I do like Jake," Hailey admits softly and begins to stare off at the bunny decor. "I think I like his heart. I think I've always liked their hearts the most. How deep they are. How you can keep reaching and reaching, but you'll never touch the bottom. It's easy to just . . . fall into." She's dazed.

Their hearts?

"But it's not like . . . it's not serious," she says, her focus returning to me. She rubs at her tired, watery gaze. "I wouldn't date him."

My frown is heavy. "Because the town thinks he's with me?" Has she wanted to be with Jake? Have I prevented my friend from having her *Mystic Pizza* romance?

"No, because I don't do relationships. I can barely take care of myself right now, Phebs." She takes strange breaths. "I feel like I'm losing . . . time. A-and honestly, the only thing that *truly* matters is figuring out where we came from and why they want us to leave this town. B-because what if it's really not safe to stay?"

"What do you mean?"

Her eyes are flooded with fear. "I have to tell you something. About the Wolfe family."

TWENTY-EIGHT

Phoebe

We haven't left the grocery store parking lot. Rain pelts our Honda, and we shelter in the backseat. Lounging longways, we face each other and prop ourselves up against the doors. Plastic bags of groceries hide our feet as we dig into them.

Hailey hands me a yellow marshmallow chick, then tears one in half for herself. "Most details about the Wolfes have been buried in old records at the Historical Society. Since Stella Fitzpatrick is the president, it's been even harder to gain entry. I asked for permission to go through the archives, and she said *no*."

Ugh, *Stella*. Claudia's snooty best friend would be an annoying obstacle. "She can shove that *no* up her ass."

Hailey smiles a little. "I did wish you were there to tell her off."

"What was her reasoning for shutting you out?"

"She said I need special access, and to get that, I need to become certified in archival research. Which she said takes *years*. It seemed like bullshit. She doesn't really like me or you. So Carter asked her for approval, and she denied him, too. I think she knew he was with me. We've been seen at the library together and mornings at Seaside Griddle on our laptops."

I think about alternatives. Sneaking into the Historical Society at night and stealing books—it isn't a safe or even realistic option. There are likely cameras galore, and the last thing we need is the sheriff taking special interest in us.

"What about Jake?" I ask. "Stella *loves* Jake, and his lineage is probably all over that place anyway. He could tell her he's interested in his ancestry, like if any relatives fought in the American Revolution."

"I had him help me next."

My smile emerges. I'm proud of myself for coming up with an idea worthy enough to already be executed by my brilliant best friend.

Hailey picks apart her chick into tiny chunks. "Jake sweet-talked her into letting him through, but then, he pushed his luck and brought me up. To try to get me in there with him."

I stiffen. "She revoked his access?"

"Yeah." She eats a tiny piece and licks yellow sugar off her thumb. "A week later, I had Oliver try. He got Stella to let him in."

My hopes rise.

"But she only gave him ten minutes. No photographs allowed, since it'd damage the paper, but he took a couple pics without flash. It was hard for him to figure out what to pull. I told him to look for the newspapers, but I only had a rough estimate about dates. He didn't have that . . . that long."

I swallow the marshmallow, and it goes down in a thick lump. Because Hailey suddenly goes sheet white. Swiftly, before I can even blink, she wrenches open the left-side door behind her and leans out into the thunderstorm. Vomiting on the cement.

"Hails!" I climb to my knees on the seat, groceries tumbling to the floor mats, and I reach out, gathering her platinum-blonde hair before it gets drenched.

With the door open, the wind roars, blowing rain into the Honda. She gags while I rub her back. We're both getting wet, but I could be partially drowned right now and it wouldn't steal my concern from her.

"It's okay, Hails. You're okay."

After a long minute, she spits, then slides back onto the seat, and I reach out to shut the door for her. She groans while I squeeze the water out of her hair.

"Here, there's a Snapple somewhere . . ." I search the grocery bags and hand her a peach tea.

She twists off the cap slowly, like her energy has been depleted. Her insomnia is one thing, but now she's getting physically ill. My worry meter just smashed through the roof.

"You don't look so hot," I tell her. She's still as pale as can be.

"I think I might be coming down with something." She wipes her mouth with the back of her hand and recaps the Snapple.

I release her hair, now just damp and not sopping wet. "Why don't you go see a doctor?"

She ties her hair back with a black scrunchie, securing it in a low pony. "That involves having paperwork under Hailey Thornhall and submitting forms about familial history. Whatever I fill out, it's permanent, and it involves more than just me."

I understand what she's saying.

Rocky and Trevor might not be biologically related in real

life, but they're her siblings in this town. She can't exactly start making up a family history of lung disease without talking with her brothers.

We've never really made aliases that are this indelible.

"I can drive you to Rhode Island," I say. "Take one of your fake IDs, so you don't have to have any paperwork under Hailey Thornhall."

"No, it's okay." She uncaps the Snapple, taking another sip. Rosy tint has returned to her cheeks. "I really think this is a twenty-four-hour bug, Phebs. I'll be fine."

"In twenty-four hours, if you're not fine, though—we're going to Providence. I won't take *no* for an answer. I will throw you in the car."

She has a lopsided smile. Her teary, sentimental eyes on me. "I love you for that."

I shove the marshmallow chicks back in the grocery bag. I'm not one hundred percent sure if they caused Hailey's sudden nausea, but I'm claiming they're the culprit. I toss the bag back onto the floor mats.

"So what was Oliver able to pull about the Wolfes?" I reroute back to our earlier topic.

"Their family tree. At a certain point, it's . . . *morbid*. It makes sense why no one in town likes to recount it whenever I ask. And I think, for a lot of people, it's been lost through the years. It's not online. It's not easy to trace back. Only those who were here at the time likely know what really happened."

I scoot closer to her as she opens her photos on her phone. Oliver took a pic of a yellowed newspaper. The typed font is faded, but it's clear what this is.

"An obituary," I say.

"He found four."

Four deaths? How many newspapers did he sift through in ten minutes? "How did he have enough time to find four?"

"Because they all died within the same year."

Chills slip down my spine.

"Emilia Wolfe's late husband died first," Hailey says, zooming in on his obit. "Heart attack in his sleep." She reads out, "'William Wolfe leaves behind his devoted wife, Emilia, and three beloved children.'" Her eyes shift to me. "Two sons and a daughter."

It dawns on me. "The daughter—she's the one who was married to Varrick?" He was Emilia's *son-in-law*, only a Wolfe by marriage.

"Yeah." Hailey swipes the photos. "Daphne." The newspaper printed a headshot of Emilia's daughter. Big teased hair and bangs, puffy sleeves on slender shoulders—it looks like an eighties prom photo. "She was only twenty-two when she died. But she wasn't the second death."

Hailey finds the right pic, then tries to zoom in. The paper is crinkled, more faded and torn. "After William Wolfe passed away, his firstborn son was next. Christian Wolfe," Hailey says. "He died in a car crash."

I have so many questions. "Was he in an accident with another car? Did he run off the road and hit a tree?"

"Those details aren't in here." She squints at the pic. "I've tried to see whether he was married, but I couldn't find those records either. Not for him or for his younger brother." Lowering the phone, she swipes to another pic of an obituary. "The second-born son, Brent Wolfe, took his life a week later by jumping off the harbor bridge."

My stomach clenches. "And then Daphne?"

"Two months after that, she overdosed, leaving just Varrick

and Emilia, who've lived in Stonehaven together for over two decades . . . until last November, when she passed away from chronic kidney disease."

"And no one thought it was strange that this entire family just died one after the other?"

She has another glazed look. "I don't think the residents of Victoria wanted this town to be known for a tragedy of this scale. It's easier to bury it under the rug than memorialize it. To pretend it never really happened." She clicks out of the picture. "Some families are cursed." Her gaze shifts to me. "But information shouldn't be this hard to find. I know it was 1986, not everything was logged into computers. Most records were still being handwritten and archived in places like the Historical Society, but I just keep thinking . . ."

"Someone is purposefully hiding what happened?"

She nods. "It feels like a cover-up."

My brain whirls a mile a minute.

Even more when Hailey adds, "I find the timing to be peculiar." She holds her bent knees to her chest.

Sitting cross-legged, I face her more. "You said this all happened in 1986?"

Hailey nods faster, her eyes widening like saucers.

Nausea builds in me now. "Hails . . ."

"I know," she whispers. "That was around twenty-six years ago." Her throat bobs. "I've matched up the dates with Carter's intel. It's the *exact* same time that the godmothers would've been in Victoria. They were *here*, Phebs, when the entire Wolfe family died."

It's not just that. My eyes sting. "Rocky is turning twenty-six soon." He was born in '86.

"We *think* he's going to be twenty-six," she reminds me.

"But it's too big of a coincidence. That they were here when this happened. And where was my brother?"

My heart swells, hearing Hailey still call Rocky her brother. I know that'd mean something to him, too.

I think about Addison and Elizabeth. "Could they have been involved in taking down the Wolfes? Maybe Varrick hired them like Jake hired us?"

Hailey leans toward the dashboard and switches on the heat. "It is the same exact job—minus the deaths. Varrick has already inherited Emilia's entire fortune."

Flashes of lightning brighten the darkness of the car. Thunder rumbles around us, and I watch Hailey's eyes ping back and forth in thought.

"But they implied a con went poorly here," Hailey says, "and that's why we shouldn't be in Victoria. So if the job was getting Varrick to inherit the Wolfe fortune, how did that go bad? It could be that Varrick isn't involved at all, but their con somehow got the Wolfes killed by accident."

"But can we trust that a con went bad? It's another thing they told us, and we know they've been lying."

She narrows her eyes at the windowpane. Rain drips down the glass. "Facts," she says. "We know they lied about our origins, and we know they won't tell us about their time in Connecticut."

"I wish we could just ask them to give us the fucking truth," I groan angrily. But asking them will get us lies or the colloquial *it's better if you don't know.*

Hailey grimaces. "It's like . . . I see the answer, but I don't. It's right there . . . I know it's there . . . but all I have are theories, and without evidence, they'll never be fact, Phoebe. Facts are real. Beliefs aren't, and we know how easy those are to warp."

I can't imagine what that feels like—knowing you have the capability to solve a riddle, but being forever one letter off because you're lacking one necessary hint.

I could be given a thousand hints, and there's a good chance I still wouldn't solve the riddle. It's not my forte, which is why I'm not beating myself up over it. On the contrary, Hailey would spend eternity in front of a sphinx, if she had to.

I admire her too damn much, but I hope our desires to figure this out aren't putting an enormous pressure on her, too.

"Maybe you're thinking *too* hard," I say. "It could be one of those things that will naturally smack you in the face the moment you stop obsessing over it."

She shakes her head wildly. "No, no. I don't have all the information yet, Phebs. That's the problem. Once I get the right piece to the puzzle, I will crack it." She twists one of her stud earrings on her ear. "And what if . . . what if my brothers and I are all tied to this town, too? What if . . ."

"You're from here?"

"It's wishful thinking, okay? But maybe . . . just maybe . . ." She rubs at her reddened eyes.

I squeeze her kneecap. "It's not that far-fetched to me, given the dates of everything. And it'd make sense why they wouldn't want us in Victoria if they were trying to hide your origins here."

"I've been thinking about genetics," Hailey says quietly. "Eye color, hair, chin dimples." She looks at mine, which I share with my brothers. "Food preferences."

I scrunch my brows. "What food preference is genetic?"

"Cilantro," she says, and her face goes pale again. She whips open the door a second time. We go for round two on the puke-a-whirl, and this time, we're both soaked from the rainstorm when she shuts the door.

"Sorry, Phebs." She downs the rest of her Snapple, still ashen. I wring out my hair, creating puddles on the floor mat.

"You puke one more time and I'm rushing you to the ER. We can make up a Thornhall backstory about your great-grandmother's chronic toe fungus. I don't care."

"I'm fine," she says determinedly.

I stare skeptically.

"*Really*," she insists and picks up the conversation where we left it like it's proof. "Cilantro. People who have a variation in their olfactory-receptor genes will more strongly detect the soapy-flavored aldehydes in the leaves."

I pull off my drenched sweater. "Rocky thinks cilantro tastes like soap." I freeze. "And so does *Jake*."

We share an unblinking *what if* look.

"Could they be . . . ?" I trail off.

"Secret brothers?" She sounds skeptical.

"And we just figured it out because of *cilantro*," I say in more disbelief.

"I'd give you an award," Hailey tells me.

"We'd have to share it, since you're the one who gave me your cilantro knowledge." The mere thought of Jake and Rocky being somehow related is too far-fetched to even make sense in my brain. It's a silly thought. Right?

And anyway, Rocky's origins are so difficult to pinpoint. It almost feels like being blindfolded and throwing a dart at a list of a million and one names.

Hailey opens the air vents wider above her head. "Maybe we can—" A knock pounds on the rain-speckled window of our car, and we jump out of our skin.

"*Fuck*," I curse.

Hailey flicks off the dim lights on the ceiling, and as darkness shrouds us, a face beyond the window comes into view.

He's crouched down to the height of the car door. And he must be holding an umbrella since he's not wet.

"Get in the front seat," I tell her, just as he bangs his fist again. We're alone in a parking lot past ten p.m. in a sleepy little town. I've seen more than enough horror movies to know what happens next.

Hailey crawls into the front seat through the middle console, and I join her, plopping down in the passenger. Just as she starts the car, the man follows to her side window and knocks again.

"I-I think I recognize him," Hailey tells me while the Honda rumbles to life.

I tighten my gaze at the window, but I barely distinguish his features in the dark.

"You okay in there?!" he shouts over a boom of thunder.

"We're fine!" I yell back, not rolling down the window to welcome his arm in our car. No fucking way. Then I look to Hailey.

She mouths to me, *Varrick Wolfe.*

What the fuck?

"It's late!" he shouts, jolting us again. "Two girls like yourselves shouldn't be out alone on a night like this!"

"Thanks for the tip!" I mouth to Hailey, *Drive.* Then I yell back to him, "Have a good night, sir!!"

Hailey reverses and peels out of the parking lot.

TWENTY-NINE

Rocky

"You're *not* talking to him," I reinforce to my brother, who's currently putting on the immaculate green of a members-only golf course. Without loaded pockets, you can't step a pinky toe here—can't even bring a friend, so yeah, I had to cough up Trevor's country-club membership dues.

Thankfully Jake did pay me back for the most senseless purchase I've ever made. Kate has Bowie the horse. I have my money. Jake has his heart. Everyone is happy.

Speaking of the third-born heir, Jake is a few feet away, possibly in earshot, while he switches to a putter at the golf cart.

My brother wears all white. Can't remember the last time I saw him in a fucking Ralph Lauren polo. But I'm trying here, I'm really trying to be a better mentor than the two he had. Our "father" never taught Trevor some of the most basic skills to infiltrate high society . . . like *golf*. My kid brother didn't even know the correct form to swing a club.

"Talking to who?" Jake asks, returning with his putter.

"Varrick Wolfe," Trevor says casually. It's only us three out on the green. The sun is rising above the hills, casting an orange glow over the course.

It's been three days since Varrick stalked my girlfriend and my sister. I don't know what else to call it, because he had to have been casing the Honda. Why else was he out there past ten fucking p.m.?

"He could hire me as his assistant," Trevor continues. "I could tell him I worked for the Prince of Wales. I literally studied everything about the British monarchy when I was ten. He'll be begging to employ someone who's been in royal circles." He taps his ball, and it misses the hole by a foot, sliding down a slope and into a sandpit. "Shit."

Jake grips his putter with a gloved hand. "Why would you need to know about the British monarchy at ten?" He rethinks immediately and holds up his hand. "Wait—I don't want to know."

I square up next to my ball. "How could you have worked for the Prince of Wales, Trev? You're a nineteen-year-old in your third year at Caufield." It was already a point of contention which grade we were enrolling him in. He wanted to be a fourth-year senior, citing the fact that he's literally been taking college courses since he was fourteen. But there's only so many grades we can say he's skipped before people start poking into Boy Genius's backstory.

"It could've been an internship," Trevor grumbles as he walks down the hill for his ball.

With little effort, I hit my ball, and it slides across the green and into the hole.

Jake politely pats his hand in a subdued clap. He's the one who asked me to a five a.m. tee time. As if I haven't had enough crack-of-dawn golf games with his brother. But that was the reason he invited me here. I'd mentioned how I hated golf, and

Jake asked, "Did you hate it before you started hanging out with my brother or after?"

I was quietly reflecting on that question when he said, "He has a habit of making you hate the things you like. Come play a round with me tomorrow morning."

He didn't hesitate when I asked if I could bring Trevor.

This morning on the course, I realize that I don't really hate golf. Trent was starting to make me think I despised it.

Besides Phoebe, I've never had someone like Jake in my life. I hate so much about everything—and to be reminded that there are things still left to enjoy . . .

Maybe I like hanging out with him.

In moderation.

Jake taps his ball into the hole. "I can alert my security personnel about Varrick being a potential threat to our girl-friend."

I make an annoyed face. *Our* girlfriend. It's grated less and less on me the more he says it—because one alternative is Jake saying, *My girlfriend.*

And she's not his.

It also reminds me that he's looking out for Phebs during this con. Protecting her when I'm stuck with his fucking dick-bag brother.

"I don't trust your security," I say. "No offense, but they're more your mother's people than yours." Everett is managing the staff at the Koning estate, but he's cautioned us that he has little control over their private security, who are usually only posted at the front gate unless told otherwise. "The best thing is to keep your security lax. They need to think there's no threats around. Let them kick their feet up and snore."

Trevor hits his ball back onto the green. "You know, I might not even be nineteen. I could be your age, Rocky."

"I'm older than you, shithead."

His lip slightly lifts.

Jake turns his back to the sun. "I asked Hailey if there was a blood test that could determine age."

I already know the answer because I asked her, too. "Nothing that'd be accurate enough," I say. "It can only estimate age within two to three years. But I remember this one when he was a baby." I point my putter at Trevor. "My eyes didn't deceive me when I had to change your diapers or when you hit a growth spurt at fourteen." I'd been twenty. Or I was told I was twenty.

Trevor's gaze relaxes on me with fondness. "'Believe nothing you hear, and only half of what you see.'"

"I've seen you," I remind him. "Throughout your whole life. I've seen you scrape your knees trying to ride a bike. I've seen you learn how to swim, then master the perfect dive. I've seen you tinker with toys, instruments, machinery, and computers, and rely *way too heavily* on your good looks to pick up people."

"It didn't take a pretty face to pick up Sidney." He rests the golf club on his shoulder.

"How's that going?" I ask him, since he's still been spending more time with Sidney ever since The Hunt. He barely talked about that afternoon bopping around town to solve riddles with her. The way he shrugged about it, I thought she bored him.

But not enough if he's been actively spotted at the ice cream parlor and coffee shop with her.

"It's going," Trevor says vaguely, nothing on his face to read.

Jake and I visibly tense, but he asks first, "She hasn't been inappropriate with you, has she?"

"What he's trying to say is, she hasn't groped your dick without consent?"

Jake side-eyes me like I'm corrupting the youth.

"He's *nineteen*," I retort.

Trevor looks between us with a slanted smile. "No unconsented passes." He clutches the golf club like a barbell over his deltoids. "She's a virgin."

I didn't want to know that.

Jake scrapes a hand through his thick hair but freezes when Trevor adds, "Or she was one, before me."

Great.

Fucking rigor mortis is setting in. Bury me.

"Are you playing her?" Jake asks cautiously.

"No . . . I think Sidney is using me to piss off her father." At least he sees that. He drops the club off his shoulder. "Her life is sad." He stares out at the green manicured valleys, a look in his eyes he's wrestling. "I'm not trying to make it sadder."

He's struggled with empathy.

"Did you wear a condom?" I ask him.

"No, I raw-dogged her."

"Wow." Jake nods a lot with flattened lips, looking like a disappointed dad. I half expect him to go into a lecture on safe sex.

"He's lying," I tell him.

Trevor raises his brows in confirmation to Jake, then says to me, "*Yes*, I wore a condom." He leans on his club. "What am I, twelve?"

"Just checking in, knucklehead." I swipe his club, and he trips.

He catches his balance and straightens up with a laugh.

"You wear a condom when you stick it in Phoebe? Just checking in."

Jake's head spins like *The Exorcist* to me.

I'm glaring. "We need boundaries," I tell my brother.

"You started it."

"Eh, I'm older, and I get to ask if you're being safe. You don't get to talk about Phoebe like that. *Ever.*"

"Like what? It's anatomical. Your dick. Your cum. Her cunt—"

"Kill me." I turn to Jake. "Just do it. Off me now so I don't strangle him."

Jake laughs hard, and the fact that he sees the humor in this weird back-and-forth is making me like him a little more. "You brought him here," he reminds me.

"Regrettably."

I don't regret it, which is why Trevor smiles more, too. It's hard to set boundaries when he knows I'd forgive him for a lot. But it's going to drive me out of my fucking mind every time he brings up Phoebe.

Trevor reclaims his putter from me.

And I'm caught on his features.

His eyes.

I stare deeper into them. *Gray.* One of the rarest colors, and yet, we're not related. Not even to Hailey, who has the same shade.

My face hardens in an instant.

"What is it?" Trevor frowns.

"Our eyes," I tell him in a haunted thought. "They picked you for your eye color. So it'd be the same as Hailey's and mine. So we wouldn't question that we were related."

Trevor leans on his putter with two hands again. "So I was

stolen or adopted into a life of crime because of my fucking eyes?"

"Yeah. I think so."

He glares at the rising sun, then faces me. "Should I be mad? Because I like my life, Rock. I like being your brother. I like traveling around the country. I liked learning about the British monarchy and getting to sit in at an Ivy League lecture hall when I was seventeen. I like what we do. No, I *love* it. I won the motherfucking lottery!" He shouts loud enough that birds fly out of the nearby trees.

"Jesus Christ," I say with an eye roll.

"I'm not you and Hailey—I don't care where I came from. All that matters to me is where I'm going."

"Okay," I breathe out, trying to shove off the weight that's compressed on my chest. But it's difficult when I feel an intense responsibility toward doing right by him. Ever since we learned he's not Addison and Everett's . . . he's felt like mine. Maybe he was always mine in a strange way.

"Where are you going, if that's all that matters to you?" Jake asks him.

Trevor lines up in front of his ball and takes a long moment to study the shot before he sinks it with one smooth hit. He smiles. "Wherever he's going." He tilts his head toward me. "I'm there."

This kid.

I shake my head, but there's an immense amount of love for him that I can't shake off. Not even as we hop on the golf cart and head toward the next hole.

Sitting in the back, Trevor leans forward to stick his head between Jake and me. "New plan. I did a summer abroad and a three-week internship with the Earl of Wessex. I'll ask

Varrick for an internship and tell him I need to pad my résumé before graduation."

Jake grips the steering wheel tighter. "Wouldn't Varrick call your royal references?"

"He would," I say and glance to Trevor. "How do you know Varrick cares about hiring someone with a royal résumé?"

"Everyone cares about status here."

"Not everyone," I shoot back. "You can't assume everyone is the same. People have different motivations, different reasons for why they drop a grand like it's a five-dollar bill. And I've said this a thousand times, there are some people you *do not* fuck with."

"Stay away from anyone who's in the dark triad," Trevor says, "I heard you a thousand and one times."

Jake frowns. "The dark triad?"

Trevor grins and places his chin on his fist, looking to me like he's enjoying this crash course in the art of confidence games.

I push his head back. "The dark triad of traits. It's a psychological theory of personality. But for us, anyone with all three traits can be harder to manipulate."

"What are the three?"

"Narcissism, psychopathy, and Machiavellianism. They lack empathy, among other things. And they're likely already running Ponzi schemes or committing crimes."

Until Trevor can tell who those people are, I worry about him choosing a mark of his own, but I also don't want to control him like our parents did.

"You think Varrick is in the dark triad?" Jake asks.

"I don't know," I sigh. "We've only interacted once." And that was a month ago at The Hunt. I don't have any other evidence besides the way he looked at me—and that instinct, that gut feeling, it means something but it's not enough. Still, when I learned about his family's tragic backstory and Varrick being the last Wolfe standing—that only intensified those same feelings. I tell them, "Varrick showing up outside the grocery store and scaring Phoebe and Hailey can't be a coincidence. He's up to something."

"Maybe he just has the hots for Phoebe," Trevor says, coming forward again.

"Sit down," I snap and push my brother back down into his seat.

Jake is glaring out the windshield. "He's in his forties."

"Older men have hit on PG before," Trevor says. "It's literally her role to entice them. Spread her—"

I grab the collar of his polo. "One more word and you're eating grass."

He looks at me like I'm the problem. "It's legitimately the fucking truth, Rock. Be mad at the person who assigned her the role, not me."

"I'm mad at everyone, how's that?" I let go of his shirt.

"Who assigned her the role?" Jake wonders.

"That's hard to say," I breathe out. "Maybe her mom. Maybe mine. Maybe my dad. Maybe all three of them."

"Her own mom?" Jake grimaces.

"You do know Elizabeth is *also* in the same role, right?" Trevor asks Jake. "She's the OG seductress."

Jake parks the golf cart at the next hole. "I didn't know that. Actually." He catches my gaze. "Phoebe said she loved her mom."

"You've never met Elizabeth," I tell him. "But there's a natural warmth to her that's hard to manufacture, and I do believe, in her own warped mind, she really loves her kids. There were times she chose positions in a job that Phoebe might have taken. Positions with older men that were far worse than anything Phoebe has done. So yeah, Phoebe loved her . . . loves her . . . maybe there will always be something there. I don't know."

Trevor jumps out of the golf cart, and I hang back with Jake. My phone buzzes in my pocket, and I groan when Trent's name is on the screen. For a second, I was actually enjoying my morning—even if it consisted of deep diving into our twisted histories.

Jake sees my screen. "Don't answer it."

"I can't let him go to my voicemail." I answer on the third ring.

"Grey!" Trent's hysterical voice is new to me. "I need you now. Shit, fuck, *shit*." He sounds like he's about to have a panic attack. "Something horrible just happened."

I smile.

THIRTY

Rocky

Trent runs two hands through his hair, pulling at the strands in severe distress.

He's pacing. He's been pacing for the past thirty minutes. Inside the Koning pool house, two empty bottles of Ardbeg line the counter, and Trent pours from a third into a shot glass. I'm not the only person he called to this little emergency meeting.

Collin Falcone and Oliver "Smith" sit on the blue toile couch, watching Trent spiral in a whirlpool of scotch and panic.

The four of us, coined the Fortunate Four (hate it) by town gossipmongers, have been playing damage control in Trent's eyes, and playing babysitter to a petulant man-baby in mine.

"I just don't get it," Collin says, leaning over the glass coffee table. "Who would've recorded you? You were in your own house."

"He was in the carriage house," I correct Collin.

"Same difference." Collin snorts a line of white powder off the table.

Trent glowers. "It's not the same, you dipshit." He waves a tensed hand toward me. "Grey understands. Facts and details matter."

Collin grimaces. "Yeah . . ." He sinks back into the couch and pats Oliver's back, nodding toward the cocaine on the table.

Oliver is quick to comply, and I look away. Try to ignore. Try not to let it get to me. My pulse thumps harder. I pull at the collar of my black button-down, heat surfacing within me. I had to go straight from the golf course to the boathouse just to change out of my wick-away polo and golf shorts. Lest Trent think I played eighteen holes without him.

"Play the audio again," I tell Trent.

His nose flares as he takes out his phone. He sinks onto a wicker chair and rests his elbows on his knees. The recording starts, and it's his unmistakable voice that arrives first.

"Celia, Celia." He laughs, and I can only imagine he's squeezing her in a hug. "You looked like a pro out on the court. Caufield's coach will be an idiot if he doesn't make you number one singles on the team."

I do everything not to grit my molars.

Celia Whitlock. *Newly* eighteen. She has a full ride to Caufield for tennis and graduates from Victoria High in May. The fact that her parents even let her play tennis alone with him is . . . something.

But they're divorced. And her mom has already *routinely* slept with Trent. So I'm guessing he was drawn to the idea of fooling around with her daughter.

"Thanks," Celia replies bashfully. "I've been working on my forehand."

"Your topspin is flawless. Just like you . . . and you know, I really like you."

"I like you, too."

I concentrate on the weight of the Rolex on my wrist. On the collar of my shirt itching at my neck. Just to stop my face from cinching in pure disgust.

"I could show you a good time, if you'd like that?" Trent asks on the recording. "Up in my room. You'll love it there. And you'll love me here." I imagine he touched her.

"Yeah . . . okay."

Here in the pool house, Trent extends his arms at me. "She *consented*. How is this fucking bad?"

Oh, let me count the fucking ways. Instead, I'm forced to appease him. "People are sensitive, man."

"I can't believe this." He has a hostile glare on his cell-phone like if he could, he'd reach into the past and sucker punch the person who made this moment public.

In the audio, Trent says, "You know I've been with your mom, right? I like you more, though. We should see if you inherited the best of her assets."

"You want me to . . . ?" There's some rustling on the recording, like she's shedding her clothes.

"Definitely hotter than your mom. Take off the bra, too." It ends with some murmuring and a grunt before they likely head to Trent's room.

Currently, his leg is jostling in pure rage. "The mother-fucker who recorded me is a dead man."

It was a woman.

One of their groundskeepers who's in charge of fresh floral arrangements on their property. Everett paid her to drop audio devices in vases around the estate.

"Look, man, I don't know if it's that big of a deal," I tell him. "No one said your name. There could be plausible deni-ability. With technology, things get faked all the time."

Highly un-fucking-likely.

Trent nods, trying to ease. "You're right. I could just say it's not me. It *sounded* like me, but that's not me."

Oliver sniffs a couple times before he says, "Deny, deny, deny."

Collin throws up his hand. "Why does this matter anyway? So you might have banged an eighteen-year-old and her mom. I've seen you finger-fuck a girl while getting your dick sucked."

Trent is seething at Collin. "Don't say it like that. I don't *finger-fuck*. You crude piece of shit." He throws a pillow at him. "Do you know what I've been through?" His face fractures like he's grasping a heart he suddenly purchased. "It *matters*. What they're saying about me isn't true. I loved Scarlett. I still *love* her. My wife was my everything. You know that, Grey?" He looks to me, seeking validation.

He does often express love for his late wife. But only to gain sympathy from others. "I know," I say, consoling. "She was your one and only."

"My one and *only*." He nods strongly. "Now they're saying I'm a pig? For what? Did they honestly expect me to never physically be with anyone else? Because that's all it was." He wipes at his mouth, incensed. "This better not get to the board. I'm a *widower*." He points at his chest. "I'm not a fuck-ing porn star."

Step two: tarnish Koning Jesus's reputation.

Weeks ago, I warned Valentina de la Vega never to accept a tennis match with Trent. How he'd been talking about her ass among his friends. She thanked me for the heads-up. And then yesterday, I slipped the audio flash drive in Val's locker at the country club. Her family owns the *Victoria Weekly*, and I thought there'd be a fifty-fifty chance she'd either post it on their website or just text it among her best friends.

No post on *Victoria Weekly*, but it's been sent to enough twenty-somethings in town that it made its way right back to Trent. And people are whispering. Side-eyeing. Scrutinizing him from head to toe.

"It'll blow over," I say casually, undeterred, like I have all the confidence in the world that Trent will ride this out. And he will. He'll skate through the barrel of the wave unscathed, because this isn't the wave that takes him down.

Trent ingests my confidence with another hearty nod. "Yeah, yeah. You're right, Grey. I shouldn't be freaking out."

"You shouldn't," I agree. "Freaking out is for the guilty."

"I did *nothing* wrong," Trent says deeply. "And do you even know how many people would kill to play tennis on the Koning courts? Celia was *happy* to be there. She even texted apologizing for this audio getting out. Everyone needs to just *chill*."

He truly believes he is a gift from God to those around him.

"I'm chill," Oliver says, then mimes taking a hit on a joint and blowing out.

Trent shakes his head with a laugh.

I join in the laughter. So does Collin.

Then Oliver.

Until we're all laughing, full-bodied, like it's all just bull-shit, and Trent's passing around the Ardbeg to commemorate his "innocence." The scotch tastes like acid down my throat. We spend the next half hour taking Trent's mind off the scandal, which involves more alcohol, six hours of *Transformers* movies, and more drugs.

Luckily, I've dodged all cocaine use by citing my employer doing frequent drug tests. I insinuated to Trent that I work for the government, but I usually tell people I invest so I don't blow my cover. He felt special being brought in on a secret that I tell no one.

Not even my ex-wife could know that I work for the CIA.

Halfway through *Transformers: Dark of the Moon*, I get a call. Casually, I glance at the screen, and then rise to my feet. "Sorry, I have to take this," I tell Trent.

And through my body language, I convey this is an important call, more important than him. Leaving through the sliding glass doors, I step closer to the Konings' Olympic-sized pool. Pink flamingo floaties drift on the surface of the crystal-blue waters.

I put the phone to my ear. "Hey," I say. "I'm outside. You can talk freely."

"Hey," Phoebe replies with the same easygoing tone. She called on her burner, but I recognized the number. There was a zero percent chance I was going to ignore her call. All I want to do is hear her voice. "Jake said you got the SOS call from Trent. Are you still with him?"

"Yep." I exhale a hot, aggravated breath.

"Shit," she curses. "Oliver, too?"

"We're on the third *Transformers* movie."

She groans. "Oh God, I wish I could come end your misery."

"Please fucking do. Bring chocolate and a chain saw."

"I'll show up in a hazmat suit," she jokes. "Tell him there's been a report of asbestos."

I'm smiling. "What are you doing tonight?"

"Hmmm. Big plans. If you can believe it, I'm actually hosting a *Transformers* watch party where we watch not only every movie but the director's commentary, too."

"That's funny because I don't believe it."

"There's nothing funny about my lies."

I run my tongue over my lips, feeling my edging smile again. "So you have no plans."

"I have a shift at the club until seven," she says, and this time I know she's telling the truth. "Other than that—I am as free as that whale in that one movie."

"*Free Willy*?" I squint into the sun and pull my sunglasses off the collar of my shirt. "You do know he wasn't free until the very end of the movie?"

"Thanks for spoiling it for me."

I laugh with an eye roll. "It's been how many years since that's been out? You're past the spoiler zone—"

The sliding glass doors open, and my gaze hooks to Collin. "Everything okay?" he asks.

"Yeah, just work. I'll be back in a second."

"Cool." Collin nods. "We paused the movie." *Wonderful.*

I force an easygoing smile before putting the cell back to my ear. "Thanks, Hank, I'll have the report to you tonight."

"Nine p.m.?" Phoebe asks. "Your place?"

I tamp down my excitement so it won't rise to my face. "Yep, that sounds great."

"Love you, bye." She hangs up swiftly, knowing I won't have a chance to tell her the same.

The sun has set by the time Oliver and I leave Trent's, and Oliver will. Not. Shut. The fuck. Up. He must have been using all his energy to "act normal," and as soon as he landed in my car, the dam busted.

"It's like the summer I found that stray cat, not knowing it had fleas, and then I brought it to our house in Raleigh and we had to flea bomb every single room. And Nova was all 'this is why you don't bring in random animals,' and I was all 'yeah, but it's not random. His name is Claude.' And now sometimes when I'm doing nothing in particular, I'll just think, *His name is Claude.* Fuck, I miss that cat. I can't believe he ran away. I was like the literal best cat dad." He takes a breath. A god-damn miracle.

"Oliver." I slow the car at a stop sign.

"Yeah?"

"Shut up."

He just smiles, and his head swings toward the window. "Isn't that Varrick's car?"

I do a double take before making a quick U-turn onto the main street. Sure enough, it's Varrick Wolfe's sixties Stingray. I would do very bad things to own that black Corvette. It's apparently just one of a hundred vintage cars Emilia Wolfe's late husband, William Wolfe, collected.

My envy for the car transforms to worry when I see where it's parked.

In front of Baubles & Bookends. Which just happens to be the shop below Hailey and Phoebe's loft. That can't be a coincidence.

Fuck this guy. I park in the open spot behind the Stingray, and Oliver jumps out first. "I'll go check on Hails." I don't follow him into the apartment stairwell.

I wait patiently beside my car, seeing the shape of Varrick through the bookstore windows. The bell chimes as he exits. He's in a navy-blue suit. Brioni. No tie. Cuff links are gold, and he's carrying a paper bag with the B&B logo.

"Surprised to see you here," I call out to him.

He jolts when he spots me as if, maybe, I caught him off guard. But the shock dims. It's instantly replaced by intrigue as he fixes his sights on my McLaren. "Nice car."

He knows his is nicer.

I flash a smile.

He cranes his neck back to the store. "Why would it be a surprise to see me here?"

"You've barely been around town since The Hunt," I say, a little casual but a lot territorial.

He shifts the bag to his other hand. "You keeping track of me?"

I lift my shoulders. "Just making it my business to keep tabs on the guy who tried to pay an absurd amount of money for my ex-wife." I smile. "You know how it is."

Varrick returns the same acidic smile. "Sure." He reaches for the Corvette's door handle. "Those lofts your sister and ex-wife are residing at—they might want to look into other living arrangements."

My stomach knots. "Why is that?"

"My family used to own the bookstore. Now *I* own the bookstore, and I'm finalizing a deal with Claudia Waterford to buy the lofts above." He meets my gaze head-on, an intensity in his eyes that borders on threatening. "Though maybe your ex-wife and I can work something out." He flashes another smile. "Have a nice day, Brayden." He opens the door.

Hearing him call me that name—it nearly steals the life out of me. I don't even flinch. I'm a solid block of ice. I catch his gaze, because he's eating up my frozen reaction like it's candy at a movie.

"Who are you?" I ask him on a public street at sunset. No one who's anything like me would utter the truth, but I'm not thinking clearly right now.

His lip rises. He's amused. "Varrick Wolfe."

"You know my parents?" I ask him.

He chuckles, tipping his head in thought. "Something like

that." His smile settles on me before he says, "I hope to see you around." As he climbs into his Corvette, a feeling wrenches and gnarls inside me.

Something like that.

Something like that.

It's in this moment I think Varrick Wolfe might be my father. And he's fucking with me.

I peel my feet off the sidewalk. I make sure not to appear shaken, but if he's anything like Everett—then he could tell he threw me the length of ten hundred football fields. With one name.

Seven letters.

Once I see him drive off, I reroute back to my McLaren and hop in the front seat. I don't start the car.

I call the man who raised me.

"Bray?" he answers.

I dig the back of my skull against the headrest, my phone in a fist against my ear. "How do you know Varrick Wolfe?"

Silence. His breath strains. Until he says, "What'd he tell you?"

"No, that's not how we're playing this. How do *you* know him?"

"You need to stay away from him, son," he cautions, his unleveled breathing unmanufactured. His fear is real. "You need to pack up everyone and *leave.*"

"Afraid he's going to tell us the truth?" I retort.

"If you love Phoebe at all, you will get her out of there—"

"Don't *ever* fucking use her against me to get what you want," I sneer, my eyes burning in their sockets.

"I'm on your side," he growls back. "I'm *actively* helping you with this job that is so massively intricate. Without me, you wouldn't be able to have eyes and ears around the estate.

If you think, for a second, that we're not the people you should be trusting—then why ask for our help? We *need* each other. We're all we have, Brayden. *That* is real love, son. Whatever he tells you, it's not real."

I don't know what to believe.

My nose flares as I restrain more emotion, and I wonder if Hailey has already thought this far ahead. Right now, I feel as fucking tormented as she's looked for the past four months.

We hang up not long after, and I climb rigidly out of the car. That's when I see the girls' Honda parked a couple sedans away. The tires appear sunken. Crouching at the front wheels, I instantly notice gaping cuts.

Someone slashed their tires.

Wonder who? Gee, let me crack a guess.

I stand back up and glare at the road Varrick drove down. Now I'm starting to wonder if he was the cause of Oliver's catalytic converter being stolen. So Oliver couldn't make it to The Hunt.

Why is he targeting us?

And now he might be buying the *loft*. With this news bearing on my chest like an elephant, I leave the sidewalk. It takes me less than twenty seconds to enter Phoebe and Hailey's place, and I toss my keys on the kitchen counter.

I need to piss, then I'll check on Hails, grab Oliver, and head to the boathouse. Phoebe is probably already there, waiting for me. All I want is to be with her right now.

So I go to the only bathroom, and I turn the knob. *Locked.* I knock.

"Give me a sec," Oliver says, sounding . . . strange. I rack my brain for how many lines he did. Worry mounts, and I don't know if Varrick or Everett or both have me on edge— but I'm digging my bump key out of my pocket.

I crack the lock on the door in under ten seconds.

One foot in, and I'm solid ice again.

Oliver is lifting his pants hurriedly up his thighs. Facing him, Hailey sits on the sink counter, and with the same haste, she slips her arms into a long-sleeved mesh shirt over a black bra.

They just had a quickie in the bathroom. Even catching them after-the-fact, it's obvious.

"Rocky," Oliver says like he's gauging my temperature, as he buttons his slacks. I am at a degree that would melt a fucking bullet.

"It's not what you think," Hailey says, more nervously.

I arch my brows, hurt in my face that she thinks I'm *that* dumb. They're *rushing* to get dressed. They're still in positions that scream, *sex.*

"Oh-kaaay," she says with wide eyes. "It might be what you think. But, *but* . . . it's not as bad as you think."

I plant my drill bits for eyes on Oliver Graves, who's quieter than a fucking church mouse. "Oh, so now you have nothing to say?" I ask him. "Claude got your tongue?"

"You have a literal centimeter of itty-bitty space to be angry at me." Oliver squeezes his fingers together. "You do realize that? You're sleeping with *my* sister—so you can't be mad that I'm with yours."

"We are not the same," I growl back. "Because I had the decency to at least inform you that Phoebe and I are a thing."

"Olly and I aren't a thing." Hailey hops off the counter. "Not like you and Phoebe."

My brain short-circuits. "What the fuck does that even mean?"

Oliver buckles his belt. Casual, unconcerned. "It means it's just sex."

"Just sex," Hailey echoes, fixing her nose ring in the

mirror. I read people, places, and rooms, and the comfort and ease between them tells me this is not new for them. This is familiar, routine.

Hot breath sears my throat. Yeah, I never pried because I didn't want to know. There've been a *thousand* times I thought maybe . . . maybe something happened between the two of them. Now I'm in too deep to leave without poking this beast.

I grip the doorframe, filling the exit so Oliver doesn't dart out. "For how long has this been going on?"

Hailey is avoiding my gaze. "Rocky—"

"You can sleep with whoever you want, Hails," I tell my sister. "But why the secrecy? Sure, I would've been irritated, but I'd live with it. Like I do everything else that irritates the fuck out of me."

"We never wanted it to be a big deal among everyone," Hailey says while Oliver sidles close to her at the sink. "We were afraid it'd affect the group dynamic, and it's just sex."

Just sex.

Just sex. I can't even imagine being involved with someone in our "group" and eliminating feelings from it. A one-night stand in Brooklyn, who you'll never see again, is not the same as getting into bed with someone you would follow to the ends of the earth. Someone you trust in ways that normal people could never understand.

Oliver cradles her *life* in his hands every single day. With the knowledge of who she is—knowledge that could send her to prison. Just like I cradle Phoebe's.

Just like they cradle ours.

They can't tell me that this begins and ends with sex. But really, what the fuck do I know about emotions—I've only spent decades trying to control mine.

"We've been sleeping around most of our lives," Hailey

reminds me, like being promiscuous is in the Grifter Handbook that we've all opened.

"How long have you two been keeping this a secret?" I ask.

Hailey slips a tiny *help me* look to Oliver.

"Why don't you drop it here?" he suggests.

"Why don't you answer my question?" I snap, aggravated now. He doesn't get off the hook just because he's Oliver Graves.

"And if I don't answer the question, what are you going to do? Shove me in the ocean like you did Nova?"

"Maybe. Give me a minute and I might come up with something more creative."

"It's been years," Hailey cuts in, exasperated. "Okay? Off and on."

"Years. *Years*." I nod a couple times, not shell-shocked. Their body language already gave it away, but still, I can't imagine being that intimate on and off for years and severing the emotion. I had feelings for Phoebe *before* we even slept together.

Hell, almost having sex on a job nearly shattered us. Maybe I shouldn't be comparing my relationship to theirs—maybe that's not right. But it's all I've got. There is no other viewpoint or window to look through than the one that exists with me and her.

"How old were you?" I ask them. "When this first started?"

They're not paying attention to me. Oliver is inspecting himself in the mirror. Hailey is on her tiptoes and drawing down the collar of his button-down. A hickey has formed on his neck.

"I'll go grab Phoebe's makeup," Hailey says, as if this has happened *many* times before.

I don't budge from the doorway. Blocking Hailey, I tell her, "Phoebe? You mean your best friend, who knows nothing about you bagging her brother?"

Guilt pools in my sister's eyes.

I immediately regret the shot I took.

"I'm going to call her, Rocky. Right now. I'll fix it. I can fix it. *I can fix it.*" She tears through my arm with panic I didn't mean to fuel, and my stomach clenches painfully.

"Hailey!" I call after her, but I let her go.

Because Oliver says, "We were fourteen."

"Fourteen?" My eyes flash angrily to him. "You took her virginity?"

"Yeah." Oliver faces me more than the mirror. "And she took mine." He's as calm as Lake Placid.

I'm not sure how I feel other than annoyed, irritated, furious that Hailey and Oliver have been hooking up since they were fourteen—but it was *Phoebe* and *me* that were somehow the objects of our parents' obsession.

Jealousy claws at my insides.

In a different reality, if Hailey and Oliver were open about their connection, would Phoebe and I be left alone? Could we have become a couple sooner without our parents' needling?

That same jealousy washes away like an ocean lapping the sand. Because in that reality, my sister and Phoebe's brother would have to deal with their love lives being pressured and controlled. We wouldn't want that for either of them.

We would choose to be on the operating table. Under the spotlight. Fighting the knife.

"What about Jake? Carter?"

"Friends with benefits," Oliver says with a nonchalant slouch against the sink.

My brows shoot up. "She's *sleeping* with Jake?" What
the . . . *fuck*? I thought he had a schoolyard crush on my sister.
Pining. Unrequited. Definitely not *fulfilled*.

Oliver hops over that to explain, "Carter is on the back
burner, which is sad for Hails because I know she liked him,
but I'm not complaining since it means I get to spend more
time with her." He slips a fallen Q-tip back into a cup on the
sink. "It's not that complicated."

"You're a friend with benefits, too?"

"Yeah. Only . . ." He shifts slightly, his gaze dragging
across the bathroom rug before lifting to me. "I'm not really
sleeping around—not while she's . . . well, you've seen her,
Rock. She's been under a lot of stress, and we agreed to keep
the pool small."

"How small?"

"She's hooking up with just me."

"Oh, just you?"

He exhales, "And Jake."

Jesus. How is that *not* complicated? "Does Jake know
about this arrangement?" Is he getting the short end of the
stick here? And why do I care about his feelings in all of this?

"I don't know. I'm not the one sleeping with him," Oliver
says. "But based on our run-ins, I'm fairly certain Hailey has
clued him in."

"And there are no feelings between you and her?"

"I never said that."

Yet, he appears to be completely fine with this situation,
and I get why. Oliver's ego is as indestructible as his heart is
big. He'd do just about anything for my little sister, including
becoming less of a playboy and staying exclusive to her. All
while she's also sleeping with another guy.

"This seems like a recipe to get hurt, man," I warn him.

"So what if we all do?" Oliver says. "The way I see it, we could be caught tomorrow. We're living on a countdown clock, Rocky, and before it hits zero, I want to know that I didn't hold back."

I spent years resisting Phoebe, and he gave in to Hailey—because time has never been our friend. It never will be, and now that I'm with Phebs, I understand it more.

To lose a single moment with her that I could've captured—it enrages me as much as it scares me.

As if Oliver knows I'm thinking of her, he says, "I'm happy you both stopped holding back." He smiles one of his dazzling, hypnotizing grins. "Oude liefde roest niet."

I'm not fluent in Dutch, but the phrase is familiar. I realize it's what he said to Jake in the grocery store. But I never looked it up. Head. Sand. Buried.

He shovels me out now.

And he translates, "Old love does not rust."

THIRTY-ONE

Phoebe

Hailey is speed talking over the phone, and I'm doing my best not to cut her off with shocked WTFs and oh my Gods.

"We were always careful—I guess today, it just slipped through. Everything is slipping. It was easier not telling everyone we were hooking up. It was just something between me and Olly, and it's sex. It's only sex, okay? It's casual and . . . and I care about him, and I know I'm also with your fake boyfriend and now you know I'm sleeping with your brother and it's so fucked-up." Her voice cracks. "I'm a terrible friend."

"That's the last thing you are, Hailey," I finally interject, the shock slowly subsiding.

In hindsight, the signs of her and Oliver were everywhere.

I've seen Oliver scoop her up and jump in a pool with her in his arms. Always making sure to toss her book or e-reader in a safe place beforehand. I've seen him bear-hug her from behind at fifteen, seventeen, twenty, twenty-four. I've seen how Hailey smiles when Oliver flirts with her—but that's what he is. A certified *flirt*. I thought he was being playful with a friend.

They were friends. They *are* friends. Friends who took each other's *virginities*.

Add in the fact that Oliver has been the one to pull Hailey out of her fixations—to help her fall asleep lately—I should've known their relationship was much closer.

I guess I thought she would've told me if she had feelings for my brother, but then I think, *I never told her I had feelings for hers*.

I adjust the phone against my ear, careful not to drop it in the tub. I took the call in a bubble bath at the boathouse. "I get why you didn't tell me," I say. "I didn't share with you how much I liked Rocky. I let you believe I couldn't stand him."

Now it makes sense why she wasn't angry or upset when she found out about me and her brother—she was just *stunned*. Basically, what I am now.

"I knew you were better than me that way," Hailey says quietly. "That you'd come clean with your feelings, even if it's hard. You're good at sharing what's in your heart."

I release a wheezy laugh. "Me? Rocky and I had feelings for each other for eons, and it took us forever to verbalize them."

Hailey and Oliver succumbed to their attraction. Whereas Rocky and I tortured ourselves with ours. If we'd had sex when we were teenagers, if he'd been my first, would we have a similar friends-with-benefits thing going on? Or would that have been agonizing just in a different way? It's difficult to play the *what if* game.

All I know is that I like what I have now, and I love even more where Rocky and I are heading together.

"You're at least better than me at it, Phebs. Your love is really big, you know? It's the sort of ride-or-die love that makes it impossible to feel alone. It's why no one wants to leave you. It's why I never would."

My throat swells up, but I express the same sentiments back. I'd *never* leave her. I slosh my foot in the water, lifting my toes into the foamy bubbles. We're quiet for a second, but the silence isn't tense between us.

She goes on. "I'm not as good with emotions."

"You don't have to be," I tell her. "I'm not angry that you kept this a secret. I'm just really, *really* shocked." And I'm not sure she would have come clean had Rocky not walked in on them. It's possible her friends-with-benefits thing could've been kept secret for a lifetime, and I still wouldn't hold it against her.

We're not made for grudges. Not with each other at least.

"And I kinda want details," I say with a smile. "But not like graphic things with you and my brother, just like . . . the good stuff, you know?"

She laughs. "If anyone understands that, it would be me." Right, she's prodded for info about me and her brother together, too. The bright sound fades fast, and I hear her deep breath. "If there's an inverse of a vampire, something that doesn't drain blood but supplies it, then that's Oliver. Because at times I feel leeched of all that I have to give, at empty, and he makes sure I'm still pumping." Her voice shakes with emotion.

My eyes try to well up. "Do you love him?"

"I can't remember a moment where I didn't," she cries, "but it's just sex. *It's just sex.*" She's panicked.

"Okay, okay," I say fast. "And Jake? You slept together?" This confession still has my jaw dropped. I never thought Jake would do something even marginally scandalous. Secretly hooking up with your fake girlfriend's best friend? That is illicit.

I almost want to give him a high five.

But then I wonder if he took the risk because it was Hailey. Because he has stronger feelings for her than I even know.

My smile softens.

"Yeah, we had sex . . . and I think I'm falling for him, Phebs," Hailey says in a quiet breath. "What he's done for his sister, the *lengths* he goes for people—I know why half the servers and guests at VCC are in love with him. But I have a feeling most of us haven't even seen how deep his heart really goes, and I can't stop uncovering him . . . it's . . ."

"Hypnotizing? All-consuming?"

"All-consuming," she says. "In the moment, at least. He's not one novel. He's the whole library."

I remember her talking about Jake in the grocery store. "But you said you've always liked 'their hearts. How deep they are.' Plural."

"I must've been thinking about Oliver, too."

Wow. She almost slipped three days ago. If I prodded a little harder, maybe she would've told me, but I'm glad I didn't. She was sick that night.

I want to pick my brother's brain *so badly* about his feelings, too. But knowing who he is, I can already hear what Oliver would tell me.

He'd say, "What's not to love about Hailey?"

I smile at the bubbles. But what if she picks Jake in the end and not Oliver? What happens then? I don't ask, because it's another pointless *what if* meant to terrify.

Hailey fills the silence. "Like I mentioned, I'm not in a place for a relationship. They both know that."

"And Jake is okay with it?" I squint trying to picture his take on the situation. I have nothing. When I moved to Victoria, he was single, so it's not like I've seen him arm in arm with a girl. And our phony relationship is very, very chaste.

"Yeah, he said he was. I was up-front from the start. Our first time was after a book club at the beginning of February. He walked me to the loft. You were already sleeping, and he came in to collect some of the books he loaned me. We were in my room, and there was a moment . . . I don't know how to describe it. But I ended up asking if he wanted to fuck me."

She says it so nonchalantly. Like she asked him if he wanted to paint her toenails.

An uncontrollable grin overtakes me. "Did you say it like that?"

"Casually? Yeah."

"What did Jake do?"

"He picked me up. Put me on the bed. And *slowly* stripped me . . . it was the most sensual thing ever. He let me take off his clothes and explore him and blow him." She does love giving head. "With Oliver, sex is like being on a roller coaster. It's raunchy and . . . untamed. With Jake, it's drawn out like an art form." She pauses in thought. "I just really love watching them come." I laugh, and she groans, "Shit, sorry. Your brother."

I'm not that abashed, and weirdly, I'm a glutton for punishment and would rather be *in the know* with the juicy gossip. Even if I regret it later. "I like that you enjoy rocking Jake's world . . ." I shut one eye. "And my brother's."

"I don't want you to think I'm hurting either of them. It's just . . . it's not serious."

"Just sex," I echo what she's said.

Clearly there *are* feelings, but Hailey isn't in a place to confront them. Sex isn't as messy as love in her head. And she already has enough to untangle. With her full plate, adding a love triangle into the mix would send me over the edge, too.

Our talk lightens when Hailey asks me about work, since she's dipped out so much. I mention Katherine's obsession with pink hydrangeas and a new chef that's being onboarded in late spring.

"Thanks for the condoms, by the way," Hailey says. "The ones you gave me on Valentine's Day." She did ask if I had any to spare, and I had a whole unused box since they were pre-Rocky, and I had no clue he had a super-specific condom preference.

"Wait, so you weren't sleeping with Liam the Dog Walker, then?" I assumed that's who they were for.

"I let you believe I was having sex with him when you brought him up. *I'm sorry.*" She's crying. "I'm the—"

"Most amazing person in this whole fucking world, and I will accept nothing less," I say into the speaker of my phone.

"Y-you're the best." Her staggered breath sounds like a hiccup. "My emotions are just all over the place."

"You're *exhausted*, Hails. You need sleep."

"I know, I know."

"Go get some now."

"I will. Love you, Phoebe."

I express the same love back, then hang up. After setting my phone on the tiled ledge that surrounds the tub, I relax back. I drift off a little as minutes pass, feeling my limbs ooze and the water become lukewarm. I drain the tub halfway, then spin the handle for more hot water.

Once it's steamy, I slowly sink underneath the bubbly water, letting my hair soak, before coming up for air. The door opens as I wipe suds out of my eyes.

My pulse skyrockets.

Rocky is already shedding his jacket, his shirt, and he pulls off his belt with a single hand. "I'm here for the *Transformers* watch party," he tells me.

"So sad," I say with a wry smile. "You're ten minutes too late. We just finished the last one. You would have loved Michael Bay's take on Bumble—"

Rocky sheds his pants with his boxer briefs, and his long, thick cock steals my words. He flashes a self-satisfied smile that abruptly closes my slack jaw, and then he confidently strides to the bathtub, stepping into the warm water. I catch the slight wince when he bends his bad knee to get in.

"Who said you were invited?" I ask, as he scoops me by the hips and draws me onto his lap. His length presses against my belly.

He gives me a pointed look. "This is *my* bathtub," he reminds me. "Who says *you* were invited?"

"This was a sanctioned bubble bath." My confidence matches his.

"I don't think it was." He spreads my legs around him and runs his hands up my slippery, bare back. "I'm going to have to arrest you."

My pulse thumps heavier and lower. We're eye level with each other, our lips teasingly close. "You can't arrest me. I've done nothing wrong. No crimes to my name."

His fingers dig into the soft flesh of my ass. "Phoebe Graves," he whispers against my ear. His hand trails between my legs. "You are guilty of a crime." His touch against my swollen clit makes me squirm, and he clutches me tighter to him. "Your crime is loving me." His arms are strength and power. "It." He has a fistful of my wet hair. "Is." He draws my head back in a fierce tug. "Criminal." He sinks his mouth against my neck. I shelter a cry as he trails hot, vicious kisses down my collarbone and to my breasts. He sucks my nipple as if it's my punishment.

A soft moan escapes me with a shortened breath. He presses a clawing kiss to my lips. The force pulls me into his chest.

Resist. Resist. I draw back, just to plant a glare on him. And catch my breath. "Guess I'm spending life in prison."

"Yeah?" He fists his cock.

"Yeah," I nod.

"Why's that?"

"Because," I say, "loving you is a crime I'll keep committing." His gaze tears through mine, as if barreling to the core of me. "I don't know how to stop."

"Don't stop," he says in a single, husky breath. His tip teases against my pussy, and while our eyes are latched with deep-seated cravings, he lowers me onto him, bucking his waist upward—plunging himself into me.

The fullness is a total body high, and I press my forehead to his shoulder and shudder against him. Wrapping my arms around Rocky, I cling. I want to be welded. Molded. Unable to be torn apart.

Instinct overwhelms me, and I grind forward on him. He grabs my hips in a vise, keeping me still.

"More," I groan into his shoulder.

"Don't fucking move," he says meanly.

Giving in sounds boring, and I stubbornly attempt to climb off his lap, but his grip is steel. He won't let me go. *Good. Don't. Never do.*

The beat of my heart won't slow. Not even when he unplugs the tub. Water begins to drain. He has a bunch of my hair again, but he won't thrust up and create friction.

I glare. "You're an edge monster."

He laughs lowly. "Okay . . . I'll do worse." He sucks my pierced nipple again, and then slowly massages the other perked bud. I arch my back, letting him have me, because *holy shit* this feels incredible. Toe-curling sensations ripple down my limbs.

"*Rocky*," I warn as I near a climax. My body trembles, and I try to fight off his hands, but he so easily responds in kind, teasing my nipple with his thumb. I'm a whimpering fucking mess against him.

The last layer of water slips into the drain. We're in an empty tub, and I start sensing how wet I really am. He's so fucking big, and without a condom, the heat of his cock ramps up pleasure and need.

He circles my hips on his shaft.

"Okayokayokay," I cry, hoping it'll ease the torment.

"Surrendering already?" he asks, amused, but he's drawn his hand away from the sensitive spot.

I meet his eyes in a fiery challenge. "Never," I say with ragged breath, but I bore my gaze into his.

He makes a low grunting noise in the back of his throat that I'm going to remember for the rest of my life.

"I'm going to fuck you now," he tells me.

Yes! my brain screams, but I try to remain reticent on the outside. "Okay, then do it." Anticipation mounts in a heady wave.

His arms curve around me while I'm sitting on his cock. He fastens me against his chest with a possession that I'm ravenous for. He holds me like I belong to him.

And he begins fucking me with the same aggression. My breath hitches, and he keeps me utterly still while he thrusts upward. His tempo is so fast, so raw—like he can't have me soon enough.

Tears pinch out of my eyes.

"*Phoebe*," he groans against my ear.

"Rock—" I cry into his shoulder. I'm just holding on for dear life.

He's clutching every inch of me in his grasp. He has all of me, and the way he works on me like my pleasure is his pleasure—like we are one—it sends me into a bliss like nothing before. How—how is sex with Rocky this amazing? Why did I wait so long to discover its true power?

Mind-numbing friction thieves oxygen and burns through me. Our lips skim, our breaths melding—the heat of an almost-kiss more intoxicating than the actual touch of one. So very quickly, I ascend to another plane. I'm lit up, and my body quakes as an orgasm bursts through my senses.

I muffle my cry in his neck.

He's hugging me. Holding me. Loving me. Never letting go of me. The affection whirls around me like thick steam. The water he drained wasn't even as hot as the sex our bodies just made.

He's still . . . no condom . . . I pant as I come down. He pulls the wet strands of hair off my cheeks and kisses me soulfully deep. Then he carefully lifts me off him.

He's so hard. He didn't come. I didn't think he would. Rocky's control is impressive and usually to my benefit.

Last thing I want right now is a baby.

As he stands, while I stay knelt in the empty tub, I look up and see the hunger in his eyes. I see the ridges of his muscles along his torso. I see the veins bulging in his cock. My pussy throbs again.

He collects a fistful of my wet blue hair. Ohhh. *Okay*. Deep breaths. I've skirted around giving a blow job for literal months . . . Maybe *skirted* is the wrong word. It's honestly just . . . never happened.

I've started believing Rocky doesn't enjoy receiving head. Even though the idea of wrapping my lips around him has been *slightly* enticing, the only part I really crave is him clenching my hair.

Which he's doing. With his other hand gripping his shaft, he says, "Open."

"Open what?" I combat, trying not to panic.

"You've never heard of a blow job before?"

"Never heard of one I liked," I mutter under my breath.

"What was that?"

My face burns. Stubbornness wins out again. Instead of answering, I unlock my jaw and part my lips for him.

He's scrutinizing me. "Is this your first blow job?"

"What?" I try to draw back, but he cups my head, not letting me jerk away. "I've definitely told you I've given head before." Maybe not while we were together, but he learned that fact somewhere along our twisty-turny history.

"You could've lied."

"*I didn't*," I snap back.

"Okay, all right," he says, seeing that I was truthful. "I'm just trying to understand . . . ?"

"Understand what?"

"Why you look like a frightened little bird every time my cock is inches from your mouth."

My heart races at an unnatural speed.

THIRTY-TWO

Rocky

"I'm not . . ." she starts to protest, but she can't finish.

I study the way her collarbone juts in and out with short, choppy breaths. I can't quite chalk it up to *fear*. Not when she's fucking obstinate as hell. I love that about Phoebe—I love *so much* about this woman, but I'm going to lose my mind if she pushes herself to a place she's A) not ready for, or God forbid B) terrified of.

She's on her knees while I tower over her bare, vulnerable frame. Is it the position? Does she feel too defenseless? I hold the back of her skull, and her combative eyes are hoisted as they never tear from mine.

"Not what?" I prod. "Scared?"

"I'm not scared," she says, sounding assured.

I believe her. "Do you want me to fuck your face?"

"Sure," she retorts. "I dare you."

"You dare me?" I look her over as she shifts her knees. Her thighs unconsciously spread. She's turned on.

"Double-dog dare."

"Oh, now I'm *really* tempted."

"You should be. The dare lasts for thirty seconds before it's rescinded."

"The *double-dog* dare," I correct.

She flips me off, then takes that same hand and wraps her fingers around my erection. Squeezing.

I let her slowly stroke my length, only to see her reaction. Blood pools south, a pounding heartbeat in my dick, and the urge to push into her mouth intensifies.

Phoebe is examining me, more interested in what I want, but I'm trying to make sense of her boundaries. We're at this weird fucking standstill that I'm going to rip through.

I pry her hand off my length, and when she reaches back, I swat her away. Then I cup her chin. "Open your fucking mouth."

"Fuck *you*," she curses.

"You made the double-dog dare. You want to take it back? Now's your chance before I fill your mouth with my erection, and you won't be able to say *Miami*."

She glares, but her breath catches in arousal. The dirty talk is a turn-on. She clutches the backs of my thighs. "Let's see what you've got," she challenges, then parts her lips.

I stare down at Phoebe. At her big brown eyes, at her knees widening on the tub. At her mouth forming an O around my cock as I slowly, slowly flex into her. My muscles coil as the sensations strike one primal urge.

Come. Inside. Her.

She sucks me and licks around my head, like she understands what to do, but I fist her hair and stop her from working my cock herself.

I guide her head forward, making her take a few more inches, then I pull her back out. Her fingers dig into my thighs.

Twice, I move her head back and forth. *Ooh* she does not like that. Her jaw tenses, likely wanting to shut.

Let's try something else.

With a firm hand against her head, I root her in place and then rock into her mouth. *Better.* She groans around my shaft, her eyelids heavy with arousal. I'm about to describe what I'm doing to her out loud, but her body stiffens like she's uncomfortable. Like this is not her thing.

So I pull out, and before she complains, I growl, "Stay still." I clasp her jaw with one hand, and I stroke myself with the other.

Her eyes spark with desire.

Yeah. She loves this.

Watching me masturbate. I get off seeing her arousal overtake her haughty attitude, and she's not fighting me. She's not rigid and locked up. She's melting. Trying desperately to stay upright.

Fucking Christ. My muscles are up in flames.

I slide my fingers into her hair, until my palm finds the back of her head again. I just hold her, the threat of forcing my cock into her lips is there. The danger. She emits this tiny, aching breath, and it sends me.

I let myself release, a groan scratching my throat, and I come on her face.

Phoebe shuts her eyes, her lips permanently parted as pleasured breaths stagger out of her. *Fuck*, that might be the hottest thing I've done to her . . . since the last time we fucked.

I scoop her up—cradling her in my arms.

"Rocky?"

"Don't open your eyes." I step out of the bathtub and into the nearby glass shower. Setting Phoebe on her feet, I shove the showerhead toward the wall. Then I swivel the knob and pull her away as cold water hits the tile. I wet a washcloth, and while the shower warms, I clean her face.

Her lips tic up, just slightly. She holds loosely to my waist.

"Cumshots over blow jobs, huh?" I ask her, seeing that she has a preference.

"I guess so."

"Bad experience giving head?"

She stiffens a little, her eyes still shut. "I've just never enjoyed it. The whole act hurts my jaw. But I did want to try with you."

I stare at her beautiful dark lashes. "Why?" I ask, tossing the washcloth aside. When I adjust the showerhead so warm water sprays down on us, she opens her eyes on me.

"I thought maybe it's something you need."

I laugh. "A blow job?"

"You mean it's not your number one fave thing in the whole wide world?" She crosses her arms. Her snide attitude back in style. "You don't dream of being sucked off by me? You're not throwing yourself into oncoming traffic every day that my lips aren't wrapped around your hard . . . *fucking* . . . *cock*?"

I exhale this graveled guttural noise. She knows how to rouse the fucking beast inside me—the one that wants to defile her pussy.

But I force the desires aside for a second. "I don't *need* a blow job." I could tell there was a hang-up with her surrounding them, and I figured I'd rip the Band-Aid now and find out why.

"But you like them?" she asks.

"Not if you don't enjoy it. And it's not a loss if you never want to suck my cock. There are too many other things I can do to you that'd turn me on more."

She tries to stifle a smile, but her cheeks flush with affection. I pull her into my arms while water slips down our bodies.

"I love you, Rocky," she says so softly into my chest.

My lungs elevate with the depth of that truth. "My Phoebe," I murmur. I press a kiss against her temple and whisper, "Still spending life in prison for me?"

"Forty years with parole."

I stare her down. "Only forty years?"

"Five years. Home arrest."

Our smiles rise at the same time, then I spin her around. She relaxes her shoulders against my chest, and I wrap my arms around her abdomen, holding her for a second while the water cascades on our bodies.

She shuts her eyes, and I feel her hands on my legs, telling me to stay. I'm not going. Our breaths are in sync, and as I track my fingers through her hair, scraping them along her scalp, she melts further against me.

And I think, *I need to tell her.*

I need to tell her everything about today. Because why? This moment is too peaceful, and I can't relax? Because I'm afraid to be calm inside the eye of the storm with Phoebe?

But then I remember.

We are the natural disaster.

Our peace is a Richter scale of 7.0 and climbing. The earth should be quaking.

When we hop out of the shower, I tell her, "Refill the tub, I'll be back." Towel around my waist, I go grab a couple green bottles of Sanpellegrino from the kitchen fridge. I've had enough alcohol today. (Thanks, Trent.) Sparkling water it is.

Phoebe and I lounge on either side of the tub, our legs threaded. A thin layer of soapsuds shrouds her body, and I'm taking a hearty swig of water as she says, "How's your knee?"

I take a quick glance at my kneecap. No scars, no noticeable issues, but it's sore as fuck in this scrunched position. "It feels like I should've gotten it looked at years ago, and I didn't."

"When did you even mess it up?" Her brows crinkle as she fights for the memory.

"Somewhere outside of Boston."

"I asked *when*, not where." She splashes me lightly.

The water sloshes at my chest. "Hey." I point my bottle at her. "Don't be pissed at me if you can't connect place with time."

"Somewhere outside of Boston isn't even an exact place," she counters. "And you never talk about it."

"About my knee?"

"Yeah."

"It's a bum knee, Phebs. There's nothing to talk about." I wish she hadn't brought this up. "I tripped."

"You've said that before, and I still can't picture it."

"I stepped in a fucking hole, and my knee decided to take a wrong turn. It dislocated. Probably tore some ligaments. I don't know. It's never been right since."

I hope she doesn't press.

She nods slowly. "Okay. You tripped." She partially believes me, and that's good enough. "Your badass cred has shot down."

"I'll cry about it later."

She motions to my neck with her Sanpellegrino. "The scar on your neck shoots it back up, don't worry."

"Oh yeah. Some shady friend of the mark almost slitting my throat at sixteen—what's more badass than nearly pissing your pants?"

"That was a bad one," she murmurs, her eyes skimming

my arms, which I rest on the lips of the tub. "Would you get a tattoo, if you could?"

Never get a real tattoo. A rule we've all followed to this day.

When you're trying to be forgotten from city to city, it's not smart to have permanent ink on your body that can identify you. It's not even to evade law enforcement. It's so these rich fucks don't hire PIs and come seek revenge if they've felt slighted. Hell, Trevor's stalker didn't even need a PI to find him.

Though, we have worn fake tattoos for certain jobs before.

Applying them constantly is a bitch.

"Probably not. Would you?" I ask her.

"I'd have a whole thigh tat," she says. "Maybe something right beneath my boobs, too. Or on my sternum between them."

"Huh."

"Huh?" She makes a face.

"You've thought about this before."

Phoebe shrugs. "I had a cherry-blossom vine on my hip for one job, and I liked it. I was sad when I had to take it off." She sips her water. "Oliver says to just do it, that I can wear makeup, but Nova says it's stupid."

"It is stupid," I say, sitting up higher to stretch out my leg. "If we leave. It's not if we stay and you quit conning for good."

Phoebe contemplates this silently. "Yeah . . . so your sister."

I'm all right with the change of topic. It seems like she hasn't figured out what she wants to do yet. Phoebe isn't a two-years-down-the-line planner. She's a week-ahead type of person, and one week from now, we're still working a job.

"Your brother," I reply.

"Did you see it coming? The two of them sleeping together?" She gathers her hair in her hands.

"I was ignoring the signs. Purposefully. I didn't want to know." I drag her to my side and reach out to do her hair.

Leaning her shoulders against my chest, she lets me collect the wet strands. "I had no clue," Phoebe says. "None. I think that's the worst part." She hands me her hair tie. "Feeling like I *didn't* catch on."

I twist the elastic into a high pony. "They're grifters, too, Phebs. They're trained to lie. It's not a knock on your skills." When I release her hair, she eases back against me.

I curl my biceps around her and hold her forearms, which lie against her abdomen. Our breaths sync again, and I finally say, "I saw Varrick at the bookstore, before I drove over here." And she listens as I recount the entire interaction, his threat to buy the loft, her slashed tires, the phone call with Everett, and how Varrick knew my name.

I end with the thing that's bugging me the most. "I think he might be my father."

"Your . . . *birth* father?" She turns slightly to meet my gaze. "You're serious?"

"There was *pride* in his eyes, Phebs. At The Hunt. It just hit me today that it's a look a father would give a son."

"Okay, yeah." She nods. "That's plausible. Why wouldn't it be? There've been stranger things in our lives. So Varrick might be your father." She's cringing.

"Yeah, I know."

"I hope he's not, Rocky. I really do."

"Me, too."

She stares off at the Venice Canal painting. "I have another theory. It's not about Varrick, though."

"What is it?"

"You and Jake . . . I think you might be brothers."

The second I realize *she's* serious, I start laughing.

She sighs. "I'm not joking."

"Yeah, that's why it's funny."

She shoves my arm, then tries to leave for the other side. I wrap my arms tighter, not letting her pull away. "Rocky—"

"Why the fuck would I be related to a Koning?"

"*Jake*, specifically," she says. "Because hating cilantro is genetic, and you both think it tastes like soap." Her face reddens. "Shut up."

I bottle the laughter and process this. "Phebs, if he's my brother . . ." I shake my head repeatedly. "I can't see it. I'm sorry. He has Dutch ancestry. More Germanic. We don't look very similar, but if you're right . . . you can have my million."

She perks up. "Deal." We shake on a million-dollar bet.

"Meat lover's, extra cheese," Phoebe tells me while she switches on the hair dryer. Wet blue tendrils soak the shoulders of her very old, baggy Strawberry Shortcake tee. One she left at my place.

I mentally file her request. "Ordering my favorite pizza for me?"

"That's been *my* go-to order since forever. Not yours."

"Since forever?" I arch my brows and knot the strings to my sweats. "You didn't even like pepperoni until you were thirteen."

Her jaw drops. "That's so not . . ." *It is true*. She steels her gaze. "I influenced you and that's the hill I will fucking die on."

"Great. Make sure it's a small hill so I don't have to climb Kilimanjaro to come visit you every day."

Her emerging smile is the last visual I have of her. Honestly, it almost coaxes me back to Phoebe, but I leave the loud *whoosh* of hot air to call the local pizza joint.

"Hi, I'd like to place an order for delivery." Phone to my ear, I'm in the kitchen. I open the high-tech fridge to make sure we have something to drink. More Sanpellegrino. Liter of Fizz Life, since we were all curious what the new aspartame-free soda from Fizzle tasted like. Not bad.

And it's still about half full. *Good enough.* I order a few large pies. Just in case her brothers haven't eaten tonight.

Oliver counts his macros religiously, so I'm unsure if he'll eat a slice. I get him meatballs and grilled chicken as extra protein.

What I don't expect is for Trevor to show up.

He has on dark shades and a slim suit. His expression is void. Flat. Emotionless. Can't read him that well right now.

He bypasses me.

The kitchen is open to the wood-paneled living room. Sliding glass doors overlook a dark, rippling sea, a crescent moon in the star-speckled sky, and he's staring into the night.

I stride over to him. The sailboat I'm demoing is secured to the dock and sways lightly with the nighttime breeze. I see no other movement.

Still, I fling the curtains closed.

Anyone from the water can see inside the boathouse at this hour, and once Phoebe exits the bathroom—no one needs to spot me with her.

"What's going on?" I ask him, slipping my phone in my back pocket.

"Just contemplating." He's quiet.

"About?"

Trevor breaks out of his thoughts to slip me a paper. The *Victoria Weekly.* "Nova texted and said to be here. He wants us all to go over the plan again."

I can't say it's a bad idea. I flip open the *Weekly*. Trevor peers over at the popular gossip column.

SIDNEY SAYS

Collin Falcone broke his leg at a Caufield kegger doing a backflip. (Go Sea Serpents!)

Rowing coach Giddeon Rosenbaum proposed to long-term girlfriend Chelsea Noknoi after a romantic date at The Lure.

Watersmith was spotted holding hands in the parking lot of the country club. Trusted sources say they looked more smitten than ever.

The Fortunate Four attended another party on the Konings' superyacht. Invited were the who's who of Victoria. (Including yours truly.)

More disturbing stories of TK Waterford's rakish behavior have been brought to the *Weekly*'s attention. He's widely known to be gregarious, but perhaps his charm is more sleaze than sweet.

I reread the part about TK. "Why didn't Sidney *specifically* spell out what Trent did?" I ask my brother.

"Claudia threatened her. She already tried to pay off the de la Vegas, so they'd remove Sidney's column. They weren't swayed, so Claudia went to Sidney. And she said if she wrote anything defaming about her son, she'd sue her, or do worse." Trevor carries anger in the pits of his eyes, but I can't see behind his sunglasses. I just hear the ire building in his voice. "Sidney is scared."

"Claudia reacting poorly over a gossip column is good for us. And if she's rude to Sidney, *Victoria's Sweetheart*, then locals will start turning on Claudia. Especially if she takes away their entertainment." I hold up the paper.

Trevor nods with more understanding. "Yeah, I get it."

I glance at the column again. "Trusted sources say Jake and Phoebe look smitten?" *Also good for us.* "Who was that source?" I raise my brows at him and push the paper into his chest. "You?"

His lip tics up in a slanted smile, and he grabs hold of the *Weekly*. "I told her they looked ready to get hitched and have a kid. She went with *smitten*."

I put a hand to his head, shoving him lovingly. "You did good, Trev."

He seems to be out of his funk. A grin spreads across his face. "Thanks, Rock."

Our attention swerves the second Nova blows into the boathouse like a powerful wind. He throws a duffel bag on the round glass six-seater table. The Edison-bulb pendant light rattles at the force.

Looks like we're not eating at the fucking table.

Nova unzips the duffel. Full of guns and ammo.

He racks a shotgun.

"Way to make an entrance, Winchester," I say.

"Is that you being nice or a dick?"

I come over. "You didn't hear the *fuck you* in my tone?" I check the mag on a Glock.

Nova has a shadow of a smile that disappears when he sees Trevor's cringe. "You might not like guns, Trev, but the girls were being cased. And we still don't know why Varrick is interested in them."

"This seems like overkill," Trevor says, as though Nova is bringing a sledgehammer to a pool party.

"Where there's rain, there's a hurricane," Nova says.

"Not true, but okay," Trevor says tensely. He backs away from the duffel.

His hatred of guns stems from being shot in the foot. He

was friends with this rich kid in Dallas whose father had a collection of prized hunting guns. They were more for display. His friend fucked around with one and accidentally pulled the trigger.

Oliver and Hailey arrive next.

He's carrying my sister in a piggyback while she reads an old textbook. I've seen them do this half our lives. Her arms hang over his chest, and she grips the book low enough that he can see the pages, too.

I'm irritated that he's acting like I didn't just catch him with his pants down. So I decide to share my annoyance. I turn to Nova. "They're fucking."

He's jarred and immediately eyes Oliver.

Jesus. I understand that look. "*You* knew?" I ask Nova. He's the most loyal brother—because he's not confirming shit to me without permission.

Oliver comes clean. "He knew."

"Since we were fifteen," Nova says. "I walked in on them."

"Glad I'm not the first," I say.

Nova shakes his head roughly at Oliver like he can't believe he slipped. "You're talking to Phoebe about this. I'm out of it."

"What's there to talk about?" Oliver says. "Nothing has changed."

"I can't look at you two the same," I shoot back. "Things have *definitely* changed."

Hailey is engrossed in her textbook. She mutters, "'The earliest known accounts date back to thirteen thousand BC in southern France inside the Cave of the Trois-Frères.'"

Oliver sets her down as I ask, "Accounts of what?"

Her nose is still in the book. "Therianthropy."

"Shape-shifting," Oliver clarifies. "She's been on a deep dive of old folklores."

"And that helps us how?" I ask Hailey.

She's not answering. She just plops dazedly on a leather chair. Flipping through her novel. Trevor lifts his sunglasses for the first time to inspect the state of our sister.

"No stone unturned," Oliver says lightly, inspecting the mini armory in the duffel.

Nova is concerned. "She's flipping over the entire ocean floor."

I rake my hands through my hair, worried about my sister if she's now cycling through irrelevant mythologies.

"She'll find the tracks again," Oliver tells me, more assuredly. "Let her derail. Addison never did."

Nova tears his gaze off Hailey. "Probably for good reason," he says darkly to me.

Yeah.

I don't know.

"Has it started yet?"

The voice of Jake Koning Waterford steals my attention. He's dressed down in jeans and a white VICTORIA COUNTRY CLUB T-shirt.

I plaster my surprised look on Nova, who sent out these invites. He says plainly, "He's important."

"No shit," I mutter. We can't do this without him. "Hope you like pizza, Jake." I pat his chest and say, "Welcome to five hours of preplanning hell."

"Five hours?" Jake asks.

"That's being generous."

"Everyone's here?" Phoebe waltzes in with dried hair twisted in a high pony. Seeing her, I almost smile.

Nova packs the guns and zips the duffel up. "Team meeting. Now."

Logistics are a major pain in the ass, but it's necessary.

Even without our parents to run the show, we've been trained on how to man the helm. We're all camped out in the living room. Three pizza boxes cracked open on the square coffee table. Glasses of Fizz Life and bottles of water slowly empty as we formulate possible scenarios for what might happen when we pull the rope.

"Let's go over scenario C one more time," Nova says, setting down his cheese slice to grab his notebook.

"You're burning those pages after tonight," I remind him.

He glowers. "Who do you think I am?"

"Someone who needs to make lists on paper instead of in your head."

Nova ignores me. The kitchen chair, which he dragged over here, creaks as he leans back and scribbles in his little book of crimes.

"Scenario C is the least likely to happen," Phoebe says next to me on the brown leather couch. I have an arm over her shoulders. She licks pizza sauce off her finger. "Do we really think Claudia will sic her security on me?"

"She could," Jake answers, relaxed on the other side of me. "My mother has had Jordan's friends escorted out before."

"That's Jordan," Phoebe counters. "I'm *your* guest, and she respects you more than your older brother."

Nova cuts back in. "It's a possibility. We need to prepare for it."

"Okay, Dad," Trevor says on the floor, lounging back on his hands.

"Nova's trying not to get us caught," I tell him. "Because when your ass is on the line, you're going to want him to be five feet away."

Nova goes silent. I can feel his deep surprise that I'd stick up for him.

"True, yeah." Trevor nods to Phoebe's brother. "Sorry, Nov."

He nods back, brushing it off easily.

I wad my napkin and see Phoebe constantly checking on Hailey with side glances. I do, too. My sister nibbles on a cheese slice and reads to herself. She's contributed to this discussion tonight, so my worries have slowly waned.

Oliver hasn't sat down. He is a live wire. He stands and paces and forks a piece of chicken from a to-go container.

"Is he on something?" Jake whispers to me.

"Oliver was with me at Trent's."

"Fuck," Jake curses under his breath and careens farther back as his muscles stiffen.

"You're not responsible for your dipshit brother," I whisper.

"I pulled all of you into this. I *am* responsible if anything happens to you," he whispers back.

I full-on meet his gaze. "You pulled in people who've done this their whole lives. Chill."

Jake sits like he's on the verge of storming a castle. I swear he and Nova together could be a pair of unrelenting legionaries.

Oliver bobs his head to the beat of nothing. "How many scenarios are there total?"

Nova thumbs pages. "I have all the way to R."

"And we're stuck on C?" Phoebe groans.

"Like I was saying," I tell Jake. "Five hours."

He twists off the cap of a Pellegrino. "I have nowhere better to be." I hold his determined gaze. His homelife is chaos and power plays, and mine wasn't that far off.

We're doing this together.

"What are we calling him?" Trevor tilts his head to Jake. "You have to have a name."

"You're the professionals." Jake stares around at us. "You tell me."

We all look to Hailey.

She's thoughtful. "It's not that you're rich. It's that you have the keys to the town. The one true heir." She says, "*The King.*"

Phoebe is grinning from ear to ear with Hailey, like we've officially just included a new person in our childhood club-house.

I'm not mad about it. I wonder if it's because Jake isn't someone I was taught to protect. He's been trying to help me. To look out for me.

Jake smiles at the girls, then turns to me. "You said I'm not a real king yet."

"You will be."

He has to be. This can't be all for nothing.

Nova tosses him a phone. "It's your burner. We'll give you our numbers. Memorize them. When you text us, you'll use a crown at the end of your messages."

"I have a serious question." Trevor sits up now.

Nova folds the cover of his notebook. "Go ahead."

"Oliver and Hailey—they should bunk up, and I should take Oliver's bed."

My arm falls off Phoebe. Jesus Christ. Here we go.

Oliver chews the grisly chicken slowly. "Was there a question in there?"

Jake wipes his hands with a napkin. Tension in his shoulders.

"It's more of a serious suggestion," Trevor says, "now that we know you're boning my sister."

"Oh God," Hailey mutters, hiding beneath her book and sinking in the chair. "It's just casual."

Trevor gapes. "No way this is just casual."

"It *is*." Hailey drops her book to her lap.

"Then casually share a bed."

No one says a thing.

Until now, I haven't heard Trevor complain about crashing on the couch. Whenever I spend the night at the loft, I let Trevor take my vacant bed at the boathouse. Essentially, he's been bouncing between Hailey's place and mine.

Oliver and Hailey share a short glance. I think Oliver would share a bed with her indefinitely in a heartbeat, but not if it'd cause her more distress.

"She can stay at my apartment," Jake offers.

Now Oliver pops the lid onto his container and wanders to the fridge. He's avoiding. My sister looks ready to coexist with the chair cushion.

Before I butt in, Phoebe says loudly, "She's *not* moving, and no one is moving in with her. Because I can live at the boathouse. Trevor can take my room."

"No," about everyone says at once.

"Moving in with your ex-husband?" Nova shakes his head at her. "Fuck no. We're not putting your fake relationship in jeopardy. The entire reason Oliver and I are still rooming with Rocky is so you two can have time together."

It's been the best alibi for why Phoebe constantly visits the boathouse. They're living with me *for* their sister. Phoebe rooming with Hailey is also the only reason I can stay at the loft.

Phoebe must feel a sense of guilt. Our relationship is causing this mess, and she's never really been selfish. But this isn't the first time we've all lived on top of each other.

Though, around this time, we'd be packing our bags and switching cities.

"Is the loft even safe anymore?" Oliver asks from the kitchen, since I told everyone about Varrick seeking to purchase it.

"I'll talk to my mother about it," Jake assures us.

"It's safe for now," Phoebe chimes in. "We don't need to add *find a new home* on top of this job. Especially when this home is free . . ." She trails off in thought, then looks to Jake. "And maybe I could . . . with . . ."

The bottom of my stomach drops. "No. You're not living with him."

"He wouldn't mind."

"*I* mind." She'd only be doing it to take one for the fucking team, and this is not it. I elbow Jake in the ribs. "You going to revoke that offer to our girlfriend, sweetheart?"

"You can't stay at my place, Phoebe," Jake tells her flat out.

I smile dryly at her, satisfied.

She threads her arms and peers past me to tell Jake, "Rocky has you wrapped around his finger. You realize that?"

"We just have mutual interests."

"Which would be?"

"Protecting you."

Phoebe's shoulders slacken. Yeah, she would live with him, but she doesn't want to. We both know that. Because living with Jake means I can't sneak into her bedroom anymore. It'll *drastically* limit our time together.

"Olly will move in with me," Hailey declares, picking at her nail polish. "Or I'll live with Jake."

"You don't have to do that," Phoebe says. "Really, we can figure something else out. Maybe we just buy Trevor a coffin to sleep in. Let him live out his Dracula fantasies."

"Maybe we just throw you to the bears, PG. Since you're so good at being bait and all."

Goddammit.

I open my mouth, but Phoebe puts a hand to my chest and says, "It's fine, I started it."

"I'll sleep on the speedboat," Nova offers.

He wouldn't even get into the hull of my sailboat for a five-minute chat. The irony of him being isolated on the *Salty Miss* most of the day—he gets fucking *seasick*.

"A life of vomit, ginger beer, and Dramamine." I flash a dry smile. "*Fun.*"

"What about the wine cellar?" Trevor asks me. "No one ever uses it here. I'll get a cot. It's big enough to be a room."

He wants privacy. "You can't bring Sidney over."

"*I know.*"

"It's fifty degrees in there," Nova warns.

"Fifty-seven, and that's fine. I can manage."

Nova shrugs stiffly at me like it is the best solution. It's only temporary, too. This situation is far from permanent. "All right," I say—just as Hailey's phone rings.

She's quick to answer. "Yeah? Yeah, everyone is here. Hold on." She puts the phone on speaker. "It's Carter."

"Hello, Ailey and mates," Carter greets. "I got a quick minute between some work I'm doing, and I found something out you'll want to know."

"About what?" I ask.

"Rocky, *Rocky*," Carter singsongs with a grating cheerfulness.

"Get to the point, Carter."

"Always so grumpy. Take a breath. Smell the sunshine." He laughs at his own dumb joke. "Get it—you can't smell the sun."

"We're hysterically laughing."

"I know Ailey is smiling."

She is.

"Barely," I snap.

"Been dabbling into this Varrick character," Carter says, "and he ain't who he says he is."

Jake frowns. "What do you mean?"

"His identity has holes. Not like Swiss cheese. Whoever built his alias did a hellava job, but it's not my work. I found some discrepancies in his identifications."

"They're fakes?" I ask.

"The fakest of fakes, mate. His birth certificate, a hundred percent forged. The parents he listed—don't exist. Passport, likely forged. I couldn't trace any past identities. But I do know he started using *Varrick* around the eighties. Then he married into the Wolfe family, and the rest—well, you know most of the rest."

Trevor stares at the phone. "So Varrick is a grifter?"

"No doubt about it in my mind. Varrick Wolfe is a con-man, and the probability he knows your parents is high."

Brayden.

I hear my name in the pit of my ear. His voice. Their voices.

Brayden.

"It's not just high," I tell Carter. "It's certain."

THIRTY-THREE

Rocky

THE BADGER GAME
Victoria, Connecticut

Don't mess with the plan, Trev." He's driving Phoebe and Hailey to the Koning estate and dropping them off. With the Honda out of commission, he's taking Nova's Pontiac GTO, which Nova hasn't let anyone behind the wheel of since he bought it at auction. He's been flush with cash after he oversold some flowerpot painting like it was an original van Gogh.

That car is his current baby. He won't even let me sit in the driver's seat. So Trevor should be fucking happy.

His insistence on wanting to shadow Varrick and integrate himself into his life is killing me. Varrick being a con artist who knows my name should be a big enough warning to stay away—but my brother doesn't see danger as a caution sign. I *just* want to keep him safe.

"When you drop them off," I say, "don't go looking for him."

He's quiet.

"*Trevor.* I don't want to worry about you getting stabbed while I'm here, and no one will be around to help you. Just think about that, please. *I won't be there.*"

"Okay," he says. "Okay." He's relenting. "This is all weekend?"

"Saturday and Sunday. We'll be done tomorrow morning," I tell him. Family and close friends are invited overnight for the Koning soiree, filled with a ten-course dinner, and then we wake up to Easter Sunday brunch. It's the first time Hailey has been hired on as staff for a Koning dinner, and we're taking it as an opportunity to get the evidence we need to bury Claudia.

This weekend, we pull the rope.

Phoebe is principal on this job. She'll take center stage, and I'm more on edge than I've been for any other gathering.

"Sounds good," Trevor says. "See you later." He hangs up quickly. Too quickly. I have a strange feeling in my stomach. *See you later.* He does mean tomorrow?

I carry this gnawing pit in my gut with me to the Koning estate. By the time I arrive and I've been greeted with an icy stare-down by the family butler, Niall Greensboro, I start walking the grounds.

Ever since I became BFFs with Trent, I've been to the estate enough to have it blueprinted on my eyeballs. Library on the first floor, west wing. Den next to the entryway. A theater room in the basement. The property covers over thirty acres and includes two greenhouses, an apple orchard, a private beach, a seventy-five-foot swimming pool with a pool house, and a main home with twenty-one rooms. It is extravagant.

And yet, it isn't the most luxurious property I've ever spent the weekend at.

Trent Waterford is in line to inherit it all, and that not only digs under my skin, but it drives me forward.

Staff mill about, mostly tending to different needs. Watering the plants on windowsills, changing out lightbulbs, and setting the table for dinner. No one gives me a second glance the farther I make my way through the property. It's as if I already belong. I walk around like I do.

The clock strikes three p.m. when I find my girlfriend's fake boyfriend outside.

"You're early," Jake tells me as he slams a tennis ball into the net. Before he approaches me, he fixes his attention on the gray-haired instructor on the other side of the grass court. "Stephen. Thanks for running me ragged with that backhand, old man."

Stephen laughs. "Not ragged enough." He hugs Jake over the net.

"Congrats again on grandchild number three," Jake says quietly, patting his instructor's back with warm familiarity. "Let Lydia know she's welcome to use the pool house for the baby shower."

I can't hear the instructor's response, but it's clear he appreciates Jake's generosity and benevolence. While collecting scattered tennis balls, Stephen peers over at me with a more guarded expression.

On a property brimming with staff, I'm not known as the ex-husband of Jake's current girlfriend. I am the best, *best* friend of Trent Koning Waterford.

Niall, the family butler, has given me an arctic breeze ever since we met. His icy disposition is shared among the staff.

It's clear which son they favor.

The tennis instructor heads toward the carriage house, which lies closest in proximity to the main house, and I step onto the grass court.

"Trent told me to come whenever," I explain. "Perks of

being *besties* with your big brother. I get an open invitation."
I wear a dry smile and toss Jake a gold-embroidered towel
hanging over a bench.

"A perk I could've given you." He rubs at the sweat along
his temples and neck.

"And then I'd have to decline your invite. Your brother
would bust a blood vessel if his closest friend ditched him for
the brother he just loves so *very* much."

"Point taken." Jake nods, then studies my white-and-blue
collegiate sweatshirt. COLUMBIA is stitched on the chest. He
knows it's all just a stage show. A prop. My wardrobe.

"It's my alma mater," I remind him casually.

"Got it," he says, but his blue eyes also tell me, *I'm not
blowing your cover.* I didn't think he would. We've been knee-
deep in this together for long enough that I do trust him.

Trust.

That word rolls over in my head. I'm surprised by myself
that I've become capable of letting someone else in this deep.
But here we are.

I watch a petrel fly over the court and toward the pool.
"Hailey and Phoebe will be here in a couple hours." I squint
out into the sun. From here, the sea laps against the rocky
ridgeline of the coast, and farther out, the *Salty Miss* is moored
with other sailing vessels. Gently swaying with the ripple of
the water.

Nova should be aboard. Our getaway. I imagine he's behind the nav table and watching the waves roll, probably obsessing over different worst-case scenarios where he'll have to
drive the dinghy to shore so we can all make a quick escape.

I hope we don't need him tonight.

Jake and I start walking back to the main house, and my
nerves are at high tide as I wait for Phoebe's arrival and likely

for Trent to come steal me away. We pass the entrance to a hedged garden, and Jake asks, "Did Niall show you your room yet?"

"I assumed I'd be staying in my usual one."

"The toilet's not working. You're being moved to the east wing."

"I was not informed," I say without much surprise. I'm sure Niall would've loved if I had to unclog a toilet all night.

Jake opens the back door himself, even though there's staff waiting in the wings to do it for him. "I'll lead the way," he says.

My new guest room is on the third floor. It has dark oak-trim windows, a four-poster bed, toile wallpaper, and a book-shelf full of works by Jane Austen. *Sense and Sensibility, Pride and Prejudice, Emma, Persuasion, Northanger Abbey,* and *Mansfield Park.* There must be dozens of different editions of each title, from leatherbound to more modern cover art.

"I'm guessing this is your collection," I say to Jake. "You being the bookworm and all."

"Those were Kate's actually." He opens the thick champagne-colored drapes, a stray ray of light seeping through. He fastens the drape with a thick roped tieback. "She begged me to read Austen, then Nora Roberts, and she started my obsession with J. D. Robb." He glances over at me. "Did Hailey ever try to get you to read her favorites?"

Hailey. My sister. The girl he's sleeping with behind my back. But is it behind my back? Is he required to share these details with me? I don't know that answer. I only know my irritation.

"No," I say, bottling my emotions for a beat. "We had an extensive reading requirement growing up. Classics, history texts, languages, all imposed by the dear old Mom and Dad." I give him a tight smile. "Hailey didn't want to add to it, but I'd pick her brain about whatever book stole her attention the most." I pluck out *Pride and Prejudice*. "You seem to be really warming up to my sister."

Jake's gaze meets mine, unyielding, unwavering. He clearly knows that *I know* he's been a little too close for friends. And then he nods slowly. "I won't lie to you, I like her."

"Good," I say. "Because I'd beat your ass if you were sleeping with my sister and didn't like her."

He sighs. "We're both going through a lot, and she's probably the most interesting person I've ever met."

"Like a science experiment," I say dryly. "You want to dissect my sister. Slit her open with a scalpel."

He laughs hard. That surprises me.

"Something funny, Jake?"

"I think it's more likely she would cut me open. I think *she* would like to dissect *me*. And weirdly, I'd let her. She's about the *only* person I would, and I don't know why. I can't even tell you why. It's been driving me . . ." He laughs to himself. "Ah, fuck." His smile fades. "I haven't felt like this about someone in a long time, and I can't . . . I can't be with her."

My jaw muscle tics. That shouldn't piss me off as much as it does. Jake rejecting my sister when she's already practically shelved him in a similar fashion. "Because of your family?" I'm guessing.

"Always because of them."

Jake gets a sudden call from his mother. He's being whisked away to speak to a florist. This is the typical Claudia/Jake dynamic that drives me batshit. Whenever he's with a guest, she calls upon him to cage his attention.

She keeps him busy.

She separates him from others. It's an uncreative power move that I have the misfortune of watching.

Once he's gone, I shower and change into dinner attire. Ready for tonight's festivities.

THIRTY-FOUR

Phoebe

THE BADGER GAME (CONTINUED)

Here's the thing, I'm not really afraid of Claudia Waterford. Even after hearing what she's done to Jake's exes—forcing a girl to eat dog food, pressuring another to cut off all her hair—it's just not that *scary*. At least not in the horrifying, fear-for-my-life sense. This is kind of . . . weirdly thrilling.

I just hate knowing Rocky drew the short straw in this job and has to entertain Trent. Fan his ego. Act like his shit doesn't stink when his stench mimics a landfill. Remind him that the whole town still thinks he walks on water when in reality Trent's name has been whispered and degraded ever since the Celia audio leak.

That scandal wasn't enough to make the Koning board turn their backs on him or for Claudia to shove him off his gold-plated pedestal. But his armor is dented, and it's a step in the right direction.

Long cons are slow decimations. Brick by brick. Until the mark is underneath so much rubble, they're suffocating.

I toss my overnight bag on my bed. My accommodations

haven't changed since my first night at the estate. A modest room with a twin bed, not large enough for Jake and me to share. Claudia said rooming together is inappropriate before marriage, but I think that's hardly her first reason.

After dropping off my things, I head downstairs and find Hailey stocking a bar cart in the parlor. She gives me a sheepish wave when our eyes meet. That's all that she can do while she's hired on as staff for the night. I hate that I'm not serving next to her.

It feels wildly unfair when she's the one who has Jake's true affections. Our positions should be reversed. I should be waiting tables tonight, and she should be wearing the glittery floor-length dress.

I leave the parlor, on the prowl for my mark.

Where is Claudia? She's usually lounging in a den or parlor, being waited on as if she hails from aristocracy and not a beer empire. After checking all three parlors and the smoker's den, I beeline for the dining room.

She might be ordering the staff to switch the centerpieces or polish the flatware. As soon as I step in the door, I freeze.

What in the . . . ?

Trevor.

As in *Trevor Tinrock.*

Outfitted in a stunning black tux, he's huddled with a violinist, cellist, and violist. As if he knows them. Not only that, he grips the neck of a sleek violin, a bow in his other hand.

He's here as a musician?!

Hold yourself together, Phoebe. I wash emotion off my face.

No one—he told *no one* that he'd be joining the string quartet for tonight's dinner. He went incredibly, wildly *rogue.*

Ugghhh, maybe we should've known. He had zero important

role for tonight, other than dropping me and Hailey off at the estate. How long has he even been concocting this side plan? For weeks? Months?

Trevor completely cold-shoulders me, and I have to give him props for that. He's not trying to make me break character.

And he was able to get an invite all on his own. I bet Rocky would be proud if he weren't so on edge. Trevor's violin skills aren't fabricated either.

Everett and Addison put him in lessons since he was four. Anything that allowed him to tinker and toil.

I need to tell Rocky—

"Excuse me, Miss Smith." Niall, the family's redheaded butler, sidesteps in front of me and blocks my view of the quartet. "Mrs. Waterford is expecting you. I'm to bring you to her."

*C*laudia." I air-kiss her cheeks upon meeting her in a humongous dressing room filled with couches, chairs, and an unlit fireplace. Candles burn on the mantel. Evening gowns are hung on several racks, and a podium faces an ornate floor-length mirror.

With his hands dutifully behind his back, a male tailor waits to be called upon.

I ignore him. "It's so, *so* good to see you tonight." I take her hands before she has any chance to greet me. "Your house is beautiful, and I'm just *so* grateful we have such a divine place to enjoy Easter weekend." I'm usually over-the-top around her, but tonight I'll have to up the eccentricities to another level.

Claudia pulls her hands away like I have diseased them. She

assesses me coldly. "I see you've helped yourself to the bar already."

I let out an ungraceful snort. "Hardly. But there's plenty of time to imbibe later."

She puts a hand to her throat, near a strand of emeralds. Her blonde hair is twisted in an updo, and she's ready for tonight's dinner, wearing a slimming green cowl-neck dress. "Why don't you stand up there?" She flicks her fingers to the round platform. "Let's get you in something a little more appropriate."

In truth, Claudia is right.

My pale pink satin dress is far from appropriate for an elegant ten-course dinner. It's not that it's off-the-rack (though I'm sure she's shuddering at this fact, too), but the neckline plunges to my navel and exposes the sides of my breasts. Very VMAs red carpet and far from the Oscars. If this were a job where I was to get into her good graces instead of light them on fire, I would've ordered a custom Atelier Versace dress and matching crystal earrings.

"You don't like what I bought?" I frown deeply and glance down at the garment, which hangs perfectly on my body.

Her smile is as fake as my name. "You *must* wear one of my pieces. It'll look darling on you. I won't take no for an answer." *Of course you won't.*

I pout. "Really? I liked this one. The lady at JCPenney said it was gorgeous on me."

She sucks in air through her nose. "I insist, Phoebe."

Blowing out a dramatic breath, I touch my dress one last time as if I'm mourning the fabric. "Fine, I'll try another option, but I can't promise I'll like it more."

A polite knock on the door shifts her attention. "Come in. Be quick."

"Ma'am." Everett slips inside, wearing a tux. "Just a word with your tailor."

"Of course, Maxwell," Claudia says and appraises me, ignoring Everett Tinrock (aka Maxwell Abbot) as he chats under his breath to him. Then he places a photo of the Koning family on the mantel next to lit candlesticks.

Seconds later, he's gone.

Claudia suspects nothing.

Why would she? She has a bajillion staff roaming her property.

She flicks a finger at the tailor, pointing at him like he's a machine she's operating. He lifts a shimmery silver dress.

I curl my nose. "I don't want to look like a disco ball."

Her eyes flame. "My son would prefer you look like a disco ball over a . . ." She bites her tongue before the insult escapes.

I challenge her gaze. "Over a *what*?" I confront. I'm too confident to bend to her will. Too obnoxious to suffer through. Too difficult to mold. I am her worst fucking nightmare for her son.

"A whore," she says, her graces lowering. "You look like a *whore*, Phoebe."

I don't balk. I just smile. "They're called breasts, Claudia. It's okay to flaunt them."

"Not in my house. You *will* change."

Claudia waves down the tailor once more. He cycles through a rack of designer gowns. She shakes her head at each one—until he halts on a royal-blue gown with a sequined bust. Modest and likely pulled from some Disney castle. Despite it being lovely, it's not something I'd choose for myself.

"That one." Claudia gestures the tailor forward. He's younger than I'd expect. Late twenties, maybe, but I evade his eyes as he brings over the blue gown. "Try it on."

"Undress here?" I ask her. My pulse has no spike. No fear. No danger. It's a flatline.

"Is that a problem, dear?" she asks me, equal challenge in her eyes as she tries to regain power in this room. Regain control.

It's a tug of the rope, and I let her have it.

"No." I hold her gaze and smile. "Not at all." I slip off the straps to my pink satin dress, and it pools effortlessly to the floor. No bra, but I do wear a lacy black thong.

Claudia's cheeks go concave, as if she's sucking a lemon. I am not bashful. I'm not tucking my arms against my body. "These, too?" I ask, fingering the hem of my panties. I don't wait for her response before slipping them off.

Completely naked, I face Claudia and give her a wicked smile. *I am the wild thing your son let in.*

Her eyes are wide saucers. Then with a finger-flick, she instructs the tailor to dress me. Blue fabric slides over my curves, cinches at my hips, and plumes out in a sea of tulle. I don't think about where the tailor's hands touch as he fusses over the garment on my body. I'm just a mannequin.

A shell.

The tailor pulls the silk laces of the corset.

Claudia bumps him away. "Let me." She takes his place at my spine, then yanks, and the force nearly doubles me over—but I right myself quickly.

Our eyes catch in the mirror as she wrenches the laces over and over, tightening them to the point of pain. "We need this nice and secure," she tells me.

Anther tug, and my ribs shriek. "I think that's enough," I tell her. Air becomes brittle in my lungs.

Claudia ignores me. "You look much prettier in this one."

I touch my chest. "I can barely breathe."

"Beauty is pain, dear."

She yanks once more, and more fire flares in my ribs.

"Enough," I snap, oxygen in short supply. Lights start dancing in my vision. I'm going to pass out. I can control a lot of things—but I'm not immortal. I need fucking air.

And if I faint, Rocky isn't here.

No one is around me. Not yet.

Claudia ignores me again, still tugging and purposefully causing the stabbing pain.

My nose flares. "I said enough!" I yell and jerk away from her. Stumbling off the podium, I try to orient myself with my vision full of spots. But I only intake sharp, uneven breaths with the corset this constricted.

"I'm not wearing this." I reach behind me to try and untie the silk laces myself.

Claudia is fast and angry and so done with me—she struts to my side in an instant, clamps my wrist in a tight hand, forces my arm to my side, and swings her flat palm at my face.

I see it coming, and yet, I let her hit me.

The soft flesh of my cheek stings, and I immediately steal a glimpse of the tailor. His gaze cements to the floor.

"Leave us," Claudia barks at him.

He's so quick to bolt from the room, and I understand. I'd be hightailing it out of here, too. "I can't breathe," I grit out to Claudia.

"I don't care," she says sharply. "You'll wear this dress."

"I won't," I argue.

She scowls. "You are an ungrateful, whiney, horrid thing." She drops my hand roughly, and I use the time to hurriedly try and loosen the laces at my back.

I think of Jake's sister in this moment.

I wonder if she was here at one point.

I wonder if this is what she endured from her own mother. My mom might've deceived me, but she's never been outright malicious. She'd never even think to lay a hand on me.

Claudia crosses the length of the room. Stopping at the unlit fireplace.

I get dizzy as she nears the family photo that Everett placed. But she disregards it and plucks a candlestick off the mantel. As she returns to me, I have just enough time to release the bindings to inhale a regular breath.

Claudia seizes my wrist again, and if this weren't a job, I'd have evaded it and likely decked her in the nose. But this is a job—and I have my role.

She forces my hand higher and drags my palm near the flame of the candle.

"What-what are you doing?" I stammer, letting fear into my eyes.

"You will respect me in my house." She lowers my palm to the flame. *Agh*, the sting is mild, then sharpens into something less tolerable. She's burning me. I pull on instinct, and she grips me tighter. "You understand?"

"Claudia, that hurts." I jerk my wrist harder. She's strong for her age, but not stronger than me. I bury the urge to body-slam her to the ground.

"You will wear the blue dress." Her gaze is cold and lifeless. I'm just a *horrid* thing that has spoken and rebelled. For her, it's the worst kind of thing. "Say it, Phoebe."

My lip curls. "I will *not* wear the blue dress."

"Then we'll stand here for as long as it takes. I'm sure we can hide the scar with a lovely set of gloves."

I'm not afraid of a small scar. Not if it means stopping her from doing this to another woman. The scorch is good.

The scorch is *rage*.

I force my eyes to well with distress, and I jerk. "*Please*," I beg. "It's just a dress. You're hurting me."

"The disrespect you've shown me by coming into my house wearing that—"

"Then kick me out!" I yell.

"If I kick you out, my son will likely marry you to spite me—and I'll never get rid of you without alienating him, and I'm *not* losing my son because of a gold-digging waitress." These are the seeds the godmothers planted in her head.

They told Claudia that she shouldn't toss me out of the estate or forbid me from entering. That it would only make her greatest fears come true.

She keeps my palm steady on the flame. I bite back the pain. She's watching me begin to cave. "You won't ever back talk again," she says. "Will you?"

How many women has she burned? How many of Jake's ex-girlfriends has she slapped? Did she also do this to Kate— or was Kate too scared to ever push back in the first place? Acid churns in my stomach.

"I-I . . ." I mumble.

"This will get a lot worse than a little burn," she threatens. "Just let go now, Phoebe."

I surrender into a submissive puddle. "I-I'll wear the blue dress."

"Say it again," she demands.

My skin is on fire. "I'll wear the blue dress." I sound meek, vulnerable, and I force down the urge to snark back, *Smile for the fucking camera!*

We're being filmed.

Unbeknownst to her, Trevor rigged a teeny-tiny camera in

a frame that matches the wooden ones around their home. Jake supplied the Koning family photo. And Everett set it up and will likely come collect it right after I leave.

The footage is extremely, horrifically damaging. To her pristine reputation, her well-respected character. She thinks being in her own home makes her untouchable.

But she's currently undergoing an *infestation*.

She releases her grip, and I draw my hand to my chest. The center of my palm is an angry, blistering shade of red. *That'll scar.* Before I can move away from her, she glides behind me with strange softness.

Then she gently reties the laces to my corset. It's no longer bone-breakingly tight.

"You're okay, dear." Her voice is sickly sweet. "The pain will pass. I'll have one of the housekeepers fetch you a cold cloth." She rounds to my front and gently caresses my cheek with the backs of her knuckles. It's affection she's *never* shown me, and I can see how others would want to feed into it. To receive it. "There you are." She gives me a look of admiration, pride. "This is a good start."

*R*ocky. He's the only person I'm thinking about. The only one I want to go to and connect with. But I purposefully gave my phone to Hailey because I didn't want Claudia to screw with it this weekend.

Consider me paranoid, but I've been taught to protect my most personal belongings. I didn't even bring a burner, since anyone could rummage through my things in my room.

To my aggravation, Claudia won't let me into the dining room until everyone arrives. I'm being held in a parlor, seated alone on a floral chaise, the tulle of the blue dress plumed out. I feel ridiculous. I might as well be her doll.

The burn on my palm is angry and painful to the touch, but a pair of white silk gloves covers the red welt.

I haven't even seen Jake yet.

"Niall, please," I whisper.

His apologetic expression hurts, because I wonder how many times he's given it. I'm being treated like an obedient debutante and forced to make my grand entrance as Claudia's new pet project.

Calm.

Be calm. I breathe out my ire and brush my fingers through my long hair. I imagine they're Rocky's fingers. I imagine he's slipping them against my scalp over and over again. *Breathe.*

I feel naked without a lifeline to Rocky or Hailey or even Nova out on the boat, but I have good directional sense and can locate the exit. I'm not in a position where I feel the urge to bail. I'm on the road to success.

Claudia has been caught. I keep repeating it to myself. *She's caught.*

I'm naked in the footage. Small sacrifices. I only cringe knowing Everett will likely watch the playback.

She's caught.

I exhale.

Jake is going to dangle the blackmail over Claudia tomorrow morning, and if he's even *semi*decent at manipulation, he can convince her to name him sole heir in exchange for destroying the damning footage.

Blackmail works wonders. It's the Badger Game. A classic con.

After it's legally binding, the plan is to show the footage to the board anyway. It will unseat Claudia—that is, if she doesn't step down herself.

And then we can focus on ruining Trent's position on the board. But Jake will be right in reach of the Koning fortune.

The door whips open. Jake charges inside with a heavy breath. "There you are . . ." He trails off, skimming the length of me for any signs of distress.

How many times has this happened?

I'm not sure I'll ever stop asking the question in my head. It pours gasoline through my bloodstream, igniting my fury toward his family. It cements my resolve that *this* is where I want to be. It's where I'm supposed to be. Cutting Claudia at the knees so she can't do this to anyone *ever* again.

"Phoebe?" he questions, his blue eyes hitting mine in a tsunami of worry.

"I'm in one piece."

"What did she do?"

My gaze flits past his shoulder to the butler.

Jake follows it. "Thank you for letting me know she's here, Niall."

"Always my pleasure, Mr. Waterford." Niall dips out of the parlor, but not before giving me a tip of the head like *take care of yourself, miss.*

Jake studies me. "I thought you were wearing a pink dress."

"Your mother liked this one better," I tell him without much explanation.

"Is it bothering you?" He's concerned like maybe it's made of blades.

"It's fine," I say gently.

He opens his mouth to reply, but a valet steps into the parlor. "Dinner is ready."

THIRTY-FIVE

Rocky

THE BADGER GAME (CONTINUED)

We're seated for dinner without Phoebe and Jake—and not knowing where they are is a static hum in my ears. There's a distracting, unstoppable itch to go find them. But I am Trent's friend first, and so I can't leave. Can't move. Can't do much more than smile into my next sip of whiskey that Trent offered me earlier.

"You *must* try our bourbon we have in the cellar while you're here." Claudia touches my wrist across the table. "It's divine."

"I'd love that, Claudia." I smile wider.

She looks satisfied with herself and with me. Together, we flank the head of the table. She's seated me where Jordan should be.

Her second-born son is relegated to the middle beside his wife, Nadia. Practically shunned to the "friend" section of the table since Collin Falcone and Oliver sit across from them.

"I don't know about you, but I am looking forward to our

Phoebe's grand entrance." Trent raises his whiskey to his lips, grinning. He's to my right. At the head of the fucking table.

While their father "sends his love" from a Switzerland trip, Claudia has let her firstborn miscreant rule the household. She should be in his seat, but sure, let your prick of a son dictate how this evening unfolds.

"She's a work in progress," Claudia says, more stiffly. "But we're getting somewhere."

Getting somewhere—that sounds like Claudia's pleased with her.

Phoebe. If she submitted to Claudia's whims, it means she must have pushed her hard enough to get the kind of black-mail we need. I hate not knowing what happened.

I'll find out soon.

Not soon enough. Because my imagination is running rampant with dark, disturbing scenarios. Boiling my blood. I want to hold her.

I want to be with her.

I don't want to be anywhere she's not.

Claudia takes a long sip of wine before continuing. "I wondered if she was ever involved in . . . well, things that aren't quite dinner talk."

"Ohhh, come on, Mom," Trent goads. "We're all adults here."

"She's just a little too . . . *free.*"

"Oh." Trent's brows spike at me. "*Oh.*" He cocks his head. "I think she's implying that our Phoebe might've dabbled in escorting?"

The way he says *our* Phoebe has me containing so much raw fury. It's contorting inside me like an animal on fire. Searing and seething. I let it feed on me.

Instead of pummeling him, I make a show of gently rolling

my eyes. "I'd know if she were a sex worker. I was married to her."

Oliver acts oblivious as they attempt to degrade his sister in front of him. He can't stick up for Phoebe without appearing defensive. It will get him axed from the friend group. All Koning privileges revoked.

He just has to take it.

Yet, he will pretend it's nothing. Water off a duck's back. But he's not infallible. He loves his sister too damn much, and I see through his carefree veneer often. When no one's looking.

Even now, Oliver has a deadened unblinking stare for a flicker of a second. It's expertly concealed disgust.

Claudia touches her earrings. "Trent, dear, we don't need to talk of escorting at the table." She looks to me. "I'm sorry, he can be so crass."

"But she loves me." Trent bats his lashes at me. I have them vying for my attention, and I'd be more amused if I didn't despise them both.

"Hush." Claudia tips a smile to him.

Jordan scoots forward. "I—"

"So, Grey," Claudia cuts off her other son, focused solely on me. "How is your portfolio these days?"

The door bursts open. "Oh my God, the tablescape is *stunning*." Phoebe blows into the formal dining room like a force of nature. Uncontrollable, disastrous beauty.

My lip tries to twitch into a smile.

She takes up double the space in that royal-blue dress. Mounds and mounds of tulle. It practically swallows her lower half, and I suspect Claudia chose it for her.

"Oh, I just love how cute this is. Look, Jake," Phoebe says and tugs Jake over to their seats, pointing out the monogrammed napkins.

Trent tilts his head. "Phoebe, you look like a princess. I didn't think I'd see the day."

I stop grinding my teeth, but before I say something, Jake snaps, "Don't."

"Don't what?" Trent mocks.

"Boys," Claudia chastises in a flat tone that I've heard a hundred times before. Unfortunately, it's not my first Koning dinner.

Oliver grins into his wine, which pleases Trent. Phoebe's brother is on *his* side in this brother rivalry.

Jake pulls out Phoebe's chair for her. "I just need him to not be an asshole for five seconds."

"*Jacob.*" Claudia is horrified.

I nearly smile.

Trent looks bored. "It's fine, Mom. Jake has no sense of humor. He doesn't know what a *joke* is."

"Were you joking?" Jake flings back.

As they bicker, Phoebe takes her seat between me and her fake boyfriend, and I check on her with a short glance.

She catches my gaze, her tenacity focusing her eyes, determined to see this through. Her lips lift into a satisfied smile. *She got it.* She has the blackmail.

It eases me in one breath and concerns me in another. Because what exactly did Claudia do?

"Thank you for inviting me, Claudia. It's been *so* wonderful so far." Phoebe rises to her feet like she means to give a toast, but instead she lifts her flute to her lips. "You've truly outdone yourself this Easter weekend. I cannot wait to spend every holiday here."

Claudia's eyes narrow into pinpoints. "Settle, dear." She holds out a hand and lowers it as if Phoebe is a toddler that needs physical cues.

Phoebe's smile glints in and out. "Yes, of course." She dutifully plops back down in her seat. Claudia seems pleased with the change of pace.

Servers, including my sister, silently place a pickled baby-beet amuse-bouche in front of us. Nobody acknowledges Hailey. We keep the attention off her.

Next two courses, Jordan hasn't stopped talking about a red carpet he walked in December for some action movie. "The publicists were barely doing their jobs. And the security was complete shit. They just let this fourteen-year-old girl stroll through like she was part of the cast. She barely spoke four words in the film."

"Definitely less than that," his wife, Nadia, chimes in.

"Exactly." Jordan sips his wine so quickly. Zero pause. "It was an absolute mess. It's my last premiere in L.A.—once you go to Cannes, there is no comparison. Leagues above the rest. And Tom, well you know, Tom is *Tom*."

"You know Tom Hanks?" Collin says, impressed.

"No," Jordan says. *"Tom Cruise."* He looks to Trent like *why is your idiot friend here?*

Trent rolls his eyes. "There are a million boring Toms in the world, Jordan." It's refreshing seeing him stick up for Collin, but I also know he's only doing it to punch his brother down. Oliver leans in, whispering something to Collin.

Jordan scowls, then continues talking about award shows. At one point, I spot him slyly pop something in his mouth. From what Jake has told me, I'm guessing it's an upper.

Three minutes later, Claudia puts a hand on top of his, a silent gesture to shut up.

Phoebe, Oliver, and I are in the front row of a dark family satire where the pillhead son can't win over mommy's attention.

"Mom, you would've loved the *Vanity Fair* party last year," Jordan tries again. Claudia looks uninterested as she swirls a spoon in her gazpacho.

Nadia peers past her husband. "Anne Hathaway was even there."

Claudia perks. Barely. "Really? What was she wearing?"

"Um." Jordan looks at his wife and whispers, "Vera Wang?"

"Balmain," Nadia says sweetly. "I think."

Claudia sighs at the answer, but then Trent raises his whiskey and stands. Her face floods with relief and gratitude.

"A toast," Trent decrees, then motions his flute glass to Collin and Oliver. "To old friends and new friends." His eyes land on me. "To best friends." I lift my glass back to him. He points like we're two peas in a rotten pod. *God help me not kill him.* He raises his glass to his mom. "To family." He never acknowledges Jake in that.

But his smirk widens on Phoebe. "And lastly, to my brother's girlfriend—I hope this Easter weekend . . . *fulfills* all your needs."

Jake is stewing. Outwardly.

His mother is shooting Jake daggers, silently warning him not to ruin the toast.

"Cheers," Phoebe says to Trent. We all drink.

I'm crawling out of my skin. I hate my black button-down. I hate the Rolex on my wrist. I hate the belt at my waist. I hate my socks suctioning to my calves. I want to rip everything off my body.

To stop from popping a blood vessel and grabbing Trent's throat by the tenth course, I concentrated on my breathing, on the feeling of my clothes against my skin, and now, the sensations are like ten-inch fingernails raking a chalkboard.

Dinner has ended, and we're in the parlor for a nightcap. The whiskey is taking the edge off.

". . . I have to wear the cast all summer," Collin prattles on about his broken leg. His crutches lean against the floral couch. He actually sprawls out across the entire couch like he's in his own living room.

Claudia slips me looks like *isn't he uncouth?*

I entertain her with ones back.

Phoebe and Jake snuggle close on a love seat, but not close enough to entice Trent to draw her away from his brother.

Trevor is here.

Playing violin in the corner with the quartet. *It's fine*, I tell myself. It's a good position for him to be in—harmless. No one will fuck with him. He'll be fine.

I only briefly acknowledged him since Trent knows he's my brother, but I worry if I act like I care, then Trent will want to bring him over for a drink. That's *not* happening.

Claudia yawns. "I think it's time for me to retire. I'll see you all in the morning. Grey, dear, it's been lovely." She kisses both my cheeks.

"Same to you, Claudia."

She brightens with faux sincerity. "Trent." She gives him the same goodbye treatment. "You behave yourself." Her smile eliminates even the semblance of a warning.

"I wouldn't *dare* do anything less." He grins.

She laughs. "Silly boys." Her smile fades at Phoebe. "Goodnight, dear." Then to her son, "Jacob. Be good. Tomorrow morning, we'll all be together." She actually hugs Jake. To her second born . . . she forgets he's even there.

Claudia leaves the parlor.

Jordan and Nadia whisper-hiss under their breath.

"Oh shut it, Jordan," Trent bemoans. "Go run after her and talk her ear off about some *lame* premiere no one wants to see."

"Goodnight." He stands in a huff, fixing his suit jacket. He catches Nadia's hand and carts her out the door.

"Bye, Jordie Shore!" Collin calls out.

Oliver laughs.

"And then there were six," I say into my whiskey, sitting in a club chair beside Trent.

He lights a cigar and puffs out smoke. "Past your bedtime, Jake?" he asks his brother. "This is when the children get tucked in."

"Then you should've gone to bed hours ago," Jake retorts.

"Oh, *oh*. He has a spine, ladies and gentlemen." Trent snickers. "For most of my life, I thought you were all jellyfish." He does a terrible impersonation of a jellyfish. He looks like he's convulsing against the chair.

Phoebe is trying not to snort into a glass of brandy.

I'm trying not to smile at her. My collar isn't bothering me to near madness. My watch doesn't feel like seven tons bearing on my wrist. For this brief second, all I see . . . is her.

I'm struck by her. Classical music pours through the parlor and triggers my senses.

And when her eyes find mine and her movements slow, it's like time reverses. Like we're both being knocked so far back. I'm fifteen and falling in love under a sycamore tree in Virginia. Lightning bugs swarm us in the sticky summer night, and we're practicing a waltz for a debutante ball. It'd be her second coming-out to high society. She's pretending to be sixteen.

But we're so young, and as she trips over my feet, I catch

her around the hips, and she's laughing off the clumsiness. A red flush stains her cheeks, and even in the night, I see her. I see how her eyes track over my features, how her breath hitches at the sight of me.

Again.

We keep going. We never stop. Not as sweat drips down our temples, as hot, heavy heat builds in our lungs, as our hands brush and skim, and our breath becomes arduous from more than the cadence of our steps. Then she trips again, and this time, I seize her from behind and yank her back into my chest.

Our bodies meld, and I hear her breath shallow. I feel her hands skating against my flexed biceps while my arms wrap around her waist. My lips brush over her neck, and her body lets out an uncontrolled, surprised shudder.

Then a flashlight glares at us. We squint, and I raise my hand to block the beam of light. It illuminates a glinting spiderweb—two inches from our faces.

Seeing the person behind the flashlight, we split apart. We're about to go inside the mansion we're staying at.

"You're not done," my father says. "Go again."

She doesn't want to argue with the godfather. I'm uncertain if he should see how much I love her. I'm concerned I can't hide it right then.

We're out there for two more hours.

It's not enough for him.

We could go forever together. Does he know that? Does he know there's no exhausting two people who can't quit?

"Grey?" Trent wrenches me out of a reverie.

I focus over on him with a tight smile and then take a harsher sip of whiskey.

He's baffled, eyeing me, then my ex-wife. "What was that?"

"The music—it sounded like one of the songs at our wedding."

"It wasn't," Phoebe snaps at me, doing a good job of flipping over the boat I capsized. "And that time is dead and gone." She holds Jake's hand tighter, making a show of how she's moved on from me.

Jake cups her hand around his.

It should work, except Trent is bored and loves trying to kick Jake down a few pegs. And I've unfortunately reminded him that Phoebe and I were once together. But there is very little that I can't outmaneuver.

Trent grins over at me, his cigar between two fingers. "How was she when you were married?"

"Vapid."

Phoebe scoffs.

"Uninteresting."

Heat flushes her cheeks.

"Destructive." I look her over. "She devastates everything she touches, like poison on a vine—I was tangled up in her. Dying from the inside. And I never wanted out." I lean forward toward Phoebe. "But there you were. And there I was." I watch her blink softly. "There will never be a day, a night, a minute, a moment, a breath where you aren't destructively mine. And I hope it fucking terrifies you."

Phoebe is doing her best to control her breathing. She's glaring, likely pissed at me for making emotion surge in her. "I hope you go to hell, Rocky."

"I'm already there, Phoebe." I raise my glass to her. "Where do you think I met you?"

Trent full-belly laughs. "Jeeeez, you two are something else." He tsks over at his brother. "Jake, Jake, Jake. You're just going to let her ex-husband say that about your girlfriend?"

Jake has an arm around the love seat. He's clinging to the furniture like it's a safety harness, barring him from standing up. "Their relationship is in the past, Trent."

He slings his head to me. "How was the wedding night?"

Fuck him.

"Ew, *no*, we're not talking about this," Phoebe protests.

"Oh, now you're a prude?"

"Knock it off," Jake warns.

Trent laughs, more unsurely. "We're all adults. We can talk about *sex*. Come on." He spreads his arms. "Is that not what we do here?" He motions to Collin and Oliver, and they chime in like seagulls.

Yes.

Yes.

"The wedding night!" he decrees. "And play something more interesting. Upbeat!" he shouts at the quartet. "Not whatever this shit is."

I purposely don't look at my brother.

Trent nudges my arm. "What was it like? Best lay you ever had?"

"Forgetful, TK." I need Jake to intervene. *Now.*

"Trent," Jake says his name like dry ice. "Don't go there with me."

"What are you going to do? Cry about it?" Trent bows forward with his cigar. He puffs smoke toward Jake, then tells Phoebe, "I have a feeling you're a secret starfish." I'm burning alive. "You just lie there and take it—"

Jake is on his feet, thank fucking God. I shoot to mine. Trent stands more leisurely. He's laughing beside me. "Big scary Jake. Come to protect his skunky girlfriend. From what?"

"Do you even hear yourself?" He waves an angry hand. "Do you know how you fucking sound?"

Trent laughs. "Oh, Jake. Always so afraid. You know, deep down, that Phoebe will realize she prefers guys like me and Grey. And I have a feeling that realization is going to happen tonight. When she spreads her legs and I—"

Jake lunges, and Trent looks to *me*, like I'm his guard dog. But the urge to slam my fist against his jaw tries to overpower me, and the only way to mitigate it is to let Jake reach his brother.

I hold out a weak arm, and Jake tears through me. He throws a violent right hook into Trent's mouth, using all his weight. His lip busts instantly, and he stumbles to his ass, dropping his cigar.

"Get the fuck off him!" I shout at Jake, pushing him in the chest.

And Jake surrenders with his hands up, but we share this brief moment of fury and fear. His brother needs to go. His brother can't be left to his own devices tonight. Not with Phoebe. Not when Jake isn't able to sleep in her room, and his mom likes to have housekeepers check on him.

I pry away from Jake quickly. "Jesus Christ. Trent? Are you okay?" I help him up, but it takes everything—and I mean *every fucking thing*—in me not to stomp him in the face.

"I'm going to bed. I've had enough of this," Phoebe says.

"Yeah, you do that!" I shout at her.

"I will!"

Oliver fakes a yawn. "Me, too. I'm beat. Collin?"

"Nah, I could . . ." He trails off as Oliver mimes a joint. "Actually . . ." He grabs his crutches, and Oliver easily lugs away Trent's friend. Likely, they'll go smoke in the garden or on a balcony.

Trent touches his bloodied lip. Seeing the crimson on his fingers, he laughs. "Nice one, little brother!" he yells as Phoebe pulls Jake toward the exit. "You do have fight in you, after all!"

I grimace at the music. "This is shrill. Do they play all night?"

"Wrap it up," he tells the quartet.

My brother hardly glances in my direction as he packs away his violin. The other musicians hurry with their instruments, and soon, it's just me and Trent. Alone in the parlor. I pour another round of whiskey and hand him the glass.

He grins. "And then there were two."

Trust me. I'm not the one you want to be left alone with.

THIRTY-SIX

Rocky

THE BADGER GAME (CONTINUED)

It's almost midnight when Trent goes to bed and I'm able to sneak into Phoebe's guest room. She hasn't changed out of the blue dress. She has her temple to the window frame, gazing out into the night.

"Watching the waves?" I ask, locking the door behind me.

She doesn't turn. "The grounds. Gardeners are still pruning the hedges."

Her room is smaller than mine. The ornate four-poster bed is twin-sized. With its ugly ruffled bedding in a Pepto-Bismol pink and a collection of old porcelain dolls on a shelf, I wonder if this room belonged to a child.

At least there's a chair. While I grab it, Phoebe gradually rotates and watches me jam the wooden frame underneath the doorknob.

She leans her shoulders on the wall. "You know how messed up it is that we're worried Trent might break into my room tonight?"

"This family is fucked up." I comb a hand through my hair,

pushing the longer pieces back, then bend down and untie my leather shoes. "You want to talk about it?" I still have no clue what happened when Phoebe was with Claudia, but I can make some great educated guesses.

"Tonight was . . ." She takes a deep breath and a hundred-watt smile lights her face. "Exhilarating."

"Yeah?" I ask, coming closer to wrap my arms around her waist. "You get off on it?"

She sways in my arms like we're slow dancing, and her brown eyes sparkle with infectious energy that pools into me. "I did. I forgot . . . I really forgot how this feels." She frowns. "Or maybe it's because *this* is different than all the other times. She won't be able to hurt anyone else."

My gaze darkens, and I tuck a strand of her blue hair behind her ear. "Did she hurt you?"

Phoebe slowly removes her silk glove. "She slapped me," she says. "And this . . ." She overturns her hand, palm up, and I see the bright red skin. A blister already forms in the center.

Caged darkness threatens to unleash in a round of violent anger. I want to lash out. I want to rip apart. I want to destroy. My lungs are charred when I ask, "Is that a burn?"

"With a candle." Phoebe's brows draw together. "It might be first-degree."

"We'll have Nova take a look at it tonight," I say, since he's the only one of us with any kind of formal medical training.

She shakes her head. "Tomorrow. I can wait until tomorrow. I don't want anything to ruin tonight."

"Until then . . ." I carefully take her hand and kiss around the redness.

Her eyes dance over me. "Oh so tender for someone so lethal."

"Believe me," I tell her. "I'm restraining myself from doing very bad things in the name of vengeance."

She glows brighter. "My favorite name."

"Hmm," I muse. "I thought that was Rocky."

"Are you sure?" She feigns confusion. "I don't recall that being on my favorites list."

"Let me fucking remind you then." I explode forward, clutching her face with a feral ferocity. She grabs on to my belt loops and hangs on as our lips collide in hunger. Cupping her skull, I lead her back toward the twin bed.

Her ass hits the mattress first, and I pull off my belt. My suit. I strip in front of her, letting her watch me with aroused eyes.

"Let me tell you my favorite word, mikrí fráoula."

Her face radiates with newfound heat. "Rocky." She says my name in a shallow breath.

I'm naked before her, and I slowly crawl on top of her body, hauling her farther onto the small bed. "What's wrong, petite fraise?" I tease in French instead of Greek as I fist the blue tulle of her gown in my hands, bringing the puffy material up to her waist.

"Stop." She fights a smile.

"Morango pequeno." I switch to Portuguese, calling her *little strawberry* over and over again in all the languages I've picked up.

"Rocky . . ." She sounds out of breath as I slip her panties off her legs.

"Still not my favorite word," I tell her and tease her opening, circling my thumb over her clit. "Try again."

"I-I . . ." Her eyes flutter, and her fingers claw at my back. I war with the tulle. Such an annoying, obtrusive— I rip the fucking thing. All of it. A flurry of tulle cascades to the floor as I tear it off the bodice of the dress. A shocked gasp leaves her lips. She's completely bare from the waist down, and I descend back to her lips. Tasting her. Having her. Mine.

I break away to let her catch her breath, a groan rumbling in my throat. My cock screams to be inside her. "Phoebe," I say slowly, sensually. "My favorite word. *My* Phoebe."

Her eyes well with a surge of emotion. "Rocky," she rasps out, her voice sultry.

"*Phoebe*," I whisper against her lips, slipping a condom along my length.

"*Rocky*." Her voice is an ache, on the precipice of a moan. She spreads her legs wider open.

I reach between them to feel her cunt, wetness against my fingers. "*Phoebe*." I make dirty love to her name, dragging my slick finger down her leg.

She's arching her hips into my cock. "*Rocky*," she moans.

Fuck. "*Phoebe*." Kneeling between her legs, I bring my finger to her mouth. The same one that was inside her. Her breath is ragged as she closes her lips around me.

She can't say it, but her eyes scream my name. *Rocky*.

I lower to press my lips against her ear. "*Phoebe*." I seize her hip and whisper, "You want to know how deep I'm going to fuck you? It's going to be worse than our wedding night. You won't be able to walk for three fucking weeks straight." I remove my finger from her mouth so she can speak.

She squirms beneath me. "*Rocky*." It's a heady, drunk-in-love *Rocky*. I capture her wrists and pull her hands above her head.

"*Phoebe*." Our eyes cling.

With one hand, I hold her wrists together, and with my

other, I lift her pelvis to align with me. My cock sinks inside her tight warmth, and I watch her face break into pleasure. *Fuck yes*.

"Oh my God," she cries and shakes beneath me. I haven't even moved yet, but I'm buried deep. Almost all of me inside her.

I flex forward, and her pussy clenches around me. Fucking Christ. I stare into her and start thrusting at a rhythmic, hard pace. It jerks her body upward—and each time, her breath catches. The noise is lighting a fire in my nerve endings.

"*Phoebe*," I growl into her ear while I pound her. "You always wished I'd fuck you on this ugly ruffled bedding in front of those dolls. Admit it, as soon as you saw this haunted-looking room, you've been dreaming of me fucking you here. That I'd hold you down and take you long and hard. You imagined this." I slam harder. "Fucking. Here." Faster. "Huh, how long did you want my cock this deep inside you?"

Words catch in her throat.

I slam.

"Uhhh-uh . . . ahhh, fuck." Her pussy pulses and tightens.

Jesus. I grit through the desire to shoot a load inside her. A groan is knotted up in my lungs. She's trying to glare, but it's smothered in pleasure as I thrust and thrust and thrust and fuck. As she jerks up. As our hot breaths and sweat meld. I can't even kiss her without stealing necessary oxygen. She's barely breathing.

"*Rocky*," she moans, her wrists pulling against my grip.

"You're not going anywhere until I've come inside you, little nightmare." The animalistic fucking *need* to fill Phoebe with my seed consumes half my brain. Penetrate. Fuck. Fill. Her.

No one else can have her.

No one.

She stretches her legs, giving herself to me.

As I fuck harder, our eyes stay latched, and I hold her face with one protective, forceful hand. The intimacy detonates everything I've ever known about sex. I see nothing but her. I feel nothing but her. I love nothing but her.

When she comes, her tightness wraps so hard around me, but it's her eyes rolling back and her limbs spasming that destroy me. "*Fuck*," I grit out, releasing deep, *deep* in Phoebe.

I wish I wasn't wearing a condom.

Not to get her pregnant—but I want my cum to seep out of her. I want to leave some of me inside Phoebe.

Once she comes off the peak and catches her breath, I pull out and toss the used condom in the wastebasket on the floor. Her half-lidded eyes fight to stay open. She's as exhausted as someone like Phebs can be.

"Signs of life?" I ask, leaning over her and combing sweaty hair off her forehead.

"Fuck you," she murmurs, her lips lifting.

I smile back. "Fuck me for fucking you so good, you mean?"

"Maybe." Her eyes flash with slight worry. "You're not going, are you?"

"No," I breathe. "Have I ever really left you?"

Phoebe shakes her head, then sits up to check on the status of the door. Chair still intact and propped beneath the knob. The reminder that it exists jolts her, and she wrangles the corset off her chest.

"He's not coming in here," I assure her.

She climbs off the bed, completely nude. Then unzips her suitcase, picking out a T-shirt and sweats. "You can't be that certain, Rocky."

"I put an Ambien in his whiskey."

She freezes, then twists her head back to me. "No." She's grinning. Drugging someone shouldn't delight us so damn much, but we're not out here delivering fruit baskets to people.

"Happy early birthday to me." I raise and lower my brows.

Phoebe is ten times more content with the knowledge that Trent is likely in a sleeping-pill-induced haze, counting sheep. Except, she's awake now, like she drank a 5-hour Energy.

"These are cool." Phoebe plucks a porcelain, blonde baby doll off the display shelf.

"Says the horror freak." I lounge against the headboard. Buck naked. It's too hot in the room to dive under the sheets.

"You love this horror freak," she slings back.

I grin, then I reach over and search the nightstand drawer. "No loose baby heads in here."

"*Shucks.*" She climbs onto the bed with the doll.

"Really?" I ask her, finding a pack of cigarettes and a lighter.

"She's precious."

"She's not sleeping with us."

"She's not *real*," Phoebe combats. "What weird superstition do you have against baby dolls?"

"It's creepy," I mumble, the cigarette between my lips. I light it, suck, and blow smoke away from Phoebe. "You're lucky I fucked you in front of it."

She smiles a little wider and then she eyes the cigarette. "You want me to crack a window?" she asks, snuggling beside me with the doll.

"If the walls smell like smoke, are you going to care?"

"Definitely not."

"Me either." The nicotine buzz vibrates my head, and I feel her body loosen against my chest. I wrap an arm around her shoulders and kiss her temple.

"You like smoking?" she wonders. "I thought you always just did it to assimilate."

"I do, but I like a cigarette after sex."

"Why?"

"Sex makes me relax, and cigarettes don't." While we're in this house, the last thing I want to do is lower my guard. I'm just happy to have Phoebe snuggled contentedly in my arms. One less worry gnawing at my brain.

My phone rings. On the other side of the room, at the dresser. I groan. There goes having her in my arms. Naked, I untangle from her.

"It might be Jake," Phoebe guesses. "He was really concerned before dinner."

"Yeah." I breathe out more smoke. Jake's been stressing about his mom's buttons being pushed. He knows Phoebe can "take it," but he still doesn't want to see her get hurt.

When I pick up my phone, my muscles tighten. No caller ID, and I don't recognize the number. I put it on speaker immediately. "Who is this?" I question, half expecting Varrick to have somehow tracked down my number.

"It's me." Oliver sounds out of breath, like he's moving a mile a minute somewhere—like he's running. I hear the howling wind. I hear his fear as the words pull from his soul: "'We loved with a love that was more than love.'"

It's our SOS phrase.

"Where?" I ask.

"Koning storm shelter. Hailey."

I hear a feminine blood-curdling scream before the line cuts out. My brain is lit up in panic. Phoebe is already jumping off the bed.

The last time any of us used that phrase, my brother had been stabbed. And he was bleeding to death.

THIRTY-SEVEN

Phoebe

The estate is asleep. Groundskeepers in bed. Housekeepers nowhere to be seen. Without pause, without conversation, Rocky and I race toward Jake's room on the softest parts of our feet. Silent, urgent *thuds* against floorboards as we sprint to him. He answers the door, pulling on cotton joggers over his boxer briefs.

"It's Hailey," I say.

He doesn't waste time grabbing a jacket. Rocky is only in drawstring pants, and I doubt any of us care if we freeze to death trying to find her. Jake guides us out, only stopping in a hallway to snag a flashlight from a utility closet.

The three of us hightail it into the dark night together.

"To the right," Jake instructs, pointing the flashlight into the foggy scattering of oak trees. Clouds hang low, and I can't see much except the stone siding of the mansion and several mammoth trunks. Old, old trees. Old, old land.

A person who can navigate this property with a blindfold

is with us. It offers a tinge of comfort. Still, my pulse hasn't slowed. It's hard to talk with the lump lodged in my throat.

At least it's the first week of April. At least it's not bone-chillingly cold.

Our breaths aren't frosting the air. Adrenaline warms me head to toe, and I welcome the slap of wind on my cheeks.

The storm shelter is apparently a good half a mile from the main house, which means we're all in a swift run.

I can't keep up with Rocky's and Jake's long legs. I'm several paces behind them, but Rocky checks over his shoulder, ensuring I'm here.

Jake checks next.

I'm here.

"Just go ahead," I call out. "I'll catch up!"

They aren't going to leave me behind.

Hot, angry tears prick my eyes. She doesn't have time! She could be dying! "Just go!" I scream, fear scraping against my lungs. Why are they like this?! "GO!"

They pick up speed, and the beam of light bounces with Jake's hurried, aggressive footfalls. They're running like the horn blew and they're in a one-hundred-meter dash for gold. Side by side, unrelenting, untiring strides forward.

Relief slams into me just watching them. *Please reach her.* As I jog from behind, darkness encases me the farther Jake distances himself, and I dial Hailey on Rocky's phone. Over and over.

"Answer," I beg.

Wind whips my hair, and the line goes to an automated voicemail for the fifth time. I send out an SOS text to Trevor and Nova. I give directions to the storm shelter, using a bocce court and a birdbath as land markers.

I stop calling Hailey when Oliver's form comes into view. Jake and Rocky are closing in on him, and the flashlight illuminates his anguished, sweaty face; unkempt pieces of maddened, dyed-lighter-brown hair; and bloodied hands. He's gripping a handle of the storm shelter door. It juts out of the grassy earth at a slight tilt, and Oliver braces his foot on the frame and tries heaving it open with all his strength, all his might.

He grits down, groaning as he pulls, he tugs, but it won't *budge*.

The storm shelter is made of steel.

My legs pump beneath me as I run as fast as I can.

"Hailey!" Oliver screams, trying harder, trying, trying, trying. "I'm coming! Hang on! *Hang on!*" Wind whistles and growls.

I can hear Hailey's shrieks of terror from within the shelter. My heart catapults to my throat.

Jake and Rocky reach the steel door, and Oliver turns to them in urgent panic, his khaki trench coat in a heap on the grass, his white button-down untucked and sleeves rolled up. His hair so wild. His eyes bloodshot—sweat dripping down his heart-shaped jawline. I've never seen my brother look this much of a mess, this ruined. Never.

Not in my whole life.

"Someone is in there with her," he says, out of breath, and I hear his labored sounds as I roll up to them.

Rocky takes the left handle of the door. Jake takes the right. While Oliver shuffles back, his hands on his thighs, he inhales sharper lungfuls of air.

"Hailey, we're here!" I call out as Jake and Rocky try to wrench the double doors open together. "We're getting you out!!"

She cries bloody murder. Like she's being slowly tortured.

"Don't you fucking hurt her!" I scream at the top of my lungs. "STOP HURTING HER!" Furious tears cloud my eyes. *Take me . . .* I'll switch with her.

Take me.

Oliver catches my shoulders, drawing me back. My entire insides are decaying, shriveling, withering, and as much as I ache to claw at the metal until my fingers bleed, I don't get in the way.

Jake's and Rocky's muscles flex in intense bands, the exertion all over their faces. They count to three and try again.

"Who's in there?" I croak to Oliver.

His usual relaxed demeanor is replaced by rattled, distraught urgency. "I don't know. I don't know. They locked her in with them."

"Who?!" Rocky yells back, the steel door clicking but not opening each time they heave. *"Goddammit."*

"We're not getting it open like this," Jake says.

"Who, Oliver?!" Rocky turns on him.

"I don't know!" Oliver shouts, talking a mile a minute. "I was on the balcony. Collin—he'd just gone to bed. I was *alone.* But I saw her—I saw Hailey walking in the grass. Barefoot. She had her service uniform on—but she looked dirty. I called down to her. She didn't . . . she didn't hear me. Then she started *running.*"

They pull again. It clicks. Not budging against the lock.

I press the heel of my palm to my forehead. Fiery tears threatening to surge once more. "Was she running toward someone?" I ask. "Or was someone chasing her?"

"Toward, maybe." His face contorts, and he rubs at the sweat lines on his face. "As soon as she started running, I left the balcony to catch her. By that time, she was already trapped in there."

Hailey shrieks again.

It's killing all of us.

"Hailey!" Rocky shouts to his sister. "Can you hear me?!"

She's not responding.

That *motherfucker*—whoever has her. Whoever is doing this to her . . . Varrick? He's not leaving here alive. He's not. He won't.

He won't.

"You can't pick it. There is no outside lock," Jake says quickly but calmly to Rocky. "It only locks from within."

Rocky lets go of the handle.

So does Jake.

"Don't stop!" Oliver yells. "We have to keep trying! We have to . . ." He stumbles forward, and I sprint after him as he tries to seize a bloody handle.

The blood, now on Jake's and Rocky's hands—it's from my brother. Blood stains my T-shirt sleeves where he touched my shoulders.

His knuckles are busted open, his palms split raw. How long has he been out here? How long has he been trying to break into the metal to get to her?

"Oliver, it's steel," I say, pained. My voice fissures. "*Oliver. It's a *storm* door!*" It's manufactured to withstand high-speed winds and whizzing objects. Tornadoes.

He reaches the door, just as Hailey wails, "Olly!" He drops to his knees, his face sheet white, and retches into the grass. As he pukes, I crouch behind him, rubbing my brother's back.

"It's okay." I intake pained breaths. "You're okay."

He touches my hand that curves around his chest. "Phoebe." He sounds like a child. Like he's stretching toward comfort, and I wish it were more than just me. I wish he had her.

"Where's my phone?" Rocky asks me in a ragged pant. Sweat glistens on his bare abs and drips down his forehead. "We need to call Nova."

"I already texted him and Trevor." I unpocket the burner phone and see a new message. "Nova is on his way. No response from Trevor yet."

"We have to get something to break the door down," Jake says. "There's a shed another half mile south with tools. I can get there and back in under ten minutes—"

"Go," Rocky says, and Jake is off. He takes the flashlight with him. Setting us in darkness.

Then Rocky yells over the growling wind, "Hailey! Listen to me! You need to open the door!"

"No, no, no!" she cries. "STOP! STOP!"

I can't catch my breath.

Jake, hurry.

"HAILEY, FOCUS!" Rocky shouts from the depths of his lungs.

"I can't! Stop! *Please stop.*" Her panicky voice is a jackhammer to my skull. I imagine someone holding her down. Caging her. Threatening her. Worse . . . *worse.*

Oliver picks himself to his feet, and I follow suit. He goes to Rocky angrily. "What are you doing? I told you, someone is in there with her."

"Have you heard another voice?" Rocky interrupts.

"What?" Oliver's frown turns into a scowl.

"Did you *hear* someone else with her, Oliver?" Rocky asks hurriedly. "Did you ever actually *see* someone else?"

Oliver runs a hand through his thick hair. "No but—"

Rocky rotates back to the storm shelter. "HAILEY! OPEN THE FUCKING DOOR!"

My eyes are flaming, burning suns.

"Rocky, she's crying and terrified!" Oliver screams. "She said someone is locked in there with her! She told me that!!" He grabs Rocky's shoulder to pull him away from the shelter.

Rocky shakes off my brother.

My stomach is a knotted mess. We shouldn't be fighting each other. "Rocky." I catch his attention. "Hailey would've already opened the door if she were alone."

"Would she?" Rocky looks between us in disbelief. "She's losing her fucking mind!"

Eerie silence grows on the other side.

I step closer to the door. "Hailey," I say, pressing my hand to the steel. "Are you okay in there? Hailey?"

"He's here. He's here," Hailey chokes out, fear lancing her voice. "Olly."

I whip my head to the guys. "She says *he's here*. Someone is with her."

Rocky is disbelieving. "No one has said a thing but her, Phebs."

"He's being quiet. He's playing with us! And what does it even matter, Rocky?!"

"She can open the door." He presses a hand to my cheek. "She can open the door."

Belief.

I've questioned what I believe more these past months than I have my whole life, and it comes down to this.

I believe in our love. I believe in the love that's high voltage, the love that raises dead towns. The love that keeps you running when you're on empty. The love that falls down with you—just so it can be there to drag you back up. I believe in love that has no room for failure because all it knows how to do is survive.

I believe in our love—the love of six people who only had each other to trust and lean on.

All I know is our love.

Oliver's bloodied hands fly to the top of his head, then he waves heatedly at the shelter. "Rocky, I'm telling you, she'd open the door for me." His eyes glass as he touches his chest. "She'd open it for *me*." His voice cracks on the last word.

Rocky approaches him and puts a hand to his cheek now. "She might not know it's you."

That pummels Oliver. Almost breaks him. He staggers back as if oxygen was stolen right out of his lungs.

Nova comes sprinting out of the darkness. A black utility backpack strapped to his strict shoulders. He has a shotgun in his hand. Jake is running from the other side with welding equipment. A plasma cutter, I think.

We all take a collective breath as they converge, reaching us at the same time.

"Jake's going to cut through the door," I tell Nova, filling him in quickly as he drops his backpack and unzips it.

Jake places the welding equipment beside the storm shelter door.

Nova hands me a Glock, and I check the chamber. Then he gives a similar gun to Rocky. "Ol?" Nova tries to capture Oliver's attention, but he's out of it.

"She's been calling his name," I tell Nova, and pain bleeds through his eyes as he studies Oliver again. It hurts—seeing our brother in this state. Hearing Hailey being . . .

I swallow nausea. It's all just anguish and fury.

Jake's gaze stays on Oliver in concern for a long beat before he throws the flashlight to Rocky. "Has she said anything else?"

I answer, "*He's here*. She said someone is with her."

"I think she's alone," Rocky tells him and Nova, then shines the light on Jake.

He's trying to power up the torch to cut through the steel. The flame flickers in and out. "Come on," Jake mutters. "Come on."

My pulse is a wave of highs and lows.

The fire dies. It goes completely out.

"*Fuck*," Jake curses, his brows knotting. He bangs the battery pack. Nothing. "It must be dead. I checked it before I left. I thought it was working."

"Where's Trevor?" Rocky asks, since he's the one who could likely tinker with and fix it.

I check the phone. "He hasn't responded."

Nova hurries over to Jake and tries to help light the torch.

I kneel in front of the storm shelter. Gun in my hand. I don't know if Rocky is right, but I just plead, "Hailey, *please*, open this door. *Please*."

Sobs come from the other side, and I take a deep, shaky breath. "Hailey, I love you. We all love you. You're our everything. We-we can't do this without you, okay? We just can't."

She cries harder.

My eyes pinch closed. We could be wrong. Varrick. He's probably grinning down there, taking sick joy in our torment. That's what this is. He's getting off on our distress. "If someone else is there," I call out, venom dripping off my voice, "then open this door and meet us face-to-face, you *fucking* coward!" I scream at the top of my lungs. "YOU FUCKING PIECE OF—"

The lock clicks.

I let out a surprised gasp, and Rocky drags me away from the door. I stumble back into his chest, and he pulls me behind him.

He flicks the safety off his gun. "I go first."

Armed myself, I try to go second, but Nova shoves me behind him, too. Then Oliver tears forward, beyond me, and Jake places a soft, gentle hand on my shoulder. He goes out ahead of me.

Nova and Jake heave the doors open.

Rocky disappears.

Everyone follows, and I'm last down the creaky old wooden steps. Descending into a dark, damp space that smells like mildew and earth.

It's pitch black. Except for the flashlight Rocky beams into the shelter. He swings it left and right. I see a bunk bed. Shelves of dusty canned goods. Beanee Weenees, Spam, SpaghettiOs.

"Hailey!" we all say.

It's utterly silent.

Jake must know where the switch is, because he puts a hand to the wall—and the small space is instantly bathed in dim yellow light. The bunker isn't any bigger than a wine cellar, and Hailey huddles in the grimy corner near the staircase.

I rush to her before anyone else can, dropping to my knees at her side. "Hails."

She's shaking, trembling. Leaves and twigs knot and tangle in her hair like she's been lost in the woods, and buttons are popped on her dirtied white blouse, exposing her black bra. Her cheeks are scratched, from branches maybe.

She's hugging her legs to her chest.

"Is there anyone else in here?" I glance over my shoulder. All four men linger and tower behind me, no longer searching the small shelter. The answer already rings in my ears. I see it on their troubled faces.

"No," Rocky says, taking my gun from me. "She's been alone."

I swallow hard and focus on my best friend. "Hailey? Can you look at me?"

She mutters incoherently, her eyes wide and horrified.

"It's me. It's Phoebe." I risk touching her fingers. She lets me pry them off her legs, and I gather her hands in mine.

I lean a little closer. "What are you saying?"

"He's here . . . he's here," she mumbles. "I followed him, and then he followed me."

"Who were you following?"

"Olly," she cries with a contorted, ugly sob. Oliver squats beside her, but she's still not focused on us. "I followed him here. He went in here."

"I wasn't on the grounds," Oliver whispers to her. "I was on a balcony."

"He followed me."

"*Yes*, I followed you, Hailstorm." He tries to steady his voice with hope and light. "I found you."

Her eyes bug out. "I-I need to tell him . . . I have to tell him . . ." She rips her hands out of mine and clutches her head. "No! No! No!" She shrieks, the bloodcurdling shriek again.

"Hailey! You're okay!" I shout. "No one is here!"

She's kicking out like we're going to kill her. She digs her back into the cement wall. "No, no, no! STOP! NO!"

"She's hallucinating," Jake says in a deep, tight breath.

Rocky lets out a sandpapery noise. "She followed a figment of Oliver to the storm shelter."

Nova ascends the stairs, his backpack strapped to his shoulders again. He stops mid-step to keep an eye outside.

"But why?" I ask them.

"She had to tell Oliver something," Jake says, concentrated on her. "That's what she just said. She wanted to tell him something."

"Hailey?" I snap my fingers in front of her face. *"Hailey."*

She rolls her head back and forth.

"'In a kingdom by the sea,'" Jake breathes, and she goes still. For the first time, her big round gray eyes rise.

She looks right at Jake.

Softly, he says, "'And so, all the night-tide, I lie down by the side.'"

Her nose flares. Tears fill her eyes. "'Of my darling . . .'"

"'My darling,'" Jake breathes, the words echoing around us. "'My life and my bride.'"

Silent tears cascade down her scratched cheeks. "'In her sepulchre there by the sea.'"

"'In her tomb by the sounding sea,'" Jake finishes the poem. I recognize it. "Annabel Lee" by Poe. It's the poem Hailey loves. It's why a line from it is our SOS call.

Her face fractures, like she's more cognizant of her real surroundings. "I saw Oliver . . . I know what I saw." She rubs at her eyes furiously. Then her chin trembles as she looks between all of us, and her gaze plants on me. "Phoebe," she says my name like we're seven years old again. "I haven't been sleeping."

My heart shatters. "I know," I tell her, my hand to the back of her head. She brings her forehead to mine. It's just us for a moment. Cocooned in our lifelong friendship.

Tears are rivers on her cheeks, tracking through the dirt. "No, you don't know," she whispers shakily, clinging tighter to my hand in hers. "I close my eyes, but I don't sleep."

I blink back the onslaught of tears. I failed her somewhere. I failed her. "It's okay," I whisper back. "It's going to be okay. We're going to get you help."

"I tried so hard," Hailey says. "I tried so hard to find answers, but I can't do it. It's all I'm good for and—"

"Hailey, stop," I cry. "You're beautiful—"

"You're *gorgeous*," Hailey professes from her core, tears streaming down her face again.

I clutch her cheeks with two hands. "You're brilliant, more brilliant than I could ever be."

She chokes on a sob. "So brilliant that I'm a useless mess here. I'm nothing. I'm *no one*."

"You're my best friend," I say from deep within. "If you're no one then so am I."

"You're counting on me to find answers."

My body caves. "You don't need to."

She's shaking her head.

"Hailey, you don't." I blink, and hot tears wet my cheeks. "You *don't* have to know everything. You could know *nothing*, and I'd still love you." We're both crying now.

She clutches my cheeks, too, holding on to me. Her chin quakes, and she squeaks out, "I'm not as smart as everyone needed me to be."

"That's okay." I rub at her cheeks. "Because I don't love you just because you're smart. You could be dumb as dirt, and I'd still love my dumb-as-dirt best friend."

She sobs harder and crumples into my body like a wounded bird. I wrap my arms around her, hugging her.

Oliver makes soothing circles on her back.

Jake is gripping the flashlight now. So tightly, the veins in his arms bulge out. Then there's Rocky . . . my Rocky.

His eyes are full of violent fury that I can't make sense of. "This ends here." He comes forward. "Give me my phone, Phebs."

I'm confused, but I don't prod. I wrestle it out of my back pocket and toss it to him.

"Who are you calling?" Jake asks.

Oliver's bloodshot gaze stays on the girl he loves. "He's calling the godmothers."

"Oliver Graves, right on the money," Rocky says tightly, then stops dialing and glances over at Nova. "Still no Trevor?"

"No."

Rocky's concern mounts.

Oliver whispers melodically, "Hailstorm. You found me."

"I found you." She peers out of my hug, and an ugly sob contorts her face again. "Oliver, it's so bad. It's so much worse than what I-I thought."

"What is?" I ask.

She has her hands to her ears. She pulls back from me.

Oh no, no, no, no. "Hailey," I choke out.

Rocky lowers his phone, not calling anyone yet.

"They lied, they lied, they lied . . ." She nods dazedly. "Prudie said, Prudie said . . ."

"Prudie," Jake says the name in recognition. "That's one of our oldest housekeepers. She's been with us for over forty years."

Rocky frowns. "Hailey must've talked to her tonight."

"Prudie said." Hailey licks her cracked lips, trying to spell it out. "Sh-she said there were three. There were three."

"Three what?" Oliver asks.

"Three children."

Oh my God. The Tinrocks. She found this information through a housekeeper at the Koning estate? I glance between Jake and Rocky. Are they really . . . could they be?

"No." Rocky shakes his head at me. "*No.*"

"Christian, Brent, Daphne," Hailey lists out. "Christian, Brent, Daphne."

Jake comes closer. "Those are the Wolfe children." He bends down on my other side. "The ones who died in '86."

Hailey's face is anguished as she stares off. "Christian married Josephine." So the oldest son did have a wife. "Christian m-married Josephine."

I take a sharp breath. "What happened to her?"

"Sh-she was in the car . . . when it ran off the bridge . . . and crashed into the river." Her breathing shallows. "There were three. There were three children in the backseat."

Hairs rise on my arms, on the back of my neck. Silence strains the storm shelter, and we all wait for her to catch her breath to tell us.

"Their three children," she says shakily. "Evan. Griffith." Her glassy, anguished eyes lift. This time, to her brother. "Brayden."

We all turn to Rocky.

"The baby," Hailey cries. "You were the baby in the backseat. You're Brayden Wolfe. The only real Wolfe that survived."

THIRTY-EIGHT

Rocky

I'm a battlefield of raw opened wounds. There's no suturing them back together. There's no medic waiting in the wings. There's only pain on pain on pain—and only three people in this entire godforsaken universe can staunch the bleeding.

I grip the phone in my fist.

It's not only about what I just found out. It's that Hailey is back to being unresponsive. She's lying on her side, her head in Phoebe's lap, who strokes her platinum hair. Hailey mutters, "I wasn't in the backseat. I'll never know . . . I'll never know who I am . . ."

I can handle the trauma of my childhood. But I can't watch my sister fade away like this—I can't fucking do it anymore.

I start dialing a number I know by heart. Putting the phone on speaker, I lift it up to my mouth as the line clicks. "It's me."

"Beds and pillows?" Addison asks, a phrase that means *is it safe and sound?* Her voice is tensed, full of worry. She knows we're pulling the rope this weekend, and it's too early to be calling.

"No beds and fucking pillows," I grit out, my lungs on fire. "Here's what's going to happen. You're going to get in your car and drive to my coordinates. We're in a storm shelter on the Konings' property. And before you tell me you can't— before you say you're not going to step foot in Victoria—you need to know your daughter is having a mental breakdown. She's not sleeping. She's hallucinating. Because she doesn't know who she is. So if you love her at all, if you have even a semblance of care for her, you will come here. You will come here right fucking now and give her what she needs. And if you don't—you will lose her. You will lose me. You will lose every last one of us. Got it?"

I don't think I'm breathing. My fingers are numb on the cell. My eyes blister. My heart is in my esophagus, waiting for a response to the ultimatum I just threw down.

There's no real reason she should agree to come here other than maybe she does love Hailey. Because there's a good chance she loses us anyway with the truth.

"Bray," she breathes out, and hearing my name from her— one I never really cared for, one that I didn't realize had any greater meaning—it nearly breaks me from the inside out. There's a long pause. My eyes sear as I fix my gaze on Phoebe. She mouths, *I love you.*

It settles the tortured parts of me. The pieces that threaten to crack. I blink for a long second and then Addison says, "Send me the coordinates."

I do. She's a half hour away, she says. Then we hang up. "Trevor," I say to Nova. "We have to find my brother."

"I'm not a guest," Nova says. "I can't waltz into the mansion and look for him, Rock."

"I'll go." Jake pushes forward with the flashlight. He touches my shoulder and tells me, "I'll search for him on the grounds and then in the house. Stay here with Phoebe and your sister."

I nod stiffly in thanks.

He nods back, then climbs the stairs, disappearing into the night. I scrape a hand against the back of my neck.

"How do you know Addison won't lie?" Phoebe asks me, caressing Hailey's head.

"Ol," Nova calls out, and Oliver goes to his brother. Nova is unzipping a first aid kit out of the side pocket of his backpack, and he immediately grabs his brother's wrist to check out his badly banged-up, bloodied hands.

I look back to Pheobe. "I don't know if she'll lie. But I believe she loves Hailey enough to offer the truth." This all banks on a mother's love of her daughter.

Have Addison and Elizabeth manipulated their daughters? *Yes.*

Have they also loved them throughout their lives? *Yes.* I believe both can be true in some twisted, crooked way, and it's the only hope we have.

"Get down," Nova tells Oliver hurriedly. "Go."

Oliver shuffles down the stairs with bandaged knuckles, and Nova points his shotgun at a figure at the top of the shelter.

"Whoa, whoa." Everett Tinrock appears, still in a tux, and he raises his hands at Nova. "It's just me. I got a call from Addy. She said to meet you all here. She's on her way with Beth."

"Let him in," I tell Nova.

"Let me in?" Frown lines crease his forehead. "Were you thinking of not letting me through?" Nova shifts out of the way on the stairs but never drops the shotgun, allowing Everett to pass with tenser confusion.

"What the fuck is going on?" he asks me between his teeth.

"You have the footage of Claudia?" I ask.

"I have it," Nova tells me. "Everett dropped it on the shoreline. I picked it up earlier tonight. It's already on a hard drive and saved in the cloud."

I stare down Everett. "So you made good on that, at least," I say with an inferno amassing in my chest. Or maybe it's been there all night. I feel it. On the verge of exploding.

Everett scans the storm shelter. Let me be very clear. He's only looking at the people. At Oliver and his bloodshot, wounded gaze—a boy who has *never* broken. At Nova and the barrel of his gun—a boy who has *never* betrayed. At Phoebe and her rage—a girl who has *never* disobeyed.

At Hailey and her psychosis—his so-called daughter.

"What happened? Hailey?" His voice is edged with paternal worry. He steps toward her. I put a firm hand on his chest and back him all the way up against the wall.

"Brayden!" He grips the nape of my neck, since I'm shirtless, to thrust me back.

I thrust him forward. "Who are we?!" I shout, pinning him against the concrete wall. "Who *the fuck* are we?! And don't lie. Because we know things. *She* knows things. So we will catch you in your own fucking web. Tell us the truth right now."

He's staring past me. He's watching Hailey mutter to herself. His jaw tics. His throat bobs. He's upset. This is upsetting him. *Good.* Join the fucking club. "She needs help, Brayden." He fixes his narrowed gaze on me. "Let's get her to a doctor."

"We're not leaving here without the truth. The *entire* truth."

He sucks in a sharp breath. "That's why you called your mother."

"Is she my mother? The woman who gave *birth* to me?"

Everett loosens the bow tie at his neck. He's tugging at his white collar. He unclips the Patek Philippe watch on his wrist. Like it's all bothering him. It's all too heavy as he controls his breathing. As he tries to control his skidding, flailing pulse.

I learned from him.

I learned *everything* from him.

"She's not your mother." Everett gets it out in the quietest breath. "Not in that sense."

"What was my mother's name?"

"Josephine Wolfe."

Now we're getting somewhere. "And my father?"

"Christian Wolfe."

Pain and wrath ball up in my throat. I swallow them down. "How did they die?"

"Their car crashed into the river."

"Did you have a hand in killing them?"

"Did I . . . ?" His brows jut up. "No, not . . ." He gets choked up. He's caught on my eyes, as if he's crawling backward. Into the past. "We were following their car. Addy and me."

"Why?"

"Because we knew what was going to happen that night." Everett curls his grown-out hair behind his ears. "The four of us were working a job in Victoria. Me, Addison, Elizabeth, and Varrick."

"You're friends with him?" I question.

"*Were*," Everett spits out in distaste. "He went rogue."

"Oh, he went rogue? How fucking convenient. Place the blame on the friend who got cut out of the circle."

Hurt flares in his eyes. He clutches my shoulder like I'm ten and he's about to lecture me. I rip his hand off me.

His chest collapses, but then he steels himself on instinct. "You know us. You've *known* what we do. We entrusted you six with thousands of felonies that could send us to prison, and how many times have you ever seen us put a hit on someone? With your own two eyes, son. Tell me the number."

Zero.

I grind my jaw.

Everett slides a hot hand across his neck. "He doesn't operate how we do. If he did, he fooled us—"

"He fooled you?" I say with thick doubt.

"I'm not the best of us," Everett admits. "Your mother— *Addison* is much better. Beth, too. But even they didn't see what he was until it was too late. We were in too deep, and we were just . . . we were hanging on." He drops his gaze for a beat, then lifts it back to me. "We were targeting the Wolfes. So when Varrick got close to William Wolfe, then when he proposed to Daphne—it was all part of the plan. What wasn't was him killing William."

"He killed Emilia's husband?"

"I didn't see it. Beth said he used potassium chloride and put the needle under his tongue. Varrick held the man down while he was sleeping. Everyone . . . everyone believed William died of a heart attack. No one suspected foul play."

"So what'd you think would happen the night my parents died?" I question.

Everett tilts his head back against the cement. He turns away from me, like this next story is misery. "Beth was in a car with Varrick. They were tailing Christian Wolfe and his family."

"I thought you said you and Addison were following them?"

"We were technically following Varrick, who was following

them. Beth was trying to convince him to turn around. Addy and I were keeping our distance. He didn't know we were there. We were afraid he was going to kill Christian's entire family. He needed them out of the picture, and this was the best chance to do it, since they were headed to Vermont for a family vacation."

My family. The family I never knew. "They never made it out of Connecticut," I say with hollowness.

"One did," Everett says to me. "You were a one-year-old boy in his car seat. Your oldest brother was next to you. He must've unbuckled you while the car was sinking. He got the window cracked, just enough to squeeze you through."

My chest tightens. I fight an onslaught of raw emotion. "How could you know this?"

"Because I jumped off the bridge and went into the water. To see who was alive."

"And you found me?" He what—he saved me? I'm fisting his shirt now, but it's not with malice.

"You were a *child*." Everett's nose is runny. He wipes it with the back of his hand. I've never seen him this outwardly overcome with an emotion that's not disappointment, frustration, or anger. "I wasn't going to let you die. The river was deep. Varrick had run them off the road and driven away. He didn't want to risk anyone seeing him." Everett fights a tremor in his voice. "I would've . . . I would've tried to save more, but they were already gone. You weren't even breathing. Addy gave you CPR when I brought you to the bank of the river. The *only* thing that we knew at that point is we had to get you out."

"Get me out? I had a grandmother, an uncle, an aunt who were all still alive—and you took me?"

"He was going to kill them—"

"Alert the sheriff."

"The sheriff was his best friend!" Everett shouts with a shrill, wounded laugh. "You have no idea, son. You think you can talk your way out of five federal penitentiaries—he can talk his way out of five *hundred*. They were all going to die, and we couldn't stop it. But we could save you."

I blink, my eyes so dry—they sear. "How does Varrick know who I am? Present day. He called me *Brayden*. How?"

"He knows you exist. He's always known. We couldn't just run off with you without him knowing, so we were trying to work around him. We told him we wanted a baby—me and Addison. It's why we saved you. It'd been our dream. We weren't going to raise you as a Wolfe, which would've been a threat to him. Instead, we'd strip you of your identity. And we were going to raise you as ours. You'd grow up as a con artist. He thought it was a great idea. We wanted to leave Varrick on good terms. So he had no reason to come after us."

Too many questions slam into me, but I just go with this one: "Why call me Brayden? Out of everything—why would you risk choosing my birth name?"

He shrugs, his eyes glassing. "Guilt. Shame. We did have a hand in killing your family, indirectly, and maybe it was our way to make ourselves feel better." He drops his gaze. "Your father was a good man—"

"Don't," I choke out. "I don't want to hear it."

He nods tensely, understanding. "They didn't deserve it, is all. William—your grandfather, maybe, but not his kids."

Nova suddenly speaks from the stairs. "Varrick has been targeting the girls. You said you left on good terms—how is that fucking *good*?"

Everett wipes at his nose again. "He's not singling out the girls. He's probably hoping to unsettle all of you. Or test you—to see how well we raised you."

"You aren't sure?" I ask, loosening my grip on his shirt.

"No. He knows all six of you are here, and he knows Addison and Elizabeth haven't stuck around. We've been worried that he's trying to threaten you all, just to lure them out to Connecticut for more than a day at a time."

"Why haven't they come out here more?" Phoebe asks angrily from the ground. "Why hide away?"

"Beth is terrified of him. For good reason." He exhales a long breath. "And Addy won't leave her. They're . . . attached at the hip, and I can't argue with it. You know how it is," he tells me, then stares behind me at Phoebe and Hailey. "Varrick is . . . unpredictable. We don't know what he's going to do, which is why we've avoided pulling jobs in this state since '86. Which is why we need to leave after this one with the Konings. We're playing roulette the longer we stay."

My temples pound.

I have this strange feeling, and the longer I stare at my father, the longer his eyes veer away from mine, the more I feel like . . . he's evading.

He's left something out.

He knows I see through him. But Nova says, "They're here."

The godmothers rush down the creaky stairs. "Hailey?" Addison's voice pitches up as soon as she sees Hailey crumpled in Phoebe's lap and how she's staring off at nothing.

"Oh my God, Addy." Elizabeth grabs on to her friend's arm, and they race toward their daughters, but I cut off their path.

Oliver does, too.

"Oliver?" Elizabeth winces. She tries to step toward Phoebe, but the fire coming out of her daughter's eyes stops her dead in her tracks.

"Wh-what?" Addison staggers at me. "Move, Brayden. Your sister—"

"She's been in pain for *months*. Because of your lies. That"—I motion behind me—"is what your deception and love does. Horrific. *Your. Doing.*"

"Let me see her," Addison says icily, painfully, between clenched teeth. She budges forward.

"Back up," Phoebe sneers at her. She weaves her arms protectively around Hailey, like there is no way in hell they will touch her. "You don't get a heartfelt reunion. Not when you caused this."

I fall in love with Phoebe a million times over in this one moment. I could kiss her. Hug her. Marry her—though we've done that a hundred fake times already.

"Brayden," Addison pleads with me.

"See this line?" I drag my foot across the dusty cement, creating a line in the dirt. "Any of you cross it, Nova shoots your leg. Which'll probably blow off since he's holding a shotgun."

"You're kidding." Addison gapes, hurt all over her face.

I'm trying not to envision her on the bank of a river, giving me CPR. I'm not thinking about the past. I'm just thinking about this moment. My sister. My family in this storm shelter. And the three people in front of me have been excommunicated, as far as I'm fucking concerned.

"*Brayden.*" She checks behind her, looks at her husband. Everett is torn up in ways that physically rattle her. "Everett, honey?"

"They know. I told them about Varrick."

Elizabeth clutches a heart-shaped locket at her neck. She seems ill. "How much do you know?"

"Why don't you tell us?" I ask her. "*Dad*, say nothing. You two, keep your backs to him and start talking."

It takes at least fifteen minutes for them to run through the same exact story. With a little more detail about the car crash. (Wish I didn't hear it.) And the deaths of Daphne and Brent.

Elizabeth is crying through these recountings of the past they clearly never wanted to revisit. Addison dries her friend's tears with travel tissues from her purse and becomes more stoic for her. It's not fabricated emotion. They'd have to be evil to play us this hard, and I know they aren't. Not when all they want is for Hailey to be okay.

"Has she been sleeping?" Addison asks, constantly peering over at my sister. "Hailey, can you hear me? *Hailey*."

"I wasn't in the backseat," Hailey mutters. "I wasn't in the backseat."

"Bethy." Addison whirls to her. "We have to tell her."

Elizabeth buries her face in her hands, then drops them. "Okay, *okay*. We'll tell them. We can tell them." She takes a readying breath, but her face punctures when she sees her son. "Nova, please don't look at me like that."

He's staring at her like she's a stranger.

"I'm your *mom*. I didn't lie, spider. We didn't lie about that."

"You lied about Rocky."

She slaps her hands to her sides. "We felt like we had no choice. If we were going to raise you as confidence men, you couldn't know the truth. We'd . . ."

"Lose us?" Nova finishes coldly.

Elizabeth claws at her heart like it's breaking. "I . . . we didn't want it to be like this." She lifts the slipping strap of her yellow floral sundress.

"*Hailey*," Addison cajoles. Her red hair is in a tightly coiled bun. Wearing a slim black dress, she bows forward like she's enticing a kitten out of a cranny. "I can tell you *everything*. Everything you've ever wanted to know."

"I wasn't in the backseat," Hailey mutters.

Addison straightens up, then glares at me. "Let me cross the fucking line."

"You can tell her everything right there. Maybe start with whether you were actually pregnant with Hailey."

Addison and Elizabeth slip each other grief-stricken, surrendering looks, then Addison unknots her bun. Red strands pool onto her shoulders. She exhales for a solid second and breathes out, "No, I wasn't."

"But you were pregnant at one point?" Phoebe says with a heated, tremoring voice. "You had a miscarriage, right? That's what you said at the Berkshires. That's why we thought you were pregnant with Trevor—but really, you adopted him."

"No," Addison says. "We made it look like I was pregnant."

"We staged it, bug, because we didn't want any of you to question where Trevor came from," Elizabeth explains further.

"We lied to you during the dinner," Addison admits outright. "At the Berkshires."

"Why?!" Phoebe yells. "Why the fucking cruelty?!"

Elizabeth winces and raises her hands, as if they're clean of misdeeds. "Bug, I promise you, we felt like this was the only way to protect you all."

Addison shakes her head in thought. "You pull a thread and then another and another. We thought we could stop you all from pulling threads, if there was a reasonable explanation for Trevor's birth."

"But you all kept pulling," Elizabeth says. "If you knew we lied about Hailey, Trevor, and Rocky, then you'd doubt us, and there is no room for doubt between each other—not in what we do. We knew you could never know or . . . or this would happen." Her face twists in a surge of grief as she peers from Nova, to Oliver, to Phoebe. "You're *my* kids. Please. *Please*. I love you, and I'm so sorry. I'm sorry." Her knees buckle, and Addison catches her, holding her friend, who sobs into her chest.

Oliver rubs his face with his bandaged hands. He's looking between Nova and Phoebe, but the triplets stay strong. They don't console their mom. They leave that to her friend.

"Who is Trevor?" I ask them, when really, inside I'm screaming, *Where is Trevor?!* He's still not here.

Fear stabs me, but I can't desert the storm shelter. I can't abandon them right now.

"And let me remind you," I tell the three of them, "whatever you say next, it needs to be the truth. Because Hailey has done enough research to find holes, and if you even have a fucking pinhole, she will know. And we will know. And you will have no chance to ever reconcile with us. We will *never* believe or trust you again. We won't work with you. Hell, we won't even talk to you. It will be a long, permanent goodbye."

Elizabeth stays knelt on the floor while Addison has an arm around her.

Everett starts, "We were given Trevor."

"In a way," Addison clarifies poorly.

"In a way?" I shoot back. "What the fuck does that mean? *In a way?*"

Addison rises to her feet, but she's unbalanced on her heels. She's nervous. She even smooths out her dress—which is her anxious tic. "He's the son of a mark."

"Of a mark?"

"Of billionaires. *Awful*, terrible people." She grimaces even recounting them. "This couple—they were so deep inside their own self-centered world, they couldn't bother to be around for the birth of their own child."

"They took a vacation to Tahiti," Everett says from the wall, his arms crossed. "While their surrogate was in labor."

"For nine hours," Addison snaps. "When Trevor was born, Everett and I paid the surrogate for the child. She believed we'd care for him more than the couple."

"She believed that, huh?" I nod strongly. "You tell her you're grifters? You tell her you'd raise that boy to nab wallets? Or that he'd be your little shill—a way for you to gain credibility wherever you went? Cute little Trevor. *No way am I screwing you over if a baby is on my hip.*"

Addison stakes a glare my way. "Judge me. But you weren't there. You didn't see their aversion and apathy toward anyone marginally less privileged than them. They didn't care for their surrogate. They saw her as *subhuman.* She felt that. It's why she called to let them know the child passed during birth. Do you want to know what they did? Hearing that their newborn died?"

Elizabeth's tears have dried. She winces at the memory. "They extended their vacation."

My brother.

He was born out of neglect. And all he's ever desired is to be included.

"We love Trevor," Addison professes. "We care for him in ways they *never* would. He would've been a forgotten child, or worse, he'd have turned out just like the men we target. Vile, cruel, and so blinded by their own vanity, they leave despair in their wake."

I look through her. "You didn't save him. You *chose* him. How many marks have kids? How many have we run by that you could've so easily robbed out of their cradles or convinced the parents to hand them over like you're a divine fucking saint? Trevor was different, though, wasn't he?"

"Of course he was different," Everett says from the wall. "He's six years younger than you all."

"At that time, we wanted a baby," Addison says like it's simple.

"Get pregnant. Adopt. I don't know, do it the normal way."

"The opportunity presented itself."

"Right."

She hears my skepticism and takes a sharper breath. "Jobs are easier with a child. We realized that really early into having you, Bray. But you all . . . you were getting older. I personally thought if the baby had gray eyes like yours, if you believed I was pregnant, it'd be easier on you and Hailey. You wouldn't question where you came from."

"This is your family," Everett says. "That's all that mattered to us. The ones we built. Tinrocks. Graveses."

"What about Hailey?" Phoebe asks, my sister's head still in her lap.

Hailey stares dazedly. Silent tears leak out of her eyes.

"*Hailey.*" Addison bends forward again. "Hailey, look at me."

Hailey blinks a slow, slow blink. "'Have I gone mad?'" she whispers.

"'All the best people are,'" Oliver replies with light in his voice, and gradually, my sister focuses on Addison.

"Hailey," Addison says carefully, afraid to spook her. "I love you. I love you so dearly, and you came into our lives with so much love. You came after the triplets. I never met your birth parents. Everett and I posed as a lovely couple from the suburbs, and we found you."

"Where?" Steadily, Hailey sits up, then more weakly leans

into Phoebe, who curls her arms around my sister's slender frame.

"The foster system."

"We adopted you under fake names," Everett says gently to her.

"Because of my eyes," she says distantly.

"And because . . ." Addison gets teary. "Because we wanted another girl."

"For Phoebe," Elizabeth explains, thumbing the locket at her neck again. "We wanted you two to grow up as friends . . . like Addison and I did."

"And look at you two now," Addison says.

Phoebe fights tears and hurt. "So you took Hailey for me?"

"*Adopted*, bug," Elizabeth emphasizes.

"W-where was I born?" Hailey asks.

"Chicago." Addison's gaze softens. "Whatever you want to know. *Any* details. I'll give them to you whenever you ask."

Hailey is drifting a little. "You're forgetting to tell us something. There's something you're forgetting. Or maybe you just don't want them to know. Maybe you'll always say you forgot. When we know. I know."

"What's she talking about?" I ask them. The feeling I had earlier with Everett—it creeps up again. "It's about Varrick?"

Elizabeth is woozy. She's on her knees. Staring at the line I drew in the dirt. "When Addy, Everett, and I left Victoria with the baby—with Brayden . . . I didn't know at the time . . . I didn't realize it."

"Realize what?" I ask.

"I was pregnant. With the triplets." She dabs at her wet eyes, but her makeup is already smeared across her cheeks.

"We didn't want to return to Connecticut because Varrick never knew the truth."

"And what is the truth?"

Elizabeth tries to say it, but the words catch. So Addison finishes, "That Nova, Oliver, and Phoebe are his children."

You could hear a pin drop.

Until Nova growls out, "He's our father?"

"No way," Phoebe mutters, catching my gaze with wide, terrified eyes. This entire fucking time, I thought he was *my* dad. I smear a hand down my face. I don't want him to be hers—probably more than I didn't want him to be mine.

"But Mattias," Oliver names their supposed dad.

"He's a friend who went to prison for fraud," Elizabeth says. "I wish . . . I wish he were your real father."

"Does Varrick know about the triplets now?" I ask her.

"Yes. He believes they're his kids. He figured it out while you've been here. He wanted me to come to Connecticut. To live with him at Stonehaven, but I won't . . . I won't."

Nova is fuming. He's pacing at the bottom of the stairs, so he doesn't see the movement at the opened doors.

My pulse pitches up, and I explode forward. "Trevor!"

My little brother climbs down the steps, the hood to his peacoat over his head.

"Where the fuck have you been?"

Trevor barely assesses the storm shelter or anyone in it. He takes measured breaths, his face flat. Void. He only looks at me. "We have thirty minutes to leave the Koning estate. It's how long Jake is giving us before he calls 9-1-1. We need to go now." He's about to turn.

I catch his wrist. "Why the urgency?"

"Because it's done."

My brows slowly lift as apprehension builds. "What's done, Trev?"

"I pulled the rope. It's over. You're welcome, everyone." He waves a hand around the bunker.

No one utters a fucking word of gratitude.

"What'd you do?" I ask while standing on a bed of nails. *Please don't say it. Please don't say it, Trev. Please. Please.*

"Claudia Waterford is dead. I killed her."

THIRTY-NINE

Rocky

TEN YEARS AGO
THE FUCKUP
Somewhere Outside of Boston

Deep into the woods at nine p.m. I can only see in front of my feet thanks to a full moon and fireworks blasting overhead. The pop of color lights the darkness in reds, blues, and greens. Each step forward, the muddy ground splatters my loafers and the hem of my khakis.

I'm sixteen.

I've always felt older, probably because I've pretended to be an adult more than once, but today—I couldn't feel less like a teenager. Because what person my age has to deal with this?

Rain has stopped. A storm from this morning left the earth soft and uneven. I hear a babbling stream nearby. My angered, dense breaths dry out my throat, but I hurry.

We're hurrying.

My biceps scream as I adjust my grip on a heavy black tarp. Carrying the weight of . . . well, a body. "You're going too fast," I grunt out to Oliver.

He's holding the other end, and his long legs outpace mine. "We don't have much ti—"

I step into an ankle-deep hole. Tripping forward, I drop the body, and a splitting, excruciating pain shoots through my knee. I bury the scream between my teeth. *"Fuuuuck."*

"Shit, *shit.*" Oliver tries to help me up.

"I'm fine. I'm fine." I push him off me. Nausea roils as I pick myself up and set slight weight on my knee. Fucking Christ. I don't look at it. I try to pop the kneecap back in, and stars flare in my eyes. I cough out. *Holy fuck.*

"Can you walk?"

"Grab your side," I say, spitting onto the ground as the urge to throw up pummels me. *"Grab it, Oliver."*

He stops hovering, and we resume course. Granted, each foot forward feels like a new blade and bullet in my leg. Pain radiates through my whole body, but I concentrate on my breath and focus on a critical task.

We follow Nova's coordinates to an area of fallen trees. He's already digging a ditch in the wet earth around the oaks. My ten-year-old brother sits on a tree trunk and picks at a chunk of rotten bark in his hands.

Oliver and I throw the tarp-rolled body to the side, then go grab the two extra shovels Nova brought.

"Should he be watching this?" Nova asks me quietly, as I stake my shovel into the ground.

"I think it's a little too late for that." I hack up and spit a loogie behind me, and I rub at my runny nose with my wrist.

Nova grimaces. "What happened to you?"

"I tripped." I toss dirt behind my shoulder. "Just keep going."

"Fucking A," he grumbles under his breath, digging with

more intensity. Nova is strong for fifteen, and we're making good work of the ditch.

Sweat pours down my temples, and I glance over at Trevor. I can't believe this happened. We were at the mark's lake house. Hell, we are *still* here. Only maybe a couple miles away from their vacation home—likely still on their property.

An enormous Fourth of July party is going on. Friends of friends of friends—all invited. I was back at the house. A half hour ago. Kids were running around everywhere with sparklers as fireworks started to shoot off.

I couldn't find Trev.

I kept searching.

My responsibility. To protect him. I checked everywhere, trying not to draw attention. Trying not to be suspicious.

I walked farther from the house. Down the sloped hill. Closer to the lake, but away from the gathering crowd of people who *ooed* and *awed* over the bursts of color in the sky.

A shingled shed sat several feet away from the bank of the lake. It stored pool chemicals. Weed killer. Yard tools. Tarps.

I walked in to find Trevor sitting close to the door. He barely rotated to look at me. He was staring at this frat boy fuckhead named Hollister. He was a friend of a friend of a friend of the mark's daughter. Lydia, a sophomore at Brown.

Hollister had pruning shears stuck in the side of his neck. His eyes were wide open. Unmoving. Still as can be—his whole body.

"Trevor," I said his name in a single breath.

He held his knees, not taking his eyes off Hollister as blood pooled beneath his dead body. "He was hurting her."

Lydia was out cold on the floorboards. She had on a red ruffled sundress, and her underwear was at her ankles. I checked her pulse. Hollister must've roofied her. There were blue Solo cups on a shelf, like they snuck in here together. His pants weren't down or even unzipped. My mind was spinning.

So I called Nova.

He came in seconds. We rolled the body in a tarp. He poured bleach on the shears, washed the slats of the floorboards with other chemicals around the shed. He called Oliver, and the two of them snuck the body into the woods. It was dark. No one saw.

Nova brought shovels from the shed to go scout a gravesite.

I scooped Lydia up and brought her back to the main house. "I found her outside, passed out like this," I told her mom, who clutched at the Tiffany's necklace at her throat.

"Oh no. How much did she drink?" Her eyes darted cautiously to her friends. She laughed a little, embarrassed, then said, "Would you be so sweet to put her in her room for me? Thanks, hun." She sipped her martini. "College these days," she prattled to her friends. "I swear, even at dry campuses, the kids find ways to drink themselves silly."

Wrath seared through me, and acid slipped down my throat with each swallow. Because she didn't know me. Didn't know my name. Didn't know my age. She only saw that I was a teenage boy at a party with hundreds of all ages in attendance.

She had every reason to doubt me. Yet, she never questioned a thing. Naïve. Vain. It should've made me happy—to gain trust so effortlessly—but I would've rather she cared enough to ask if her daughter was breathing. At the *minimum*.

I would've rather not had to walk into my kid brother staring at a dead body.

I would've rather not had Trevor walk into an act of violence, only to feel like he had to be violent to end it.

I would've rather not have been apart this long from her.

From Phoebe.

I would've rather been playing horseshoes with her and pretending she was a girl I hated at school.

I would've rather stolen glimpses of her as her big brown eyes looked up into the firework-lit sky.

Instead, my kneecap is shrieking. Splinters dig into my palms from the old wooden handle of the shovel. Mud continues to splatter my pants and button-down.

"Can we take his eyes?" Trevor suddenly asks from the tree trunk.

Oliver stops shoveling, sharing a disturbed glance with Nova. "Sure, that's a reasonable request." He pants hard. "You want to pluck them out, Nov, or shall I?"

Nova shakes his head so hard and stakes the earth more aggressively this time. "I can't fucking believe this."

"I'm serious," Trevor says.

"You don't say?" Oliver says lightly, then cocks his head at me like *something is wrong with your brother, man.*

Yeah. "Why do you want his eyes?" I groan out.

"I don't think he should have them."

Great. I spit to the side again. "What'd you see, Trev?" I finally ask.

"I was watching them. Through the window of the shed. She was drinking with him, then she passed out. He caught her in his arms, but . . . he didn't help her." His frown deepens. "I thought he'd help her."

"Is that all?"

"He was messing with her clothes." He scratches his nail over the bark. "He didn't see me coming . . . no one ever sees me." His gray eyes lift to mine. "I got him in the neck."

I nod a ton, my lungs roasting alive with each heavy breath. He's *ten.* I think our mom has taught him about sexual assault, seeing as how we're walking a minefield of shitty peo-ple doing shitty things. She wanted to ensure the people we screw over don't rub off on any of us. I don't know if she mentioned rape. I don't tell him he might've prevented that. I don't give him kudos for killing.

I just say, "This stays here. With the four of us."

Nova hesitates. "Your dad should know—"

"*No*," I snap back. "How is he going to help the situation? We shouldn't even tell our sisters. You want to put them at risk of being an accessory to . . . ?"

Murder.

I say out loud, "Self-defense. And that's what we're going with if this all blows up. I can talk our way out of it."

Nova relents, then throws more dirt onto a pile.

"We should cut off his ears, at least," Trevor says.

"You think the dead can hear?" Oliver muses, as if my brother isn't currently imagining butchering a body.

"Next time," I tell Trev, "run out and call an adult. This isn't the way."

Trevor just nods. "Sorry, Rock."

I want to hug him. Ditch. Body. Bury. No time. Once the body is packed beneath dirt, we all head back to the lake house. Fireworks still pop in the sky, and with my enflamed knee, I limp my way toward the docks.

As soon as I'm in view of people, I walk normally. I even run—and I leap into the dark water, plunging deep. Then I breach the surface and wipe a hand against my face. Dirt—I'm washing off the dirt.

I laugh and holler out like I'm having the time of my life.

It entices half the student body to rush down the hill. Se-niors begin cannonballing and splashing into the lake.

Causing raucous, chaotic noise. Nova and Oliver join like they're part of the pack, but they're doing it to get clean, too.

Trevor dives off the dock in a perfect arc.

The only relief in my body is from the water. And seeing Phoebe jump in after me.

The laughter in my chest is real now. It expands in me like a balloon as she swims closer, as her pissed-off eyes sink into mine, as I tread water around her, circling.

"*Peggy*," I taunt.

"*Kieran.*" She scoops water in her mouth and spits a stream at my face.

I fight a smile. "Mature." I splash her back.

"The most mature." She splashes me, then I dunk her, and we're wrestling in the lake with dozens of happy-go-lucky, oblivious teenagers swimming around us.

For a minute, I feel her holding on to me. Hugging me. I cup the back of her head, more affectionately, and I consider kissing her. I would if I knew it wouldn't ruin our positions in the job, which would infuriate Phoebe.

Then she ends the embrace and plants two hands on my head, trying to dunk me. I have her by the waist, and we're fighting all over again. On repeat.

Over and over.

When she slows, water beads down her face and catches in her lashes. Her lips dip beneath the surface of the lake.

I'm so in love with her.

I can't control it. I just feel it growing, intensifying, devastating me.

And I hope it obliterates me.

Every single day of my life.

FORTY

Rocky

Claudia's funeral has double the turnout of Emilia Wolfe's. Trent Waterford makes sure of it.

"He doesn't want an autopsy. He's adamant," Jake told me at the florist shop down the street from Baubles & Bookends. Several days before the funeral.

We met there since Trent wanted me to ensure Jake didn't order the wrong type of flowers for the memorial service. He'd never said which flower that was, but it didn't matter if it was tulips or carnations or fucking lilies—as long as Jake didn't choose it, it'd do.

The florist snipped stems of pink peonies at the counter. Phoebe's favorite. We browsed the vases near the shop window, out of earshot of the florist. "Let me guess, Trent doesn't want her body tampered with," I said quietly.

"Yep," Jake said, just as hushed. "He thinks it's a desecration, and the coroner is already ruling it as a stroke."

We're going to get away with this.

Because of vanity and ego. Because Trent can't even consider, for one second, that foul play might be involved. Because he was there the night she died, and surely, *he'd* know if she were murdered.

But it's not how we do things. It's ruined everything, *everything* we had planned. "Did you talk to the lawyers?" I asked.

"We're reading the will tomorrow, and it's likely everything will be split fifty-fifty between me and him. We might be fighting over some of the properties. But my father told me it's legit. She did update the will to include me."

Turns out, Claudia didn't want to give her favorite son everything anymore. Because it wasn't smart to leave a hundred percent of her family's legacy to Trent, a son who'd been dragged in the mud for something so . . . minor—an audio leak. What if an uglier skeleton fell out of his closet? That's what Addison and Elizabeth stressed to Claudia for days. That she needed to hedge her bets.

Claudia had listened to them. And so it really turns out, we did need the godmothers after all.

It's good that Jake walked away with something, but Trent was supposed to have *nothing*. Now he has ten times more power than he did. And killing his mother has only endeared him to the town. They knew he was Claudia's favorite son, and he's milking their pity.

We've been slowly setting him on fire. It extinguished with one wrong move, and he's risen from the fucking ashes.

Jake plucked out an orchid, twisting the stem between his fingers. Hailey's favorite. "Honestly, man . . . I wish we were burying him instead."

I nodded stiffly. "Sentiment is shared."

Phoebe has said my brother killed the wrong Koning. If there were a choice, I think we all would've targeted Trent over Claudia.

Why had Trevor chosen her? He'd given me a runaround answer. "It was a one-step solution. It helped, didn't it?"

Not really.

Claudia was never blackmailed. She never made Jake sole heir before she died.

Trevor chose to kill her either because Phoebe was the principal and he wanted to show he could execute it better than her, or because Claudia was threatening Sidney. And he cares more about Sidney Burke than I thought.

Whatever the motive, the Koning matriarch is gone.

"How are you holding up?" I asked Jake.

"I keep waiting for the guilt, the sadness, but it's just not there." He set the orchid back. "I keep thinking about Kate." Jake faced a giant poster on the wall.

I turned with him.

It said VICTORIA'S MOST CELEBRATED FLOWER with an art sketch of a giant mountain laurel—prominent pollen stems arched toward purplish-pink petals like spider legs. The mountain laurel is on lamppost banners. It's on the logo of the country club. It's on brochures for the town. It's everywhere.

Including in Claudia's bloodstream.

I started laughing.

Jake side-eyed me, and then he started laughing, too. "Your brother either loves poetry or has a sick sense of humor."

"The latter, probably." He killed Claudia with a mountain laurel. Toxic if consumed. Lethal in large quantities. He muddled it in her bedtime tea.

Before we left the florist shop, Jake asked me, "How old are you then? For real?"

"Like you ever knew my real age," I said under my breath and slipped my sunglasses on. "How old did you think I was, Jake?"

"I never believed you were younger than me. I'll just say that."

"You could just keep believing that." I flashed a tight smile.

Jake ground out an annoyed sound, like I was a shithead little brother. "Or you could tell me the truth."

The truth. "I thought I was going to turn twenty-six on the nineteenth."

His brows jumped. "Holy shit," he said with a laugh, like I just descended into puberty.

I made a face. "That's barely younger than you." He's twenty-eight now.

"Meh, it's pretty young." His lips rose, and he shoved his wallet in his back pocket. "Real age then?"

"I'm turning twenty-seven." Addison and Everett found me when I was one, but they made me believe I was a year younger. One when I was truly two. And so on, and so forth.

"You were born in '85." He smiled at me like he saw me. "Do I call you Brayden, Grey, or Rocky?"

"From you, I prefer *jackass*." I backed up to the door. "Every time Victoria's Sweetheart curses, a baby bird dies in the sky."

He laughed. "Phoebe did say you're afraid of geese."

"Christ." I rolled my eyes.

"Bye, jackass," he called out.

"Bye, sweetheart." I middle-finger exited.

Now at the funeral days later, it's setting in. The finality of what happened that night. Not just with Claudia.

But in the storm shelter.

All of it.

Us.

Once the crowds disperse and the casket is lowered, I distance myself and walk the old cemetery.

It takes me several minutes.

But I find them.

I stuff my hands in my leather jacket and stare down at four headstones—the engravings badly chiseled. Names and dates nearly illegible. They were reburied farther back in the cemetery in the nineties. Away from the other Wolfes.

Left to be forgotten. To be written out of history.

I crouch down to one. The earth is soft beneath my boots, and I pick up a fresh white rose at the base. Since they've been back in town for a couple hours at a time, the godmothers have made a point to leave flowers at the graves of the Wolfes, they told me. *Find the ones with the fresh white roses. That's your family.*

A knot is in my throat. My eyes burn as I make out the start of a name. *Ev* . . . for Evan. I run my tongue over my molars, and I somehow manage to get out, "Thanks for saving my life, big brother."

I didn't think it mattered to know where I came from. I didn't think I'd care.

Because I wouldn't trade the family I have for another, but this one—this one was ripped out of the ether. I was what was left. And the man who did it has parasitically consumed their entire legacy, all they ever built through the generations—*his.*

All they were—*gone.*

They weren't the type of people we prey upon.

"I hate cemeteries because I don't like disturbing the dead," I say quietly.

I'm not talking to myself.

I sense her beside me. Phoebe sinks her knees into the grass.

"But I hope they feel me," I say. "I hope they know I came back. That I didn't leave them." *Fuck.* I pinch my eyes and bury the crashing, searing emotion.

She places a hand on my thigh.

We check over our shoulders. Jake waits by an old poplar tree, keeping an eye out.

Our gazes return to each other, and I touch her hand on my leg.

"They know it, Rocky—I believe they do, and everything I believe is true, so . . ." Her emerging smile floods me and centers me.

I lace her fingers with mine.

She swallows hard. "I still can't believe it. Like when I say it out loud, it—"

"Sounds ridiculous?"

"And fucked up. My father killed your whole family." She lets out a sharp laugh. "I didn't even want a dad. I never felt empty without one. And now that I have one, I'd really like to give him back."

"Yeah? How are we going to do that? Send him to the returns and exchanges at T.J. Maxx?"

"I would a hundred percent return him for a knockoff purse."

I laugh a little, but the sound fades as I gaze at the headstones of two brothers I never knew. Of a mother and a father who never got the chance to see their children grow up. "The Alcon blue butterfly," I say under my breath.

"What?" Phoebe frowns.

"It's something Hailey once told me about ants and this specific caterpillar. How it can take over an entire colony by tricking the ants into believing it's the queen."

"Like what Varrick did," Phoebe realizes.

I rise with her hand still in mine. She follows suit, and I stare one more time at the headstones. At Christian, Josephine, Evan, and Griffith.

Defenseless, unsuspecting, prime, easy targets for him. But I'm not one.

I was raised to mimic the fucking queen.

As we walk back to Jake, my fingers slowly, slowly, *slowly* slip from hers, and then I stuff my fists in my leather jacket. She's still his girlfriend in public at the moment. With Claudia gone, there's no reason for their fake relationship to continue, but Phoebe breaking up with her "boyfriend" the week of his mother's death is callous and would do irreparable damage to her reputation in this town. We all agreed to give it some breathing room.

I try not to fixate on her hand in his hand as they head in the opposite direction of me.

Looking backward, I catch Phoebe risking a glance at me, too, and we share a furtive smile made of passionate, loving, volcanic years.

This isn't forever. But her hand always staying in mine—that will be. One day.

It's just not now.

I put my sunglasses on and hike down a hill. To the Pontiac GTO idling on the street. Nova waits outside for me with crossed arms and tension in his stern-lined face. Some things never change.

And then some things do. "No more mustache?" Stubble has grown along his jawline. His dark brown hair is even an inch or so past the buzz-cut stage.

"You hated the mustache."

"Yeah. But *now*, I'm worried you're reversing to eleventh grade where you looked like Crash Bandicoot."

"You want a ride or not?" he retorts.

"Am I driving?"

"Fuck no." He gets in the front seat.

My lips tic up, and I stare around the cemetery one last time. History. My history. Then I climb into the passenger seat, and I look ahead as Nova peels out onto the road, driving into town. Home.

How do you make a place safe when you're the thing that tears homes apart?

For the first time, I want to find out.

FORTY-ONE

Phoebe

Hailey and I sit side by side on a hospital bed, the paper crinkling underneath our butts. Neither of us are wearing those flimsy patterned gowns, but in solidarity, I got a physical and blood work done with her.

Color has returned to her fair cheeks, which might just be blush, granted. She brushed mascara on her lashes and even did a smoky eye.

"Do you have any family history of insomnia?" Dr. Kent asks Hails. She was nice enough to let us stay in the same room together.

"Not that I know of. I was in foster care."

My lungs inflate. I love that she can offer this info and feel that it's true. Especially at Victoria Internal Medicine. Going somewhere local cements the notion that we're remaining here.

We're staying and choosing to weather the Varrick storm. Whatever that may be.

Running away isn't in me anymore, and I think for my

brothers and Rocky's siblings, the idea of planting roots together has taken hold, too. Finding out your parents weren't completely honest with you can make for Gorilla Glue bonding.

And we were already pretty tight to begin with.

Dr. Kent scribbles on her notepad while seated on a stool. "Are you taking any medicine to help you sleep?"

"No."

"How's your caffeine intake?"

"I might have a couple cups of coffee a day. It's not a ton."

More jotting. "Have you found that anything helps you sleep now?"

"Uh . . . sex. I sometimes have sex to the point where everything shuts off and I can fall asleep."

I did not know this, and maybe I shouldn't know, because now I'm wondering if it's Jake or Oliver who rocks her world to sleep. Dr. Kent takes a note, not criticizing Hailey's sleep tactic.

She asks a few more questions, then says she'll be back with our blood-work results.

"Do you think you'll reconcile with them?" Hailey asks me, chains on her black cargo pants jingling as she shifts a little. "Our moms?"

I stare down at my strawberry sundress and my strappy pink heels. *Those are so cute on you, bug.* I thought about Elizabeth . . . my mom, this morning when I chose the outfit.

My heart pangs. "Maybe . . . I'm not as angry anymore. I guess . . . I get why they did what they did. But maybe it's more than that." I hold her gaze. "I would've never known Rocky. I would've never had you as my best friend. If it weren't for them. And I love you both more than humanly comprehensible—it's impossible to hold that kind of anger in my heart when you two fill it."

Hailey rests her temple on my shoulder. "I know exactly what you mean." I wonder if she's also thinking of Trevor.

It reminds me of Easter weekend, and I thumb the scab on my palm where Claudia burned me. All for nothing. That riles me a little . . . a lot, if I'm being *super* honest. The rope was never really pulled. There was never a high of triumph.

I don't take pleasure in Claudia's death.

The amount of crocodile tears at the country club could sail a fleet of Viking ships. The lack of Jake's mom doesn't resolve things. It complicates them.

Five more minutes pass. We get bored and start meandering around the room. I flip through a *Celebrity Crush* tabloid left on top of a *Health* magazine. Then Hailey blasts music from her phone. I recognize the old Avril Lavigne song from our youth.

We exchange a giddy grin before we burst out scream-singing the angsty lyrics, jumping up and down like we're in a concert pit. I grab her hands as we bounce, and then we spin in a circle at high speed.

Which is how Dr. Kent finds us.

We slow to a halt, crashing into each other, and the music hits a little different seeing Dr. Kent's flattened lips and serious eyes.

"Is everything okay?" I ask.

She motions to the hospital bed, and Hailey and I reclaim our seats side by side, paper crunching under us. The noise adds to the tension and makes my heart pound.

"Hailey, I'm going to prescribe you some medication for your insomnia and refer you to a psychiatrist."

She nods nervously.

Dr. Kent flips through papers on our charts. "Good news. You're both negative for all STDs and STIs."

Okay, great, not that either of us thought we had an issue with one. "That's positive—well, it's negative," I say, "but you know what I mean." I laugh unsteadily. Why am I so anxious? It's her face. Something is *clearly* wrong.

She offers me a pity smile.

Lovely.

"I realize you didn't come in here for this, so it might come as a shock." I can't tell who she's talking to. Her attention descends to her charts. "It looks like you're pregnant."

I choke on air. "Excuse me?"

"No, *no*," Hailey says adamantly. "I've *always* worn condoms."

"Same." I don't mention the times Rocky has pulled out and come on me.

"Oh, sorry . . ." Dr. Kent is flustered, embarrassed as she switches charts. "It looks like only one of you is pregnant. And condoms aren't one hundred percent effective in preventing pregnancy."

I shake out the unhelpful fact floating in my face. "Um, ma'am, Dr. Kent, which one of us is pregnant?" I sound hostile. Is that a pregnancy symptom? Irritability—because I am feeling really fucking irritable right now!

"It can't be me." Hailey crinkles her face. "I've barely slept. I've been stressed. What can grow in that condition?"

Am I pregnant?

Rocky. I feel myself trying to call out for him. The powerful need for him to be next to me—it slams into me like a head-on collision.

I feel sick.

Morning sickness? It's not even the morning. I'm battling with the desire for him and the fear of telling him. We've never had these talks. We've never discussed what a year looks like together, because I haven't created a vision board of our life. Okay, I need to go to Staples. I need to get cardboard. Tape. Some construction paper and cute strawberry stickers.

What if one of us doesn't want to stick *babies* on the board? What if I don't want a minivan ever? These are things I don't have answers for. I'm not ready—I'm not ready.

We're not ready.

"You'd be surprised"—Dr. Kent peers up from the charts she's reorganized—"how strong new life can be." Her smile tries to console us. "Hailey is the one pregnant. It looks like you're about seven weeks along."

She squeaks out a shocked breath.

I hold her hand tight. Then I suddenly remember how she was ill outside the grocery, how she's been more emotional lately, and I just attributed all these signs to exhaustion.

"And Phoebe's not . . . ?" she asks.

"No, Phoebe isn't pregnant."

I release a breath, but it's staggered because I also remember, "I gave you my condoms. You were using *my* box of condoms." Guilt piles up on my rib cage. Did I . . . did I cause this? Should that have been me?

That was supposed to be me? If Rocky wasn't particular about condom preferences, we'd be the ones expecting.

Is that how it works?

"I don't have the stats," Hailey says softly, "but a defective condom is probably like one in a million, Phebs. You didn't know."

When Dr. Kent gives us a minute alone, I rotate to my best friend. "I'm here. I'm here for *whatever* you need or want to do, Hails. You don't have to figure this all out today."

She's biting her thumbnail.

"Do you know who . . . ?" I start to ask.

She shakes her head wildly. "It has to be . . . either Oliver's or Jake's baby. Neither one wants a serious relationship with me, Phoebe." She wipes at her watery eyes. With more words of affirmation and reassurance from me, Hailey calms a little.

But I tell her, "I'll cancel my date night. Let's just eat pints of Rocky Road and stay in." She loves ice cream when she's sad.

"No . . . no, you go," she says. "It'll make me feel better knowing I'm not bringing you down."

"Hailey Thornhall. I enjoy my time on the floor with you. How dare you say otherwise."

Her smile turns into a laugh, and it's the sound that carries us out of the doctor's office. It also carries me into my date at ten p.m.—a horror-movie screening.

Months into fake dating Jake, I learned that the Konings own the eight-screen theater in town. A bit of a shocker, considering Jake rarely ventured there, but I suppose in his childhood, the public theater was seen as a bit dingy compared to his lavish private home theater.

When I brought up how it'd suck if Trent obtained the movie theater in the division of assets—because chances are, he'd turn it into some gentleman's club—Jake said we should go more often.

He, very sweetly, requested they start screening horror movies at night.

So *A Nightmare on Elm Street* plays in the dark theater, and I get comfy in my seat among many, many rows of empty chairs. Nightly horror showings might not be the most lucrative idea, since Jake and I are literally the only ones here.

But I bought popcorn.

He even purchased Sour Patch Kids.

"Freddy!" I shout in a crunch of popcorn. "Don't do it!"

Jake laughs.

And then my pulse goes from about twenty to one hundred miles per hour—as I sense Rocky. I brave a quick glance behind me. He sinks in his chair, his brooding face lit from the bright glow of the screen. Before his dark gaze shifts to mine, I face forward.

I smother a smile.

He's never abandoned me. Not a single moment when we challenged ourselves through this job. Not even when I have to slowly cut off my fake relationship with Jake. He's always, always going to be here.

This is our date. And I wonder what it'll look like ten days from now. I wonder if the intensity will amplify until we both just explode. Become particles floating in the air. Merge as atoms.

The chair creaks behind me. Rocky careens forward, and his dominating, dangerous presence closes in on me. I do my best to concentrate on the screen.

My breathing catches, but I shout, "FREDDY! Come on!"

His jaw skims my cheek as he whispers, "Shut the fuck up. I'm watching a movie."

A smile tries to burst through me, but I push it all down to retort, "No one is in here, so no, I will not shut the fuck up." I pop another kernel in my mouth, chewing slower as anticipation shifts me to full throttle.

He's not moving backward.

Rocky slides an arm down my shoulder, past my collarbone. The force of his clutch pulls me back into the seat. I catch a needy noise in my throat, especially as he grabs a fistful of my breast. *Jake is right there.* My eyes dart to my left.

Jake sips his fountain drink. Not paying attention to the devil behind my chair. I bite the corner of my lip.

"You're smiling," Rocky whispers.

"Am not," I retort. "And I thought you were watching the movie, not me."

"I can watch two nightmares at once." His other arm slinks down my other shoulder. It feels like he's right up against me. He steals a handful of my popcorn.

"Thief," I accuse. "I will call the theater attendant."

"Try me." He even drinks my soda. "I have a pretty good feeling they'll believe I'm innocent."

I tighten my eyes at the screen. *Do not turn and look at him. Do fucking not.* My heart swells at a vicious rate, making it harder and harder to breathe. "I know what you are."

His whisper hits my ear. "And what's that?" A bolt of electricity courses through me as Rocky holds me against the chair from behind.

I'm gripping the armrests like I'm going to plunge and free-fall. Then I let go and touch his arms, which strengthen against my body.

"You're the same as me," I breathe.

I imagine his eyes flitting from the screen, back to me, and his lips graze my cheek. "Then we must want the same things."

"And what exactly do you want?"

I feel him looking forward. "You," he says deeply. "And revenge."

My smile takes wicked shape.

Acknowledgments

If you've made it this far, *thank you so very much*. Looking back, we know our teenage selves would be very, very happy and emotional to know you enjoyed Rocky and Phoebe's romance enough to embark on book two and reach the end. As we mentioned in the last acknowledgments, this series was a childhood concept between us, and bringing it to life decades later has been a true joy. But because of so many of you, it's been a more overwhelming and joyous experience than we could've ever imagined.

Thank you to those who rushed to the bookstore and snuck art and bookmarks into copies. You are the most beautiful people. Thank you to those who took time to make *Dishonestly Yours* baked goods. (They looked delicious!) Thank you to those who made the trip to see us on tour and to those who showed up in strawberry outfits!! To those who created art on social media. Those who made fan videos. Those who gifted us strawberry merch. Those who posted about Phoebe and Rocky. Every little thing meant the world to us, and to see so many readers rally behind our new series made our whole careers.

It was such a force of love, and it's what we'll remember most about the series. We are beyond grateful for you. And we can never properly name everyone. It'd be impossible. But just know that we know who you are, and we hope you feel our love in return.

Writing *Destructively Mine* was a labor of love. It was one of the most challenging novels we've ever written, but it quickly has become our proudest. Thank you to our mastermind agent, Kimberly Brower, for again helping us make our books so much better. We can't imagine not having your input on this one. You were invaluable to us.

Thank you to our brilliant editor, Kristine Swartz, for always helping us have those lightbulb moments and finding the best story. We think this was the biggest lightbulb moment yet! Likewise, thank you to the rest of the amazing Berkley team: Mary Baker, Rosanne Romanello, Kristin Cipolla, Jessica Plummer, Kim-Salina I, and the copyeditors, proofreaders, and all those in between who've made Phoebe and Rocky's story reach readers in all its beauty.

Thank you to our most wonderful, beautiful mom. There are no words to really convey how happy we are that you joined us on tour to celebrate *Dishonestly Yours*. To spend that time with you was *everything*. We would've been messes without you! Thank you for all the help and all the love, always. And thank you to our awesome dad for your unwavering support with the Webs We Weave series.

Thank you to Jenn, Lanie, and Shea—you three are absolute treasures to us. Your friendship from the start will always hold the biggest place in our hearts. Much like Phoebe's love of strawberries, it's never going away! Thank you to more extraordinary friends we've made along the way who were the best cheerleaders two dorky twins could ever ask for: Haley, Alyssa, Juana, Andrea, Maria, Marissa, Rowena, Zoë, Angelina, Abby, Andressa, Margot, Em, Laura, Marie, Sarah,

Olivia, Kenny, Allyn, and so many more. *Thankyouthankyou-thankyou.*

Thank you to our bestie, Ashley, the Hailey to our Phoebe! Thank you to our big brother, Alex, for coming out to the launch event! Having that moment with you, our sister-in-law, and our baby niece meant so much. Thank you for all the support you've given us.

Thank you endlessly to our patrons on our Patreon! It's our happy place, and you all are the reason we could continue writing. We'll never forget, and we hope you've loved Phoebe and Rocky's fiery romance as much as we loved writing it!

To our significant others—thank you for being there every step of the way. You two saw how much work, brainpower, and heart and how many late nights went into *Destructively Mine*, and it's the first book we've written where the two of us were split apart. To say we needed you would be an understatement. Thank you for being there. Thank you for reminding us that we are badass and we can do anything, even the things that feel impossible.

Thank you, again, to you—the reader. The mystery about who this merry little gang of heathens are might be over, but there is so much more still to come as they figure out what *home* means. Phoebe and Rocky will be returning in all their volcanic glory, and we truly hope you'll be there to see what happens next. ;)

—xoxo, Krista & Becca

KEEP READING FOR AN EXCERPT FROM

DANGEROUSLY OURS

Phoebe

"Yeeeeee-haw!" Oliver howls and tucks a cowboy hat on his natural dark brown hair. "This round is on me, boys." He barrel-chest-bumps the bachelor, Bradley Wheeler, who's a city boy from Toronto and looking to experience Nashville's nightlife before the big wedding day.

Bradley is also loaded.

Like *flew a private jet here* loaded. *Buys the most expensive liquor at the bar* loaded. *Wears a Chopard diamond watch* loaded. That's probably twenty-five million just on his wrist.

Lucky for him, he just so happened to run into three "Nashville locals." After striking up a great conversation, Oliver, Rocky, and I offered to take his bachelor party on a honky-tonk bar crawl. To show Bradley and his groomsmen the *best* music, the *best* drinks, and the *best* time.

Bradley is all grins, pumping his fist as he follows his new friend Oakley (*ahem*, Oliver) to the packed bar.

"Tequila with lime, Penelope?" Shane, the best man, asks me, on his way to the bar, too. He's bought me shots at the past three stops. I drank two Jägerbombs, then dumped the third when no one was looking.

"Just a water!" I shout after him, my Tennessee twang more subtle than Oliver's. Per usual, my brother is going above and beyond. Just hopefully not too far.

"Aw, come on!" Shane shouts back. "Don't be a Debbie Downer! I'll get you a tequila!!" He disappears into the sweaty throng with the rest of the bachelor party, not giving me the opportunity to decline.

"He wants in your pants," Rocky says huskily, a toothpick between his lips and his elbow perched casually on a wooden barrel. He's Rhett. My "college friend." Same with Oliver. We all supposedly met freshman year at Vanderbilt.

Rocky hangs back with me, and I'm momentarily hooked on how hushed and deep he speaks. Like we're slipping clandestine notes to each other.

"He'll have to try a little harder. I'm waitin' till marriage." I thicken my twang. "Thank the good Lord."

Rocky almost smiles at my lie. *Almost*. "Praise be."

"Praise be," I joke, too, but Rocky looks straight into me. He's holding my gaze for longer than any man ever does. It's more intimate than a full-body once-over. A flush tries to roast my cheeks.

If attraction is a scorch, then Rocky is the only one who gives me third-degree burns. I'm hooked on more than just the photogenic planes of his cutting jawline, more than just his annoyingly perfect hair, a few tendrils of which lightly brush his forehead. More than just his toughened stance that commands *You fuck with her, you fuck with me* to the rest of the bar. More than just how he wards off other men from approaching me.

More than just how I feel safer when he's close.

I'm hooked on the entirety of him. On how he's choosing to be at my side. How his real, coarse nature flickers across his striking features for only me to notice. *For only me to see.*

His dark, smoldering eyes still transfix me in a vise I'm not readily escaping. Not now. Maybe not ever.

"Rhett," I warn half-heartedly, not wanting him to stop staring.

"Penelope." He bites on the toothpick, never tearing his gaze away. My heart thumps harder, faster.

Last thing I need is for Rocky to believe a falsehood—that I'm *infatuated* with him. I'm not some obsessed puppy about to slobber on his lap and beg for a fucking pet. I don't want to be petted. I want to be *ravaged*.

I'm simply a twenty-one-year-old woman with a high libido. And I can admit to myself that it's highest around him. I can't help that my hormones go haywire in his presence. I can't help that I *love* the feeling of my racing, skidding, flyaway pulse when he's inches from me.

It's human nature, and these are just *biological* problems.

Gathering my bearings, I face forward. The fun part of tonight is the best distraction from Rocky.

Live country music booms from a stage. Blue lights bathe a guitarist and a fiddler, along with the dance floor. Girls in cheeky Daisy Dukes and cute leather boots are line dancing with belt-buckle-clad guys. Most are bachelor and bachelorette parties. I see bedazzled Barbie-pink cowboy hats, sashes that say LAST RODEO, and penis straws.

I'm trying to enjoy tonight, especially since it's our last one in Nashville.

"Do you think Hails will come out?" I ask Rocky more quietly. I've already texted his sister. She can pop in as a college friend who's meeting up with us for a drink. It'd be an easy ruse to pull off.

"The godmothers specifically told her no, so no. You both don't break rules."

"That's a good thing," I point out.

"Being good gets you stepped on." His deep voice sounds even more gravelly with his twang. "You must love looking at the bottom of your mom's heels."

"We all can't be anarchists wanting to *burn it down*."

His lip twitches into a slanted smile. "Does it look like I'm burning it down?"

He's not setting fire to our lives. We are a well-organized machine of deceit. "You aren't lighting any matches," I recognize, resting my forearms on the barrel in a casual lunge. It doesn't draw his attention to my ass or my breasts. His focus remains on my face as he reads me.

It's intrusive. Intimate, again.

In a hot blip, I imagine Rocky moving behind me, sliding his possessive hands against the crook of my hips, and fucking me *hard* against the barrel. I brick-wall my expression so he can't read those desires, but he has all the tools to knock me down if I'm not careful.

I don't want to be careful with him. That's the exhilarating, yet terrifying, part.

I skim his features. "Why not try to usurp them if you want to so badly?"

"Y'all don't want me to try." He eases out a sexy drawl and moves the toothpick with his tongue.

He might as well be saying, *Because I love y'all more than I hate them.*

My heart swells and pangs, and I should probably distance

myself from Rocky—I *should* go entertain the bachelor party instead of sharing his company. I have a job to do, and so does he, but neither of us moves.

I wonder when we became a vortex together. Exiting the EF5 winds takes hellacious effort, and I'm not fighting against the pull or the force of nature.

"*Y'all?*" I ask in a tight breath. "As in . . . ?"

I want him to say, *You. Mostly you. I love you more than anyone I know, Phoebe.*

He shifts the toothpick again. "You know who."

Right.

His siblings: a younger sister and brother. My siblings: two older brothers—granted, older by minutes.

I nod and say out loud, "You love Hails more than you hate the godmothers."

"Astute," he says. But he's not adding me into the equation. He's not putting me before his sister, and why would he? I'm just her best friend.

I'd put Hailey above myself, too.

I bend a little more. "I've been known to be perceptive."

"Not more perceptive than me," he says thickly. I'm unsure if it sounds like a challenge or a come-on.

I open my mouth to combat him. Instead, I take in a strange, shortened breath of arousal. I hope he doesn't comment on it. And he doesn't, not as his muscles flex, as if he's controlling something carnal within himself.

We *are* perceptive. I think we both know attraction exists, thrives, *terrorizes*. Tension thickens at the unsaid things. Our bodies are mere inches apart, and still, neither of us shifts away or nearer.

I breathe hard.

He does, too.

Feelings are thorns we let puncture us. Sometimes I believe Rocky and I like bleeding out together.

I finally straighten up, and he slides his darkened gaze off me. If he had a beer, he'd likely chug it right now.

I wouldn't say the tension snaps. It's buried in my core, and I try to ignore it by checking my phone.

No new text from my best friend. I frown, wishing Rocky was wrong—that his sister would sneak out. Which is a funny phrase: *sneak out*. She's twenty-one, too. Sneaking shouldn't be a thing for us, but I guess it's more like being held up at work. She's clocking in overtime since she's helping our parents preplan the next long con.

After this, we're heading to Miami.

I shove the phone in the front pocket of my frayed jean shorts. My ass peeks out. It's been burning hot in each bar, so I've loved my skimpy outfit for comfortableness. Plus, the matching bejeweled jean vest is seriously cute.

"She wanted to be here," I remind her brother. "The original plan was better."

Hailey had concocted a Bar Bill job. It would've taken at least a month, if not two, to pick out a mark and for one of us to be hired as a bartender, but our parents rejected it. Now we're just passing through Nashville with this short con.

Last night, when we were told the change of plans, Hailey looked so defeated and said, "I just wish they gave me better constructive feedback over why they axed it."

"They said it wasn't personal," I told her. "It wasn't a bad con or setup."

Hailey fell flat on the bed, dejected. "I'm pretty positive they don't think I'm ready to plan a job of that level yet."

I lay back with her and held her gaze consolingly. "It's probably just timing."

Hailey's Bar Bill job would've meant she'd be having fun with us at Rowdy Rooster's Watering Hole tonight. We could've even ridden the mechanical bull.

Now she's stuck alone at the Ritz—which, *yes*, isn't a Super 8 or an RV park. But seeing Hailey's devious dreams get shot down offends me as her best friend. The universe should be better to her.

Hailey ended up taking her blues out on a pint of Moose Tracks. Rocky had gone to the nearest convenience store last night to get her the ice cream. I imagine she's finishing off the last of the container while we're here.

"The original plan," Rocky says under his breath, not dropping the subtle Tennessee accent. "Did you like it because your best friend came up with it? Or because it involved her being here?"

"Both. And because of Nashville." I watch the line dancers. "I'm not ready to leave." The catchy tempo from the fiddle is invigorating. "Are you?"

I feel him studying me. "I could stay."

I try to pry my eyes off the rhythmic bodies, but I'm latched on to the heel-toe taps of cowboy boots as I say, "You finally fell in love with country music?"

"Yeah," he deadpans. "It's growing on me like a cold sore."

I snort. Why would he even want to stay here for longer? "I bet it's the toothpick," I tease. "You've always wanted something to gnaw on."

He flips me off.

I laugh, and I see the start of his smile before I'm entranced by the dancers again. Girls smack their heels and hop-jump to the beat. Guys tip their cowboy hats as they shimmy to the side.

Rocky pushes off the wooden barrel and suddenly captures my hand, leading me to the dance floor. My pulse rushes ahead of me.

I pick up speed with glee. We slip into the line dancers, and, side by side, we mimic the moves in seconds, sharing smiles at the ease of our inception. Shuffle to the right, toe forward, heel back, clap our hands. Spin. Twirl our hips.

Rocky looks like a skilled country boy from *Footloose*. I'm captivated for a heady moment by how effortlessly he becomes someone else—and by how deeply I still see him through the veneer. In a way, this is all of him, and this is all of me. We're every skill we've learned, every lie we've created, every secret we've shared.

Even dancing, he's still attentive, observant. As we rotate, his eyes land on me, then the bar—where Oliver hands the groom a shot—then the fiddler on the stage.

We glide closer to each other. With the music blasting, we can have a private-enough conversation, so I ask him while we dance, "What would you be doing tonight if you weren't working?"

"Is it work?" He claps, then we spin side by side.

Our eyes are fastened with our movements. "It's called a *job*."

Rocky passes close, his lips brushing my ear. "It's a *life-style*." My skin vibrates with electricity, especially as he whispers, "Think about it. Have you ever gone out and not done it?"

It.

As in, lie.

Scheme.

Con.

Hailey and I got tickets to some underground heavy metal band she loves, and even at that concert, we fucked over this raging dick who purposefully spilled a drink on his girlfriend's head. The girl was mortified. Crying.

So we stole his wallet and his phone (unlocked) and found his passcodes typed out in the Notes app. Including his ATM PIN.

We emptied his checking account.

It was impulsive. Unplanned.

And I rode that high all the way to our hotel, where we ordered the entire dessert menu from room service.

"I usually do it," I answer Rocky, knowing that in little instances and bigger ones, I've always cheated my way through a day. "I can't imagine *not* doing it."

We shuffle back together and dip forward.

"Same," he says with the raising and lowering of his brows.

My pulse skips. I stumble over my boots on a side step, and before I can brush off the momentary lack of coordination, Rocky rotates out of sync with the dancers and catches my hips. He spins me into his chest.

Breath evacuates my lungs.

His arms around me are familiar, devoted, protective, powerful.

And he says, "I'd still be doing this. It's not work to me." His gunmetal grays dive deep into me, and I imagine his hands rising to my cheeks. I imagine him possessing me with a forceful, agonizing kiss.

It's not work to him.

Rhett could have the hots for Penelope.

Penelope definitely has feelings for Rhett, even if she shouldn't. Even knowing that this will all end when the job ends. Because Rocky *does* clock out.

He's still never kissed me outside of a job. Practicing when we were younger doesn't count.

Just when I think he's easing in, he veers to my ear and whispers, "I'm getting you a water."

"Yeah." I nod assuredly a few times, forcing down the aggravating flush. "Okay." We both see the bachelor party at the bar. They're searching for us.

Get the job done, Phoebe.

Rocky is likely going to try to keep them at the bar, away from me. He leaves after a deep "Be careful." And I don't need to imagine his dark gaze lingering on me. I feel the heat of it stroking the length of me in a red-hot caress before he peels away from my side.

I struggle to intake breath. It's like he took my oxygen with him.

In the next minute, I miss his presence. It's hard to have the same energy dancing alone.

I slide to the brick wall for a breather.

"Was that your boyfriend?" a girl in a disco cowboy hat asks me, her face full of glitter.

"No, he's just . . ." *Rocky.* ". . . a friend."

She gasps. "Oh my God! Is he single?!" She's about to flag down her friends to share the *terrific* news.

My face burns, heat gathering in my lungs. "No," I lie fast. "He has a girlfriend."

Her shoulders slump. "Really?"

"Yeah, she's not here. She's super nice, too."

The blatant side-eye she gives me is deserved. Penelope was a little too cozy with a taken man, but I want to brand him with the name he gave me. I want him to brand *me* with the name I gave him. *Phoebe. Rocky.* Deep, thick, bleeding scars visible over our thrashing hearts. More permanent and painful than ink.

I shut my eyes, my breath deepening, and I picture the bloody mess as his lips crash against mine, as our limbs tangle. I picture how everyone can see who we are to each other—ingrained, embedded, entrenched.

And I wonder how long I've really been in love with him.

Photo © Kelley Raye

Krista and Becca Ritchie are *New York Times* and *USA Today* bestselling authors and identical twins—one a science nerd, the other a comic book geek—but with their shared passion for writing, they combined their mental powers as kids and have never stopped telling stories. They love superheroes, flawed characters, and soul mate love.

VISIT KRISTA AND BECCA RITCHIE ONLINE

KBRitchie.com
KBMRitchie

Ready to find
your next great read?

Let us help.

Visit prh.com/nextread

Penguin
Random
House